OVER EXPOSURE

OVER EXPOSURE

HUGO RIFKIND

CANONGATE

Edinburgh · New York · Melbourne

First published in Great Britain in 2006 by
Canongate Books Ltd, 14 High Street,
Edinburgh EH1 1TE

1

British Library Cataloguing-in-Publication Data
A catalogue record for this book is available on
request from the British Library

1 84195 858 1 (10-Digit ISBN)
978 1 84195 858 3 (13-Digit ISBN)

Typeset in Adobe Garamond by
Palimpsest Book Production Ltd, Polmont, Stirlingshire
Printed and bound in Great Britain by
Creative Print & Design, Ebbw Vale.

www.canongate.net

For Fran

'Mr and Mrs Nipple have popped
out to say hello . . .'

It starts, on a Thursday, at the *Gazette*'s Diamond Awards at the Mandarin Oriental. It is a glitzy affair, one that the articles in the papers tomorrow (and, indeed, the article that I have already written) will rightly describe as 'star-studded'. Everybody is here, or rather, everybody who the *Gazette* believes to be anybody, and who didn't have anything better to do. Look one way and you'll see Sir Elton John in a large crown, followed by David Furnish in a smaller one. Look the other and you'll see Sarah, the Duchess of York, and her daughter Beatrice. Both wear strappy black dresses with diamond pendants, giving them something of the air of a coven. Liz Hurley and Arun Nayar are here, smiling showily near the entrance. He opts for the simplicity of a studded cummerbund, she does something sparkly with her garters. No one will notice, poor love. These days even the *Telegraph* prefers Keira Knightley.

Elsewhere, moving between the aisles of this extravagant buffet, other stellar heads bob and weave. There's Graham Norton, chatting manically with Ant and Dec. There's Vanessa Feltz and Ruby Wax working as a team, scavenging at the canapés like a pair of rotund meerkats. There's Victoria Beckham, trying to catch Elton's eye, there's Ewan McGregor, succeeding. There's Damon Albarn, Nicky Haslam, Caroline Aherne, Amanda Holden. There's Angus Deayton, Julien Macdonald, Nigella Lawson, David Jason, Cat and Edith, Nic and Nat, Geri and her damn little shit of a dog, Kate Moss, Peaches Geldof, Honor Blackman and that kid of George Best's with the raging libido. Everybody wears diamonds, or at the very least diamanté, and everybody is frightfully pleased to see everybody else.

I'm here too, of course. I've battered my Jewfro into something more like Lenny Kravitz and less like Art Garfunkel and I'm wearing a black tie and kilt combo. The kilt isn't my first choice for what is essentially a work do, but I was stuck. My dinner jacket, I discovered this evening to my horror, is still screwed up at the bottom of my cupboard, now covered in mould from the guacamole Liam Gallagher flicked at my back at the Brit Awards. I've a plastic dagger in my sock with what looks like a diamond in the handle, but is actually a bit of glass. Nobody would mistake me for a celebrity, oh no.

The star of the show, even before anything happens, is of course Gemma Conrad. You'll have heard of her by now. On a normal night, she might not stand out – she's got a face you are sure you recognise, maybe from *Big Brother*, maybe from *Hollyoaks*, but one you can never quite pin down until you read the words 'Satellite TV Weathergirl' in the caption under her photo. Tonight though she's making heads turn. A 'perky' brunette, below the waist she's wearing a shimmering silver wrap-around skirt. Above, she's not really wearing anything. Instead, her entire bosom (no small area) has been plastered with individual gemstones. The highlight of all this, the focus point if you will, is the stone that was once known as the Glare of the Kalahari, now dubbed the Bushman's Thimbles.

The Glare, as most of Britain will read tomorrow morning, was the seventh largest diamond ever discovered. A hundred and ninety-six carats and hollow, it would have been almost spherical, were it not for a flaw that ran from pole to pole, leaving one hemisphere slightly misaligned with the other. Several years after its discovery (in 1866) the decision was taken to split the wonky sphere. This created two hollow cups, each weighing slightly under a hundred carats and each about the size of . . . well. Each about the size of a weathergirl's nipple.

But not just any weathergirl. Stick 196 carats to the front of Ulrika Jonsson and you're talking stretched turkey meat and grazed knees. Gemma Conrad though, perky twenty-three-year-old Gemma Conrad, she's firm enough to handle these gems with aplomb. She's already been like that for about six hours though, poor girl. Our photographers shot her this afternoon for the front of tomorrow's paper, and she's had that lot stuck to her ever since. From tomorrow she's not just going to be a Satellite TV Weathergirl, she's also going to be ours – the new management having decided that even patches of cloud and drizzle can help sell a paper if they're fronted by a nice piece of tit.

This is very much the new management's style. Image over content is the new philosophy, and not just because it sells better. It's usually cheaper too. The bash tonight is a good case in point. Diamonds, sure, to celebrate the paper's 'diamond jubilee', but they've left everybody to bring their own. The only stones that the *Gazette* has provided tonight are the thimbles on Gemma's modesty and the rock around the neck of Marge Randall, wife of our demonic new CEO. Even the editor's tie pin is on loan from Ratners. The rest of this evening suffers from a similar budget

3

mentality. There's a buffet, not a meal. In the kitchens the wine comes in boxes and a large percentage of the caviar – I would bet my life on it – is actually fish paste. The only reason the hall itself looks vaguely showy is that some German princeling got married here last weekend, and someone persuaded the hotel not to clear up too fast. None of this has gone unnoticed by the celeb guests or the resident hacks, or indeed the sniggering rival hacks invited along from other papers.

Anyway, until 11 p.m. or so, shabby or not, everything is going according to plan. Graham Norton is up on the stage, cracking gags and inviting people up to accept or present various awards. It's all slightly spurious, this awards business. Nominally, being 'Diamond Awards' they are meant to be given to people who have done incredible things over the last decade – made films, sold albums, presented game shows, lost limbs, that kind of thing. In practice, if you haven't made headlines in the last five years you haven't got a chance. Mainly it's actually a star vehicle for those who are presenting the awards – a host of young wannabes and gonnabes who are keen to make their name. Norton flirts with the men and asks the women deadpan questions about their vaginas. Gemma Conrad is presenting one of the last awards, the inanely-titled 'Mockney Diamond Geezer' award, the nominees being Guy Ritchie, Jamie Oliver, Sir Michael Caine and, bizarrely, Kathy Burke. Clutching the envelope, she pushes her way through the throng of hacks and photographers at the bottom of the stage, and heads for the podium.

To my eternal shame I actually miss all of this. At this precise moment I am in the gents, sharing a pure skunk spliff with a member of the So Solid Crew, my ex-girlfriend Elspeth and a lanky former youth TV presenter who, for legal reasons, I should point out is absolutely not Jamie Theakston. Nevertheless, I gather things go as follows:

4

The weathergirl reaches the podium.

'Gemma, darling,' trills Graham. 'You are looking radiant. Quite the eyeful, if I may say so.'

'You may Graham,' purrs Gemma, no poor mockney herself, 'you may.'

'And the nominees are?'

Gemma flashes her weathergirl smile, and rips open the envelope. 'The nominees are,' she says, and stops. 'The nominees . . . no. I don't understand.'

'Poor lass,' says Graham. 'Blonder than you look, aren't you? What does it say on the card, love?'

Gemma looks bewildered. 'It says . . . it says "*Thanks for the stones. Yours aye, Fingers*".'

Norton blinks.

'And there's a picture of a hand,' adds Gemma. 'What does it mean?'

'Oh my,' says Norton, and looks down.

Gemma follows his gaze. 'What? What?'

'It means,' says Graham Norton, ever the professional, 'that Mr and Mrs Nipple have popped out to say hello. You're looking a little chafed, dear.'

Eyes widening, Gemma Conrad stares at her breasts. Her hands scrabble to cover them, but she is too late, too late.

The flashbulbs pop and the hall erupts.

And that's how it begins.

'Which cretin wrote that?'

In the film that I have no doubt they must one day make of my life, I should like to be played by Jude Law. It's not a perfect likeness, largely as a result of Jude being about as Semitic as a bacon crucifix, but still. Stick an extra bit on his nose and add a touch of pallid greyness to his cheeks, and I reckon he could do me justice.

In the same film, should he deserve depiction (which is doubtful, frankly), I am at rather a loss as to who should play Trevor Brainchild, the *Gazette*'s managing editor. I suppose John Prescott would do, if one could knock a few years off the man, but I'm not sure if his thespian skills are up to much. Still, if he can shout and quiver indignantly, then the role is his.

Brainchild is shouting now and quivering fit to burst.

'You!' he hollers, 'are in shit!' A podgy finger wags over his head.

I watch this with an air of aloof interest. This enrages him further. He's talking to me, you see. I'm not meant to be watching with aloof interest, I'm meant to be cowering. I would, but I'm hungover and I don't have the energy. It's Friday morning, the day after the diamond heist, and I only made it to bed four hours ago. I am not at my best. 'Bed', incidentally, is something of a euphemism. I did not make it to bed. I made it back to the office (a long story, the key ingredients being a blonde called Lucy from the marketing department who clearly thought I was more important than I am and a gramme of whatnot I mistakenly remembered my old boss stashing in his pen pot), where I dozed fitfully for three hours in the photocopier cupboard. Fortunately one of Daniel Kemp's suits was still under his desk, so at least I'm not still in the kilt. Still, I stink.

'Are you *listening* to me?' screams Brainchild.

I give him an encouraging smile. I'm not, really. I'm looking across the room towards the newsdesk, where there appears to be some kind of commotion. Rebecca Leighton, possibly the only member of the *Gazette*'s editorial staff of whom I am truly afraid, is leaning forward across her desk to berate Willie Fowler, the almost-certainly-outgoing deputy news editor. There are two uniformed policemen standing next to them: a dumpy lady PC and an equally dumpy gent. They look thoroughly out of place, like vicars in a lingerie store. Leighton must be in a rare old fury to be sounding off in front of them.

Although plainly far too clever to ever have the remotest interest in sleeping with me (and she's said as much, more than once), Rebecca Leighton is gorgeous: high cheekbones and the kind of swept-back semi-dreaded hair that management would never permit if she was even a tiny bit whiter. She's wearing suit trousers and a fitted pink shirt that sculpts her athletic upper body pleasingly. If she was twenty foot closer, I'd probably have an unrivalled view of her cleavage. I squint, and Brainchild's hand slams down on my desk.

7

'Jesus, Trevor!' I focus on his tomatoey, apoplectic face. 'What?'

He's so taken aback by my 'what?' that I have a few seconds' respite, and return to gazing at the lovely Leighton. He's a professional though, Brainchild, so he recovers fast.

'I'll tell you fucking what you cocky little shit,' he begins, and somehow something tells me that there really is a degree of actual annoyance here. I get hunches.

'The Boss,' continues Brainchild, 'just called about your front page. He's spitting.'

I glance at Philip, to my left, but he's intently studying his fingernails. Not fair. It's his front page too. I shrug wearily. 'That's unreasonable.'

'Is it?' asks Brainchild, voice squeaky and eyebrows raised. 'Is it indeed?'

I nod. It is indeed.

'Well perhaps you can tell Mr Randall this,' says Brainchild, near hysteria. 'Perhaps you can tell him just how *unreasonable* he is being in objecting to the fact that *every single other paper*, even the *Express*, managed to lead with last night's debacle and we, the people who actually *paid* for it, who *sat* there and *watched* it *happen*, did not. Perhaps, Lewis, you could explain to him just how *unreasonable* he is being in *minding* this?'

It drives me spare the way Brainchild speaks likes this, the way he *stresses* every *other* word, slightly nodding and widening his eyes as he does so. He looks like a frog being given an enema. It's disgusting.

'But it's his fault,' I tell him. 'Nobody else had it in their first edition either. Our problem is that we only have a first edition. His brainwave. This kind of thing is bound to happen from time to time. You should know that, Trevor.'

'Oh I *do* know that. I *do*. But I'm hardly going to *explain* it to the Boss, am I?'

I yawn. 'No? Why not?'

'Because *you* are,' says Brainchild and smiles. And not nicely.

As if. Fifteen minutes later, Brainchild is safely closeted in his office with the police, and I firmly delegate the matter to Philip, my pointy balding sidekick. (Gunther from *Friends* could play him, but he'd have to lose the hair.)

'No way,' he says, instantly. 'You're not my senior. You can't delegate to me.'

'But I have to,' I explain airily. 'I'm going out.'

Philip does a kind of hesitant shuddering sigh of disgust. Very weird manoeuvre. 'Where?' he asks. 'Why?'

'Religious holiday.'

'No.' He shakes his shiny dome. 'Today isn't a religious holiday. It would say so in my diary.'

'Scottish,' I tell him. 'Might not be there.'

'Scottishness isn't a religion, Mac.'

'Course it is,' I say, standing up. 'And today is a celebration of St . . . erm . . . Dougal. Patron saint of haggis. So. Love to stay and chat but piety beckons.'

'No!' Philip is positively quivering. 'What about Randall? I won't cover for you if he comes around.'

I pinch him on the chin, which he hates. 'Yeah you will. Anyway, he won't come himself. He probably doesn't know the way. He'll just send Jensen.'

'Yansen,' says Philip quietly.

'I beg your pardon?'

'Yansen. It's pronounced "Yansen".'

I sigh, rub the back of my stiff neck and walk away. 'Well it shouldn't be. Look, I'll be back . . . ah . . . probably. And I'll have my mobile. But it might be turned off. Bye now.'

'You're a cunt,' says Philip suddenly, shocking himself pink.

As I reach the newsdesk I swivel on my heel, turn and bow. If it weren't for the two inches of pasty builder's arse I inadvertently display to Rebecca Leighton, it would be an extremely suave exit.

I'm not heading far. Daniel Kemp, my former boss, lives about ten minutes from the offices, just to the south of Victoria Station. It's not a nice flat and it certainly wasn't a cheap one. Daniel swapped it for his semi in Clapham three months ago so he could walk to work. Which he did, for about a month. Then they sacked him. How we all did laugh.

Daniel leans over the edge of his miniature balcony when I push his buzzer. He's two floors up and has a coffee in one hand and what I would warrant must be his fifth or six Dunhill of the morning in the other. He's wearing a ripped, silk dressing gown, and looks every inch the faded English gent. Grey-blond hair hangs, aristocratically, over one eye. His skin is pale and patchy.

'Macaulay!' he calls, faux Scottish. 'Have they let you out for play time?'

'No,' I reply. 'I'm bunking off. Can I come up?'

'Surely, surely.' He nods and disappears and a few seconds later the door goes buzz. I head up to his one-bed flat which is, not to put too fine a point on it, disgusting. The place smells of dead flies. Expensive but threadbare tailoring lies strewn about the place, and empty wine bottles huddle along the walls, like penguins at the edge of an iceberg. Papers are piled by the door, a laptop flickers blue on an ironing board in one corner. On a coffee table in front of the sofa stands a single leopard-print Jimmy Choo stiletto, with a length of pantyhose spilling out of it, through an ashtray and onto the floor. I raise my eyebrows.

'The lady left early,' says Daniel in the doorway to the balcony. 'I lent her my trainers. Nice suit, by the way.'

'Oh. Yeah. I'll have it cleaned and send it back. The lady being Michelle?'

'Michelle's away. Skiing or something. Just a girl I picked up last night.'

I extract the tights and pick up the shoe. 'A tart in Jimmy Choos? Very nice.'

'Not a tart, Macaulay, you sexist rogue. A lady.'

I redden, and very nearly stammer. 'Right. Of course. Where were you?'

Daniel gives me a withering look and turns back outside. 'I lent you twenty quid. Don't you remember?'

I follow him, and slump into a plastic chair. If I squint, at just the right angle, I can make out a tiny piece of the top of Big Ben. 'No,' I say, and close my eyes as the sun glares from behind a cloud. 'Where?'

'At the Mandarin, you imbecile. At that bloody diamond thing.'

I shiver. It's freezing out here. I can see my breath. 'You were there? Why?'

'Why not? I had an invitation.'

I hear the hiss and scrape as he lights a Dunhill. 'No thanks,' I murmur, just in case he's offering me one. 'I'd have thought you would have been struck off.'

Daniel chuckles. 'I still get all the invitations. Whatever fool took over my job obviously hasn't got round to redirecting them yet.'

'Ah,' I say, and open my eyes to check if he's giving me a scornful look. He isn't. 'Ah,' I say again. 'Philip's fault. I swear it.' I pause and look up. It's too bright. Above me, a pigeon circles. I feel vulnerable and ill.

'Are you sure I owe you twenty quid?'

'Positive.'

'But what did I do with it?'

'Frankly, Mac, the mind boggles.' Daniel peers into his coffee cup. 'Quite a night. *Fingers?* How tacky. But enough to piss off Randall and his little goblins, I'll wager.'

I relent and horizontally waggle the first two fingers of my right hand at him. After a moment's rather meaningful pause, he reaches over and slots a cigarette between them.

'Ta,' I say. 'Yeah, they do seem a touch miffed. That's kind of why I jumped ship this morning, actually. Police all over the office. It's in all the papers. Pretty much all of them have led with it. Most have got a photo of that weathergirl looking all wide-eyed and covering her breasts.'

'So?' says Daniel.

'So we don't. We've got a ton of pre-written gushing drivel about how much of a success it all was.'

Daniel sits forward, raising his eyebrows. 'Jesus. Which cretin wrote that?'

I hang my head over the back of my plastic chair and stare up at the sky. The pigeon is still there, probably taking aim. 'Me,' I say.

Nothing happens for almost thirty seconds, and then Daniel explodes. He's rocking in his chair, almost crying with laughter. His face is on his knees, with his cigarette hand holding the back of his head. Smoke spirals away from it, mixing with the foggy condensation from his breath.

'Oi,' I say, hurt. 'OI!'

He sits up and wipes his eyes, pulling a poker face. 'Forgive me,' he says, and his face trembles. 'But congratulations on your first front page.'

He's off again. Resentfully, I watch him.

He used to be my boss, Daniel, did I mention that? He's a

twinge under forty, maybe a decade older than I am, and he's been around the block. Occasionally I'll get little flashes from his conversation that, ten years ago, he wasn't that dissimilar to how I am now. As far as I know, he's always done gossip. I think he started on one of the tabloids, before moving to a Sunday and then to the *Post*, a weekly London rag where an old friend of mine from home works. He was at the *Indy* very briefly before he came to the *Gazette*, and I gather everybody thought he was destined for great things. Then the Antichrist bought our paper and the cuts started. Aside from various illicit private enterprises, I shouldn't imagine that Daniel has worked since.

'They can't sack you,' he says now, still chuckling.

'You reckon? I doubt that Randall will see it that way. It looks pretty bad.'

'Relax,' says Daniel. 'They won't sack you because they can't. They haven't got anyone else. The pair of you are hopelessly out of your depth as it is. Without you, Philip would go to pieces.'

'I hope you're right,' I say. 'I'm sure you are.'

'Of course I am, Macaulay. I see all.'

I stand, and grind my cigarette into the concrete floor. 'I'd better get back,' I say. 'Philip will be frantic.'

'Please. Don't let me hold you back.' Daniel gestures into the flat. 'As you can see, I have many pressing projects to be getting on with.'

I smirk. How does he spend his days? Illegally, I'd imagine. My friend Will Ramsey, on the *Post*, once told me that half their office used to get coke from Daniel.

'Sure you do,' I say. 'Like tracking down the foot that fits that Cinderella stiletto on the table there.'

'Oh her.' Daniel waves the back of his hand dismissively. 'She said she'd come back for them. Friend of yours, actually.'

I stop, halfway out of the flat. 'Really? What's her name?'

Daniel blows a smoke ring. 'I forget,' he says. 'In fact, I'm not sure she told me.'

'What did she look like?'

'Like the rest of them. Maybe,' says Daniel, with a twinkle in his eye, 'she's somebody you've painted.'

I redden, horribly. 'What? What? How do you know about the painting?'

'Common knowledge.' He turns away from me and looks back over the grubby skyline. 'You little lothario, you.'

I don't quite have the nerve to follow this one up. I let myself out.

'My dad isn't a knife-wielding psycho.'

L isten. Don't let this veneer of apathy fool you. It's a front, a pose, something I put on to give myself extra depth. That's what you want, isn't it? A bit of depth? I have fathoms. I'm a rising star. They could never have sacked Daniel if I wasn't. I'm hip, I'm fashionable, I'm wonderfully promiscuous, and I have exactly the right kind of colourful, ethnic, semi-troubled background that is requisite for your standard movie hero.

I'm a top-notch character, and I've been waiting all my life for a top-notch plot. Heading back home that night, and pondering this Fingers business, I'm beginning to think I might have found one.

Macaulay Lewis. Not a bad name, I've always thought. Better, admittedly, pre-*Home Alone*, but acceptable still and, when shortened to Mac, possibly rather funky. It suits me. My voice, despite the best efforts of my parents (and yeah, depending on company, the odd effort of my own) still picks up a bit of a Scots burr when I get drunk or angry. My height, beneath my 'fro, is somewhere around five foot ten. With it, I manage six, no problem. I'm skinny, with the makings of a pot-belly (a cruel twist of physiognomy, it's true) and the 'fro itself is shot with just enough copper to look acceptably Celtic. You'd never guess I don't have any blood in me from west of Warsaw.

That's the ethnic background. It's a Jewfro, you see, not a Scotchfro. The differences are subtle. In its most traditional form, the Scotchfro has a certain dryness and gingery luminescence which I myself am lucky enough to lack. My grandfather was a different story. Forget simply looking Scottish, in his youth, J. J. Lewis was ginger enough to have come from *Newcastle*. Every day I knew him, except for Saturdays, he wore the same Macleod of Lewis tartan kilt, the same Masonic tie and the same green tweed jacket. He looked like a walking racial joke – honestly, like a fucking porridge commercial. All of which might have been acceptable had my granddad not secretly been the wrong race entirely. He didn't wear the kilt on Saturdays simply because on Saturdays he had to go to the *shul.*

Born Joachim Laszkiewicz, Krakov, 1903. Died John Jack Lewis, Edinburgh, 1991. He must have been mortified when he found out that 'Jack' was a diminutive of 'John' anyway. 'Johnjohn' was what his kids called him behind his back. And God only knows how long it took him to spot that he'd given himself the same name as a department store. Poor man.

He was a pioneer really, old Grandpa Johnjohn. Most Jews waited until at least the 1930s before they started fleeing across Europe. Not him. By the time that Hitler started strutting about collecting bits of *Lebensraum*, Johnjohn Lewis was a firmly established Scotsman, running one of Edinburgh's pre-eminent tartan wholesalers. He'd been able to bring quite a bit of money with him, you see, getting out so early. His wife was a bit of an embarrassment, being a stocky, black-clad type, with absolutely no desire to be anything other than a displaced Pole. She died before I could know her, but, knowing the women in our family, I'm guessing she had nothing but scorn for his social desperation. Johnjohn just kept her at home, like you could with wives back then. And while, despite his best efforts, his own English never progressed beyond heavily accented slang and conversational pleasantries, he counted himself lucky to have a strapping son who spoke as a Scotsman should. That was my dad.

As a child, I had a truly romantic image of these early years. I saw my dad, dressed in his own mini-kilt, behind the counter, rosy-cheeked and eager to please, swapping cheery Scotch pleasantries with the customers, while his equally kilted father, a kind of gingery Santa Claus, beamed proudly from the storeroom. My heritage. A merry Brigadoon.

This, needless to say, is sheer bollocks. Not all that long ago, I ended up drunk at a wedding with Graham McLean, grandfather of my friend Elspeth. He told me that Lewis Cloth was a 'dingy fucking place' and also ventured the opinion that in his youth my father was 'an evil wee tyke who was lucky no' tae end up in the gaol'. Moreover, for all Grandpa Johnjohn's desperate attempts at Scottishness, he was still known to Graham and his peers as 'the Jew' in polite company, and far worse out of it.

'One time,' continued old Graham, as I plied him with Famous Grouse by the bar (and ignored Elspeth's increasingly elaborate mimes of rolling joints, snorting powders and, unless I was very much mistaken, actual penetrative sex, from over his shoulder by the toilet door), 'a gang o' heidcases frae south were up fer the fitba. This was the fifties, aye? Yer old man would have been about ten. Now, I dinnae ken how ye'd describe these lads today. No' fascists, because it was a wee bit late for them, an' no' skinheads, as it was a wee bit early. These lads had a bee in their bonnets about the Bolsheviks, aye? Anyhoo, they heard about the Jew, an' that he was, well, Jewish, like, and decided tae put his windows oot. An' they did, but only just. Seconds later the Jew himsel' was oot there wi a fuckin' claymore, and I heard that your wee da stuck a laddie or two wi' a skean-dhu. Nobody died, like, but they were messed up bad.'

Excuse me, but *what?* My dad and my Grandpa fighting off louts with swords in the 1950s? How cool is this? It's like something out of *The Godfather*. To be honest, though, I take it with a pinch of salt. As far as I have ever been aware, I absolutely do not come from this kind of family. I am respectable. My dad isn't a knife-wielding psycho. He's an accountant, and on the board of his company. He's called Peter, and he's a dad. Imagine your own bloody dad having 'stuck a laddie or two'. Can you? If you can, your dad is nothing like mine. I don't think Mad Old Graham was making it up, though. I just wish I could get my dad to talk about it.

As far as I can make out, my dad was bog-standard second-generation immigrant, in that he got posh, and studied hard. He pretty much sounds English now. Add to that the fact that my mother was born in Manchester and it maybe explains why my own voice is so totally shafted. I have no idea where I'm meant to be from. It only takes me about a week to pick up an accent. I went to St Lucia on holiday for a week when I was fourteen and talked like a Yardie for months.

As a family, I sense that we're still finding our feet. Does that make sense? We don't really have a theme yet. Elspeth has about a million siblings, of all sizes and professions, but they are all fundamentally the same grounded Scottish stock. I only have two, and if you met us, you probably wouldn't even think we were related. There's me, there's my older sister Janie, and my younger sister Mary. Janie, Macaulay and Mary. Good Jewish names, eh? Somehow, I get the impression my dad wasn't too keen on the whole Jewish business when we were younger. Recently, he seems to have acquired the same weird cultural doublethink that my grandfather had. I can't see it ever happening for me.

I'm back home now, changing out of Daniel's ugly-ass suit, and finally subjecting myself to my tiny flat's meagre excuse for a shower. I think this is all going to turn out pretty well. I get excited just thinking about it. It's going to be a hell of a movie, my one. A mix of *Fight Club* and *The Pink Panther*. I can feel it. It's happening, finally. And it's mine.

'You are going to paint me, right?'

Embassy. Nine p.m. Friday. I'm sitting, alone, at a booth between the DJ's podium and the kitchen door. I am well-placed – waiters coming out of the kitchen are forced to stop here to allow their colleagues to squeeze past. I, of course, am forced to lighten their trays when they do so. I'm about eight glasses down, I think, and feeling rather garrulous. I'm waiting for Lucy from Marketing and she's at least half an hour late. Possibly I have been stood up.

Let's take a look around, shall we? Isabella Hervey, Jade Jagger, Clarissa Mountejoy, Iain Bovery, Dan Macmillan, Normandie Keith, Tessa Compton, Tim Jeffries, Daphne Guinness and Gabriella Windsor. I have to say, I'm spotting a theme. Look at them all: haughty, clear-skinned, and gulping down champagne like it's bloody Tizer. And none of them more than a phonecall away from their own column in *Tatler*. It's so unfair.

To be honest I've only the very faintest glimmer of an understanding as to what I'm doing here. This is not like me – as I hope I have made plain, I am normally the consummate professional. Philip was meant to be on tonight, but there was some kind of heated debate in the office this afternoon which resulted in everybody deciding that it was actually my task. Why, I'm not sure. I wasn't really listening, being more concerned with relocating my impending date with Lucy from Marketing.

There's a lot of gold about, I've noticed that – chokers, waistcoats, cufflinks, even the odd wig. Also, in amongst the Sloanes there are more Euro-types than usual – I've also spotted Laetitia Casta, Sophie Gerad, Audrey Tatou, the girlband t.A.T.u, Luc Dernier and that bloke from *Eurotrash*. I did see a press release about all this, I'm sure of it.

'Mac,' drawls a voice above me. 'Nice spot. Mind if I join you?'

I look up, into an elaborately bearded chin. 'Neil,' I say. 'Thought you might turn up. Be my guest.'

Neil Hammond. Secret Liverpudlian. Tries to look like Joseph Fiennes looked when he was trying to look like Shakespeare. Fat, though, and five foot four.

Neil is one of the oldest friends I still have these days, bar Elspeth. He sits down opposite me, and starts reciting some lengthy anecdote about Mariella Frostrup. I have never met Mariella Frostrup. I'm pretty sure that neither has he.

Neil and I shared a house in Brixton six years ago, fresh out of university, when both of us spoke rather differently. I'd come straight from Cambridge, he straight from Bristol. Our mutual friend was Sandy, a podgy, balding guy from my college who wanted to be a musician. Oh! What a creative bunch we were! Neil and I both wanting to be journalists (or 'writers' as we called it back then), Sandy with his keyboards, Jacob with his decks and Ray with his tireless yet fruitless attempts to get into drama school.

I last saw Sandy six months ago, at a house party in Tooting that I only went to by mistake. He's in IT these days. I haven't seen Jacob or Ray for years, but I gather one is a lawyer and the other does something for a charity, very possibly in Nepal. Neil, conversely, I see about once a fortnight. He's a photographer these days, you see. He works for one of the glossies. Unlike the other three, he's still a character in the drama of my life. Although he is, on occasion, dull as piss.

He's saying something now. By his tone, it appears to invite response.

'What's that?' I ask.

'David Baddiel,' he's saying, for some reason. 'Did you know?'

'Yeah,' I hazard. 'I think I read it somewhere. Listen. I'm going mad here. Do you know what all this is about?'

'All what?'

'This,' I say, and wave my hand elaborately. 'The gold, the booze, the sloanes. Mr Eurotrash. What's going on?'

'MOFO,' says Neil, and I very nearly hit him.

'Merchandise of French Origin,' he adds hastily. 'It's a trade bash. Luxury goods.'

'MOFO. I remember. What a totally un-chic name.'

Neil doesn't look very impressed. 'I think it's deliberate, actually Mac. It's an FCUK thing.' He pauses. 'Are you okay? Why don't you know this?'

'I'm a slacker,' I tell him nonchalantly, despite being genuinely shaken. This is not like me. I do not usually forget things like this, ever. Must be the booze. I reach for a fresh glass and eye Neil hopefully. 'Do you have any fags?'

He doesn't, so we pass the time trying to impress each other by pointing out obscure semi-famous people that we've never spoken to. I'm winning, and I can tell it is driving him insane. I've just let him have Jean-Paul Gaultier's ex-boyfriend (even though it plainly isn't) and Tanita Tikaram's elder brother Ramon (who I spotted hours ago) to keep him calm, when Jessica Kapur and Carolyn Somethingorother saunter up and start blowing smoke at us. Jessica sat next to me at my first job when I was stuffing envelopes for *Poshbird Monthly*, and Carolyn used to live with Elspeth. I had a bit of a thing with her at one of Paxy's sordid gatherings about six months ago, and I have a notion that she now hates me. How or why she and Jessica know each other, I have no idea.

'All right?' says Jessica, who is petite, Asian, from Newcastle, and mildly dreadful. She prods me in the thigh with one toe of her red strappy shoes. 'Saw yer froont page. Dozy fooker.'

Neil laughs merrily at this. I grimace. Carolyn, who is one of those tall, freckly, flat-footed girls, stares around the room, seemingly ignoring all of us.

'Yeah, well,' I start to say, and then catch sight of Elspeth over by the toilet door, trapped by that fucker Jensen Randall, twisting as though she is trying to get away. Jensen is the son of the ogre who bought our newspaper, and his views on women would make a Saudi blush. No way is he getting anywhere near Elspeth. I stand up. 'Excuse me.'

'We were trying to figure out who it was in our office this morning,' says Jessica, 'I reckon we've got it.'

I sit down with a thud.

'Oh yeah?' I say.

'Yeah,' says Jessica. '*Little Britain.*'

Neil blinks. 'Excuse me?'

'*Little Britain,*' repeats Jessica. 'Those two guys. It's a publicity stunt. It's exactly the sort of thing they'd do.'

'Christ,' I mutter, and Jessica kicks me again. I yelp. 'Stop *doing* that.'

'It could be them,' she says, looking hurt.

'It couldn't,' I tell her. 'The *Gazette* would sue them. We look ridiculous.'

Jessica pouts. 'Maybe you're in on it.'

'*I'm* not,' I say, and stand up again.

'But there'll be another tonight though, won't there?' she says, and I sit down again with another thud.

'Eh?'

'That's why I'm here,' says Neil seriously, and I stare at him. 'Everyone in the office reckons he's going to go after that gold choker on Sophie Gerad.'

Jessica nods.

'Everybody *reckons?*' I ask, wishing I'd paid more attention to what was going on in the office today. 'What did he do, send out a press release?'

'There was an email going round,' says Jessica.

'I saw it on Popbitch,' says Carolyn, sounding bored.

'Jesus,' I say, and scan the room until I spot Sophie Gerad. She's standing over by the bar, flashing her teeth at a polo player who used to go out with Jodie Kidd. Normally described in the press as 'France's top export to London', Gerad's a B-list model with A-list pretensions. You can do that if you're posh or foreign. Actually Belgian by birth, she is a touch too small to be a proper model (five foot five or so) but must have a friend working on one of the society glossies. She's a platinum blonde with an impressively Gallic upturned nose, and she probably appeals to the kind of people who'd really fancy Patsy Kensit if she didn't sometimes look like she should be shunting a pram around Croydon. She turns up occasionally in the broadsheets' gossip pages, and I'm pretty sure was once engaged to somebody Guinness. Basically, she wears things that her friends make, and gets paid for it. Tonight her entire neck from jaw to collar bone is encased in a yellow gold sheath, linked together around the back by a series of hoops. The look is part African Queen, part orthopaedic post-op. It's certainly eye-catching.

'That,' I say slowly, 'would not be an easy thing to steal.'

Neil points out that diamonds glued to a lady's nipples can't really be that easy to steal either, and Jessica starts suggesting ways that Fingers (or Lucas and Walliams) might have managed it, most of which involve turpentine and a good hard twist. Carolyn doesn't really say anything, but gives the occasional sigh of weary disbelief. I don't think I like Carolyn very much.

'Why should there be another theft?' I ask, once her breathing is really beginning to bug me. 'Why should he do it again?'

'Why not?' says Jessica. 'Why should *they* only do it once?'

Carolyn yawns.

'He'd have his work cut out on this one,' says Neil. 'It's hardly the kind of thing you can just sneak off with, is it?'

It isn't. Sophie Gerad is now being fawned over by an Italian guy who works for Gucci and one of those lumpy Etonian lordlings that seem to be employed full-time to be friends with Prince William. She's leaning against a wall, resting her head at an odd angle and very slightly grimacing. She has one hand against the top of her collar bone and a thumb under the edge of the choker. She looks tired.

'She'll take it off,' says Jessica, nudging Neil out the way and squeezing into the booth alongside him. 'No question. It must weigh half a kilo. She'll take it off and leave it in the cloakroom.'

I move along to allow Carolyn to sit next to me. She eyes me with distaste, but does so.

'That choker is the *Collier d'Or*, made in 1638 by Louis XIII's chief jeweller,' Neil points out. 'According to FT.com, it is worth an estimated half million euros when twinned with the matching wrist-cuffs, and something over 200,000 on its own. It is not the kind of thing you leave in a cloakroom.'

I look over towards the toilet, but Elspeth and Jensen have disappeared. Together? Almost certainly not. All the same, I feel a familiar quiet rage.

'You're seeing Thingy Denton, aren't you?' says Jessica, and Carolyn gives an astonishingly rude snort.

'Er, who?' I say, ignoring the noise. 'I don't think so.'

Jessica rolls her eyes. 'Lucy. Lucy Denton. From your paper.'

'Oh. Right. Lucy. No, I wouldn't say that. We're just friends. Why?'

'Because she's over there,' says Jessica, and points towards the bar. 'Waving at you.'

Lucy is gold, shimmery, sequined and apologetic. She says that she was late because she's been drinking with her cousin and they lost track of time. I am grateful for this, because it also means that Lucy is drunk. I vastly prefer drunk girls to sober girls in situations like this.

'You are going to paint me, right?' she says when I bear down on her at the bar, and already I know my work is done. From then on, it's just a matter of patiently waiting until it's time to leave.

Lots of my friends, and especially my female friends, refuse to believe that people like Lucy exist. In a nonchalant, rushing-to-the-lift-at-the-right-time kind of way, I've had my eye on her for a while. Lucy likes white wine, Top Shop, Maroon 5 and boys. She works in our marketing department, where I'd imagine she spends most of her time filing and putting up with old men checking out her arse. I have a hunch that Lucy likes old men checking out her arse. She probably finds it flattering.

When I finally struck up a proper chat with Lucy at the diamond bash at the Mandarin she was wearing a smooth silk silver-white balldress which clung to her like a membrane. I remember thinking that something about the way the silk gave way to skin where her limbs protruded was almost obscene: biological, like a tongue flicking from a glistening mouth. Remember, I was stoned. Her own mouth was lipsticked scarlet in pout. Her hair was piled up, like a film star. Obviously, I wanted to sleep with her. Obviously, she wouldn't have been surprised to hear this. So instead I told her I wanted to paint her.

That's pretty obvious too, you might think, but it works. It would have worked with Lucy I'm sure, had I not dragged her back to the offices in search of further drugs. That, I now acknowledge, was a tactical mistake. It might have worked on a weekend, when a night out can turn into an adventure. On a schoolnight it just broke momentum. There were no drugs, and I was too drunk to get to my home without them. She wasn't drunk enough to have sex in a photocopier cupboard. She went home by herself.

Tonight she's wearing loose black hipster slacks, pointy black heels and a gold sequined halterneck. She has on lots of black mascara, and her hair is in bunches. When she cocks her head and pouts, which she does a lot, one side of the halterneck rides up her hips and displays a small tattoo of a fairy and the tiny strap of her G-string.

'I'll paint you,' I say, and escort her to the bar.

We drink a lot. More than necessary, even, but it's Friday night and it's a free bar and there is frankly no reason not to. I keep an eye out, but I don't see Elspeth again. Neil and Jessica spend the next few hours at the booth arguing violently about (I think) blaxploitation and pornography, before taking to the dancefloor and snogging equally violently to Destiny's Child. Carolyn vanishes with a Belgian prince. Sophie Gerad doesn't take the choker to the cloakroom, and gamely lasts until almost half twelve before making her exit. She has two bodyguards with her, I notice. Nobody will be making off with the *Collier d'Or* tonight.

Lucy and I leave at about two, and pick up one of those weird little rickshaws that crusties with pink dreadlocks use to clog up the streets of central London from 8 p.m. onwards. It takes us over half an hour to get to my flat in Knightsbridge, and costs something like £50. Extravagant, I know.

It's a warm night. We share a scorching joint made of chalky resin, which Lucy picked up in a café in some hellish part of South London, while chatting about nothing and enjoying being watched. Nobody bats an eyelid in Soho, but we're unusual from Marble Arch onwards, and by the time we reach Park Lane people are openly nudging each other and pointing us out. Lucy sits up straight and grins and starts imagining, I can tell, that she's some-body famous and cool and classy like Denise Van Outen or Jo Whiley. Our pedaller (a crusty with pink dreadlocks, natch) keeps arching his neck and giving us little conspiratorial winks when-ever we pass the joint, so, feeling magnanimous, I hand the lucky sod the last two inches, which he then enjoys so theatrically that we skip a red light at Hyde Park Corner and very nearly get wiped out by the N22 nightbus. No tip for him.

Back at my building, I wink at Lenny, the granite-faced porter (who detests me, I just know it) and take Lucy into the lift up to my flat. I've left the curtain drawn over the kitchen cubicle, and the easel propped against the oven. When I go to bring it out into the main space, I do that softly-fading-into-the-distance thing with my footsteps, thus cleverly giving the impression that the flat is at least twice its actual size. At my suggestion Lucy removes her top as I start to wave a brush around, and ten minutes later, without my suggesting anything, she has flipped one strap of her shiny aquamarine bra down over her shoulder and her panda-bear eyes are staring directly into my own. Five minutes after that, her left hand is inside her bra massaging her left breast, and two minutes after that, this time at her suggestion, I am beside her on the sofa, pressing the paint-daubed fingertips of my right hand against her lips, while my left frees the drawstring ties on her loose black slacks and slides, silkily, into the enchanting aquamarine world beyond.

Art. Everyone's a sucker for it.

Now. A few things I don't see.

At 9.45 the following morning, not a million miles away, Sophie Gerad sends the shoebox containing the *Collier d'Or* choker downstairs with her own doorman after he brings her the morning papers. At 9.51, the doorman hands it to a courier, who is expected, flashes some identification, and claims to have been sent by the French Embassy. And then, at 9.58, the doorman hears a furious banging on the front door and opens it to find the real embassy courier, holding a nearly-empty shoebox and demanding to know why the hell it had been left unattended on the doorstep. Inside, between them, courier and doorman discover a handwritten note. '*I do hope this fits,*' it says. '*Yours, Fingers.*'

'You lost a thin one. I'm so sorry.'

Nine thirty a.m., Saturday, and I am huddled in the small corner of my queen-sized bed that the voracious Lucy has left me. Too hungover to properly awaken, I play a favourite game; I imagine I know nothing of my surroundings and try to establish as much as possible without opening my eyes or using any prior knowledge. It is similar to another game I often play – imagining seeing myself now through the eyes of myself as a child. All deeply significant in some deeply psychological way, I'm sure.

So. The dark blue sheets feel creased beneath my back. Of course – I remind myself – I don't know that they are dark blue. Merely sheets, and creased. I think I can feel a soft, smooth thigh cushioning my knee, but do I actually know it is soft or smooth, or even a thigh? Here and now, it is merely flesh. In a bed, next to flesh. Could be *Basic Instinct*, could be *The Godfather*. But then there is the smell – no horseheads here. I smell paint. I smell sex.

I smell cigarettes and hairspray and very possibly, if I really strain, the overflowing dustbin from the kitchen next door. Not, of course, that I should know of any such thing.

Sounds. Traffic and shouts, plainly from outside. Inside, feet away, a soft, warm snuffling. Honestly, the noises women make while they sleep. Elsewhere in my building pointed footsteps clip the floor, a door slams, a woman sneezes and I begin to form a picture in my mind. I'm cheating now, but sod it. I'll be properly awake in a minute anyway.

My mobile rings ('Reach For The Stars', by S Club 7, although I'm thinking of changing it because it's been two months and not a single person has asked me *why*) and I sit up and open my eyes, replacing the mental picture of my surroundings with a real one. Reality shifts like a focusing kaleidoscope; my room is darker and smaller than I had imagined; I, fatter and less brown. Christ I am hungover. Stretching over Lucy's hip, I scoop the mobile from the clothes-strewn floor.

'. . .,' I croak.

'Mackie? Mackie, is that you?'

'Princess,' I mutter. 'How are you? Isn't it *shabbas*?'

'Janie,' says the voice. 'Not Princess.' There is a sniff.

'Janie? You okay?'

'Ross left.'

'Ross. Ross was the fat one?'

'Ross was thin.'

'Jesus, you lost a thin one. I'm so sorry. I'll be right over.'

The phone goes dead and I scramble over my bed-guest's ample curves, inadvertently wiping my penis against her belly. Her nose wrinkles, but I don't think she actually wakes up. Fumbling in the stifled light, I shove the easel back behind the fridge and grab what clothes I can — the slate-grey trousers from Daniel's suit, trainers, an orange T-shirt. I take my huge army-surplus jacket from the back of the door and shuffle down to the lobby. I feel like a glue-sniffer. The porter, who probably hasn't even set eyes on anybody else this morning who earns under £200k, pretends not to notice me. I pretend not to notice him. Moments later I'm blinking in the vicious glare of Brompton Road, dodging shoppers and waiting for the number 52 bus to Victoria.

Janie is my sister. Or rather, Janie is my South London sister, two years older than me. My North London sister is Mary, two years my junior and more usually known as 'the Princess'. Janie is a quasi-Buddhist hippy, the Princess is dating the son of a rabbi. Janie lives in Brixton, the Princess lives in Hendon. I live in the middle. We really are quite the most ridiculous family.

Janie's flat is up towards the Herne Hill end of Brixton, where the streets get a little cleaner and the crack dealers fear to tread, in case they get collared by some wild-haired sociology professor in a woollen tie who wants to share a cup of lentil tea and discuss their views about *Amistad*. The Princess thinks it's 'dodgy' round here. Janie prefers the word 'multicultural'. It is a weird and disturbing area, but not for the kind of reasons that it likes to think it is. It suits Janie perfectly.

In the film that they must one day make of my life, Janie, poor girl, should probably be played by Tim Roth. She has the same sandy hair, the same red lips, the same snarl and the same only slightly mannish jawline. Really, now I think about it, this is ruder to Tim Roth than it is to Janie. Janie looks like a man who looks like a woman who looks like a lesbian. I really can't think of any better way to describe her.

Jane believes that she is a hippy. I have never figured out quite what she means by this. To my mind, hippies have messy hair, take drugs, are a bit smelly and enjoy a comfortably elastic morality. I do all of these things, and I don't think I am a hippy. Janie does none, except maybe for the last. She eats organic food, works out, wears patchwork and has a rotund black and white cat she calls Orca, after the killer whale.

I remember well the day that Janie started calling herself a hippy – it was in 1994, the day that we put a headstone over Grandpa Johnjohn's year-old grave. My dad, in one of his periodic bouts of mildly combative Jewishness, had been insisting that we all go along. Mary and I had no problem with this (Mary for her own, secret reasons, which wouldn't become apparent for a few years yet, and me because I've always felt suitably distant from my relatives to view them as would a social anthropologist). Janie, though. Janie wasn't having it.

'You have to be joking,' she told dad over the breakfast table, glowering through her purple fringe, and doing her best not to dip her black lace cuffs in her Coco Pops. 'I'm not going. No way.'

Cuffs? Purple fringe? Perhaps I should explain. Janie was at the end of her Goth phase back then. She wore black or red velvet bodices, the fronts of which were usually stained with yoghurt. She never really carried off the whole crow-like dignity thing all that well. Two years her junior and into grunge, I was loftily disdainful of her image, but always raiding her tape collection. Two years my junior, Mary wore a lot of pink and was not yet into anything much.

My dad just stared at her, spoon hovering over his Ready Brek. Yes, I know. Ready Brek. The mark of the wannabe Scot. 'Not going? Why in God's name wouldn't you want to go?'

'It's just so totally bogus,' snarled Janie, in that stabbable Bill and Ted manner in which we all used to talk. 'You're, like, totally imposing a mindset on us that you yourself abode.'

Dollops of Ready Brek splattered from my dad's spoon. 'Abode?' he said. 'Abode?'

'She means "abhor",' sighed Mary, aged fourteen. 'Shut up, Janie.'
I sniggered.

'Shut up yourself, you prissy little bitch,' spat Janie. 'Abode, abhor, whatever. I'm not going. I don't believe in organised religion. And you're hardly a proper Jew anyway, Dad.'

He put down his spoon. 'I bloody am actually, young lady.'

'No you aren't,' said Janie. 'There's bacon in that fridge. We had prawns the day before yesterday. But suddenly you're pretending to be all religious, just to impress a bunch of old men you haven't seen since you were a teenager.'

'Janie,' said my dad. 'I'm Jewish. We're all Jewish. So what if we stray from time to time? It's still there. I'm simply asking you to honour your grandfather in the way he would have wanted.'

'Well why should I?' demanded Janie, batting her mascara-heavy eyelashes. 'You never did. Face it, Dad. You simply don't consider yourself to be Jewish.'

'I do! I am absolutely Jewish.'

'Well I'm not,' said Janie, and tucked into her cereal. 'I'm not Jewish and I'm not going. I believe in natural things, rather than the dogmas of the mind. I'm not going to be a Goth anymore, either. I'm going to be a New Age hippy.'

'A what?'

'A New Age hippy.'

'Jesus Christ,' said my dad, rather proving Janie's point.

So that was that. Over the next few months the black lace was replaced by beaded flares and countless T-shirts with little pictures of aliens on them, usually smoking joints. Then came yoga. Then came crystals. Then came a degree in Psychoanalysis and Massage at an ex-poly in Newcastle. Then – and yes, I'm aware that I'm condensing about a decade here into a mere paragraph, but I'm

hoping I'll be forgiven for the sake of smooth narrative – came a
shitty flat in Brixton, a part-time job at a Holistic Bookshop ('A
what?' cried my father, 'a bloody what?') and a huge succession of
unsuitable boyfriends, most of whom smelled vaguely of cider and
many of whom came and went in a matter of hours, rather than
weeks, months or years. Then came her late twenties, and then
came the realisation that, unless something pretty dramatic
happened, not much else was going to come for the rest of her
life. Then came the depression, and then came Ross, although
Ross, I suppose, probably falls into a category already mentioned.

Janie answers her door in a leotard, which is a bad sign.

'Hey,' I say, gently.

'Hey,' she says, and marches brightly away back down her
grubby corridor, with a camp little bounce like Geri Halliwell in
her 'It's Raining Men' video. 'Just finishing my workout. With
you in a moment. Help yourself to a cup of chai.'

Chai, thank God, turns out to refer to regular tea, rather than
any more unusual eastern brew, and I sip gingerly at a cup in the
kitchen while Janie thuds about next door in the living room to
the sound of some hideous Goa trance. Janie only works out when
she's thoroughly miserable. Consequentially, she's in pretty good
shape.

It's not nice in here. The kitchen is small and smells, constantly,
of drains, teabags and incense. The floor is made of cork tiles,
scratched and bleached pale, and Orca, bloated parasite that he
is, has merrily shredded the edges. The sink is chipped enamel
and full of brightly painted but wobbly plates. The chairs are
plastic. The table is a nice wooden one, but old and grooved, and
boasting enough food packed into its scratches to have fed my
shtetl-dwelling ancestors for a matter of months. One look tells

you that the occupant of this flat went to Ikea, once, five years ago. Holistic bookery does not pay well.

The tape stops. Janie comes through from the living room and starts crying.

'Hey,' I say. 'Hey.'

She just looks at me. I ask her if I can smoke. She stops crying for long enough to say no, which is just as well as I am fagless, and then gets going again. I unfold one of her plastic chairs and set it down next to me.

'Sit down,' I tell her. 'Drink tea. Talk to me.'

She does the first two. My eyes itch. This always happens. I am allergic to her damn cat. After a few minutes, I take her hand.

'What happened with Ross?' I ask.

'He left,' says Janie, tonelessly as well as obviously.

'Why?'

'Some little bitch,' says Janie, and there is fire, suddenly, in her eyes. 'Some prepubescent slag who worked with him at the station. Lola. The same one as last time.'

Now I remember who Ross is. Ross is one of the regulars, in that he goes out with my sister for a couple of months every six or so, generally until somebody better comes along. He's a skinny, lanky dopehead, with long hair and a thing about the Foo Fighters. He works at a South London radio station, and has a reputation for shagging all his interns. When I first heard about him, I was insanely jealous of the guy. Then I found out he was thirty-eight.

'I thought you split up with him about a month ago,' I say, carefully. 'You were seeing that fat guy.'

'Gerald,' agrees Janie. 'But I threw him out when Ross came back last week.'

'Why did you throw Gerald out?'

'Because I thought it would be different. Ross needed somewhere to stay.'

'Why did he need somewhere to stay?'

'Because Lola threw him out. But now she's taken him back. And Gerald . . . Gerald . . .' Her voice cracks.

'Gerald?' I prompt.

'Gerald won't take me back. He won't even see me.'

'Why not?'

'Because he says I'd just do it again.'

Jesus Christ. Jesus fucking Christ. This is my sister's life. This is it. Before Gerald and Ross there was Jon and Nick, and Jeremy and Ben, and Will and Alec. There's no end to the fuckers. This is what she does, over and over again. She's been doing it for a decade, and she'll do it forever, until some bastard gets her up the duff and even sad, desperate wankers like these won't go near her. Don't blame bloody Gerald. Gerald is absolutely right. Really, my heart goes out to the guy.

'Forget Gerald,' I tell her. 'Forget Gerald and Ross and Jon and Nick and Jeremy. Forget all of them. Find something to do. Not a boy. A hobby. A proper job. A life.'

'I have a life,' sniffs Janie. 'I have my shop, and my yoga.'

'Find a new one. Go somewhere. Go travelling. Go home.'

Janie mumbles something that I don't catch. I ask her to repeat it. She looks at the floor.

'I haven't got any money,' she whispers. 'How can I go somewhere with no money?'

'Not even enough money to go home?'

Janie just cries.

I push myself away from the table and stand up. This is not right. This is the wrong way around. Older sisters are meant to look after their siblings, particularly in families like ours.

'Christ,' I say, and after a moment I say it again. 'Christ. Are you sure you haven't got any cigarettes?'

'Rollies,' says Janie. 'On top of the fridge. Ross left them.'

So the man has some uses. Behind a box of cat litter (on the fridge! on the bloody fridge!) I find a plastic pack of Golden Virginia. Inside are some kingsize blue Rizlas, which I chuck onto the table, and around a tenth of hash, which I smuggle into a pocket. Janie would just make me bin it if I told her.

'Want one?' I ask.

She screws up her face. 'No,' she says, and looks at me, as if for the first time this morning. 'You look like shit.'

'Thanks.'

'Were you out last night?'

I nod.

'Did you pull?'

I don't answer, but I hold her eye as I sit down and begin rolling a cigarette.

'You did!' Janie leans forward and actually claps her hands, wiping her eyes. 'Who? Not Elspeth?'

'Ancient history, Janie. This was just a girl from work.'

'Who? Who, who, who?'

We are both leaping onto this new topic of conversation like stricken sailors leaping for a life raft. It's obvious, and we both know it's obvious, but that's okay.

'Not telling,' I say, but I grin, causing her to almost grin back. 'Really. Just someone from work who thinks I'm more important than I am.'

'Work being the paper?' asks Janie.

I nod.

'How's that going? The Princess left me a message the other day. Said you were on the front page. I didn't actually buy it though, sorry. What was it about?'

So I tell her – about the Diamond Ball and my first front page, about Gemma Conrad, and about last night; about getting so drunk that I slept in a cupboard and about the trouble I got into

38

at work, through no fault of my own. She laughs and I laugh. She is grateful, and so am I.

'That was your paper?' she asks, wide-eyed. 'I saw something about that on the news. I didn't know it had anything to do with *you*.'

I tell her it doesn't really, but share the theories we were discussing last night, none of which she really understands. Then she starts telling me about how sick she is of the whole London thing, and how much she'd like to go home. Or if not home, then to India, where a guy she knows has opened an ashram-cum-guesthouse place on the banks of a holy lake in Rajasthan, just like in that car advert. India is her new place. It used to be Japan. Janie could bore for Europe about Japan. She'd also like to go to Ethiopia, and to Iran, and to New Zealand, Malawi, China, Ecuador, Alaska, South Africa, Malaysia and, although I'm sure she's confusing them with somewhere else, the Falkland Islands. Janie would like to go everywhere, but she hasn't been anywhere. Except for Ibiza, and that was five years ago. I start wishing I had a lot of money, stupid money, so I could buy her a ticket to fly around the world. Then Orca slips fatly through the open window, and, as my eyes brim with itchy tears, I realise that if she did go away I'd probably have to cat-sit.

Once I start sneezing, Janie lets me out the front, and closes the door behind me. I take two steps along the path towards the pavement, and then stop. I take out my wallet. Sixty quid. Not enough to get her to Rajasthan, but maybe enough to get her to Edinburgh. I push it through the letterbox and head for the train, feeling slightly happy, but in a sad way.

'You're looking at it all wrong.'

Sunday morning, and there is a note on my desk scrawled in Brainchild's spidery hand. *'Be in conference'* it says. This alarms me, not least because conference started fifteen minutes ago.

'Philip!' I holler automatically, but Philip isn't in yet. Working on Sundays is a bitch. The one consolation is that the majority of us can usually get away with not turning up until half ten or so. I'm in earlier because Elaine, Brainchild's secretary, left a message on my mobile telling me that I had to be. She didn't mention anything about *conference*, though. Why not? I start to feel slightly panicked.

Lucy had gone by the time I got home yesterday. She didn't seem too cross about my leaving unannounced – she just left a note apologising for finishing the milk, and said I should call her sometime. I sent her a text in the evening, saying my sister had been having a crisis. I shouldn't have left her alone in the flat,

40

though. She'll have seen how small it is. I just hope she didn't find the easel. That could be embarrassing. I toyed with the idea of actually calling her, or maybe even going to see her, but decided that my best bet was to remain attractively aloof. Does that work? I suppose it's what Elspeth does all the time. Not an approach I've tried before.

So. On to conference. 'Conference', for those of you lucky enough to work in the real world, is the meeting at the beginning of the day, when we journalists sit around and decide what will be going into tomorrow's paper.

I say 'we'. Personally, I don't usually actually go to conference. I'm not sure why. Daniel always used to, back when he was my boss. The morning after he was sacked, when I – technically – took over his job, I strolled confidently down to the little anteroom outside the editor's office and took a seat. I was the new Daniel. I had my own column. I'd probably have my own table at the annual Wrexham House party. I was a player. I sat there, smiling confidently at most of the top-level editorial staff as they filed in, and determinedly refusing to meet the eye of the newsdesk's lovely Rebecca Leighton who, a mere eleven hours previously, had rudely refused to have sex with me in a carpark behind Liverpool Street station. She'd be sorry already, I decided.

That morning didn't pan out how I had expected. Rudie Andrews, our ageing and largely irrelevant editor, gave me a surprised look when he came in but, fool that I was, the alarm bells didn't ring. Andrews looks like Ronald Reagan looked in the last years of his presidency: baffled and slightly concerned. I'm not sure he actually fulfils any real function these days, thanks to the Big Boss's omnipotence. He was followed by Jensen Randall, son of the CEO. We'd been out for a drink earlier that week; I gave him a little wave. He did an immediate about turn, and returned a few seconds later with Trevor Brainchild at his heels.

Brainchild went to the front of the room, put his hands on his hips, and spoke to me over the heads of everyone else.

'Lewis,' he said, with his usual bullfrog smile. 'Don't think we *need* you actually. Why not *pop* along back to your *desk*, eh? Anything comes up we'll let you know. There's a *good* lad.'

I actually laughed; can you believe that?

'Aye, right, Trevor,' I said easily. 'And you'll be today's celeb specialist will you?'

A few people laughed, but not Trevor Brainchild. 'Lewis,' he said, and I realised he wasn't joking. 'Go.'

So I did. In front of every even mildly important person in my place of work (and, more importantly, in front of Rebecca Leighton) I stood up and went away. Jensen was staring pointedly out of the window, a wry smile on his face. That two-faced fucker. I still don't know why he was even there. He's meant to work in *marketing*.

Jensen is there again when I turn up today, but he doesn't notice me. Nobody does. Numbers are down, what with it being a Sunday, and the ten or so people present all have their eyes fixed to the front. Martin Priest, the goblin who took over as foreign ed. when the old one took a bullet in Afghanistan (good story, but maybe now isn't the time), is ranting on about the origins of the power struggle between Hamas and the PLO in the Gaza Strip. He's quite animated and sweating like cheap cheese. He's also completely wrong in almost everything he's saying, but I don't think anybody would expect me to interrupt and point this out. Just as well. That kind of thing exhausts me.

Neither Trevor Brainchild nor the real editor are in today, what with it being Sunday, so the editor's chair is filled by Robin Hargreaves, one of the deputies. I can't really figure Hargreaves out. He's an officious little chicken of a man, but he seems to like me. Perhaps he spots a kindred spirit. Close-cropped hair, elaborate speech patterns. The kind of clothes that turn up in the short-term memory as expensive suits, even if they aren't. Think John Malkovich, but softer. Hargreaves used to work elsewhere with Daniel, but I don't think they really got on.

'Thanks, Martin,' he says now. 'Just the foreign pages for that one, I fear. Highly stimulating, I'm sure, but I still think we'll be leading with Rebecca's rapist. The battle for Palestine will still be with us tomorrow. Mr Spike, God willing, will not.'

There is a mumbling restlessness in the room. Hargreaves raises a hand for quiet. Beside him, Melvyn Nottinger, the lanky chief sub who talks like Catullus, rolls his eyes.

'Enough,' says Hargreaves. 'Now. This Fingers business. I don't think we can really ignore it, can we? Very glam, very celeb. Perfect water-cooler chat.'

Priest sighs, loudly and theatrically. Hargreaves shoots him a sharp look.

'Problem, Martin?' he says.

'No,' mutters Priest.

'Yes,' announces his neighbour who, what with it being slightly past 9 a.m., is almost certainly drunk. This is Willie Fowler. Red-nosed, long-haired and shabby, Fowler looks like a Musketeer who has spent the last two decades drinking paint thinner. Nominally he's the paper's news editor but his days are numbered, and almost certainly in single figures. Beside him, Rebecca Leighton has her head in her hands.

Hargreaves turns to him as might a weary kestrel surveying a chirpy vole. 'Willie.' he says, too brightly.

'It's fucking bollocks,' explains Fowler, and everybody freezes.

'Excuse me?' says Hargreaves.

'Randall bollocking shite,' says Fowler, and one of his eyes twitches downwards, as though staring in consternation at the wayward mouth below. 'It's drivel. Pop gossip nonsense that has no place in the news pages of a serious family newspaper. Water-cooler chat? If we weren't owned by that brown-nosing bloody Russian, we wouldn't even consider running this kind of thing outside the diary.'

There is a deathly hush, during which nobody looks at Jensen Randall. Did I say days? Willie Fowler has hours. Or possibly even minutes.

'Comments noted,' says Hargreaves (bravely, I can't help but think), and then adds, 'but dismissed. And I'll thank you, Willie, to keep your prejudices out of this room, at least when I'm in it.' He glances at Jensen, whose tanned face is ruby red. 'Perhaps, if you have nothing better to contribute, you'd do best to remove yourself from this meeting.'

Fowler looks rather stunned. 'I'm staying.'

'*Verbum sat sapienti*,' murmurs Melvyn Nottinger.

'Fine,' says Hargreaves and takes a breath. 'As I was saying. Fingers. We *will* stick with this story. It *is* water-cooler chat, and we *want* water-cooler chat. As, these days, does everyone. So. What do we know?'

Rebecca Leighton stands up, dark, plaited hair framing her face like the Predator, and reads from a printed sheet, in a monotone bored-robot voice. Rebecca has a face like an Egyptian, African dark, but pointy as a Slav. It must be awful, looking as good as that. How do you get through the day? How do you even get the *tube*?

'Saturday morning at about ten,' she reports, flatly. 'A man pretending to be a courier pulls up outside a Gloucester Road apartment block and steals the *Collier d'Or* from a shoebox. The previous night, it had been worn by French model Sophie Gerad at the Merchandise of French Origin party in the Embassy night-club, just off Piccadilly Circus. Evidence left at the scene of the crime suggests that the criminal was the same thief who made off with the Bushman's Thimbles at our own party last week.' She looks up. 'According to the guy who has taken over the case, one Detective Inspector Tom St Eccles at the Yard, the Met currently has no leads.'

Hargreaves frowns and, to my surprise, shoots me a quick glance. 'Right,' he says. 'A high-profile theft. Good story. What are you thinking in terms of presentation?'

Rebecca shrugs. 'Front page,' she says. 'Tell the story straight. More quotes from the police and eyewitness reports from people who were actually there.'

'Colour,' growls Nottinger. 'Fluff. Flibbertigibbets.'

'Mmmm,' says Rebecca, after only a moment's pause. 'We could get someone to knock up an artist's impression of the card he left behind. Not hard. We still have pictures of the old one.'

'Fine,' says Hargreaves, but he doesn't look delighted. I don't blame him. 'That's the front. And inside?'

Everybody frowns, intently. Jensen taps his teeth with a pen. He looks dim and eager.

'Maybe put it into context?' suggests Rebecca. 'What other high-profile robberies have there been?'

'The Dome,' yawns Priest.

'Ronnie Biggs,' slurs Willie Fowler.

'The Golden Fleece,' declaims Melvyn Nottinger.

'This is daft,' I say.

Every neck in the room twists, the older ones with audible cracks. From somewhere in the vicinity of Jensen there is a hiss. I stare at him, and get to my feet. *Finally.*

'Hark,' mutters Nottinger, 'at the interloper.'

'Thank you, Melvyn,' I say. 'Listen, folks. You're looking at it all wrong. This is not just a theft. This is celebrity. The whole thing. This is a bigger story than the Great Train Robbery. This is a celebrity event. We shouldn't think of this as a crime story. Totally dull. It's more like a film launch. It's a *happening.* It's *cool.*'

I hear titters.

'Calm down,' mutters Rebecca.

'Why is he here?' demands Jensen. 'Who asked him to come?'

'I did.' says Hargreaves. 'I like this. Go on.'

'Right,' I say, and feel a small flush of triumph. 'This isn't a news story. Willie's actually right about that. It's a lifestyle feature. This is a trend. Like . . . some weeks everybody dyes their hair red, or has babies. This week, anybody who is anyone is getting robbed. It's the new black.'

'No "new blacks" in this newspaper,' chides Hargreaves, 'But I like the approach.'

'Bullshit,' says Rebecca. 'This is a crime. It is *wrong*. We shouldn't glamorise it.'

'Bullshit yourself,' I snap back. 'It's not very wrong. This guy isn't stealing from the public. He's not stealing from us. He's stealing from *them*. From celebrities. He's a criminal, but he's not scary. People love that. He might turn out to be the new Robin Hood. Let's be on his side. Why not?'

'*Facias ipse quod faciamus suades*,' says Nottinger, but everybody ignores him.

Rebecca glares at me. 'I don't believe this. Why not? Why do you think? Morality? Reputation? Call me old-fashioned, but I think we have a responsibility to come down on the side of the police when a crime gets committed. No?'

I laugh, not because this is in any way funny, but because I've found in the past that it's a good thing to do when you are collecting your thoughts in an argument. 'No,' I say finally. 'You want old-fashioned? Fingers is old-fashioned. If all crims were like him, Britain would be a much nicer place. He's old-school. An honourable rogue. We should celebrate him. Let's put the chivalry back into crime.'

Jensen doesn't look up. 'I don't understand a word he's saying. I'm with her.'

'*She*,' says Rebecca, a touch acidly, 'is called Rebecca.'

Jensen smiles into his lap. 'That's nice for her.'

Hargreaves claps his hands. 'Rebecca is wrong,' he says, firmly. 'I'm with Macaulay. This guy chose us as the first people he was going to rip off. So he's ours. Macaulay, write up what happened the other night. I want enthusiasm, excitement. Editorialise it a bit. That's our lead.'

'I'm not happy with this,' says Rebecca.

'Tough,' says Hargreaves, and heads for the door. 'Meeting over.'

Everybody follows him out. I'm still scribbling on my pad, so I'm one of the last through the door. Out in the corridor, Jensen is waiting for me. He puts a hand to my chest, which I stare at, pointedly, until he removes it.

'Lewis,' he says.

'Jensen,' I say.

'Yansen,' he says.

I blink at him. 'What?'

'My name,' he growls, 'is Yansen. It's pronounced Yansen.'

'Lovely,' I say, and push past him. He grabs me on my shoulder, spins me around, and pushes me against the wall. I'm too shocked to even hit him, which is probably a good thing as Melvyn Nottinger has stopped at the door to the features room and is staring back at us. 'What?'

There is a finger, long and possibly manicured, hovering under my nose. It curls, and then straightens again. Jensen's voicebox is bobbing up and down. He seems to be fighting to control himself. I'm thinking of how I saw him, once, in that pub around the corner, with that bottle of Grolsch lifted high above his head.

'You shouldn't be doing this,' he manages.

'Doing what?'

'Getting,' he breathes, 'in my way.'

Does this mean anything? It seems as close to nonsense as I can imagine. I harbour no great designs towards the marketing department. I glance across at Nottinger, but his face is expressionless.

'Okay,' I say, although I don't know what I am agreeing to. 'Point made.' I shove Jensen lightly in the chest, extract myself, and back away. He stays were he is, frowning slightly, clenching and unclenching his fist.

'*Iacta alea est*,' says Melvyn Nottinger as I pass.

'Well, quite,' I say, and return to my desk.

'And you like that, do you? Being flexible?'

Sunday night, and as bloody usual I end up at Paxy's. This was not my intention when I woke up this morning, satiated as I was, Lucywise, but the triumphs I enjoyed at work today seem to have given something of a jump-start to the old libido. I'm disgusting, I know. Like a dog. Tickle me on the belly and I start humping the furniture. Still, if I am going to end up here then better a Sunday than a Saturday. Or, dear God, a Friday. Fridays are just sordid.

I first met Paxy when I was at university, although he wasn't. I met him at a house belonging to a guy called Ivor, who was the second cousin of a bloke I don't see anymore called Douglas, who was the aristocratic gay buddy of a lipsticky Mancunian faghag called Macy, who herself was at Queen's College with a (in retrospect, utterly cunty) guy called Jason. Elspeth wanted to sleep with Jason. Bing. The link. She had met him at a warehouse party in Hoxton (back when there actually were warehouses in Hoxton) and drove up to Cambridge a few weeks later, ostensibly to see me. We were going through a sort of accidental 'open' phase at that point, Elspeth and I. All very Geldof and Yates.

It was one of those idyllic June weeks that we always forget actually ever happen in Britain. Elspeth had turned up on a Wednesday, but we'd gone out clubbing that night and I'd lost her. Sometime around 10 a.m. the next morning I was woken, still in my jeans, by the sound of the illegal European horn on her garish beige convertible Escort. By my heavy bowels and ashtray mouth I could tell it had been a big night. I hoisted up my window. There was a camp floppy-haired guy I didn't recognise in the driving seat, in a stripy shirt and a cravat.

'Morning!' he called, as I wiped the sleep from my eyes. 'Elspeth sent us. She went ahead.'

'Where are we going?' I asked, grabbing a T-shirt and swinging my legs out the window.

'To the country. My cousin's house. Jump in.'

So I did. There was a twitching guy in a tracksuit and sunglasses in the passenger seat, so I clambered into the back, alongside a pouting skinny girl in too much make-up, a vinyl miniskirt and a short fake-fur jacket. She clasped me on the inner thigh the moment I sat down, which I neither objected to nor read too much into, as her other hand was playing with the camp guy's hair. Elspeth is always meeting people like this. Even now.

'I'm Macy,' she whispered into my ear, before sticking her tongue into it. The poor girl. I hadn't even washed.

'Douglas,' said the camp guy, twisting his neck. 'And this is Mikey.'

'Wotcha,' said Mikey, without turning.

'I'm Macaulay,' I told them. 'And this is my stench.'

Douglas smirked and winked at me. I winked back, and then we both laughed. As though somebody had said something that was actually funny. Picture us. Loud, ostentatious, young and carefree. We were driving an open-topped car through the centre of Cambridge, doing what we weren't meant to be, and desperate for everybody to notice it. A sunny day and, while the world walked to work, there we were, dripping with freedom in the middle of it all.

Fuck me, but we were insufferable, weren't we?

An hour and a half later, we were in deepest Huntingdon somewhere. The whole journey should only have taken about forty-five minutes, but Douglas got us lost, and Mikey, sitting beside him, was rolling and smoking a succession of rather anally constructed joints, and refused to interrupt this strict regimen in order to read the map. Macy, sitting behind Douglas and by now sucking a strawberry lolly, also refused to map-read because she 'didn't know how'. This left me responsible, carsick, hungover and increasingly needing a shit, shouting instructions to a guy I didn't know (and kept calling Duncan), in a speeding open-topped car, while that bloody Macy girl scratched at the seam of my jeans and Mikey wafted smoke back into my streaming eyes. Eventually, Douglas pulled off the road in the middle of a long stretch of eight-foot hedge, and we found ourselves on a winding gravel drive. I lay back in the seat with my eyes closed. The sun played crazy stoned patterns on the inside of my eyelids and I could hear the crunch of our tyres, and the chuckling of a stream nearby. My bowels were torture. I smelled sap and tobacco. I was tired and blinded, and I think I must have drifted off.

When I awoke, clenching, the car had stopped in front of a house and Douglas was standing up, leaning over the windscreen and chatting to a middle-aged lady on a four-wheeled motorbike. She wore a green quilted bodywarmer and a headscarf, and had a loud piercing laugh, and for a sleepy moment I quite honestly thought she was Penelope Keith. But she wasn't. She was Douglas's aunt.

'Come in, come in,' this aunt was saying. 'Ivor and the rest of the advance party have set up residence by the summerhouse. Julian and I are off this evening, so you'll have the run of the place. What a lovely skirt, dear. Is that lino?'

Macy removed the lolly from her mouth and peered over the top of her Snoopy sunglasses. 'Vinyl,' she said, sullenly.

'How delightful,' trilled Douglas's aunt. 'But you will be careful not to lean on the Aga, won't you?'

Macy nodded slowly, at which point I ran out of patience and climbed over her out of the car. 'Hi,' I said. 'I'm Macaulay. Sorry to be so rude, but I urgently need to . . . uh . . . visit your smallest room.'

'My what?' said Douglas's aunt.

'Your . . . um . . . bathroom.'

'You need a bath?'

'No. Well yeah, but . . . no. Your . . .' I was out of euphemisms. 'Your toilet. I need to go to the toilet.'

'Piss or shit?' asked the aunt, unexpectedly.

I blinked at her. 'The, um, latter. Why?'

'There's a urinal by the front door,' she explained, merrily. 'But if you want to crap, I'd head to the loo in the kitchen. There's no lock, so in this house we just sing. Okay, dear? Hymns are best.'

I ran inside, up some steps and through an open double door and I could see the kitchen on the other side of a large, stone-floored hallway. I began racking my brain for hymns I might have sung at school, in assembly. Wasn't there one about a pilgrim I used to like? Tum-tum-tum tumtumtumtumtum, to be a . . . oh.

Never mind there not being a lock on the toilet. There wasn't even a door. Instead there was a tatty maroon curtain, not unlike the one I have these days over the kitchen in my own flat. And on the other side of it somebody was singing 'Get in the Ring Motherfucker' by Guns 'n' Roses.

That was how I met Paxy. He drew back the toilet curtain a few moments later, muttered 'so what you pissed off your dad gets more pussy than you do,' and looked up from his fly.

'That,' I told him, 'was not a hymn.'

'I don't do hymns,' said this apparition, sweeping hair from his eyes. 'I'm a heebee.'

'A what?'

'A heebee. I'm Jewish.'

I stared at him. Tall and thin, this guy was wearing a tweed suit and a pink T-shirt that said I AM THE GOD OF SEX on the front in lurid green letters. In the film that they must one day make of my life, Paxy will be played by a stoned Pierce Brosnan. This man couldn't possibly be the same kind of thing as me. He was chic, alternative England incarnate. He could have been an off-duty catalogue model.

'Me too,' I said.

Paxy was from North London. He'd met loads of Jews. Being from Edinburgh, I'd only met about eight, and I'd been related to all of them. This kind of thing can really mess up your thinking – it did then and it still does. Whenever I meet a new Jew, which is pretty often these days, I always assume that we must have some kind of special bond, as though they are more like a family member than a stranger. I guess that's because when I was a kid they usually were. Paxy, to this day, finds this hysterical.

'You think Celts feel a special bond with other Celts?' he asked me later that night. 'Normans with other Normans? Britain is a nation of tribes, Mr Mac, and nobody cares which tribe they come from anymore. We are just one among many.'

This is half-baked gibberish of course, but at the time it sounded pretty profound. I was feeling impressionable. After Douglas's aunt and her doughy husband had finally left, Ivor, their son, had instructed us to carry their entire set of living-room furniture out onto the croquet lawn. It had taken us ages. There were two priceless old sofas, a couple of armchairs, a seriously decadent purple velvet chaise-longue and a big kind of footstool-meets-coffee-table thingy, which we put in the middle. We'd spent the afternoon out there, drinking cocktails and smoking weed, and it was now about 10.30, a rich, scented summer night. I was slumped back on one of the sofas, chatting to Paxy, my new friend. Macy, the plasticky tart, had spent much of the afternoon rolling around on the chaise-longue with Mikey (still in his sunglasses, nightfall notwithstanding) but had relocated to the ground in front of our sofa, having been usurped by Douglas. She was now lying back, with her head resting between my legs and her hand, once again, scrabbling at my thigh. She seemed comfortable. I let her be.

The other sofa was at right angles to us, and was occupied by Ivor, our host, and a couple of girls I hadn't properly met, one of whom I think had something to do with Paxy. Elspeth and that guy Jason had appeared very briefly at about five, padding barefoot across the grass from a distant gardening shed where I assumed they had spent the afternoon. They had waved, and headed straight into the house. I'd caught sight of Jason, shirt-less, as he'd yanked open a top-floor window a few minutes later.

Cries, grunts and giggles would occasionally drift down across the grass, causing everybody else to smirk.

'How do you fit in?' Paxy asked me one time, when he caught me looking ruefully towards the window. 'Are you her boyfriend?'

I shrugged. 'Kind of. Sometimes.' I glanced down at Macy's foraging hand. 'It's flexible.'

'Yeah?' said Paxy. He was smoking a Marlboro menthol, and he stared at me as he spoke, breathing into my eyes, mintily. 'And you like that, do you? Being flexible?'

I stared back, not quite sure what he was saying. 'Yeah. I do.'

'Good.' Paxy looked away. 'Good. You should come to my place sometime, in London. Big place. Bit derelict, but funky. We have some good times there. This lot come around. Miss Macy here too.'

He looked back at me and said something quite shocking, very audibly. He said, 'She's a very good shag.'

Macy let out a snort and pushed herself to her feet, pressing hard onto my thigh. 'You're well grim, Paxy,' she said. 'I am fookin' here, y'know.'

'Forgive me,' murmured Paxy, 'for offending your delicate sensibilities.'

'Ponce,' said Macy, and yawned, shaking her hair. 'I'm off for a dump. Where's the crapper?'

'Kitchen,' I told her. 'But be careful. There's no door.'

Macy stopped still and stared at me. 'No door?'

'No door,' I confirmed.

Macy looked bewildered. 'So how am I meant to get in then?'

Not really girlfriend material, Macy.

But enough reminiscing. I did go and check out Paxy's place about a month later and, six years on, I'm still something of a regular.

It's a large five-storey Georgian place on a very posh street in Hampstead. Paxy's dad, who is some kind of disgustingly rich bond broker, bought it to do up as a family home about a decade ago. Then something bad happened: Paxy's mum either died or left him (Paxy will not be drawn) and the place just got moth-balled. The recession hit, and while Paxy senior didn't have the heart to sell the place, he didn't have the cash to do it up either. It sat empty for a few years, and then Paxy moved in himself, along with an ever-shifting circus of friends. I lived there myself for about six months, before moving into the flat I have now. I couldn't really deal with it. That kind of faded glamour is all very well for the occasional evening, but even an NW3 address doesn't make up for a lukewarm shower, a kitchen that looks like a cave and floors you can see through. Plus, it was exhausting.

Like most of the original lot, I now treat it as a private members' club. You never know who will turn up, which is both good and bad. Some nights I barely recognise a soul. Paxy's always there, of course, but I'm not sure he's got a soul anymore.

Tonight, there are about ten people nodding around in the living room. This part of the house is notably less shabby than the rest, with plush rugs and luxurious furniture, and actual working radi-ators on the walls. Paxy, who has grown rotund and sedentary in the years I have known him, reclines limply in an armchair oppo-site the fireplace. He has a redhead I don't recognise balancing on one arm, and a generous tumbler of something amber balancing on his belly.

'Mr Mac,' he says when he sees me. 'Thank heavens. There's barely a person here worth speaking to.'

Paxy doesn't mean this. He says it to just about everybody.

'Evening,' I say, and survey the room. Semi-recognisable faces loom out of a tobacco mist and give me semi-sincere smiles. I reciprocate. 'Who else is about?'

'Oh the usual,' he sighs, and proffers a bottle of whisky from down the side of his chair. 'Everybody is feeling somewhat sedate, sadly. We had a big one last night. Mr Donny has just gone to get some pizza. This lot aside, Messrs Rich and Kulwinder are jousting with the twins upstairs, and I think Little Misses Carolyn and Debbie are also about somewhere. They may have left this morning, I'm not sure. Your Lady Elspeth was here yesterday, along with sirs Douglas Bolton and Will Ramsey.'

'Quite the old gang.'

'Indeed. Tell me, have you met Miss Leila?'

Leila, it appears, is the redhead. A newbie in a short polkadot skirt, making slightly too much of an effort. She glances at me nervously and then, possibly reading something in my face, flashes me a warm smile.

'Leila,' I say, accepting the whisky and settling into my usual chair. 'Delighted.'

'Moreover . . .'

The next week is Fingers' week, and we are right at the centre of it. Obviously, we aren't the only paper to run a story about the latest theft on Monday. However, thanks to my efforts, we are the only paper to take a jokey, pro-Fingers stance, and do it on the front page. The uproar, frankly, is astonishing. By 8.17 a.m. on Monday, Dermot Murnaghan (pro) and Vanessa Feltz (against) are waving copies of the *Gazette* at each other on BBC *Breakfast*, in the midst of a screaming argument about the ethics of the whole thing which is only stopped by Natasha Kaplinsky loudly declaring that they have to cut to the weather. By lunchtime Radio 4 has had a brace of bishops denouncing our ungodly ways, and by 2.30 p.m. the Media Guardian website is claiming that we've been reported to the PCC. ITV's *News At Ten* has a three-minute segment entitled 'Fingers: Where Will He Strike Next?', and even the dour old Beeb has a slot on their rival show, with Jeremy Bowen pacing through the ballroom at the

Mandarin Oriental, and lowering his bushy eyebrows every time he says 'nipple'.

That's just Monday. The following day our stance is vehemently denounced in leaders in the *Telegraph*, the *Mail* and the *Mirror* and slyly cribbed by the *Indy*, the *Sun* and the *Express*. Dapper in a new Paul Smith, Robin Hargreaves appears on *Newsnight*, successfully defending the *Gazette* to a wryly amused Jeremy Paxman while, over on the other side, Norman St John-Stevas, Vanessa Feltz (again) and a bloke who used to polish shoes for Prince Charles engage in a shriekingly fierce spat about crime, punishment and the examples we are setting to the nation's youth. Trevor McDonald looks on helplessly, only occasionally reminding them that they're meant to be talking about an historic royal visit to Taiwan. Fingers is everywhere. He's a supernova. He's mine.

That Wednesday I meet Daniel for lunch at the Wrexham Rooms in Soho. Do you know the place? It's a club owned by the Wrexhams, the family that used to own the *Gazette*. You'll have heard about it. It's that media-centric private drinking hole that hit the headlines a few weeks ago when one of those hotel heiresses was photographed staggering out the main door, covered in vomit, on the arm of a nephew of Osama Bin Laden. They also have a high-profile drugs crisis (doorkeeper arrested for selling cocaine/minor royal shoots up in toilets/toddler swallows ketamine etc) every six months or so. Daniel, who treats the place as a second home, tells me that the hack count has tripled recently, as the latest one is long overdue. It's a hellish, cunty place. I love it.

We arrange to meet at the rooftop restaurant, which isn't nearly as glam as you might expect and always makes me feel slightly like I'm having a picnic in a carpark dotted with palm trees. Daniel is late, predictably, so I order a Long Island Iced Tea and play with my phone, somehow managing to avoid staring, goggle-eyed, at all the celebrity chefs, *Coronation Street* stars and dropouts from Big Brother who are yakking nearby in impractical clothing. I'm strong, me.

A Harris tweed overcoat is thrown into the chair opposite me, and Daniel follows it, collapsing theatrically and waving his ludicrous legs about. One hand sweeps back his unruly fair hair and the other, as if from nowhere, produces a Dunhill and sticks it in his grinning mouth.

'Well,' he says. 'If it isn't the man at the eye of the storm. What's your cut, Macaulay? One of the Bushman's Thimbles? Or are you just taking the standard agent's fee? Twenty per cent of Fingers' next five crimes, with options for any outstanding?'

I grin back. 'Now, now,' I say, stirring my cocktail with its straw. 'I am a mere scribe. I am impartial. I simply report. I am but Watson to his Holmes. Boswell to his Johnson. St John to his Jesus, if I may be so bold.'

'Bunny to his Raffles?' suggests Daniel.

I frown. 'I don't know that one.'

'Oh but you must,' says Daniel, craning his neck and nodding for the waitress. 'Raffles? The original Gentleman Thief. Talk of London. Scourge of society. An amiable, affable rogue, drawn like a moth to a flame to the rich and famous, and intent upon making the latter less like the former. And assisted, reluctantly yet ably, by his close friend Bunny. Ah yes. Samantha dear. I'll have a Grouse and a menu.'

'I'll have another one of these,' I tell the waitress, and twitch a hand to distract Daniel from watching her bottom sway out the door. 'When was this?'

'No time and all time. It's a fiction. The work of E. W. Hornung. Turn of the century, I believe. Yet the parallels between that case and your own are remarkable.' Daniel raises his eyebrows and lights a Dunhill. He offers me one, which I accept. 'Really. Remarkable.'

'I don't see how,' I say, flicking open a matchbook from the table. 'You say Bunny was Raffles' assistant? I'm not anyone's assistant. I'm just writing about it. I'm a journalist.'

'As,' says Daniel, 'was Bunny.'

I'm trying to strike a match as he says this, and I fail. A splinter lodges itself under my thumbnail. I stare at him. 'Are you suggesting something?'

Daniel grins, slightly wildly. 'Are you suggesting I'm suggesting something?'

'Okay.' I try again, and succeed in creating fire. 'I'm suggesting that you are suggesting that I know more about all this than I am letting on. Fair?'

'Fair-ish,' says Daniel, and looks, sweepingly, around the rooftop. 'And why would I be suggesting that?'

'Because you're a nosy bastard,' I tell him, trying to see who he's looking at. 'And this is how you get information. You're well wrong, anyway. I don't know anyone who's even nearly organised enough to get away with something like this.'

'Don't you?'

'No. I don't. And moreover . . .'

Daniel nods, with mocking encouragement. 'Moreover what?'

'Don't moreover me.'

'I'm terribly sorry.'

'You should be. Moreover . . . if I did, I wouldn't tell someone like you, when I was sitting somewhere like here.'

'I see,' says Daniel, just as the waitress returns with our drinks on a tray. Just as our silence begins to imply some kind of conspiracy, he says, 'Is there anything you'd like to tell me if we were elsewhere?'

'Absolutely not.'

He gives the waitress an inclusive wink. She blushes and looks away, as though she's just overheard something she shouldn't have.

Has she? I squeeze my thumb, hard. The splinter pops out, and a tiny spot of blood oozes from the wound under my nail.

In the film that they must one day make of my life Daniel will be played by Rhys Ifans, but only because Nigel Havers is a couple of decades too old. Of course, you might object that Nigel Havers looks nothing like Rhys Ifans, and you'd be right. Nonetheless, Daniel is halfway between the two of them, in much the same way that Rupert Everett is halfway between Pierce Brosnan and Dale Winton, or John Malkovich is halfway between Morrissey and Michael Stipe. I do hope this kind of thing makes sense to you. It is how I see the world.

I don't know Daniel nearly as well as I ought to, considering I sat next to him for the best part of a year. In fact, I could probably tell you more about the private lives of Elton John or Madonna. I do know that Daniel has a long-term on-again/off-again girlfriend called Michelle. She's exactly the kind of slightly withered coke-head semi-aristo you might expect to find on the arm of someone like him – with a wayward eye, and a tendency to slip in the tongue when she kisses you hello. That's about it. He never talks about school or university, but because of that it's a fair bet that he went to either Eton or Harrow, followed by either Oxford or Cambridge and simply – as I've found is common of people like that – assumes that everybody else he meets did too. Possibly he lived in Swaziland until he was about fourteen, but I may have got hold of the wrong end of the stick on that one. Not sure. That's men for you. We don't talk much, and when we do it's largely bollocks.

Daniel stops digging eventually. He's got a story to tell me, about Jensen Randall. Apparently the creepy, leather-skinned one has been in here quite a lot lately. It takes some nerve, that. Everybody knows his old man would give his right bollock to own this place. Or somebody's right bollock, at any rate. He'd probably buy a truckload of bollocks, in bulk.

Give or take the odd million, Jensen Randall's background is much like my own. Despite Willie Fowler's slur (his slurred slur, really) he's not actually Russian – he's Ukrainian. He's not Jewish. His grandfather, or possibly great grandfather, was some kind of plutocrat in the Old Country, and had to leave under the Reds. Or, at least, he had to leave if he wanted to keep his money under the Reds. He went to Canada, bought a chunk of Toronto and, in some form or another, banked. They kept banking until Jensen's dad came along. Torquil (Yes. Torquil. And you thought my family had silly names). Randall also banked, in a sense, but he had the good fortune, or wit, or whatever, to spend half his time in London as a young man, and invest in a British packaging company. Apparently, they invented the tube that toothpaste comes in, or something. Cue untold billions (or, at least, millions) and, after a while, the desire to buy a newspaper.

He found it hard to buy a newspaper. Nobody wanted to sell him one. Despite having lived in Britain most of his life, and having married a cockney showgirl (not that you'd know it to look at Marge Randall now, the great toadwoman), he was regarded as foreign, subversive, not of the right cut of jib. But he persevered. He must have known that he was never going to be a Murdoch or a Rothermere, but he wanted his invitations to the Palace and his Christmas card from Number Ten. Eventually, in one of those elaborate take-overs that stick in the other papers for weeks and nobody else gives much of an arse about, he got the Wrexhams' backs against the wall. They'd been in newspapers for 200 years, and they'd been rubbish at it from the start. What had been theirs became his, and one of those things was the *Gazette*.

Not everything that was theirs became his, mind you. At the last moment, with a deftness that they had been notably lacking for the previous two centuries, the Wrexham family lawyers managed to wrestle both the Wrexham Rooms and Wrexham House, out in Surrey, into a trust. There was quite a battle, but the trust, most of whom hadn't wanted the bloody man to buy anything at all, could not be budged. Randall has a say in this trust, but not a decisive one, so it was a bitter blow. He lost out on a few million quids' worth of real estate and, most gratifyingly for all those sneering media columnists, he lost out on the Wrexham Cup. That's the goblet on our masthead, just between the '*The*' and the '*Gazette*'. You'll have heard of it. It's awarded each year, like a sort of low-rent Nobel Prize. That writer got it last year. You know the one. He wrote that novel that everybody read, about the Inuit jockey who died.

Well, I say 'awarded'. Winners get some sort of trinket. The actual cup lives in the nineteenth-century East Gallery of Wrexham House. It does not live in a glass case in our Victoria entrance hall. Not at all. Because of that, we don't control the award, and we don't control the guest list for the annual party at which the winner is, briefly, presented with it. It's the latter that annoys me. They'd better bloody invite me this year. It's surely my turn.

Anyway, despite all this, or more likely because of it, Jensen Randall has taken to breezing in here and pointedly hanging around in the bar. The staff are terrified of him. A few people used to jeer, at first, but rumours have started spreading that he might have the power to get their membership revoked.

'He's lowering the bloody tone, actually,' says Daniel.

'I wasn't aware,' I say, lightly, 'that it could be much lower.'

'Foolish boy,' he drawls. 'Although you may have a point. I first came in here in 1987. You had to wear a suit back then.'

I look around. Is that Jade Goody's ex over there? 'I shouldn't imagine that most of this lot even own a suit.'

'Well exactly,' says Daniel. 'And speaking of which, you owe me one.'

'One what?'

'One suit.'

'Oh, right. That. God, yeah. Sorry. I've been wearing it, actually.'

'It fits?'

'Not really. I'm a bit low on suits right now. You don't mind, do you? It's pretty foul.'

'It was cut,' says Daniel acidly, 'by an extremely expensive chap on Jermyn Street. He makes all my suits.'

'Well it's bogging. I'll get it back to you. Listen, I'd better head off.'

'Working you hard?'

'Trying to. No, I just need to check in. Email and that.'

Daniel laughs. 'Goss at the *Gazette*?'

I pull a face. Goss at the *Gazette* (or, rather, goss@gazette.co.uk) was my major innovation when I started work for Daniel. I had the brainwave of sticking an email address at the bottom of the column, and inviting anonymous tip-offs. It was a terrible idea. A beacon for lunatics, and we just didn't have the staff to filter it. 'No,' I say. 'Never look at it. Only mad people write in. They put it on the Popbitch board once, you know. We were smothered with shit. It's not even on the page anymore. It probably doesn't even work. No, I'm waiting to hear from Greebo.'

Daniel doesn't want me to go. He tells me that Greebo is rubbish, and always has been. He tells me that I ought to just nip out to the Internet café and check it remotely from there. He offers to come with me, to show me how. He even offers to buy me a drink when I get back, for God's sake.

I resist. I am a professional. As I leave, as he orders another whisky. For all his haughty detachment, Daniel is a mess. He really, really needs a new job.

'I just don't think I like you very much.'

There are good things and bad things about my flat. I am blind to neither. And the good things are very good. I am in Zone 1. The reception area of my building has a elaborately tiled mosaic floor, on which the pointy heels of London society ladies (and the chunkier heels of the men who actually buy their shoes) can be heard, frequently, to skitter and clip. My building has a porter, no matter that he loathes me. My building has a rooftop terrace, to which residents have unlimited access for sunbathing and stargazing. My building has a lift, in which I have not yet had sex. My building's location allows me to walk to and from almost anywhere in London I should have any desire of reaching, providing I'm not visiting one of my sisters in the sticks. Indeed, my building allows me to talk about 'my building', which is just so wonderfully A-list and Manhattan that I sometimes catch myself dropping this phrase into conversations with strangers when I am talking about something else entirely. But best of all, my building (aahhh) is almost directly across the road from Harrods.

Those are the good things. And the bad? Well. There are but two. Firstly, my flat costs me slightly under one and a half thousand pounds a month – something like three quarters of my post-tax monthly salary. Secondly, my flat is the size of a broom cupboard. Actually, no. That 'secondly' is a little disingenuous. My flat is a broom cupboard. Or at least, it was. They shifted out the brushes and vacuums two years ago, and stuck in a sink, a bed and a hotplate. Along with somewhere in the region of thirty proper apartments, we now have a broom-cupboard flat on all four floors of the building. Two of the others are occupied by sweet old dears whose offspring have pissed away the family fortunes, and the third houses some young foreign countess, who seems to make a living out of society magazines by writing articles about how small her home is. Where the cleaners now keep their brooms I cannot imagine.

I read about my cupboard in the property section of the *Evening Standard*, just before the building's committee started letting them out. It was a bit of a joke article, but Paxy's was getting embarrassing and I wanted out. Paxy's was only meant to be a stopgap. I hadn't meant to stay there for nearly so long.

I was in Brixton before, with Neil. I moved out in order to live with my last girlfriend. She was called Naomi, and we lasted three months.

Naomi lived in Vauxhall, and she was a ballet dancer. I didn't know she was a ballet dancer when I met her. She wasn't dancing at the time. She was handing out leaflets for *Chitty Chitty Bang Bang*, just down the road from Covent Garden tube. I'd just finished work for *Poshbird Monthly*. I guess it must have been November, and I was freelancing, but not very well. I'd been having a pint with my old friend Will Ramsey, in the Nag's Head.

I was hoping there might be some work at his place. There wasn't. He left, but I stayed. I had nowhere else to go.

I was sitting right up by the window. I could see Naomi out there in the street, huddled against the cold in a fur-lined parka, frayed jeans and pixie boots. Some people were taking leaflets, most weren't. She looked miserable. Eventually it started to snow and she came inside. I told her I'd been watching, and I bought her a drink.

'I think I like you,' she said, by the second, and I could tell she did.

Naomi was a sweet girl. A couple of years younger than me, she was from Hertfordshire, or Derbyshire, or something shire, and had only been in London for a couple of months. She was attached to a ballet company, and she was very diligent. From the moment I met her, I was a new person. I didn't even think of Paxy's for weeks. Instead, we went on dates. Cinemas, with chocolate. Restaurants, with white wine. Bedroomwise, nothing happened for weeks. After it did, I started staying at hers most nights, and, eventually, I made plans to move in.

Then, she started having dreams.

In Naomi's dreams, I was unfaithful. Horribly unfaithful. I had sex with all her friends, sometimes all at once. She would wake in a betrayed fury, and take hours to forgive me. In real life, I was as model a boyfriend as I have ever been. I cooked. I cleaned. I held her hand. I put Paxy's out of my mind, and didn't go near the place. It made no difference. In her mind, only in her mind, I was a cad.

At first I resented this horribly. While I did fancy all of her friends – except for Clara, the one with the face like a pumpkin – I was on best behaviour, and enjoying it. She was too sweet, life was too good, I was basically just too nice. It seemed terribly unfair that I should be stifling all my most base urges, and still getting grief for them.

Eventually, though, I kind of started to enjoy it. For two months, I couldn't wait for morning, just to hear about what imaginary sexual athletics I had got up to the night before. It was like porn, with me as the star. Our real relationship kind of went off the boil, but I didn't mind. I began to live, vicariously, through her paranoid dreams. Any man would. They were great. Even the ones about Clara, the one with the face like a pumpkin.

Ultimately, she dumped me. She cried. 'I just don't think I like you very much,' she explained, and there wasn't much I could say in return. I suppose I just wasn't a terribly likeable person.

Like I said, Naomi was my last girlfriend. I don't do that anymore. When I moved out of her house, I moved into Paxy's. And when I moved out of Paxy's, I gave my spare key to Elspeth and decided to live alone. It seems better this way.

'Tug MY diamonds.'

E very once in a while, a band comes along which is supposed to change the world. You know the sort. The Stones did it. Jimi Hendrix did it. Led Zeppelin did it. Oasis did it. Tragic as it might sound, the Spice Girls did it. And for every band that manages it, there are ten that don't, but are supposed to. Remember The Auters? Or Mother Love Bone? Remember Northern Uproar? Remember Gene, or Transvision Vamp, or Jay Mackenzie and the Dogs? Bands that set out to make a splash, and do, but sometimes only for a couple of weeks.

Here and now, at right this minute, The Zekes are the biggest band in Britain, if not the world. They don't have a record deal, and you wouldn't recognise a single one of them if you passed them in the street. Not even Zeke, the guitarist. Like most people I can see in this sweaty and crowded room, I have never heard any of their songs. They are so cool it almost hurts.

The hype around The Zekes has been growing for months.

Their sound is rumoured to be the usual kind of shouty guitar nonsense, but they've got a certain glam-trash look which won them the cover of *Dazed and Confused* before they'd even put out as much as an EP, simply because some photographer liked their publicity pictures. After that they had *NME* and *i-D* over here and *Details, Nylon* and God knows what else across the pond. As always happens after a start like that, things then exploded. If everybody says that something is the next big thing, then it is, already. So, broadsheet lifestyle columnists started namedropping them in an effort to sound hip, and last week – slightly over a month since *Dazed* stuck them on the cover – even the *Sun* devoted half a page to telling its readers that, if they hadn't heard of The Zekes yet, they would have done very soon.

The four band members have always insisted that they originally met in an orphanage in Detroit, a claim rendered only slightly suspect by the recent revelations that the singer, Jacx, is a first cousin of Michael Stipe and the bassist, Wazzo, is the son of the daughter of the man who played Hammond organ for Bob Dylan. They have 'next big thing' written all over them. They're tall and they're skinny. They have lank hair that hangs over their eyes. They wear a combination of seventies punk bondage gear, old-school tweeds and Captain Beefheart hippy trippy tie-dyes. These people are the new, authentic face of rock, and the world is about to change. Again.

How odd that 'authentic' bands like this can enjoy the kind of relentless hype that Kylie would receive for baring her bottom on Regent Street without even releasing a single, and still have nobody question their authenticity. The Zekes are the emperor's new clothes, and nobody wants to be the first to shout 'naked'. Their debut UK gig is tonight, in Brixton Academy, and it's the hottest ticket since . . . well. Since the last bunch of unknown prettyboy US mop-tops with decent PR decided to jet over here and milk our credulity for all it was worth.

To get a ticket, I have fought tooth and nail.

So, tonight that's where I am. Ticket or not, I've blagged my way into the VIP room at the top of Brixton Academy by, quite honestly, pretending to be one of the Stereophonics. There I was, hanging about in the lobby with grommets, idly enjoying the spectacle of a top youth TV presenter failing to persuade a bouncer that his date – an Arabic-looking girl nearly twice his height, in eye-wateringly tight brown leather trousers – ought to be let in without a ticket, when they swept by in a swirl of pointy hair and slightly outdated angry Welshness. Their old drummer (the one who looks like a clown from a horror film) was at the back of the group, and without really thinking about it, I fell into step behind him, pressing myself up so close that my Jewfro and his Welshfro slid together like combs, and making us look from above, no doubt, like a pair of large hairy bollocks. Nobody really knows how many Stereophonics there are (Clownman, singer, bloke who looks like singer . . . others), least of all the bouncers, so by the time the whole dispute started getting whiny ('. . . but Dermy . . . I need to pee . . .') I was slipping up the stairs and into the stellar inner sanctum with my new bandmates.

Inside, by the door, I spot Neil. He's looking twitchy.

'Hey man,' he says, not really looking at me. 'How's it going?'

'Hey,' I say, and glance over his shoulder. 'Yo Peaches. Looking trim, baby. Not bad, yeah, not bad. You here by yourself?'

'Jessica's about someplace. You want an E? Love the new hair, Patsy, love it.'

'Maybe later,' I say, winking at Gail Porter and pointing a

finger like a pistol at Mark Owen. 'You guys been seeing a lot of each other?'

'Ah, y' know. A bit. Wayne? Catch you by the bar, yeah?'

'Yeeuch. That sun-visor is a mistake. No question. Did you . . . Pete! Dude! Hope that's an orange juice, yeah? . . . um, stay late at the MOFO thing?'

'Pretty late, yeah,' says Neil, eyes darting around the room. Then he looks at me, so suddenly and directly that I am momentarily taken aback. 'So how come you haven't been returning my calls?'

'What calls?'

'Oh, Mac. Don't.'

'I'm not,' I tell him, adding, 'Coxy! Shoes! Nice one! What calls?'

Neil spins, incredulous. 'Patrick Cox? Here?'

'Sara Cox. Over there.'

'But shoes? What's she got to do with shoes?'

'She's wearing them. What fucking calls, Neil?'

Neil looks at me as if I have the remains of a human baby soufflé smeared across my chin. 'About your Fingers. We want to do a spread. I need your inside line. Evening, Meg. New breasts! Splendid.'

'You haven't called me. And I haven't got an inside line.'

''Course you do. Everyone says so.'

I stare at Neil, but he's already looking away, mouthing intimacies towards a busty non-entity who I think might be Dwight Yorke's current girlfriend. First Daniel, now Neil. Why does everybody think I know more about this Fingers than I am letting on? And why didn't I get those calls? And more importantly . . .

'Hold on. A spread? You want to do a spread?'

'Hmm?' says Neil, looking back. 'Yeah. A spread.'

Now it's my turn to give him the baby soufflé look. 'A fucking

73

spread, Neil? Like . . . what? "At home with Fingers?" "London's latest enigmatic crim shows us around his secret lair?"'

'Sure,' says Neil. 'Why not? That's why I need you to tell me where to find him.'

'The world,' I mutter, 'has gone mad.' Shaking my head, I compose myself. 'Hey Dannii? Love the new single. Very street, honey, very street.'

Neil almost stamps his foot. 'Jesus, Mac. Why are you being so difficult?'

'You've got the wrong idea,' I tell him. To change the subject, I catch somebody by the shoulder as they slip past. 'Whoa, man! Haven't seen you since the Brits. Neil, you want to see this guy with a spoonful of guacamole. Lee Harvey Oswald, know what I'm saying?'

'Who the fuck are you?' says Liam Gallagher. 'Touch me again and I'll break your fucking arm.'

There is a short pause.

'Might go find Jessica,' says Neil.

'Mmm. Right, yeah. See you later.'

I'm dressed tonight in what I call my 'plainly-famous' look: high-necked leather biker jacket, skinny black flares and sunglasses. It's part of a couture strategy Neil and I devised a few years ago, when we first started blagging our way into expensive clubs in search of stories. We both realised quickly that it's not enough to look smart – bouncers don't give a shit about smart, smart says boring, or, worse, eager to impress. The secret is not only to choose something that makes you look like you'd fit in wherever you are going, but also to be able to give the impression that you'd be dressed like this even if you were just slumping in front of the telly with a pizza. Consequentially, Neil has always favoured the 'Eurotrash' pose: a suit with a T-shirt or plain silk shirt, twinned with medallions, bracelets and Brylcreem – suggesting that, while he's aware he looks a bit rubbish, he's far too wealthy to care. My wayward hair has always made the 'Eurotrash' hard to carry off (I'm too pale to be Greek), so the 'plainly-famous' was my alternative. This basically involves wearing clothes that are so wanky that bouncers will assume you are some kind of cuntish style icon, of whom they, through their own failings, happen not to have heard. This can involve anything from the smacked-up-*Matrix* garb I'm in tonight, to twinning a Hawaiian shirt with a thrift-shop white dinner jacket. It's a strategy that rarely fails, the only minor downside being that I feel a bit of a cock on the tube.

My clothes work well. Squeezing in between Annie Lennox and the guy who used to be the guitarist from Skunk Anansie, I battle to the bar and order myself a Red Bull and vodka. Thus armed, I mingle, slipping through the sea of fame and semi-fame as though I actually have somewhere to go on the other side of it. This also works well – little asides and half-conversations make celebs much less suspicious than actually pinning them down in a corner and subjecting them to interrogation. So I pass comment on Emma Bunton's necklace and I give Kym Marsh an ashtray in which to stub her cigarette. I laugh at something scathing that the artist Alice Caligula says to Jake (or possibly Dinos) Chapman. I even (and I'm proud of this one) tell Martine McCutcheon that I spoke to Barbara Windsor the day before (I didn't) and she said to pass on her regards (she wouldn't). I mingle, I fit in. It's what I do. The wonderful thing in such situations is that, if people think they should know you, they invariably assume that they do. Or better still, if they think you know people higher up the celeb ladder than they are, then they want to.

Tonight, rather wonderfully, the chatter is all about Fingers. *My* Fingers. Screw The Zekes – the next big thing is a black-clad style-icon with a penchant for glitzy baubles. And without me, he'd just be a tealeaf in a balaclava. I'm in heaven.

Everybody has a theory, everybody has something to say. It's glorious. Most people think he's a publicity stunt of some sort, but nobody has much idea why, or by whom. In the space of only a few minutes, I hear that . . .

. . . Fingers is a member of the Russian mafia, stealing to order for wealthy American collectors . . . Fingers is a minor member of the British royal family, a fact that is known, but being suppressed by both the government and the media . . . Fingers is part of an advertising campaign for mobile phones . . . Fingers is a disaffected SAS serviceman with Gulf War Syndrome . . . Fingers is part of a secret society of cat-burgling students from Oxford University . . . Fingers is an Arab . . . Fingers is Irish . . . Fingers is Dom Joly . . . Fingers is something to do with *Jackass* . . . Fingers is a black militant, a white supremacist, a gay icon . . .

. . . so that's my article for tomorrow sorted, then.

My favourite theory so far is the one that he is actually a piece of performance art. Over by the toilets I hear a confident sub from *i-D* inform an ice-blonde teenage model that Fingers is being funded by Charles Saatchi, is represented by Jay Jopling, and will be having a show at White Cube in Hoxton some time in the autumn. How fantastic is that? I suppose it might even be true. They could all be true. Who knows?

After about a quarter of an hour, there's a commotion by the door and Kate Moss and Bobby Gillespie appear. These two are sufficiently stellar to cause a stir even in company like this. A few cameras flash as the tame paps get their shots and Kate twists her back and pouts, thrusting out her chest. She's wearing a brown suede skirt and a green custom T-shirt which says 'Tug MY diamonds' in shimmering silver across the front. As the flashbulbs catch this and people begin to get the joke, a wave of approving laughter ripples around the room. When Jodie Marsh makes an entrance a few moments later, in a T-shirt screaming 'LICK MY CUPS OF LUST' (or similar), people only snigger and the cameras stay resolutely away. She looks perplexed, poor girl. There's a moral in that, somewhere.

The Zekes, needless to say, don't live up to the hype. They're pleasant enough, in a winsome, sub-Ramones kind of way, but they don't rock my world. I doubt they rock anyone's – impressing a crowd that has never heard any of your songs before only works if you sound like Bon Jovi. They (except for their 'ironic' cover of 'Smoke On The Water') don't.

Still, it's fun. I venture down to the dancefloor only twice; once with Neil and Jessica (who are pawing at each other like rabid dogs on Viagra) and once with a gorgeous American-Japanese girl in a tight blue satin vest, who – if I remember rightly – has come over from New York for the week and is connected, in some oblique way, to David Blaine. Somewhere near the stage, we share a sweaty and badly-rolled joint I make with the hash I nicked from my sister's flat, and then I lose her as the crowd swells half-heartedly towards the stage. A shame. Her shimmering top makes me think of aquamarine-clad Lucy, and I text her. She's out with friends in Kensington, but promises to 'drop by' my flat on her way home. I didn't see her at work at all today.

I don't stay long after that. Of course, most of the people here who are anyone in particular only turned up in order to be seen arriving. By the time the band starts and the world conspicuously fails to change, they start slipping out. I do the same.

By the time I'm at the tube, with the noises still ringing in my ears and the sweat evaporating from my warm, damp shoulders, it occurs to me that I could have invited Janie along tonight. It could be simply that I'm in Brixton, or it could be the oniony fumes of the incense that the Rasta at the top of the stairs pretends to peddle in order to mask the stench of his real wares, but I'm suddenly struck by how crap I am as a brother. She'd have loved it – the noise, the celebrities, the sensation of mild yet magnificent bohemia. Why didn't I think of this before?

But then, perhaps it's for the best. Perhaps she'd only have embarrassed me. Perhaps she'd have been like those Big Brother winners at TV Awards – charging drunkenly about the place, with no idea of quite how low-rent their sniggering and gawking makes them appear. Perhaps it's for the best.

'Yarrwanga,' says the Rasta, or words to that effect, adding 'Hash? Weed? Good puff, man' when I look his way.

'Nah, mate,' I tell him and head underground and home to Lucy, hating myself all of a sudden for a host of reasons I can't quite pin down.

'Cme bck NOW. we hav nEWS.'

'What on *earth* is this *sheer* drivel?' lilts Trevor Brainchild's voice some time the next day, and my eyes flip open in a panic. Where am I? A plastic coffee cup, stained and sideways, sits about three inches from my nose. Beside it broods a hole puncher, looming at me like a JCB. There is, I note with alarm, part of a diced mushroom under my keyboard. Odd.

'Fingers,' continues Brainchild, reading from a proofsheet, 'is a *wayward* member of the *aristocracy*. Would you credit it? Fingers is in *league* with the *Triads*. The Triads, Lewis? Fancy!'

I sit up, my face parting company, audibly, with the beige Formica of my desk. Beside me, Philip has his head in his hands. He looks up, sees me looking at him, and looks away. Treacherous sod.

'Hold on,' I say, and I lever myself out of my chair. I can't bear being spoken down to. I can feel one side of my face throbbing red, and my hair must be ludicrous. I feel gawky and alarmed. 'What are you talking about, Trevor?'

'Forgettable,' agrees Brainchild. 'Isn't it? But there's more.' He turns towards the newsdesk, as though inviting an audience. He gets one. 'Fingers is a *modern artist*. Fingers is on drugs. Fingers is *selling* drugs. Fingers wants to be a pop star. Fingers *used* to be a pop star. Fingers . . .'

'Trevor, I know what it says. I wrote it, remember?'

'Wrote,' says Brainchild, 'or *fabricated*?'

Philip and I exchange looks. The room is almost silent; an unusual state of affairs for the offices of a national newspaper at 11.45 a.m. If I strain, I can hear only two things: the photocopier churning away in the stationery cupboard next door, and the muted tap-tap of Rebecca Leighton's keyboard. She has her plumed head down behind a monitor, and quite definitely isn't looking this way. It can't be easy for her. Everybody else in the room is.

'Wrote,' I say, picking sleep out of my eyes. 'Very much wrote.'

Brainchild sighs, causing his eyelids to flutter. He always flutters his eyes when he sighs, just as he always widens them when he speaks. I hate the man.

'Lewis,' he says. 'All this is *complete* speculation.'

'Well exactly. So I can't have fabricated it. I wouldn't know how to fabricate speculation if I tried.'

'Don't get fucking smart,' snarls Brainchild, suddenly no longer playing.

'I'm not being fucking smart,' I snap back, and hear Philip suck a breath in between his teeth. I swing around to stare at him.

'Um, you are actually being a bit smart,' he whispers, apologetically. 'Sorry, Mac.'

'Judas,' I hiss.

Brainchild very nearly screams. 'Lewis! I shall *sack* you and I shall *punch* you, so help me *God*. This *fantasy* will not do! We are a newspaper! We demand news! I demand news. *News* is what you are *for*.'

I deflate. 'But it is news. It's what people are saying. Famous people. Isn't that news?' I'm whining, I can tell.

'No,' says Brainchild, and turns his back on me. 'News is something that has *happened* that nobody *knows* about yet. *News*. Find some.'

I watch his chunky back as he stalks away. People start talking again as he passes them, like . . . like . . . like a wizard might move through a frozen scene in *Buffy*, with all the human statues coming to life one by one, like *he* was something *special*. As he passes Leighton's desk, she pops up, stares at me, and then disappears again. I throw myself back into my chair and spin it around to face Philip. After a moment, I grin at him.

'Oh no,' he says, shrinking away.

'Oh yes,' I say. 'You heard the man. *News!* I *demand* it.'

Philip quivers. 'Don't,' he says.

'Don't what?'

'Don't speak to me like that. You find the news.'

I smile at him, indulgently, and lean forward to pinch his cheek. 'Ah! Resistance! I shall make a man of you yet, young Philip. Trust in me.'

He twitches, batting my hand away. 'I can see what you're doing.'

'Yeah,' I say, and get to my feet. 'Good lad. Find me news, Philip. I'm off for lunch.'

'You always do this. Why should . . . ?'

'Discipline,' I tell him. 'That's what you need.'

'Mac . . .'

'Silence, my son. *News!* Failure will not be tolerated. *News!* I'll see you in an hour.'

'But . . .'
'News!'

Out of the office, I take a left, then a right, then a left again, and I'm nearly at the river. I am painfully hungover. I need a bench.

Today wasn't meant to be like this. Blame Daniel. No sooner had I walked through the door of my surreally small flat last night, than my landline started ringing. Answering said landline, in such situations, is no easy matter. Due to the peculiarities of Japanese cubicle-esque architecture (and the fact that, when drunk, I tend to push the door slightly too hard), simply getting to the rather chic matt black walkaround that usually lives on my desk can be a problem. The door opened too far and got stuck against the sofa, which meant that I had to climb over the sofa, lift it up, and heave the door back to where it ought to be, by which time the telephone had stopped ringing. Which, of course, meant that I couldn't find it. Once I had located it – after phoning it myself, from my mobile – it started again, startling me so much that I dropped it.

'Jesus,' I murmured, and picked it up.

'Ah, Macaulay,' it drawled, in a languidly sozzled voice. 'You're home. Have you wine?'

'Have I . . . Daniel? Is that you?'

'You have? Splendid. I shall be there shortly. Which . . . place do you live in?'

I had never heard him this drunk. 'You've been here,' I said. 'Knightsbridge. But I haven't got any wine. Where *are* you?'

'Knightsbridge. But I haven't got any wine.'

'That's what I just said.'

'Yes,' said Daniel, vaguely. 'I seem to recall.'

'Right,' I said, and stopped taking my jacket off. 'I'll meet you outside the V&A. Okay? I know a place that should be open. Are you okay?'

'I'm fine,' said Daniel. 'I was in the area. I thought we needed to talk.'

'About what?'

'Ahahaha,' mumbled Daniel, like a very weary parody of enigma.

'Whatever. I'll see you in ten minutes.'

'Bring wine,' said Daniel.

'I haven't . . . never mind.'

Knightsbridge is strangely haunting at that sort of time on a weeknight, probably because very few real people live around there. With the streets relatively deserted and the moon fullish and high overhead, one really notices how extravagant all the buildings are. Plenty of ledges, oodles of cornicing, myriad little windows of myriad shapes. What is inside them all? Offices? Homes? What a city to be a cat-burglar in. I only wish I had thought of it first.

Daniel was where I had told him to be. Ramrod straight and leaning against a wall, he was hugging his camel-hair overcoat around his beanstalk frame, looking surprisingly trampish for one so bespoke. I led him around to Monkle Street, where a Greek Cypriot I once met on a nightbus runs one of those seedy semi-legal middle-class cocaine and vodka taverns above a Turkish Cypriot's kebab-shop-cum-greasy-spoon. All plastic furniture and sticky floors, inhabited by mobs of sneezing bankers and burping mini-cab drivers. You know the sort. Grim, really.

I steered Daniel – quite literally steered him – to a table by the door, wedged him into a chair, and gave the owner's son (who, if he gets a look-in in the film they will make of my life, could only be played by Ali G) a tenner to grab us a bottle of Jacob's Creek from downstairs.

'So what's up?' I said to Daniel.

Daniel blinked and looked around, as though waking from a deep sleep. 'Have we wine?' he asked.

'It's coming. What did you want to talk to me about?'

'Are there bees in here?'

'No.'

He looked sad. 'Right. Yeah. This Fingers of yours . . .'

'Of mine? Why is he of mine?'

Daniel showed his teeth and stuck a Dunhill in his mouth. I sighed, just as the bling-bling waiter thing returned with the wine and a stack of Styrofoam cups.

'Ta,' I said, letting him keep the change. I poured myself a glass and downed it, then poured another and one for Daniel. 'Go on,' I said.

'Whoever Fingers is . . .' began Daniel, grappling at his drink and rather theatrically failing to light the cigarette hanging wetly from his lips, 'No. Let me start again. If I knew who Fingers was, I could make a lot of money. Right?'

'If you say so,' I said, grabbing the matches out of his hand and lighting it for him.

'Oh I do,' he insisted, mistiming a swig and actually biting a chunk out of his cup. 'Anyone could.' Wine sloshed around the teeth marks and curled around his fingers. Daniel looked puzzled.

'This is not coming as news to me, Daniel,' I told him, snatching his cup and decanting its contents into another one. 'What's your point?'

'A journalist who wasn't working,' he slurred, snatching back at the replacement, 'such as myself, would soon be working again.'

'Obviously.'

Daniel grinned at me, little bits of polystyrene still crumbling from his lips. 'We journalists,' he said, 'ought to trust each other. We ought to . . .'

'Christ!' I interrupted, grabbing his Dunhills and appropriating one. 'Enough already. I don't know who it is, and I don't know why everyone thinks I do. And if I did, frankly, I wouldn't share that knowledge with you. Now. Why so drunk?'

'Michelle,' grumbled Daniel, a little sadly, and leant forward onto the table.

'You were out with Michelle?'

He shook his head. 'She's gone. My fault. She minded . . . the whole Jimmy Choo thing.'

'Oh.' I didn't quite know what to say. 'Who was that?'

'Michelle. Girlfriend. Slutty. Teeth. You never met?'

'Of course we met. I had dinner with you. She went for a snog at the front door. I meant the Jimmy Choo person. You said I knew her.'

Daniel twitched. 'She knew you,' he muttered, and I couldn't quite tell if he was correcting me or agreeing with me.

'Who was she?' I asked him, but he was already asleep. I let him sprawl there for the next twenty minutes while I finished the wine, before dragging him outside and bundling him into a cab. I went through his wallet and gave the driver a tenner. He's loaded, Daniel. Must be peddling coke again. I wondered what he was complaining about.

Hence the hangover. Not helpful, midweek. Lolling here on this bench just along from Vauxhall Bridge isn't too bad a way to be spending my time, but I'll have to head back sooner or later. It's a shame. There are ducks down there, actual ducks, and some kind of tug on the other side is battering away at one of those weird boats-cum-trucks they pack full of tourists. Just up to my left I can see the block in which Jeffrey Archer owns the penthouse, and just behind it, peeking out like a demon from behind a tree, is the bigger, brasher, shinier one inhabited by Jensen Randall and his dad. I've been in there, once. It was a couple of months ago. Jensen has a whole duplex at the north-west corner, full of granite and spotlights, and expensive pornography. He has a mirror on the ceiling above his bed. He really does.

Lucy told me a story about Jensen the other day. I'm not quite sure whether to believe it. Apparently he took her friend Linda away for the weekend a couple of months ago. Linda works a couple of desks along from Lucy. She's a brunette with short curly hair. Slightly Essex, built like a pole-dancer, but strangely quiet and shy. Jensen picked her up in his Ferrari (Yes. He has a Ferrari. The cunt) on a Saturday, and took her out to this little B&B somewhere along the coast from Brighton.

Now, Linda didn't know they were going to Brighton. She thought they were just going out for lunch – he'd come over to her desk and asked her the day before. But Jensen started going south, and didn't stop. Didn't tell her, didn't explain, didn't even answer when she started screaming at him. When they stopped at traffic lights, Lucy says, Jensen hit the central locking to stop her from getting out. Eventually they pulled up outside this B&B and Jensen opens the doors. In the boot, he's got his own case and one for her. Inside, hers just has this collection of underwear, suspenders, negligees and stuff, all new and all in her size, and a toothbrush. 'What's a girl to do?' says Lucy. 'Wasn't anywhere she could go, was there? They didn't leave the room until Sunday.' Jensen dropped her off home that night, and didn't even speak to her on Monday.

What really got to me about that story isn't that Linda went along with it (although that does make me feel a little . . . odd, it's true) and it isn't the suitcase (although, now I think about it, perhaps it should be). It's the fact that he drove her all the way to Brighton on a Saturday morning – maybe two hours in a car – and he didn't say a word to her. That freaks me out. That's dark.

The thing is, Jensen probably wouldn't understand how dark it was. He wouldn't have a clue. I didn't exactly know him before his dad bought the paper, but I knew of him. I'd seen him at parties; promos and launches, that kind of thing. He'd always turn up early in the evening and vanish after half-an-hour or so, with some kind of textbook blonde. Somebody introduced us once, possibly Jessica. I thought he was an arse, but I didn't read too much into it. I think this about lots of people, and I'm usually wrong.

We went out for drinks a few times, he and I, after he'd arrived at the paper, before we'd decided to be enemies. On a purely theoretical, mercenary level, I quite liked the idea of having him as a friend. I think he thought the same about me. It was a doomed endeavour: we didn't match. Humour was taken as fact, and he asked questions about the strangest things. He's done time in property and television, but he didn't want to talk about that. He just quizzed me on my job, and paid for all the drinks. I just couldn't get a handle on him. He sort of got into a fight once, as well, and it was the same: calculated and savage, yet somehow uncertain. Like there was somebody else whispering in his ear, telling him exactly what to do. Or like he was a robot, getting fed instructions on how to act like a human being. Go there. Do this. Hit him. Fuck her. And so he does, because he thinks he's supposed to. He's a freak.

———

In my pocket, my mobile twitches with a text message, jerking me back to the now.

'fuk R u?' it reads. 'Cme bck NOW. we hav nEWS.'

Back in the office, Philip is in a state of high agitation. There is a red patch on his forehead, just above the bridge of his nose, exactly where he always pinches himself when he is stressed.

'What news?' I demand, flinging my coat over the back of my chair. 'How on earth did *you* get news? Did Greebo ring?'

Philip shudders at me, wearily. 'No,' he says. 'It was on the telly.'

I stare at him. 'The telly? Hardly an exclusive, Phil.'

'Doesn't matter,' he says, and he's right. Fingers has struck again.

There are too many people like Turino in the world. I think everybody would agree about this. I think even Turino would agree about this. A pretty half-Bangladeshi girl from Swansea, Turino was, until three years ago, earning an uncomplicated, unremarkable income as a bog standard model. Catalogues, housewifey afternoon TV shows, the *Daily Mail* – you get the idea. Too short to do catwalks, too normal-looking to do magazines, and too flat-chested to do Page 3 (although I think she managed it, once, for the *Star*), she was a nice face in a world of nice faces, destined to go on doing nothing much until her face went saggy or she had the good fortune to get knocked up by a Manchester United footballer. Then came the breasts.

And what breasts! Each one the size and shape (and quite possibly consistency) of a medium-sized cannonball, they were works of art, silicon masterpieces, crafted at knock-down rate by some cut-price tit-butcher in South Africa. Newly breasted, Turino dyed her hair blonde, bought herself a few corsets and schoolgirl outfits, and took the world of tabloids and lad mags by storm. Within a year she'd been on the cover of *Front*, *Loaded*, *Zoo* and *Nuts*, she had a contract with the *Sport*, an advance on her auto-biography, and a ghost-written column in the *Sunday Express* magazine about sex tips. In the meantime she'd spent a week in Hugh Hefner's mansion, co-hosted a show on *Men & Motors* and had a brief but high-profile fling with Mick Hucknall. As it happens, rumour had it that she'd also been knocked up by a Manchester United footballer, but had very swiftly dealt with the consequences. She's not quite in the Jordan league yet – or even the Nell McAndrew or Alicia Douvall league, to be honest – but she's getting there. A fortnight ago she announced her engage-ment to 'North London businessman' (read 'second-generation Southern European trustfunder') Troy Basco by displaying a vast, pink diamond ring – that Carmen Soprano would have consid-ered vulgar – in a photoshoot with *OK!*

And last night, it seems, Fingers stole it.

'Get onto the designers and see if they can knock up a time chart,' I bark at Philip, kicking my swing chair backwards towards the printer to grab the reports that the newswires have just started culling from Turino's on-air press conference. Halfway there my phone rings and I snatch it, stretching the curly cable taught. Just as the base leaves the table, Philip hurls himself on top of it, deftly preventing catastrophe.

'Ta,' I say, and cough on dust. I never use my work phone. 'Yup?'

It's Brainchild. Rebecca's rapist is taking a back seat again – it seems we've got another front page. I punch the air as he says this, and wink at Philip. He grins back, the tip of his nose going pink. Bless him.

'Don't *fuck* this one, Lewis,' Brainchild is saying.

'Turino? Couldn't hold me back if I had the chance, Trevor, old chum.'

'Are you *incapable* of conversing like an *adult?* I mean it, lad. Don't you get us *sued.* You *check* everything you *print,* okay? No *rumour,* no *conjecture.* I don't care if she's been linked with *Prince William* and given birth to his bloody *puppy.* If it's not a *provable* fact you don't *print* it. Kapish?'

'Didn't know you spoke Italian, Trev,' I tell him, allowing Philip to pull me back across the room by the telephone cord.

'*Lewis!*'

'Yeah, yeah. Take a chill pill, Trev. I'll take care, okay?'

'See that you do,' says Brainchild, and, putting down the phone, I start to type.

'You didn't even check it.'

A plainclothes chap from Scotland Yard turns up in the office later that afternoon. I hate him on sight. He's taller than me, wider than me, and has a face like a young Christopher Reeve. He's been reading my stuff, and he thinks we need to talk.

We go into the editor's office. As usual, it is in no way burdened by the presence of our editor.

The cop sticks out his hand. 'Good to meet you,' he says, and gives my hand a squeeze like a python might give an antelope. Then he tells me his name is Detective Inspector Tom St Eccles.

'I've heard your name before,' I say.

'Your colleague? Miss Leighton? I've worked with her.'

Rebecca. On that rapist story. Of course. 'Bet that was a riveting pleasure from start to finish,' I say.

'Not a friend of yours?'

'I don't think she does friends.'

'Really? Rather smitten, myself. I'm a big fan of her mum's.'

Have I mentioned Rebecca's mum? She's Kathy Leighton, that human-rights lawyer from Nottingham. The one they always wheel out to talk about immigration on *Newsnight*. This guy is so wholesome it's loathsome. What sort of policeman is a big fan of a human-rights lawyer?

'I'm sort of busy,' I say. 'What can I do for you?'

DI Tom St Eccles looks me straight in the eye, public schoolboy style. 'I think we need to work together.'

'Excuse me?' I say.

'I'm heading up the Fingers case now. I think we need to work together. You seem to be on top of this story like nobody else, and maybe we can help each other out. I've been authorised to allow you full access to our investigation, provided that you share any tips you have with us.'

I stare at him. 'Is this a joke?'

'Why would it be a joke?'

'It's just . . .' I feel a bit flustered. 'I've dreamt about moments like this. It's like something out of a film.'

Eccles grins. 'Live the dream,' he says.

I start to grin back, then I stop. I'm thinking. I'm thinking of all the movies I've ever seen in which a hack and a cop team up. The cop is the hero. The hack is just some nasty piece of grubby underworld he's forced to co-operate with. I can see what Detective Inspector Tom St Eccles is doing, breezing in here with his hand-shakes and his charm and his Superman looks. He's turning me into a sidekick. I have my own sidekick. I have Philip. I will not step down the ladder. It's not his movie. It's mine.

'I'm not sure that's such a good idea,' I tell him.

'Why not?'

'Lots of reasons.'

Eccles cocks his head. 'Are you telling me that you have information on this case that you are *not* willing to share?'

I shrug. 'I might be.'

'Because I can get a warrant, you know.'

'In which case, I know nothing at all. Zilch. Nowt. Completely in the dark.'

Eccles looks me up and down, and sighs. 'That's not what I've heard.'

I remember Neil. And Daniel. And everybody else. 'What have you heard?'

'All of a sudden he wants to swap information,' says the policeman. 'Listen, Mr Lewis. I offered you a deal. Either you're taking it, in which case we can keep talking, or you're turning it down, in which case I believe you're making quite a mistake. Which is it?'

'Are you threatening me?'

Eccles winks. 'Of course not. I'm an officer of the law. We don't make threats. We don't need to. We bludgeon people over the heads with our truncheons and call them *'orrible little men*. If I need to know what you know, I can find out. I'm just offering you the chance to play nicely.' He gives me a card. 'My number is on there. You change your mind, you give me a call.'

'I probably won't.' I tell him.

'As you wish,' he says.

'You want to watch the TV news, mate,' I say. 'This Turino business. Shouldn't you be out investigating that?'

Eccles smiles, and heads for the door. 'As I understand it, the TV news doesn't quite tell the full story.'

It's my turn to frown. 'You're bluffing. You don't know anything.'

'As you wish,' says Eccles, and steps outside. 'We should do this again some time. It's been very special. And do give my best to Miss Leighton.'

'Oi!' I call after him. 'Plod! You're bluffing!'

Eccles waves.

Very much to my surprise, I manage to lure Philip to the pub in the evening. I attempt this most nights – being the kind of sly, directionless, alcoholic young adult that is giving the nation a bad name – but he invariably declines. I've never been able to figure out whether this is because he has something very important to get back to (a boyfriend, a girlfriend, a teddy-bear that needs washing) or simply because he doesn't like me very much. Tonight we're a team, and things are going well. He says yes.

'Why aren't you afraid of losing your job?' he asks me, some-where between the third lager and the first whisky and coke. We're sitting in the Dick Whittington, which is one of the nicer pubs in the vicinity of our office, but still a shabby, varnished hole. Why do the poshest parts of London have only horrible pubs in them? Where do all the old men come from? Do they bus them in? It's a mystery.

I laugh when Philip says this. 'Why should I be?'

Philip twitches his hands, as though looking for something to fiddle with. He's already rolled up the sleeves of his fussy M&S shirt and loosened the knot of his green M&S tie. Now he just tugs at it. 'Because you're such an arsehole,' he says, miserably.

'And you're a fey little shite,' I snap back. 'What the fuck do you mean?'

He goes pink. 'That came out wrong.'

'So did you, ladyboy. How was it meant to come out?'

He sighs, and studies the ceiling. I stare at him.

'I just meant . . .'

'What? You just meant what?'

'The way you behave . . .'

'Yeah . . . ?'

'With Trevor and the rest . . .'

'Go on.'

'Well,' says Philip, looking at me then looking away, '. . . is like an arsehole. The way you *talk* to them. You're just so *rude*. The way you shouted at that policeman, in front of everybody. You are aware of it?'

'Oh, that,' I say, relieved. 'Yeah. Course I am.'

'I'd be terrified,' he says, looking a little bit terrified just talking about it. 'I just couldn't spar with people like that. Not over my job. There's just too much to lose.'

'It's only a job, old bean,' I tell him, casting a meaningful glance at my empty pint glass. 'Plenty of other jobs around.'

'I wouldn't get them,' he says, immediately. 'I don't have the experience. I don't even have your experience.'

'Less of the even,' I say huffily and, as an afterthought, tap the glass with a forefinger.

'Sorry, but it's true. Daniel only took me on as a favour to a friend of mine. And since he left . . . well. If I lost this, I'd be screwed. And . . .' he hesitates. 'Can I tell you something?'

I gaze at him. 'It's not about me, is it? And how I sometimes look at you? And how, although we're just friends at the moment, you've always harboured this dream that, if you'd only buy me a pint, we could . . .'

'No,' says Philip, and he's blushing. 'It's about Jensen Randall.'

'Jensen? Didn't think he was your type.'

'Don't be a dick, Mac. I think . . . I think he wants to get me sacked.'

I shrug. 'Probably. That's just what he's like. I think he wants to get us all sacked.'

'No, but me particularly. I've seen him talking with Trevor, and, from the way they look over, you can tell they are talking about us.'

'Paranoia, old chum. You want to lay off the weed.'

Philip gets pinker. 'Stop it. I'm being serious. Jensen is scary. You think so too. I can tell.'

I just chuckle, but in a way Philip is absolutely right. I'm thinking of Linda, Lucy's friend. I'm also remembering the final time I ever went for a drink with Jensen. It was in here, only a few feet away, that he picked up that bottle and lunged, ever so casually. I wonder how much damage he'd have done to that fat, drunk accountant if I hadn't pulled him off, or how much damage he'd have done to me if the connections in his nutty robot brain had pulsed the other way. Jensen is scary, but so scary that he's hardly worth worrying about. He's like a patch of oil in a road tunnel, or a lightning bolt hitting a jet.

'Confidence, lad,' I say. 'You need confidence. And I need beer.'

'Maybe I do need confidence,' says Philip, thoughtfully. 'Maybe that's it. Like, today? I couldn't have written that story the way you did.'

'Ah,' I say bashfully. 'Well no. You probably couldn't. Few could.'

'You didn't even check it,' he says, seemingly ignoring me. 'You didn't phone the police, or even her agent. And after everything Trevor said . . . well. I'd be terrified. I couldn't do that. Too much to lose.'

He's got me thinking about Eccles now. Drunken introspection. I hate it. 'Goddamn, boy,' I snarl. 'Are you going to the bar or not?'

'Sorry,' says Philip, and stands up.

'Good lad,' I tell him, stifling a burp. 'You'd be fine, anyway. Nice posh chap like you? Surely mater and pater would keep you on your feet.'

'I don't speak to my parents,' says Philip, and turns his back on me.

———

He doesn't as well. The things you learn about people when they've got a drink inside them, eh? He's a dark horse, that Philip. It seems I had him all wrong. For one thing, he's only twenty-three, which amazes me. And for another, while he is gay, he's certainly not the kind of little sheltered dink I had assumed. He comes back to our table with a pair of whisky and cokes, and sets them down. 'I haven't spoken to them for two years,' he tells me, and it all just kind of gushes out from there.

Philip grew up in a wee village outside Bath. As a child he lived in a manse; his dad was a vicar and his mother was a vicar's wife. The same vicar, luckily. Philip tells me that the manse cottage had roses and creepers up the outside, which is neither relevant nor pertinent, but I suppose adds a bit of local colour. All very idyllic. The young Philip was a bookish and slight lad who liked fishing and ornithology. His happiest childhood memories involve hiking with his father to a pond in the middle of the New Forest, looking for a great crested grebe. When Philip got tired, his dad would swing him up and carry him on his shoulders – Philip says he can remember the feel of the pine twigs brushing his scalp. Was he going bald even then?

I can't really visualise the vicar, probably because Philip doesn't tell me very much about the way he looks. In my mind, he's the spit of Friar Tuck from the Kevin Costner Robin Hood film. Philip says that he and his father are very much alike in temperament, to the extent that when he went off to boarding school, aged fourteen, he cried because it felt like he was leaving his best friend behind.

He pauses here because it's my turn to go to the bar. While I'm gone he barely moves. He doesn't fiddle with his tie, he doesn't rip up a beer mat, he doesn't play with his phone. Nothing at all.

———

School, says Philip, was a little boarding place, on the outskirts of Bristol. I'd imagine he was one of the geeks – too inoffensive to be bullied, but too little and pointy and strange to make that many friends. He won prizes in French, Geography and Classics. Ma and Pa were delighted.

Philip goes on to read Theology at Edinburgh. People like him. Adorably, he finds this a little surprising. After a while he meets a boy. This doesn't surprise him. He hasn't thought about it so much, but it's not exactly a shock. The boy doesn't work out, but then there's another. And then another. Philip senses a pattern emerging. He decides he'd better tell his parents.

His mother cries and says he'd better tell his father. His father cries and punches him down the stairs. Then he chases after him to deliver a kick that leaves him with a four-inch scar that you can still just make out running along the side of his (now largely theoretical) hairline. Mother screams, father rages, Philip leaves.

'Jesus fucking Christ,' I say.

'Nice guy, eh?' says Philip. I expect to see tears in his eyes, but they are hard and dry. You could almost tap them with cutlery, like Daniel Day Lewis in *Gangs of New York*.

I look at the table. 'Er, no. Wouldn't really say that at all. Wow.'

'Get me a drink,' Philip instructs, and I do, even though it's technically his round.

I'm feeling a little shaken, if the truth be told. Does this kind of stuff actually happen? Like, to real people? I had no idea. I thought it was the stuff of news stories, of fiction and celebrities. It was . . . *other*, like HIV and appearing on *Big Brother*. One of those things you just don't expect to happen to somebody you know.

'I've shocked you,' says Philip, when I return with another brace of whisky and cokes.

'Not at all,' I say, then come clean. 'Well yes, actually, you have. I had you down as being slightly more, uh, sheltered. Traditional. Boring, frankly. I'm sorry.'

'Don't be,' he says, and I notice with some alarm that he's already sunk almost half of his drink. 'Everybody has something like that. You aren't going to tell me that you have a normal family, are you?'

'Um, yeah. Pretty much. Sorry.'

'Stop apologising,' he says. 'But really? The full set? Two point four siblings and a pair of parents?'

'Three siblings,' I tell him. 'Well. Two plus me. And just the one parent. Just a dad.'

'Oh God, I'm sorry,' says Philip, and looks almost comically contrite. 'I was being pushy. I'm such an insensitive berk. How did your mum die? No. You don't have to answer that. I'm sorry.'

I laugh. 'Now who's apologising too much? Don't worry. She's not dead. She just doesn't live with us.'

'Oh. Right. Where does she live?'

'Israel,' I say. 'On a kibbutz. Don't suppose you've got any fags, have you?'

Philip stares at me for a moment. 'No. Since when?'

'Ages. Since I was about seven. Is there a machine? Bollocks. I need another quid. Do you have a quid?'

'Probably,' says Philip, without moving. 'I've wondered why you're always reading up on the Middle East. I thought it was just because you're Jewish. When did you last see her?'

'God knows. Couple of decades? Go on, check. See if you've got a quid.'

Philip knocks back the rest of his drink, seemingly ignoring me. 'So that means . . . what? You haven't seen her since she left?'

'No,' I say, staring back at him. 'I haven't seen her since she left. Please. Can I have that quid, Philip?'

'And you don't think this is a big deal?'

I stand up. 'No. I don't. Am I going to have to go to a cash-point?'

'Sit down,' says Philip, and grabs me on the shoulder. 'You're being ridiculous.'

I grab his wrist and twist it. Our eyes meet, and I feel my lip curling into a snarl.

Philip sounds slightly breathless. 'So what?' he says, pleasantly. 'You're going to hit me now? Purely because you don't have any cigarettes?'

Time passes with a thump, like a planetary heartbeat. For a moment I don't know what is about to happen. Then I let go of his wrist and fall back into my chair, suddenly and ragingly drunk. Philip is off by the bar, and the room feels like it is spinning. How much have I drunk? I need to go home.

After what feels like only a couple of seconds, he's back, with another pair of drinks and a pack of Silk Cut. I rip into them, like a lion with a wildebeest.

'Sorry about that,' I say, lighting one.

He shakes his head. 'Don't be.'

I'm baffled, about more or less everything. I sip at my drink, but it tastes like acid.

'Look,' I begin, and try to think of something to talk about. 'You didn't explain. Your parents and everything . . . why did you tell me that? What has it got to do with anything? With you not being able to lose your job?'

He chuckles, mirthlessly. 'Isn't it obvious? They read the *Gazette* every day.'

'So?' I say. 'So?'

'So,' says Philip, and looks away. 'So I want them to see my name in it every day. I'd like to think it hurts them.'

Poor Philip. Of course he's a fuck-up. You can always spot a fuck-up, can't you?

'Are ye blind?'

Edinburgh, 1992. It was June, I think, and I was up late, sitting on my bed and reading about Asterix and Obelix and their mission to save a divided village from the Machiavellian schemes of a sallow-faced ginger called Codfix. Summer light was knifing into my room from the crack between the two halves of my Thunderbirds curtains and, drifting through from the garden, I began to hear the breathy sounds of Janie and a hairy bloke with a nose ring having a grinding shag against our garage wall. I'd skinned my knees against the very same wall more than once, climbing up onto the garage roof and knew its spiky harl well. One of them, most probably Janie, must have been doing some serious damage to their back. I'd like to think that this occurred to me at the time, but that's probably a bit fanciful. I was engrossed in my book and, at best, angry at the distraction. Mary was asleep in her own room next door. Dad was out at the hospital. That was the day that Grandpa Johnjohn fell out of the attic at Lewis Tartans, and the whole of the Royal Mile came to a standstill while the ambulance came and scraped him up.

Disturbed by these panting fumblings, I remember slipping out of bed and making my way to the kitchen to see what I could find in the fridge. Sleep was out of the question. Sororal copulatory affairs, and the combined distractions of Goscinny, Uderzo and the health of my grandfather aside, the rest of Janie's friends (i.e. those who weren't currently doing her up against the garage wall) were making far too much of a din. She was never what you might call a responsible child, Janie. Charged with babysitting her two junior siblings while her father went to visit a critically infirm relative, she opted instead to have all her friends round and get pissed on cider in the garden. I suppose it was a plea for attention, of sorts. Worked, too.

Anyway, I was in the process of pillaging my fill of sliced ham and processed cheese for a late-night sandwich when a voice from behind me said, 'Oi.'

Startled, I spun around, dropping a Kraft Cheese Single to the floor with the kind of sticky slap that tells you immediately that the underside is going to be grimy when you pick it up. Behind me, sitting at the kitchen table, was Nina McLean.

'Hello,' I said.

'Hello yourself,' said Nina McLean, and stopped fiddling with whatever incomprehensible thing she had in her hands. In retrospect, I suppose it was probably a joint, but it's not impossible it was a wrap or even a syringe. She'd have been about sixteen at that point. Nina was Elspeth's second oldest sister, the one who was to choke to death in a squat in Glasgow four years later when something which she wrongly understood to be ketamine caused the contents of her stomach to expand in a viscous white foam. She was also (and I hope this doesn't sound disrespectful in the light of the above) soon to be the subject of my very first wank.

She was a beautiful girl, Nina. I can still see her, leaning forward over the table at me, with the loose grey cotton of her stretched sweatshirt slipping over one shoulder and almost down to her elbow. Had I seen a bra before? Probably not. She was wearing a purple one and most of her breasts spilled out of it, mushed together by the sides of her outstretched arms. She had big dark hair and black lipstick, and I didn't even know about the hard little twelve-year-old branch straining at the flannel of my pyjamas until she peered at it and made an amused coughing sound.

I turned away, mortified, and opened a drawer to hide my shame.

'How's Elspeth?' I managed.

'Fine,' said Nina. 'We've no' seen you around the house recently. How's that?'

'Just been . . . busy, really,' I said, which is a lie almost by definition for any twelve-year-old.

'Aye right.' Nina sounded amused. 'Nothing tae dae wi' her boyfriend, then?'

I blushed. Nina laughed.

'You're cute. I'll put in a good word for you. Okay, wee man?'

I muttered something awkward, and bent down to clear up the cheese. I could see her legs, in green Doc Martens and fishnets, protruding from a small red kilt.

When I turned back, a blond boy in a Nirvana T-shirt was coming in the glass door from garden, behind the table. He had his hands on Nina's shoulders. 'C'moan back through,' he murmured in her ear.

'Just a minute,' said Nina, shrugging slightly.

'C'moan,' said the boy, almost wheedling. As I watched, one of his hands went down her collar bone and into her bra, quite visibly tweaking her nipple.

'Get tae fuck!' she snapped, turning around and slapping at him. 'Are ye blind? There's a fuckin' bairn in here.'

The boy looked at me and sneered. 'So?' he said. 'So fuckin' what? Doesnae look like he minds, does it?'

'I'm just going,' I blurted, and did so, red-faced and waddling. I could hear his booming laughter behind me, along with Nina, high-pitched and annoyed.

'He's only a bairn,' she was saying. 'They've no' had it easy. Their ma . . .'

I leapt into the bathroom and slammed the door, loudly and deliberately. Inside, I crossed over to the window and slammed that shut as well. There were maybe six of them out there, smoking and laughing, most likely listening to some drivel by Ned's Atomic Dustbin. Drawing the curtains, I stepped towards the toilet and dropped my pyjama trousers. It was still there, a small fleshy prod. I needed to pee. I wasn't sure how to make it go away. Then I heard a whimper from the shower.

Snatching up my trousers in a fury, I spun around. Not more of them, please God. Why the shower? Couldn't they just leave me alone? 'Get out!' I shouted.

'Mackie?' said a small voice.

I whipped aside the curtain. Mary, my younger sister, was curled up in a ball on the floor, in pyjamas and dressing gown and clutching a stuffed rabbit. She must have been ten, I suppose.

'Go to bed,' I commanded, sensing weakness and falling into the role of older sibling.

'Don't want to,' said Mary, which was a significantly less aggressive response than the one I had been bracing myself for. I peered at her, uncertainly.

'Why are you sitting in the shower?'

She's cleverer than me, Mary, and she's always been able to baffle me with the greatest of ease. She did so now.

'Why shouldn't I be?'

I couldn't answer that. Instead I pushed past the curtain and squatted down next to her. For a time, we sat in companionable silence. Mary's snuffling grew gradually less teary and petulant, and eventually she stuck the rabbit in the soap dish and rested her head on my shoulder, watching me out of the corner of her eye.

'What?' I asked, but she didn't say anything. I sighed. 'Are you worried about Grandpa Johnjohn?'

'A bit,' said Mary. 'Will he be okay?'

'Of course he will,' I declared, absent-mindedly trying to stuff the rabbit down the plug hole. 'Or he'll die, maybe.'

'Aye,' she said with a nod, and didn't stop nodding. Eventually I glanced at her, and noticed that the nods were turning into shudders, which themselves were turning into sobs.

'Hey,' I said, 'hey,' and shoved the rabbit at her, desperately.

'It's wet,' she complained, but took it anyway.

'Sorry.' I put an arm around her shoulders and hugged, tentatively. 'Don't cry. He probably won't die.'

Mary shook her head. 'It's not that.'

I blinked at her, baffled. 'So . . . what, then?'

'Janie,' whispered Mary, 'and Grandpa, and Dad, and you, and me, and Mum, and school, and *everything*.'

'Right,' I said, and tried to look knowledgeable. It didn't last. 'No. I don't get it. What do you mean?'

'*Everything*, Mackie,' said Mary, and looked at me imploringly. 'We're so *different*. Don't you hate it?'

I was baffled. I thought of our modest detached Victorian house, with its patch of garden and widespread lino. I thought of the yellow, bobbled wallpaper in the living room, and the raggedy rug my father had laid out in the hall. I thought of our school, private but hardly elitist, with its endless sportsdays and maroon blazers that smelled of cowshit when it started to rain. I thought of evenings in front of our one telly, of *The Man from Uncle* or the *A-Team*, of *EastEnders* and *One Foot in the Grave*, and I thought of dinners of burgers or fish fingers, always with chips. I thought of my rebellious older sister and my frightened younger sister, and I was baffled.

'But we're normal,' I told her. 'We're *exactly* normal.'

'Oh Mackie,' said my sister, almost sadly. 'We're not.'

I shook my head, and squeezed her shoulders. 'We are. We're normal and I do hate it. I don't want to be normal. I want to be different. We're all going to be special, Mary. I promise you.'

'How?' said my little sister, genuinely intrigued. 'Will we be the cool people?'

'Of course we will. We're going to live in London, and we'll be the coolest people anyone ever saw. Except for our friends. They'll be even cooler.'

'Like Jason Donovan?'

'Cooler,' I said. 'Like Madonna, and Michael Knight and those guys from A-ha.'

'Cool,' mused Mary, although I remember thinking, even then, that she was humouring me.

'That's a little harsh . . .'

Heading into the office the morning after my night with Philip, I feel distinctly shaky. My mobile tells me that Daniel called last night, twice (presumably chasing his minging suit which, yes, I am wearing yet again). I have no recollection of this whatsoever.

The bus from Brompton Road to Victoria lurches unpleasantly, and I find myself resting my forehead against the sticky, smeared glass as we pass the green grass of Hyde Park. Something in the back of my mind tells me that the window should feel cool and soothing. It doesn't.

He's there before me, Philip, which surprises me – not because I am not late (I am, slightly) but because he was surely in a worse state than me last night. Still, there he is, pale brown shirt with creases as jagged as a Toblerone, and scalp as shiny as ever through the sparseness of his hair.

'Hey baby,' I call. He shoots me a look like thunder.

I'm about to take issue with this when Trevor Brainchild walks past me, fairly thumping me on the back as he goes. 'Lewis,' he barks. '*My* office. *Now.*'

Philip looks away, quickly. I stare at him for a moment, and then hurry after Brainchild, anger growing. What has the little shit been saying to people? Few people will meet my eye as I pass through the office – Willie Fowler actually turns his back on me. I catch one of the fashion girls staring at me and she panics for a moment, before screeching something about picture credits to a worky. What on earth have I done?

Brainchild reaches his office some seven paces in front of me and slams the door. I frown for a moment, and then knock on it. This is surreal; it's like the time I was called to see the headmaster at school after the CCTV camera caught me pissing against the side of the chapel (it wasn't a religious statement, I was drunk. I remember making this point – perhaps unwisely – at the time).

'Come!' he barks.

He's sitting at his desk now, which makes me think he must have really flown across his office to get there before I stepped through the door. Between his hands, he's holding a rolled-up copy of the *Evening Standard*. And he's not alone. Robin Hargreaves is sitting to one side, with a loosened tie. This is a worrying sign. Rebecca Leighton is in one of the two chairs that faces Brainchild's desk; her back is to me and the other chair is empty. And behind Brainchild, lounging against the bookcase like some kind of fucking *consigliore*, is Jensen Randall. He's grinning at me.

'Jensen,' I say, nodding at him.

He stops grinning. 'Yansen.'

'Whatever.'

'Sit!' yaps Brainchild, who may feel he is being ignored.

I don't sit. 'What's going on?' I demand.

'Macaulay,' says Hargreaves, almost wearily. 'Sit down.'

I take the seat next to Rebecca. She doesn't even acknowledge my presence. Brainchild looms at us over the desk, eyes popping more than ever. He looks like the Nazi at the end of that Indiana Jones film, when the ghost swoops out of the Ark of the Covenant.

'Seen a *paper* today, Lewis?'

I shake my head. 'Nope, Trev. Wrote one yesterday, though. Any use?'

Brainchild's arm swings out across the desk suddenly, and I flinch, momentarily convinced he is actually about to hit me. But he doesn't. Instead he flings his copy of the *Standard* in my face.

'Sit down, Macaulay,' thunders Hargreaves, and it's only then that I realise I'm back on my feet. 'Read it.'

I sit. I read. I understand. I look up in disbelief.

'He issued a statement?'

'He did,' agrees Brainchild. 'A *statement*. And *not* to *us*.'

This, to me, seems to be beside the point. What kind of thief issues a statement?

Fingers does. This morning, at around 9 a.m., a motorcycle courier pulled up outside the Associated Newspapers building in Knightsbridge and made his way to the *Evening Standard* offices on the first floor. Here he delivered (*by hand* no less) a silver envelope to the editor herself. Inside was one of his cards, with the famous silhouette and one line of beautiful calligraphic text. '*Turino?*' it read. '*Please! One might as well burgle an Argos catalogue. Yours, Fingers.*'

The courier, needless to say, could not be traced. He was caught on the building's security cameras, but the number plates on his bike were gleaming and unreadable. Courier plates often are – they smear them with clear nail varnish to avoid speed cameras. Somehow, though, I suspect that this courier wasn't really a courier.

'Jesus,' I say. 'Turino made it up? All of it?'

'Of course she did,' sneers Brainchild. 'You stupid little shit.'
Rebecca looks a little shocked. 'Steady,' warns Hargreaves.

Brainchild closes his eyes for a couple of seconds. 'We're a laughing stock. *Again.* Because of you. *Again.*'

'That's a little harsh,' I mutter, but my heart isn't in it. 'It was on the telly,' I add, weakly.

He ignores me. 'You're a *fantasist,*' he says, as though struggling to stay in control. 'You *can't* be trusted. You have *no* idea what is news and what isn't, and it *won't* do. From now on, every *word* you write goes through Rebecca here. Your contacts, her skills. You will *investigate* this story like *journalists* and you *will* have *results.* Do I make myself clear?'

I blink. 'I'm being baby-sat?' This is too much. 'I'm being baby-sat by *her*? Oh come on!'

'You ought to be sacked,' says Jensen Randall, loftily.

I'm on my feet again almost immediately. 'You want tae fucking . . .'

'SHUT UP,' screams Brainchild, and I'm shocked into silence. He is rocking, almost throbbing with anger. 'You're *lucky* we didn't sack the *pair* of you. Now get out.'

As I walk back through the office, I wonder who he meant – me and Rebecca, or me and Jensen. Must be Rebecca. They couldn't sack Jensen. Could they?

It shows, really, how badly it is possible to misread somebody. Once, I genuinely thought we were going to be friends, Jensen and I. Not good friends, perhaps, or indeed even real ones, but happy pretenders. I think I mentioned, I even went to his house. Astonishing place. We went to the pub together, three times. Granted, shortly before closing time on outing three, he did have to be forcibly prevented from ramming a broken bottle into that cheery accountant's eyes, but for the most part he was passable company. He was awkward, and nervy, and a little hard to . . . *connect* with, in a way that reminded me of some Americans I've known, but he seemed to mean well. He always wanted to know what parties I was going to, and who else was going to be there. Strangely deferential, really. Like I've always wanted Philip to be. He wasn't halfway as likeable as Philip, of course, but I never minded that. It's a bad thing about me, I think, that I don't need to particularly like somebody in order to class them as a friend.

It's only when I reach my desk and see Philip, that I realise Brainchild wasn't talking about Jensen or Rebecca at all.

'Hey,' I say to Philip's back. 'It's going to be okay. I'm sorry, man.'

He doesn't turn around. After a few moments I sit down and start wondering what on earth I am going to do.

'The dark and fetid reaches of pleasure . . .'

The rest of the day is a nightmare, and I don't really want to talk about it. Eccles calls, presumably to gloat. I don't answer, and he doesn't leave a message. At about 2 p.m. I get an email from Lucy, who I'm meant to be seeing tonight. '*Hear you fucked up,*' it begins, tactfully. '*Want some sex and sympathy?*'

I do, but not from her. I don't reply. Instead I file a short, made-up story about a Premiership footballer buying a new home in Amersham, and then I go home and get stoned. Then I go to Paxy's.

'One can never be a true libertine until one has opened one's mind to the tantalising mystery that is defecation!'

So announces my host, holding forth in his living room. It's slightly shy of midnight, and Paxy is balancing precariously on the right angle of the arms on a crumbly velvet chaise-longue.

He's wearing an open red silk dressing-gown, and polka-dot boxer shorts. From my position across the room, I can see his sallow penis poking out of one leg. He has a spilling tumbler of whisky in one hand and a billowing cigar in the other. His face and belly are flushed mauve, his hair is disarrayed and his eyes are gleaming, wet and lascivious.

'Filth!' he shouts, and his voice reverberates against the flaky stuccoed ceiling. 'Excrement! That chocolate stew of intrigue is the last bastion of repression! The portal that must be breached! The gates that must be ripped asunder! The murky pool in which we must dip if we are to be true to our desires of love, lust and pleasure!'

Vintage stuff. Half the room are cheering. The rest look concerned. Melissa, a boyish ITN researcher I have cornered by the fireplace for the last two hours, pouts her purple painted lips and looks unimpressed.

'This is nonsense,' I whisper to her. 'Don't worry.'

She raises her eyebrows 'Who said I was worrying?'

'Crap, poo, and shit!' hollers Paxy, before pausing, momentarily uncertain. 'Are there any more?'

'Turd!' shrieks Xani, a Chinese girl who does make-up for *CD:UK*.

Paxy beams at her, majestically, arranging his features in a manner that makes him look oddly like Brian Blessed. 'Turd indeed,' he bellows. 'Turd indeed. Young lady, I am in your debt. Turd! Crap, poo, shit and turd! These, fine people, are terms we must escape! They exist to ridicule, to suppress, to make ludicrous. We make things ludicrous, people, in order to counter their threat. Ludicrous, people, is not sexy!'

'Rubbish!' I shout at the fat, shiny, naked libertine. 'You are the living disproof of that rule!'

Paxy winks at me, gravely, plainly not taking in what I have just said at all. 'Who will join me?' he booms. 'Who will journey with me to the dark and fetid reaches of pleasure? Who will come with me this night . . . to a Cadbury's heaven?'

People roar, but non-specifically, just in case. 'I'll come with you!' screams the Chinese girl.

'Young lady,' says Paxy, and bows, 'to bed. First floor on the right, where together we shall attend to the sludgy magic, forthwith.'

She's in for a disappointment. For all his talk, I have it on good authority that Paxy's pleasure is a highly conventional beast. He's like me, with my ex Naomi. Just as I once lived a wild and varied sex life through her paranoid dreams, he now lives one through these ridiculous evening speeches. He'll declaim shamelessly about threesomes and foursomes and fivesomes; about bottomy and bondage and scat-love; and then he'll pop off upstairs and have an unremarkable knee-shaker against his great-grandmother's French dresser. Quite sad, really.

Melissa crosses her legs towards me. She's wearing some smooth tights under a knee-length tweed skirt, and one shin brushes against my knee. I stroke it lightly with a finger nail. She looks at me for a moment, and then moves her legs away. Confusingly, just as I am about to conclude that I have been wasting my time from the start, she leans forward, with her elbows on her knees, quite deliberately giving me a view down her shirt. She has on a dog-collar thing (as in a dog, please note. Not as in a vicar. It's not *that* kinky here). It works well, with her smart shirt, in an incongruous sort of way.

'So,' she says, sitting up. 'How long have you been coming to this delightful place?'

Aha. This is very much changing the pace of our courtship. Up until now, we have been talking about ourselves, showing off and trying to sound important. Basically we have been blowing our own trumpets in order to convince each other that sleeping together would not just be a mind-blowingly intense and frankly trendy experience, but also a rather shrewd career move. This kind of thing happens a lot at Paxy's. But now . . . hmm. Relative intimacy. Sneaky.

I laugh at her, deliberately to annoy. 'I see what you are doing. You're asking me if I come here often.'

'No, I'm not.'

'Yes you are. You're just pretending you aren't.'

Melissa smiles at me. One hand scratches at her short blonde hair. The other raises a glass of red wine to her lips. Both look a bit like they'd rather be gouging out my eyes. 'Okay,' she says, with slightly forced pleasantry, 'how about you just tell me how long you've been coming here, without being a total arse about it?'

I nod. Seems fair, I suppose. 'Right. Um, about six years. Six or seven. You?'

'Months. About six months. Why haven't I seen you before?'

'Hmm,' I look around with distaste. 'Week nights. I don't usually do them. It can get a bit . . . exhausting. I used to live here, actually.'

'Oh,' says Melissa, and drains her glass. 'A regular. So you must have penetrated the inner circle then?'

'The dark and mysterious chocolate inner circle,' I say, gravely, which makes her laugh, although not as much as I'd hoped. 'Guess so, yeah. I've known him for ages. He used to go out with an ex of mine, actually. Girl called Elspeth.'

Melissa nods. 'I think I know her. Light brown hair?'

'That's her. How come?'

'Met her here. What does she do again?'

'She's an, erm, actress. Basically.'

'I can see that. Very elegant.'

'Yeah. You could say that. So you and Paxy haven't . . . ?'

She looks positively shocked. 'Eeeuw. God no. He's a bit . . . piggish for me.'

'He's become that way,' I concede. 'It's a tragedy.'

It is, as well. When I first started coming here, almost seven years ago, there really was something fresh and exciting about all this. Was I just young? Maybe to some people, there still is.

I first visited this cavernous sexual Babylon in the summer holidays of my second year at university, not long after I met Paxy at that house party thing. It was a spur of the moment occurrence – Elspeth had vanished off up to the Highlands with some random lordling she'd picked up at the Royal Garden Party (don't ask), none of my school friends seemed to be around and the Princess was at a pre-university Jewish student union get-together in Leeds. I was bored, and I'd started to bicker with my dad. Early one afternoon I left him a note in the spout of the kettle and jumped on a train to King's Cross.

Seven hours later, I was ringing the doorbell of a large house in Hampstead. I was a touch concerned, if truth be told. This wasn't what I had been expecting. I didn't know London very well back then and, from the brief chat I'd had with Paxy about 'his space', I'd assumed I'd be heading to some crumbly warehouse in a seedy meat-packing district. Instead, I was on a cobbled pavement in a leafy suburb, ringing the brass doorbell of a house that must have cost around eight times as much as my father's. Dear God, I thought suddenly. He didn't live with his parents did he? Perhaps I should have phoned to say that I was coming.

'What?'

The door opened, and I found myself facing a plumpish girl with short black hair. She was holding a small white towelling dressing-gown closed at the front, but it wasn't quite up to the job.

'Jesus,' I said. 'I'm sorry. I haven't got you out of bed, have I?'

She scowled at me. 'None of your business. What do you want?'

'I'm, uh, here to see Paxy. He in?'

She eyed me critically. Did I, I wondered, look like too much of a tramp? It was possible; I was a lot scruffier back then. My jeans were baggy and frayed, and it's not impossible that my shirt was made of cheesecloth. 'Paxy?' I said again. 'He . . . uh . . . oh. I don't know his real name.'

This was turning into a nightmare. I had nowhere to sleep. The girl sniffed at me, turned her back, and flounced into the house. It took me a moment to realise she'd left the door open, and another moment to pluck up the courage to step inside.

Inside it was dark. I could dimly see the white, fluffy expanse of her arse heading off up a staircase to my right. Straight ahead, however, was a corridor with a vague yellowish glow and what sounded like the hubbub of a party at the end of it. Was that Portishead I could hear? Lots of voices. The house was quite so ludicrously large that I hadn't heard it from outside at all.

I made my way towards the noise, thinking, quite inanely, of that story about the Hollywood star who put that hamster in a tube and made it run up his bottom. At the end of the corridor was a crowded room, and in that room were three sofas, on one of the sofas was a girl of about seventeen, and under that girl was Paxy. The girl was wearing a red, sequiny cocktail dress thing, which was pushed up around her hips, and she was straddling him, oddly, just above the knees. She seemed to be almost in a trance. Paxy himself appeared barely aware of this. He was lying, stretched out, with his head and back propped up on a cushion, and talking in an animated fashion to a guy who looked like a skinnier version of Russell Crowe.

'Hi,' I said.

Paxy's eyes swivelled. 'I know you,' he mused.

'Erm, yeah. Mac. Mac Lewis. We met at a guy called Duncan's house.'

'Duncan?' said Paxy, mystified.

'Douglas,' I corrected myself. 'There was a girl called Macy, and a bloke called Mike and . . .'

'Good lord, yes!' Paxy swung himself off the sofa, tipping the seventeen-year-old onto her back, like a drunk, skinny turtle. 'Mr Mac! Thank God you've come,' he cried, wringing me by the hand. 'There simply isn't a person here worth speaking to.'

Nobody else seemed at all fazed by the stunning rudeness of this comment. There were maybe twenty people in the room, the youngest of which was the aforementioned dazed teenager, now tottering to her feet and tugging her dress down over her naked thighs, and the oldest of which was a chap with a forked beard (it was. It was forked) who must have been in his early thirties. Most were Paxy's age: a few years older than me. They were people very much of a sort, the sort which, I suppose, I have since become. They worked in television, magazines, public relations and advertising. Trendy and affluent; not people at the top, I suppose, but inching towards it from a very comfortable middle.

House of ill-repute Paxy's may be but, as I learned that night, there are firm rules. For one thing, sexual aggression, at least in public, is not tolerated. For another, etiquette dictates that whenever a couple leave the room, regardless of their gender, orientation or sexual preferences, they take a condom from the large fruit bowl on the central coffee table. This serves a double function. Aside from enforcing a message of safety first ('Right, kids?'), it's also an indicator that both parties agree to whatever is about to happen next. To be honest, I think it's largely superfluous in practical terms, as most temporary unions here tend to result in slaps and tugs rather than bumps and grinds, but it's strangely reassuring nonetheless. It's a symbolic thing, like car keys in the seventies.

It's odd how these things work out, isn't it? Thinking about it, it was the seventies when things like this started to go wrong. There must have been set-ups like Paxy's forever, since the Greeks thought up Dionysus. How tawdry is the modern age! Eighty years ago, Paxy would have had assorted Wildes and Woolfs and whatnots queuing up to be part of his brave little bohemia. Royalty even – he's posh enough. Instead, he has to make do with media scum like me. He was born in the wrong age, really. He's become a sexual facilitator, a pimp who works for free. Before, even thirty years before, he would have been a legend.

I had sex with three people that night, including Lesley, the fat girl who answered the door. I stayed a week.

It's an edited version of this story that I give to Melissa. Hers is odder. She doesn't, socially, know anybody here at all. She first came along incognito, to research a story about a group of swinging members of the Young Conservatives. Plausible as this might sound (Paxy's has suffered an upsurge in Tory numbers lately, while the New Labour fuckists seem to be in decline), it turned out that her source had been mistaken, and the particular ones she was after weren't around. She toyed, she claims, with the idea of trying to get a story out of it anyway, but decided in the end that there could be career advantages in keeping schtum. She's right, too. My first job (a menial hell at *Poshbird Monthly* which I may have already mentioned) came about as a result of somebody I met here, and many of my best stories have too.

It's important to understand, there are plenty of people who come to Paxy's regularly, and never have the slightest intention of shagging anybody. I personally make a firm distinction between people who might give me work (absolutely unshaggable), people who give me stories (potentially shaggable, but usually only afterwards) and people with whom I have no professional connection whatsoever (you work it out). Melissa, I am happy to say, falls squarely into the last category.

By the way she has been content to let my hand creep slowly up her thigh for the past hour, I'm pretty sure she has similar designs on me. However, we've been talking a bit too long. It's almost two, and I will need to sleep eventually. More annoyingly, the living room has all but emptied out, which means that all the bedrooms upstairs will already be occupied.

'It's late,' I tell her, and increase the pressure slightly on her leg.

'It is,' she agrees.

'Where do you live?' I ask.

'That doesn't matter,' she says. 'I want to do it here.'

I'm not surprised by this sudden forwardness. This is how it almost always happens – endless verbal fencing and jousting, and then a sudden unspoken acceptance by both parties that whatever is about to happen is about to happen, and there is no point pretending otherwise.

'There won't be any rooms,' I tell her.

'We'll get by,' she says, and springs to her feet, grabbing my hand and leading me towards the room's back door, the one that leads away from the staircase. As we pass the low, flat coffee table in the centre of the room, she plucks a condom from the pot. She lets go of my hand to open the door, and as soon as she does I'm pushing her through it, up against the wall outside. Our teeth clash and her hands are in my shirt. I start pulling up her skirt, but she stops me.

'Not in the corridor,' she breathes.

I pause for a beat and nod. 'Billiard room,' I say, and step backwards towards another doorway, hand flapping loosely behind me for the handle. We stagger together through the door, like spastic dancers, and then fall back against it, slamming it closed. My shirt is around my elbows now, and my hands are opening hers, ripping at the buttons and delving inside at her small, pointy breasts. She kisses like she's looking for something, with a hard, cold, inquisitive tongue that tastes of smoke. It's dark in here. Headlights from cars passing outside flicker crazily across the room, reflected in the giant dusty mirror on the far wall.

Melissa pushes away from the door and we stumble across the room, her hands fumbling at the zip on Daniel's trousers. As she reaches inside I spin her around, pushing her forward over the grey plastic tarpaulin which covers the billiard table. With both hands, I push up her skirt, feeling her wriggling her hips to help me. Confronted with her opaque tights I pause for a moment, and then gouge in with my fingertips, tearing a hole. My thumb hooks around her G-string, yanking it to one side, and I'm in, hands on the back of her neck, tugging at her hair, pulling her shirt down over her shoulders and her back. As the lights slash across the room, her face, illuminated, flashes in the mirror. Hair disarrayed, chest bare. Eyes closed, mouth curled like an endless, inky 'O'.

The thing is, I'm not actually paying much attention. I don't realise at first, and when I do, it hits me like a horsekick. I'm going through the motions, but all I can think about is my job, and how soon I'm going to find myself out of it. That shouldn't really be happening, should it?

'Fingers did it.'

And the weeks go by, and slowly my stock at the *Gazette* sinks even lower. I write, I drink, I make frantic phonecalls, and nothing, really, ever comes of anything. Eccles calls, frequently. Sometimes I answer, sometimes I don't. Usually I'm pretty rude to him. And Fingers? Fingers is just taking the piss. I'm at Alice Caligula's White Cube opening (alongside Keith Allen, Jay Jopling, Nigella Lawson and endless YBAs who aren't all that Y anymore) when her self-portrait *Sin* – a life-sized sculpture made of her own frozen blood and naked except for a ruby pendant – is unveiled, minus the pendant. I'm at the launch of Froth.com (a luxury goods website fronted by a member of Pink Floyd, a former Russian mobster and that woman from those 1980s coffee commercials) when, in the midst of people as diverse as Helena Bonham Carter and Carole Caplin, the vast pearl that is meant to highlight the sheer exclusive pointlessness of the Froth.com product list, is suddenly no longer on its pedestal. I'm there. I'm there, but everybody is there, so simply being there doesn't give me anything approaching a story.

And, as Jimmy Cricket might have said, there's more. At the National Portrait Gallery, rock legend-turned-photographer Willy Zilder displays his photo portraits of the faces of today. Zilder, who is going for a Dickensian look these days, arrives with a mahogany, platinum-topped cane that once belonged to Frank Sinatra. He doesn't leave with it.

. . . At the St Martin's Lane hotel, Poppy Levant, that milliner who famously denied sleeping with both Gallagher brothers (what is it with milliners? Why are they always milliners?) displays next year's autumn/winter range of headgear. The centrepiece of the show is a ridiculously impractical creation; a silver latticework in the shape of a Stetson, overlaid with ripped and fraying raw silk. You'd need a neckbrace to wear it. And now, you'd need to find it, as well.

. . . At the Tower of London, Topaz Wilton, the trashiest daughter of the trashiest member of the trashy seventies rock group Shazaam! launches her trashy jewellery range for Ricklers, probably the trashiest High Street jeweller. Ricklers are desperate to be burgled. The room they hire in the tower is positively littered with glitzy (but ultimately cheap) baubles, simply begging to be surreptitiously pocketed. He doesn't touch them. Instead he somehow swipes Topaz's keys, drives to her apartment in her own Porsche Boxter (it was caught on CCTV), helps himself to the contents of her own personal safe, drives back to the tower and then tips off the police *himself* from the call box by the main gate. He left cards in both her handbag and the safe, the former saying '*I'd head home if I were you*' and the latter saying '*See?*'. Genius.

———

It goes on and on. He's making the police look stupid because they can't find him and, even worse, he's making us look stupid because we're running out of things to write about him. THIEF STEALS THING is all very well for your average news page, but we've got an investment in this guy. I do, personally. I've become the big Fingers expert and, somehow, I've dragged a whole newspaper along with me. Even now we're leading the pack, but we've got nothing new to say. We repeat ourselves, and talk in clichés. We make spurious comparisons and draw fantastic conclusions. We have become absurd. *Private Eye* has even created a new column, 'Fingersballs', in the style of the regular 'Colemanballs' slot. I've been in it three times. Once, I'd have been delighted by this. Now it seems as though every mention is another nail in the coffin of my career. Hargreaves said that Fingers was ours. Somehow, things seem to have turned around. Somehow, we've become his.

Aside from that, Philip and I barely talk anymore. We've been joined in our little square by Rebecca Leighton, who hates us. I think she's about as unhappy about her role as baby-sitter as we are about our roles as babies. She's in a filthy mood. Her rapist hasn't raped anyone for weeks, the selfish bastard, and the story seems to have faded away. I think top brass feels she could have done better with Mr Spike. We are her punishment.

The problem is, she's out of her depth. She knows nothing about the celeb scene, and she cares even less. She's a hardnosed newsy type, a journalist version of her mother. Every time I go to a party and come away with nothing, she stares at me in disbelief, semi-dreads twitching and mouth curled into a sneer. She made me arrange invitations so that she could check out a couple of likely-sounding bashes herself (a book launch by a woman who used to front a Britpop band, a champagne reception at Select Models), but Fingers steered clear. I think she hates him almost as much as she hates me. And to think that there was a time when we were on speaking terms. We even got drunk together! I shouldn't imagine she'll ever sleep with me now. I think she'd get me sacked if I even winked at her.

I'm growing to hate Fingers myself – this flashy thief with his attention-grabbing targets and his oh-so-witty epithets left at the scene of every crime. Gentleman Thief my arse. I'm sick of him.

But nobody else is. The remarkable thing is that everybody seems to feel Fingers belongs to them – media hacks, giggling sloanes, the glitzy party crowd, the Brixton bling kings, the indie music press, the gay lobby, the Church, everybody. The week they start the 'Fingersballs' column, *Private Eye*'s cover is a picture of Tony Blair and Gordon Brown. 'Explain the budget deficit,' says Tony. 'Fingers did it,' says Gordon.

The more time passes, the sillier it gets. *Alastair McGowan's Big Impression* begins to feature a regular Fingers character, a guy in black with a mask. Avid Merrion's *Bo' Selecta!* does the same, but his version is secretly Paul Daniels. *Have I Got News For You* invites him on as a guest presenter and erects an opaque screen over the podium 'so he can turn up and go if he feels like it'. Prince Charles confesses that he always wanted to be a cat burglar. *Tatler*, blithely assuming that Fingers is a toff, profile a list of people who they think it could be, alongside a rather confusing disclaimer pointing out that they aren't actually implying that it really is any of them. They name James Archer, Piers Adams, Tim Jeffries, Ben Goldsmith and, to my intense annoyance, Jensen

Randall. In an interview with *Q* magazine, Damon Albarn from Blur suggests that his side project, Gorrillaz, may record a Fingers tribute song. He must be devastated when, days later, he's beaten to it by the Crazy Frog. Caught on camera at the Leicester Square première of *Charlie's Angels VII*, while Lucy Liu simpers in the background, Cameron Diaz names Fingers as the person she'd most like to meet in the UK and says that Drew would say the same if she could only be here, but can't be because she's in LA 'gettin' married or divorced or somethin''. Appearing on *Parkinson*, Kevin Spacey confesses his admiration for this 'very English charlatan'. Appearing on *CD:UK*, Jon Bon Jovi attempts to do the same, but refers to him as 'Fingernails'. Everybody, everywhere, everything. It's insane.

And all the while Philip glowers and Leighton fumes. I feel like I'm shrinking. I'm like a graphic from *Ally McBeal*, getting ever smaller and smaller. Destined, soon, to fall into the sweat-drenched, crumb-filled grooves of what was once Daniel's chair. Soon, I'll be down there with him, and whoever came before, and whoever came before that. This isn't a career. It's Death Row.

'Miriam and Mordechai, that's us . . .'

n the film that they must now, doubtless, one day make of my life, the Princess should be played by Catherine Zeta Jones. She'd have to lose a stone. And about a foot, actually, although the hair is spot-on. It's a bit of an oddity. The Princess was born with a dark wayward frizz, like the hair I have in chestnut, and Janie has in mouse when she doesn't shave it. But these days . . . I dunno. She must iron it or something. She went off to university in Leeds with the familial crinkly mess on her head, and came back to Edinburgh with the kind of sweeping glossy curtains that a Sioux would be proud of. God knows what she'd look like in the rain. Brian May, I'd imagine.

She spots me now, through the pock-marked window of Joshua P's Kosher Café on Hendon High Street. She steps away form her table, waving. Six identical heads in shades from blonde to black turn with her, locks bouncing like a pack of showdogs. I catch myself smirking. Misunderstanding this, the Princess sends a smile back, and I feel mine become genuine. I am so soft. My sisters change me utterly.

'Mackie!' she coos as I step through the door.

'Hey,' I say, and kiss her on the tip of her nose. 'Look at you! Did you just step out of a salon?'

While she preens, I shoot a winning smile towards her friends – all equally sleek and indistinguishable. That said, one particular blonde in a tank top catches my eye, and I feel the smirk returning. I look away. It smells *Jewish* in here: of onions and fish, with a hint of expensive leather. I ruffle my sister's immaculate hair and she hits my hand, playfully but savagely.

'Yowza, Princess,' I say, snatching it away.

'Don't *call* me that,' she hisses, and steps back. 'Oh Mackie. Look at *you*. Your clothes! Your . . . *crazy* hair. Where did you sleep? On a bench?'

'At home,' I tell her, and look down at my rumpled army jacket and faded jeans. 'It's Sunday, okay? I'm relaxing.'

The Princess sighs. 'You are embarrassment personified,' she declares, but squeezes my hand as she leads me towards the table. 'Sit down there. We're just about to order. Any idea what you want?'

'Ba . . .' I say, and then, from the look on her face, decide instantly that the 'bacon and eggs' line I have been planning all the way here isn't actually all that funny. I mumble something about a smoked salmon bagel.

I'm shown to the opposite end of the table from my sister, in between a girl called Leoni who looks like a pug in a glossy wig (and it may, in fact, be one) and the blonde I spotted earlier, who turns out to be called Sarah. Immediately, I'm pretty keen for the latter to have a large role in the movie of my life. I'd cast Mel Blatt, the former All Saint. Down the other end, by the Princess, there are a few guys. They're all pretty much of a type: very hairgel.

Tans, open shirts, gold-chains; all that. All a couple of years younger than me. They talk in deep, spiky voices, play with phones, take out their wallets and put them away again. The girls either ignore them or laugh at them, cackling and doing that weird inverted thing with their wrists.

'Hey,' I say to the blonde.

'Oh hi,' she says, in one of those voices that people put on when they want you to think that they are making an effort, but also want you to be aware that they can't really be bothered. 'I'm Sarah. You're Miriam's brother, right?'

'Ah, no,' I say and nod down the table. The Princess doesn't meet my eye. She looks like she's just burped up something nasty.

With a frown, Sarah follows my nod. 'Who?'

'Ma . . .' I start to say, and then stop. 'Oh, Miriam?' I call.

'Hmmm?' squeaks my sister, my sister *Mary*, who didn't even have a *batmitzvah*, the bullshitter. She has rolling eyes, like a horse.

'Nothing dear,' I call across the table, and turn back to Sarah, still speaking loudly. 'Yes, I am *Miriam's* brother. *Miriam*, that's right.'

'I've heard all about you,' says Leoni, the pug. 'It's Mackie, isn't it?'

'Yea . . . no,' I say. 'Mackie for short. Actually it's Mordechai. Mordechai Lewis. Miriam and Mordechai, that's us.'

'Wow,' says Leoni. 'You must have very religious parents.'

'Oh yes,' I say.

Behind us, two American Hassidics in shiny black suits are arguing loudly. They sound like Zoidberg from Futurama. 'He has connections, so I'm telling you!' says one. 'He has a pile of diamonds already, never mind the ones from the breasts. And also famous ones. I'm asking you, how can he move them along without the connections?'

The other is saying things like 'absolutely!' and 'but of course!' and 'of that there is no question!' but in the kind of outraged voice that suggests he disagrees utterly. I'm so engrossed in the theatrics of it all that it takes me a few moments to figure out what they are talking about. When it clicks, I start laughing.

Pug-girl Leoni is listening too. 'That's your story,' she says. 'Fingers? That's what you write about, isn't it?'

'Um, yeah,' I say, taken aback.

'Oh my *God*,' says Sarah, all of a sudden sounding genuinely interested in me. She leans across the table and waves at the two girls opposite us. 'Guys! This is him! She shows us, like, *all* your articles. That's *you*. That's so cool.'

'Oooh,' flutter the girls. Hair is everywhere.

I blink, wondering if I am blushing. 'She . . . Who does? The Princess?'

'The what?' says Sarah.

'Ma . . . Miriam. My sister. Wow. That's so sweet of her.'

'The Princess?' asks Leoni. 'Why d'you call her that?'

'Bec . . .' I begin, and then stop. Sarah has one silver two-inch fingernail pressed to her lips in puzzlement. Leoni's hand, glimmering with gold, has paused in her glossy locks. Across the table the two other girls stare at me, glittering with Gucci, daubed in Dolce & Gabbana.

One does that Rikki Lake thing with her wrist, and I hear her bangles clink.

'No reason,' I murmur.

Some time later, once we've eaten our bagels and the café becomes filled with the hubbub of muttered after-dinner prayers, Leoni leaves. Mary (the Princess. Miriam. Whatever) comes down to our end of the table and appropriates her seat.

'How's it going?' she asks.

'Fine,' I say. *'Miriam.'*

For an instant, her face contorts. 'Leave it,' she hisses, and then she's all smiles again. 'No, really. What have you been doing? It's been about a month.'

It has. 'This and that,' I say. 'I saw Janie the other week.'

Mary doesn't say anything.

'She's a mess,' I continue.

'Big deal,' says the Princess, tersely.

I sigh. 'And other than that . . . well. Nothing much. Working a lot. I've been seeing this girl a bit. Works at the paper, on the business side. And before you ask, no. She's not Jewish.' I think about this for a moment. 'I assume.'

My sister rolls her eyes. 'Honestly, Mackie. All these *shikses.'*

'Listen to you! How do you even *know* that word?'

'It's a Jewish word.'

'So? I'd never heard of it until I read *Portnoy's Complaint.'*

'Oh, be quiet,' says Mary, crossly. 'You're too good for these sales girls. You're a rising star. I could set you up with any of my friends.'

Outwardly I'm laughing at the way she is talking (I'm *pretty* sure it's a joke, this whole Jewish aunt business), but I still surreptitiously shoot a glance towards Sarah. She's talking to one of the slick boys. It looks like he's showing her something on his mobile phone.

'I'm not sure I'm really rising any more, actually,' I mutter.

'Of course you are,' says Mary, confidently. 'You're in the paper every day. You know it, and you love it. You're almost a celebrity.'

I smile. Mary is new blood, and her world is seen through different eyes from mine. Like me, she wants to be noticed, but her ego is of a nobler hue. Ultimately, I think, she'll end up running UNICEF or the World Bank. Or both. While being President and Prime Minister, and becoming the new Aga Khan.

These days she's just starting out. Since she left university last year she's been doing PR for charities, mainly ones that deal with the poverty-stricken remnants of Jewish communities in Eastern Europe. All very worthy. As far as I can tell, she sees me in much the same way as I would see a *Big Brother* contestant.

'No, really,' I say. 'It's been a bad couple of weeks. I've been having a nightmare. They might even sack me.'

The Princess snorts. 'You're exaggerating,' she says. 'You're such a drama queen. Daniel thinks that this could make your career.'

'I think Daniel should be more concerned about his own career,' I start to say, and then stop talking for a moment. '*Daniel?*'

'Daniel Kemp,' says the Princess.

'I know Daniel. Do you know Daniel?'

'Of course I know Daniel.'

'*How* do you know Daniel?'

'You introduced us,' says my sister, 'you idiot. About a year ago. In that dreadful nightclub full of footballers.'

'But you kept in touch?'

'A bit. Why shouldn't we keep in touch?'

I shrug. 'I don't know.'

I feel unsettled. I'm not sure I'm happy about any kind of connection existing between Daniel Kemp and my precocious little sister. Is this jealousy? Or is it just because he's quite so flamboyantly depraved? Dear God, I've never introduced her to Paxy, have I? A horrible thought strikes me.

'Jesus Christ. You don't own any Jimmy Choos, do you?'

Mary kicks me under the table, and for a horrible moment I think she does. Then I click. 'Oh. Sorry.'

'No,' she says. 'Although Reuben bought me some Blahniks for my birthday. Why?'

'No reason,' I say, but she's not listening anymore. She's leaning forward and speaking to one of the hairgel boys.

'Blahniks,' she's saying. 'My Blahniks. No, they're lovely. I was just telling Mackie about them? What? Haha. Not really, no.' She turns back to me, apologetically. 'I'm sorry. He's convinced you're gay. I'm just going to pop over there for a moment, okay?'

'Not *really*?' I start to say, but she interrupts me.

'Oh, yes. Daniel. I saw him the other day. He's helping me with this ball we're sorting out. Sarah? Sarah! Tell Mackie about the ball, yeah?'

With that, she's gone. Sarah gives me a bright smile.

'You guys all work together?' I ask.

'Oh yes,' says Sarah, doe eyes wide. 'Your sister is inspirational. Tony adores her.'

'Who's Tony?'

'You don't know Tony? Tony Manstell? He owns the company. Very well known. He's always in the JC.'

The Gucci girl, who I think is called Deborah, nods solemnly. 'Always.'

'I'll look out for him,' I tell them. 'But what's this about Daniel?'

'Oh.' Sarah nods, knowledgably. 'He's the journalist, right?'

'One of them,' I point out.

'Oh yah,' says Sarah and laughs, falsely. 'Gosh, how embarrassing. Um, yeah. I think, like, Miriam and Tony wanted some advice about, um, celebrities and things, yeah? For this ball we're doing?'

This is outrageous. My sister seeks advice about celebrities from *another* journalist? I am distraught.

'Right. What ball?'

'It's a ball,' says Gucci Debbie, helpfully. 'It's for, like, all the young adults from all the different communities across London. Right the way from Hendon to, um . . .' she glances at Sarah, 'Wimbledon?'

'Wimbledon,' agrees Sarah. 'All the usual crowd. Twenty-one

to thirty-five. We've got the *hugest* mob coming from Golders Green. We're trying to figure out what celebrities to invite, so we get the right press coverage. We just,' she sighs, 'need to figure out what we are going to call it.'

'It's a problem,' agrees Deborah. 'It had to be something witty. You know, catchy. It was going to be the Jew Ball.'

'Jew Ball,' Sarah agrees.

'But that sounded a bit too much like "chew ball".'

'Chew ball,' repeats Sarah, and clarifies: 'like for *dogs*.'

'Then we thought of the Kippur Convention.'

'But that was no good either.'

'No,' agrees Deborah. 'That made us sound like fishermen.'

'Ugh,' says Sarah, quietly. 'Fishermen.'

'And then,' continues Deborah, almost sadly, 'we went through, like, *hundreds* of other names, using words like "Fellowship", "Under-21s" and "Community" and "Kosher", but they all, like, had problems of their own.'

'Acronyms, usually,' sighs Sarah.

'Nasty,' I sympathise. 'So what now?'

Deborah shrugs. 'Now we're not sure. Miriam and Tony will think of something.'

It's funny, I reflect as I bounce along the Jubilee Line on my way home, how little we think of other people. Or rather, we think of other people, but we think of them differently. We don't think of them at all how we think of ourselves. This is my movie, my world, my plot, and it concerns my life, my career. But the rest – Philip, Janie, Lucy, Daniel and the Princess – they have movies too. In their movies I'm the peripheral character, not them. These people opposite me on the tube. We're cameos in each other's films. But we all have them.

I don't think I'd ever thought about the Princess's movie until now. She's trying to make her own career, trying to make her own name with this nameless ball of theirs. If she does, says Deborah, then she's going to be responsible for something even bigger – some huge country house affair in a couple of months. I suppose she is excited by this. I suppose, to her, it must be every bit as important as my job is to me. I suppose she must generally care about mine as little as I care about hers. Odd. What is her story? Where does it start? Am I even in it? Or am I on the cutting room floor?

So many movies. Everyone I've ever met, living their own film. Everybody on the train, everybody out there sighing and sweating on the crowded Baker Street platform, everybody out past them, in the street, in the city, in the world. And somewhere, out there, not too far away, is Fingers. Right now, his movie would probably make better watching than mine. And I doubt I'd even figure in it.

Damn him. I'm not having this. I refuse to let somebody be a character in my film when I'm not equally important in theirs. I'm not having it. We'll meet, he and I, in the finale. A show-down, atop a skyscraper. Lightning flashing, thunder crashing. His tragedy, my redemption.

Credits roll.

'It's only a small toe.'

Finally, when these dark, dark weeks are becoming almost too dark, dark to bear, I get a lead. It happens the day after I go to see the Princess, when I'm sitting at my desk. It's when Greebo calls.

'Mac,' says Philip, and something about the slightly weary way in which he addresses me makes me think that maybe he doesn't hate me so much anymore. 'Mac, it's Greebo.'

My reclining office chair is almost fully reclined (as it tends to be these days) and as I lurch forward it nearly catapults me into my desk. I flap my hand at Philip and, ignoring Rebecca Leighton's suspicious gaze, say, 'Pass him over.'

'Colombo,' says Greebo, the instant I put Philip's phone to my ear. He sounds impossibly self-assured. Ooh, I think. The slimy creep. He's got something good.

'Greebo,' says I. 'What have you got for me?'

'Everything you could possibly want,' says Greebo, slightly

sleazily, 'and more. I think you want to take me for lunch. Two o'clock. Usual place.'

He puts the phone down, assuming I'll be there. And he's right. I spin around in my chair and whoop, drawing stares.

'Anything?' says Philip, pinkly.

'Something,' says I, and do a Roger Moore trick with my left eyebrow. He clenches a fist towards his face, Tim Henman style.

Leighton stares at us, like we're some kind of monkey circus double act. 'Who was that?' she demands. 'What's Greebo?'

Philip looks away. The hate may be going, but his allegiance is leaving with it. Bloody Leighton. Of late, the body language between him and this invading Athena has been most alarming. I fear my pointy, balding sidekick will soon be mine no longer. I shall be Brannigan, without my Kif.

'Contact,' I say, airily. 'Top showbiz mole. You have contacts, don't you?'

'What does he want?'

'Lunch,' I say, and glance at my watch, which reads 11.45 a.m. 'Best be off, actually.'

'I'll come with you,' she says.

'No,' I say, standing up, 'you won't.'

'You can't stop me,' she says, but she doesn't move. She's already insisted upon accompanying me to the Piss Streak Planes bash this evening. She looks hesitant, as if fearing that, if she pushes this one, I might have a tantrum. She's right. I might well.

'I can't,' I agree, and click my fingers. 'But Philip can. Philip! Restrain this woman!'

With that I leap aboard a copy of *Tatler* that's lying on the floor and ride it like a skateboard for a couple of feet towards the door. It hits the rubber doorstop, and I travel the last few feet in a flailing stagger.

'You're such a wanker,' sighs Philip, to my back.

'God,' I hear Leighton agree. 'God, he is, isn't he?'

Greebo is my oldest contact and certainly my best. I met him about two years ago, through an internet messageboard. Glamorous, huh?

Have you ever used an internet messageboard? Most people have, at one point or another. I met Greebo on the Popbitch one, back when Popbitch was something exclusive and exciting, rather than the *Heat* online it has turned into since. These days it's mainly office workers and students. Back then it was hacks, PRs and hangers-on, and on occasion genuinely famous people. Online, Greebo gave every impression of being one of the latter. He isn't of course. He's not even a hanger-on. He's a hanger-on hanging on a hanger-on.

There's somebody like him on every anonymous showbiz gossip board, I'm sure. Not necessarily the wittiest poster, and certainly not the most popular but blessed, somehow, with a camp, self-assured confidence that makes them impossible to ignore. And the gossip he had! Either he was an insider or a stalker. Both were good. I had to meet him.

I did. He was neither. He was a fat, gay, bald banker, with a face like a peach, fuzz and all. Greebo isn't his real name, obviously – it's his online alias, and all he wants me to know. But once, when we met for a drink in Teatro last year, I noticed he'd inadvertently left his office passcard dangling from his breast pocket and I read his real name off that. Gavin. Gavin Burton. Bland name, bland guy. He was so far from what I had been expecting that I was too surprised to even express surprise. Instead I bought him drinks, listened to what he had to say, and wrote it down. 'Who is this guy?' Daniel used to say when I filed my copy, and I'd tell him, 'He's nobody.' It's true. He is.

Given the right circumstances, though, it's not actually that hard for utter nobodies to end up on the peripheral asteroid belts of the social circles of somebodies. Real nobodies are no threat. They're easy. And while Greebo is an utter nobody, his marginally less grotesque boyfriend is marginally less of one. Greebo's boyfriend is the trendy side of their partnership. He makes rugs, or chairs, or pots or some such thing, and, on occasion, he makes them for famous people. This, in the weird and presumably lonely world of UK celebrity, gets him invited to endless barbecues, dinners and garden parties, and he'll frequently drag his gargoylic other half in his wake.

I meet Greebo an hour and a half later in the Cinnamon Club in Westminster. This is his favourite meeting place because 'it's more *Economist* than *Hello!*,' and he 'simply couldn't bear' to be spotted by 'anybody else in the scene'. He really does talk like this.

Having left work so prematurely, I'm absurdly early. In a very *me* way, I pass the time leafing through a biography of Disraeli in a nearby Waterstone's and find myself getting so engrossed that I actually manage to arrive at the restaurant late. Greebo is already a third of the way through what looks like a distressingly pricey claret – most of which he seems to have dribbled onto his brown silk tie – and there are three soggy cigarette butts crumpled in the ashtray.

'Sorry,' I say, and he pauses in the process of lighting a fourth.

'Colombo,' he says. 'So nice of you to join me.'

I sit down. 'Mac, please.'

'Colombo' is my online name. It was a mistake. I got it from the guy in the raincoat in the TV movies, being momentarily under the impression he was a journalist. Stupid, really.

My guest frowns, like I knew he would. 'I don't think we should let this get too personal,' he says, as I help myself to one of his cigarettes.

'Of course,' I agree, and turn to the approaching waitress. 'I'll have the Rogan Josh, please. And you, Gavin?'

Greebo stares at me in horror. 'What did you say?'

'And you're having?'

He gives me a worried look. 'I've already ordered.'

The waitress scurries away. I pour Greebo another glass of his own claret and, as an afterthought, help myself to one. 'So,' I say. 'What have you got?'

Greebo grins fatly and touches his fingertips together. He loves this bit. It provides the only clue I have as to why he bothers to speak to me. It's not like I pay him. I buy him lunch and he spills all, often literally. He could afford his own lunch. I think he just likes the way it makes him feel.

'My friend,' he says, 'was on a boat.'

'Which friend? Gustav?'

He looks pained. I'm not supposed to know about Gustav. 'Let's just say a friend, okay?'

'Sure.'

'Right. This friend was doing some work for Jackson Pirelli. You know Pirelli?'

'Italian?'

'Yes.'

'Something to do with tyres?'

Greebo rolls his eyes. 'Oh for heaven's sake. No. He's a jewellery broker. A stupidly rich jewellery broker.'

There is a pause while the waitress deliver Greebo's dish. Looks like I'm going to have to wait for mine. Greebo attacks his like a bulldog eating . . . well. Like a bulldog eating a chicken korma. Incredibly, scientifically speaking, this doesn't prevent him from talking. 'You know the guy. Made his money after the war, when all the Austrian gem traders temporarily weren't around to trade gems anymore. Was rumoured to be dating Fergie.'

'Alex Ferguson?'

He snorts in disbelief. 'You do this on purpose, don't you? Sarah Ferguson. Duchess of York.'

I nod. Since that snort, something small, cold and wet has been oozing slowly down my right cheek. Very slowly, I remove it with a napkin. Chicken. 'Mmm. The guy who owns the vineyard in Tuscany. I remember about him.'

'Not him. That was Count Gaddo della . . . something.'

'Gherardesca.'

'Right. Gherardesca. Not him. Pirelli was the one before. Ring any bells?'

I shrug. 'Maybe.'

Greebo stops talking to slurp down some wine, and I get a fine view straight down his gullet. Does he actually eat food, I wonder, or does he just mush it up and keep it in his mouth? Not nice.

'So anyway,' he continues. 'Gustav was on the yacht.'

'Which yacht?'

'Pirelli's yacht! The bloody yacht!'

'What was he doing on the yacht?'

'He lives on the yacht.'

I frown. 'Gustav lives on Pirelli's yacht?'

Greebo raises a chickeny hand to his forehead. 'No. Pirelli lives on Pirelli's yacht.'

'Makes sense,' I concede. 'What was Gustav doing there?'

'Making a . . . never you mind.' says Greebo. 'This isn't about Gustav. This is about Pirelli. Apparently he's a collector.'

'A collector? A collector of what?'

Greebo shrugs, messily. 'Paraphernalia. Celeb stuff. Items and icons. Mementos. Apparently he has one of Elvis's toes.'

'Fuck off does he have one of Elvis's toes.'

'He does.'

'How would you get hold of one of Elvis's toes, Greebo?'

'It wouldn't be that hard. After he was dead.'

'Obviously after he was fucking dead, Greebo.'

Greebo is pained. 'It's only a small toe.'

I cannot do this. I cannot watch Greebo eating lumps of chicken in a brown korma sauce, and simultaneously talk about severed toes. 'Forget the toe.'

'Right,' says Greebo, agreeably. 'The toe isn't important. He's got loads of stuff. A dress of Marilyn's, a bearskin that used to belong to Katherine Hepburn.'

'After it belonged to a bear?'

'Yes. Oh, and the Mini that Marc Bolan died in.'

'And this is all on a yacht, is it?'

He stares at me, his fork, for a couple of incredible seconds, actually stationary. 'I don't know if it is all on the yacht, Colombo. I doubt it. I haven't been on the yacht. None of this matters. Why do you always do this? You always ask questions about the wrong bits.'

'I'm sorry,' I say. 'What are the right bits?'

Greebo starts eating again, which I take as a sign of forgiveness. 'Well. Pirelli was bitching about his friend Itotaki . . .'

'Itotaki? Is that Japanese?'

'Of course it's bloody Japanese.'

'So who is he?'

'How should I know? He's Pirelli's friend. He's also a collector. Apparently he'd been in touch to tell him about some new stuff he was getting. From London.'

I sit up. Very suddenly, there is a point to all this. 'Go on.'

My source grins at me, meatily. Despite my best efforts, I have made the classical error in dealing with Greebo – I have shown interest in what he is saying. Equipped with information that he knows you want, Greebo's pomposity can become insurmountable. 'I thought that might get your attention,' he says.

'Och, it's probably nothing. New stuff from London. Big deal. Must happen all the time.'

He bristles. 'Not like this, Colombo. That's why Pirelli was so annoyed. Apparently this stuff is hot. Very hot.'

'Hot? How hot? Hot as in how? Hot as in good?'

'Hot as in *stolen*. So hot that collectors don't want it. So hot that Itotaki was looking to shift it as jewellery alone. That's what he wanted with Pirelli.'

'Christ,' I say, despite myself.

'Oh yes,' says Greebo.

'How can I speak to Itotaki?'

'You can't.'

'Well, how can I speak to Pirelli?'

'You can't.'

'Dammit, Greebo. When can I speak to Gustav?'

Greebo looks positively terrified. 'You absolutely one hundred per cent cannot. I thought you knew the rules here, Colombo. You think he knows we have these chats?'

I snatch a cigarette from his packet and light it from the tabletop candle. 'Come on, Greebo. I have to. This is dynamite.'

He folds his arms across his chest. 'Not going to happen. Period.'

I stare at him for a moment, making a calculation. 'You can't stop me,' I say.

He goes pale. 'You wouldn't.'

'I might have to. My career is on the line with this one. I have to find out who that contact in London is.'

Greebo hasn't eaten anything in almost a minute. He must be seriously upset. 'Gustav doesn't know that! I've already asked him!'

'Doesn't he? Maybe he'd remember a little more if the questions were coming from me.'

'I'll ask him again!' Greebo gibbers and, for a moment, I feel horribly guilty. I harden myself. This is my movie. Occasionally you have to decide whether you're to be played by Sly Stallone or Woody Allen. Rebecca Leighton wouldn't feel guilty right now. Nor would Daniel Kemp. Am I one of them, or one of Philip?

'I'd be grateful,' I say, levelly, 'if you could. Any more information. I enjoy our chats, Greebo. I'd hate to have to jeopardise them.'

'I'll do it,' he says.

'Splendid,' say I, and nod subtly towards the spattered menu. 'Now then. I see my dish approaches. Would you care for pudding?'

'Is this a sex thing?'

Of all the millionaires I've ever met, Apollo Rosakis has to be my favourite. It's not just because he's Greek, and thus manages to combine Northern European class with Middle Eastern brash extravagance, although that is a big plus in his favour. And it's not just that, on encountering British royalty, he always manages to be photographed with a hand shockingly near a princess's pert rump, but I love that too. It's not even that he appears to own a thousand impeccably tailored Savile Row suits, yet persistently seems to twin them with a pair of ancient, stinking Dunlop tennis shoes. This is a man who invested millions, borrowed millions and begged millions to set up a British budget airline. He revolutionised European air travel at a single stroke. He employed God knows how many thousands of people. And not one of them thought to tell him that it might be a bad idea to call it Yellow Jet.

I love that. I just love it. Perhaps because of my own messily monikered Grandpa Johnjohn, the Yellow Jet of Apollo Rosakis will always have a special place in my heart.

Rebecca Leighton and I share a taxi to the party that evening. She's not happy, mainly because while I've told her that Greebo told me great things, I won't give her a clue as to what. There's a big story in this. I want it to be mine. I think she's particularly annoyed because, in my position, she'd do exactly the same.

'You're impossible to work with,' she tells me in the taxi, as I slip off my shoes and rummage around in my bag.

'Philip has no complaints.'

'How can you say that? He thinks you're a prick. Everyone thinks you're a prick. You are a prick.'

I loosen my tie. 'You don't think that.'

'Don't tell me what *I* think. I know what *I* think. What are you playing at?'

'Back off,' I tell her, rolling it up. 'I have my methods. I get results.'

She slams her hand down on the fake leather seat. A thrilling sound. 'But you *don't*. The whole point is that you *don't*. I wouldn't be stuck with you if you did, would I? I'd be chasing the story I had to give up to come and hold your hand.'

'Yeah. Like *that* was going well.'

'It was!' she insists, but she knows I know she's lying. 'I'm better than you. Prick.'

I untuck my shirt. 'Didn't manage to get yourself tickets for this bash tonight, did you? I seem to be better at that.'

She stares at me. 'Oh right. Sure.' There is a pause. 'But how did you do that?

'Give it a shot, did you?'

'If I'd tried, I'd have got them.'

'Sure. I had to stand somebody up tonight, you know. Thanks to you.'

'Well you should have said. I would have managed it.'

'Of course you would. But you didn't, did you?'

She's smiling now, but only with her mouth. Her eyes look scary. 'Didn't get round to it. How did you do it?'

'Why do you want to know?'

I think she might hit me. She's looking out the window, intently. 'Professional curiosity.'

'Oh. Right. You should have said. It was easy. I just called up Apollo and asked him.'

Rebecca looks back at me now. 'You *know* him?'

I start unbuttoning my shirt. 'A bit. I've spoken to him enough times.'

'But doesn't he hate you? Piss Streak Planes. That was you, wasn't it?'

'It was. He loves it.'

'Oh come on. You're making this up. He loves the fact that every shitty gossip columnist in the UK refers to his business as *Piss Streak Planes*? I don't think so, Mac.'

'At least they refer to it. He gets more press than EasyJet and Ryanair combined thanks to that.' I start taking off my belt.

Rebecca presses herself against the taxi wall. 'Is this a sex thing? Touch me and I'll have you sacked. And jailed. Ugh. You're repulsive. Why are your legs so *pale*?'

I muster as much dignity as the situation allows, 'I am getting changed,' I tell her. 'No offence, but this isn't my idea of a romantic situation.'

'Like that would stop you,' she snorts, and then falls silent, looking back out the window as I drag on a pair of black jeans. Neither of us says anything, but it's obvious we're both thinking of the time we snogged, drunkenly, in that carpark behind

Liverpool Street Station. It was a brief and pitiful thing, that. A mutual lunge, a clash of teeth, and then a world of excuses, regrets, pleas, and, ultimately, a slap.

Next week, Piss Streak Planes start running flights to Cape Town. Tonight's party at Picadilly Circus's Thrust is nominally in honour of that. Not that Apollo Rosakis normally needs much excuse to have a party. Considering the pittance he pays his staff, one could almost consider it criminal the amount he spends on corporate entertainment. Mind you, he also spends a pittance on advertising, so it seems to pay off. His parties are always lavish affairs, thronged with identifiable rent-a-crowds. Invariably Apollo will be photographed looking bumblingly lascivious around some newsworthy skimpily clad starlet. In our tirelessly xenophobic way, the British press are always queuing up to sneer at him. It's damn clever, really. I can imagine him sitting in a hot tub with Mohammed Al-Fayed and Stelios Haji-Ioannou, each of them showing off about the latest ruse they've hit on to make credulous hacks like me go out of our way to take the piss.

The taxi drops us just by Eros, and we push through the evening chaos towards the club. Rebecca strides ahead of me at first, but soon hangs back when it becomes clear that she doesn't really know where she is going.

The pavement outside Thrust is roped off, and there is a gaggle of grommets with cameras and autograph books herded into a corner. Obviously, they ignore us, not least because Tamzin Outhwaite and Denise Van Outen are just stepping through the door as we arrive. 'I can see your nipples, Tamzin!' shouts one, but I strain, and I can't. I point out our names (Macaulay Lewis + 1) to the crop-haired blonde on the door, the bouncers step aside, and we're in.

Inside, the place is sleazily heaving. Most nights, Thrust is a pole-dancing club, catering to a variety of bankers and businessmen. Tonight they've been kept away, and the dancers are wearing bikinis made of fake fur. Presumably, this is meant to refer to the African theme. Subtle. Lightly, I grab Rebecca by the arm.

'What?' she says.

'Try not to look so horrified,' I tell her.

She shrugs me away. 'I'm not *horrified*. I just think it's all totally pathetic.'

'Never been to anything like this before? Not even with your mum?'

'My mother is a lawyer, Mac. Not a celebrity.'

'She does an awful lot of telly. Wasn't she up for the Wrexham Prize?'

'No. Are you trying to wind me up?'

'Yes. And speaking of the Wrexham, if you think this is nasty, just wait until that.'

'Where,' says Rebecca, 'can I get a drink?'

I lead her to the bar where, predictably, we find Neil.

'Hey man,' I say. 'Who've we got?'

Neil shrugs and takes a swig from a bottle of Becks. 'Jade Jagger,' he says. 'Keira Knightley, Mick Hucknall, Anthony Worrall Thompson, Dean Gaffney, Amanda Redman, Justin Hawkins, Fran Cutler, Simon Cowell, Ben Bradshaw, Anna Friel, Will Self, Peter Pike, Lauren Laverne, Trinny but not Susannah, most of Liberty X, Jo O'Meara, Rachel Stevens, Kym but not Jack, Sadie's sister but not Sadie and Des but not Carol.'

'Sorry. Lost you there. Des who? Not O'Connor?'

'Lynam.'

'Also strange.'

'That's what I thought.'

I try to catch the barman's eye, but fail. 'So then. Pole-dancing. By the end of the night we'll have Jade and Anna, I reckon.'

'At least,' says Neil. 'I'd say Kym and Amanda as well. And Justin, possibly. And who knows, Des is always a possibility.'

'Not Trinny?' I ask. 'I'd pay good money for that.'

'We can but hope,' says Neil. 'Oh, and I heard Cheryl Tweedy is coming.'

'Whoopie-doo.'

Rebecca is staring at us. 'What are you two on about?' she demands.

I smile at her. 'Just talking shop.'

'I didn't understand a word of it.'

'You'll learn.'

'I'm not sure I want to.'

I grimace. 'Rebecca, meet Neil, an old, old friend. Neil, meet Rebecca, a right pain in the arse.'

Rebecca has a band sweeping her hair back from her face, and some kind of purplish blusher on. She looks incredible but also, in here, somehow out of place. Perhaps she's just wearing too many clothes. 'Hi,' says Neil, and looks her up and down.

'Yeah, hi,' says Rebecca, leaning over the bar and physically grabbing the barman by the shoulder. 'Vodka. Now. You?'

'Vodka,' I agree.

Rebecca arrived at the *Gazette* before I did, but only by a matter of months. Along with the more serious nature of her work, this makes her slightly higher up than me in terms of newspaper hierarchy. Only slightly, mind. You wouldn't know it from the way she carries on. For a time we were almost friends. You wouldn't know that, either.

These are different days, but, before Satan bought our newspaper, we used to have a relatively big staff. On the lower rungs of the professional ladder were a host of bright young things like me, lifted from magazines and websites. It was a fun time – we weren't expected to actually do too much, and we were frequently made to feel very important. Moreover, in the weeks leading up to Randall's arrival (and, I suppose, for a few weeks thereafter until it all just became bleak and horrific) there was a rather wonderful devil-may-care feeling in the air. For a while it looked like we might shut down, and then for a while longer it seemed we'd survive, but not all of us. I remember endless, tortuous conversations in pubs about who could stay and who they could afford to get rid of. We felt like conspirators, revolutionaries living on borrowed time, and the air was heady with lust and desperation. It was glorious.

Rebecca and I tended to dominate these conversations, partly because we're both arrogant and forceful popinjays, but mainly because we were both more comfortable than most that, in some way, we'd be staying. Considering the *Decline and Fall of the Roman Empire* environment in which we were working, it thus seemed inevitable that we should get together. Or at least, it did to me.

'When are you going to sleep with me?' I breathed in her ear as we sat, holding court in the pub. She smiled, and squeezed my knee, and said nothing. 'When are you going to sleep with me?' I murmured, squeezing my bottom past hers as she clipped past me in a corridor with her swaying boss. 'When are you going to sleep with me?' I asked in that carpark in Liverpool Street, with a string of her saliva hanging from my bottom lip, and the tight smell of her, high in my nostrils. 'I'm not,' she said, and threw a punch when I tried to press the point.

That was the day before they sacked Daniel. The day before Brainchild ordered me out of my first conference. The day before

I stopped being second in command on an important part of the paper, and became the temporary custodian of an outgoing joke. It makes me wonder how much of an insider to the whole thing Rebecca really was, all the while pretending to be an outsider like the rest of us. When she saw me the following morning, eleven hours later, she didn't even meet my eye.

'Who did you stand up?' she asks me.

It's about 10 p.m., and we're still at Thrust, sipping vodka Red Bulls through straws, and doing a very passable impression of people who actually like each other. The night is still young, obviously, but thus far there has been depressingly little pole-dancing. Nonetheless, I've been having fun. Only a few moments ago I left Rebecca chatting awkwardly with Carolyn Somethingorother (tall. Whippetish. Friend of Jessica's. Doesn't like me) while I sneaked off with a former *Big Brother* contestant who now presents a chart show (no, not that one. The other one) for a wee toot in the gents. I'm feeling puckish in the extreme.

'Eh?' I say, and sit bolt upright. 'My God. Is that Johnny Depp?'

'Fuck Johnny Depp,' says Rebecca, somewhat ungraciously. 'I'm asking you, who did you stand up tonight?'

'Oh. Nobody special. My, uh, girlfriend. It is. I'm sure of it.'

Rebecca laughs, and waves her empty glass at Carolyn, who is over by the bar with Neil. Carolyn nods. 'Your . . . uh . . . girl-friend? Nobody special? Who is this lucky princess?'

'Not a princess.'

'What?'

'Not . . . never mind. She's Lucy. From the paper.'

'Lucy?' Rebecca frowns. 'I don't think I know a Lucy. Is she one of the subs?'

'Yeah you do. Lucy. Use to come to the pub sometimes. Works in marketing.'

'Oh my God.' She has a hand over her mouth. 'Lucy *Denton*? You're shagging Lucy *Denton*?'

I scratch my nose. The room is spinning. Rebecca is grinning, and not nicely.

'Indeed I am. Why such hilarity?'

'Lucy Denton. God help me. That must have been a challenge.'

'You're being rather rude, you know.'

'Oh, I can be ruder. Make you wait until the second date, did she?'

I open my mouth and then close it again. I look away. 'It is Johnny Depp,' I mutter. 'I'm sure of it.'

It isn't. It's Orlando Bloom. Rebecca checks him out on the way back from the toilet, and pronounces him dishy, if a little small. 'Look at him,' she says, sitting down. 'He's even smaller than Davina McCall.'

'That's not Davina McCall,' I slur. I'm too wasted to see that far, but I'm pretty sure I know who she's talking about.

'Of course it is.'

'It isn't. It's Claudia thingy. Winkleman.'

Rebecca looks shocked. 'These are two people?'

'Allegedly. Davina is not Claudia. But Davina could be played by Claudia, most assuredly.'

'Come again?'

'In the film.'

'What film?'

'The film. The film of my . . . never mind. The film. Everybody has to be played by somebody.'

Rebecca crosses her legs, sheer grey pins flickering in the slit of her tight navy skirt. I am transfixed. 'What film?' she repeats.

I drag my eyes away. 'Oh, you know. At the end of it all. When they make it all into a film. If she's in it. Me, I'll be Jude Law.'

Rebecca must be humouring me. 'Won't Jude Law be Jude Law? He is an actor, Mac.'

'Of course he's an actor. I'm hardly going to play myself, am I?'

'Oh,' says Rebecca. 'Oh right. *He'll* play *you*. Of course. So who plays me?'

'Whatshername,' I say promptly. 'From *28 Days Later*.'

'Jesus,' Rebecca looks away. One of her legs stretches out enticingly towards a nearby stool. Is this for my benefit? Not sure. 'That's pathetic.'

'Naomie Harris, that's the one. Or that girl from *Teachers*. She'd be perfect, actually. You have very nice legs, you know?'

'Shut up about my legs. Why them? Why not Gwyneth Paltrow? Why not Anna Friel?'

'She's over there.'

'I know she's over there. So what? Why not her?'

Almost absent-mindedly, I shift my stool and catch hold of her wandering leg by the calf. She doesn't seem to mind. 'Um, sorry. What?'

'Why not Anna Friel? Because she's white?'

I give her an exasperated sigh, but I suppose she's got a point. In a distant sort of way, I suddenly feel a little jealous. Here's me, with the fuss I make about my own colourful roots, and there's her, with a famous mum and a black dad. I've never really thought about that before.

'Yes,' I say, finally. 'And also . . . no. I don't know what I'm meant to say here. Are we about to have an argument about my . . . like, institutional racism?'

Rebecca yanks her leg forward, pulling me off my chair and onto my knees in front of her. She leans forward. Our faces are millimetres apart. 'No,' she says, and I can smell the Red Bull on her breath. 'We're about to have an argument about your shameless and affected vacuity.'

'My which?'

'You know what I'm talking about. You're . . . infuriating. You read the foreign pages every day. I've seen you. I've seen the way your face screws up whenever Martin starts talking about the Middle East. You know this stuff. Yet you're not even going to have your own job for very much longer.'

'You'd sack me? Oh baby. After all we've been through?'

'Don't baby me. We both know who's taking your job.'

'Do we? Who?'

'Who do you think? That fucker over there. He keeps staring. Do you think he's trying to pick me up?'

I glance over. '*Mick Hucknall?*'

'Oh, stop it. Think, Mac. Is your brain really so full of froth and drivel, or do you do it on purpose? It's not like he's going to stay in marketing for ever, is it? He wants your slot, and he's going to get it. I mean, come off it. What did you think all your cosy little chats were about? Are you really so self-obsessed that you didn't even *suspect?*'

The next few seconds are a bit of a blur. Things are a mess. I'm aware of moving forward, perhaps quite swiftly, and there's a soft sensation, followed by a hard one, possibly similar to touching lips and clashing teeth. Then there's a hand on my collar and I'm on my feet, staggering backwards as though being pulled. Somebody says something, nastily, and I reply, feeling terribly witty.

'*Yan*sen,' snaps that somebody, and there's a blow like a car crash in my stomach. Then I'm stumbling, out into cold air, and landing hard, cheek first, onto cool, comforting concrete.

———

'Mac?'

The voice is familiar, but unplaceable.

'Mac?'

So is the face. Male. About my age. Bearded.

'You okay?'

'Fucked,' I hiss. 'Buggered. Totally doolally.'

'You seem it,' says the stranger. 'Haven't seen you in years. You want a taxi?'

I nod. He has his arms around my shoulders, rather tenderly. Stripy jumper. Black and red. Smells of wool. 'You still in that posh commune place? Up north?'

'Knightsbridge,' I mutter.

'Blimey,' he laughs. 'You've come up in the world. I'm back in the old place, with Sandy. You should come round some time.'

A door opens, and I'm in a taxi, staring out of the window, into this friendly, bearded familiar face.

'Take care,' he says. 'And call me. Same old number. We should meet up.'

I nod, and the taxi moves away. I'm drifting away, but something clicks. Ray. Old housemate from Brixton. Wanted to be an actor.

Odd.

'Unrepeatable things about hamsters . . .'

wake early the next morning, shivering and ill. Blackouts are nothing new to me – especially recently – but this is different. My eyes are smeared shut with sleep, sleep like wallpaper paste that I'm forced to chip away in flakes with the nail on my little finger. I rub my face, and notice that my hands come away grimy and black. Earth? Oil? Greasepaint? Why?

Newsprint. Yesterday's *Gazette* is splayed on my pillow. I seem to have slept on it, face first. Black is smeared across my pillows and the top of my duvet. I could have been sharing my bed with a miner. My throat feels like mottled leather (as do my ears. My *ears*. A bad sign) and my heart is beating fast, thudding in my chest like an erratic but enthusiastic military band. This isn't a hangover. It isn't even a come-down. It's all wrong.

Bad things happened last night. Shame hovers, enigmatically poised above my conscience. Did I kiss somebody? Did I try to? Did I kiss Rebecca? Somebody hit me, I remember that. Oh God, and Ray. Was that really Ray? I was on the pavement, wasn't I? What must he have thought? I'll have to give him a call. Same old number? What was that? Neil will have it.

Or Elspeth, maybe. Ray was a friend of Elspeth's. That's how I met him. He and Neil were the only two in our house in Brixton who I hadn't been at college with. Sandy – who looked like Matt Lucas at the time, and probably looks more like Phil Mitchell now – had found the house. None of us were earning anything. Sandy was gigging with some God-awful swing band, I was pestering dull style mags for work experience and Jacob, who had been on my course, was trying to be a DJ. Sandy had found the house advertised in *Loot*. It was perfect, by which I mean it was hideous. Huge, sprawling, semi-detached and halfway to Clapham North, it had damp on the walls and bogweed in the garden, and we had to put buckets on the landing when it rained. Neil, who was a friend of Sandy's from home (Somethingden, a commuter town on the outskirts of Thingyshire) took one of the spare rooms, and the four of us clubbed together to cover the rent of the fifth for the first few months. Then Elspeth introduced us to Ray.

I'm not sure where she met him. Random Ray, we christened him. Random guys orbit Elspeth like satellites. She picks them up at parties, hangs around with them for a while, and then either drifts away from them or has sex with them. And then drifts away from them. I don't think she and Ray ever had sex. Possibly this was his choice – he was a pretty down-to-earth sort of guy.

We got on very well. I expected Sandy or Jacob to be my best friend in the house, seeing as I already knew them, or failing that Neil, seeing as we were both trying to 'write novels'. Ray was nothing like me. He was sporty and wholesome, and he wanted to be an actor. He was, I think, the most blithely style-free man I had ever met. He bought new clothes when his old ones fell apart, and bought them cheap. Because he was so good-looking, he got away with it. He had stubble, constantly, but only because he couldn't be bothered to shave.

He was clueless. I remember, once, when Jacob had a small gig DJing at some achingly trendy MTV-linked affair in a gallery out east. The rest of us went to town on our outfits. Neil and I spent the afternoon clipping weird bits out of our hair and trying on strange items of forgotten clothing (sweatbands. Ties. Superfluous belts etc) in order to get the right kind of dishevelled, post-Grunge Hoxton look. Even Sandy, if I recall rightly, squeezed into his girlfriend's fake-fur coat and a pair of flares. Ray, on the other hand, trotted down the stairs just as we were about to leave. He was cleanly shaven, had gel in his hair, and was wearing a freshly ironed Ralph Lauren shirt. I think he might have even been wearing aftershave. He honestly did not understand why we were laughing at him. And he pulled that night, as well – a gorgeously messed-up artschool chick who looked like Wendy James. It just wasn't right.

Ray was a great person to be poor with. He was a real celebrity addict, but in a rather charming, fanclub sort of way. He'd spend free mornings in Brixton Library, devouring the latest copies of *Heat* and *Now!* He was a shameless grommet. He used to drag Neil and me along to Leicester Square a couple of times a month, so he could stand outside premières and use a disposable camera to take pictures of Hollywood stars. We had great fun. He'd bring picnics, Neil would bring hash and I'd bring vodka. Pretty soon we worked out that great unspoken secret of all paparazzi photographers – that to get the best pictures, all you need to do is yell something unspeakably rude. Drunk, well-fed and slightly spacey, Neil and I would shriek unrepeatable things about hamsters or buggery or Jesus, and the star in question would be captured, looking suitably incredulous, by the plastic shutter-click of Ray's Kodak Compact.

I liked being poor. It suited me. I made a good aspirational person. I'm still aspirational, of course, but in a different way. Back then I had nothing, and I wanted everything. That's a beautiful situation. These days I have an average amount and I want a greater than average amount. That's a bit dull, isn't it? Human nature, I suppose. Fear and compromise and all that. It's funny. I used to want everything, and now I'm losing my edge. Janie still wants everything, but has never done anything about it. And the Princess? The Princess was born compromising. It's rare, I suppose, that you'll find somebody who wants it all, and gets a bit of it, and still keeps wanting everything. I doubt I've ever met anybody like that.

Except for Elspeth. Elspeth has always wanted it all. When we were teenagers we used to sit on the rocks on Arthur's Seat in Edinburgh, smoking Regals and dreaming of London. She wanted to live in Camden so she could shag pop stars. I wanted to live in Sloane Square so I could shag public school girls.

'They're just . . . different,' I'd muse. 'They have hair like honey, and these really cool small noses. And I gather they go like trains.'

Elspeth would ask me if I'd ever met any.

'Not really,' I'd say.

Elspeth would call me a prick. Then we'd go back to her house, go up to the attic, and put a chair in front of the door.

We grew older, we left school. This is the difference between myself and Elspeth: I then went to Cambridge and studied Philosophy. She went to Camden and shagged pop stars. We'd both meant it. She just meant it more.

She didn't just shag pop stars, of course. She also shagged managers and journalists and trustafarians. For a brief period she was shagging the coolest man I have ever met – before or since – a dreadlocked Essexer called Bobbin, who sold *Planet of the*

Apes T-shirts and hand-painted DMs from a stall by the canal. When Elspeth moved to London she embraced London, much of it quite literally. She slipped lightly into this world that we'd read and dreamed about as though she'd been born to it, exiled temporarily by a simple quirk of geography. Which, in many respects, I suppose she had.

Elspeth and Ray. These were the people who used to be at the centre of my life. And now look at me. Hungover and alone; blacked-up and naked in my stinking bed, after an abortive night out with a collection of people I don't even particularly like. Last night was the first time I'd seen Ray in years. I haven't had a proper conversation with Elspeth in . . . God. Possibly even longer. I used to see her all the time. My phone would ring, and she'd be there, summoning me to some dingy bar in Elephant or King's Cross or Vauxhall. Somewhere resolutely uncool, where we'd drink and smoke and bitch about the world. Then, if I was lucky, we'd go back to her flat. I was her escape, I suppose, from the world she'd thrust herself so enthusiastically into. I'm in it too, now. I suppose that's why she has no use for me. What a miserable thought.

Do I have actual friends these days? I'm not sure I do. I have Neil, who reminds me so much of the bad things about myself that I can hardly bear to speak to him sober. Not that I often have the opportunity. And I have Daniel, who I only class as a friend because I don't work with him anymore. After that I have Philip and Rebecca. Paxy and Lucy. Janie and the Princess. Furniture and families, not friends.

Is Fingers like me? Is he drifting? Has he pulled up so many anchors that he now feels attached to nothing? And is he now sitting alone, in a tiny over-priced flat, raging with a hangover and asking so many melodramatic introspective personal questions that even Kevin from the *The Wonder Years* would have given him a slap?

No. He's not. He's out there, making a mark. He's like those characters in *Natural Born Killers*, who know they are alive by virtue of the fact that they stop other people being. If he disappeared, the world would feel it. He'd leave a gap. The bastard.

Janie drops round, unannounced, at about five. She's strangely cheery, which depresses me. I let her in and scramble back into bed.

Like a virgin bride, I draw the covers up around my neck. 'Go away,' I wheeze.

'Oh Mackie,' she chides, in her maddish way, leaning over me to whip open the curtains. 'Look at you. It's foul in here. It's like . . . a squat.'

'You'd know,' I mutter.

Janie puts one hand on her hip and looks at me. She does wear the oddest clothes. Think dungaree shorts, made of a thin, oxblood denim, but low at the front, so that the workman's pocket sits around the navel. Under them she has a white and black stripy longsleeved thing that wouldn't look out of place on a Frenchman, and green nylon leggings that wouldn't look out of place on a roaring fire out the back of the HQ of the Taste Police. Oh, and hiking boots. Let's not forget the hiking boots.

She frowns, but pleasantly. 'What are you staring at?'

'Nothing. Sorry. What do you want?'

Janie flops down on a stool by the sink. She's being kittenish. I hate it when she's kittenish. 'I want,' she says, 'to talk about two weeks today.'

I gaze at her for a few moments. 'Sorry. What?'

'Two weeks today,' she says, and then looks away. 'It's Mum's day.'

'Janie, I'm really ill. Can we not talk about this now?'

She's so bright-eyed and enthusiastic she could be a fucking American. I can't bear it. 'We *have* to, Mac.'

'No we don't. And don't look at me like that.'

'Like what?'

'Like that. Like Mindy looking at fucking Mork. I hate that understanding smile of yours. It makes me want to . . . I dunno. Hit you in the face with an iron.'

Janie is smiling.

'Don't laugh at me. I do *have* an iron, you know.'

'You're being ridiculous.'

'I'm not. I don't care if I am. I don't want to talk now. Look, I needed to give you a call tomorrow anyway, about Japan. Let's talk then.'

'What about Japan?'

'Never mind Japan. Go away. I want to sleep.'

Janie comes and sits on the side of my bed, her presence trapping my arms in the duvet by my sides. I hate this. I want her to go away and let me sleep. I want a cigarette. I want to be running along a beach at twilight. I want to climb a tree.

'I'll be quick,' she says. 'Two weeks on Wednesday. Mum's day. There's a problem. It's also the day of the Princess's Ball. She can't get out of it.'

I nod. 'The Jew Ball, yeah. I got an invite for that. Shame.'

'Maybe I'll come too,' says Janie, and, despite my agitation, I laugh out loud.

'You? At a ball? In a *frock*?'

'We'll be together,' says Janie, brightly.

I shudder. 'Fine. We'll talk about it. You go now.'

My sister stands up and moves (by which I mean takes a couple of very short steps) towards the door. 'Oh,' she says. 'What was that about Japan?'

I think for a moment. 'Itotaki,' I say. 'Does that name mean anything to you?'

Janie frowns. 'It's not a name.'

'I, um, have it on rather good authority that it is, actually.'

'I don't care,' says Janie. 'It isn't. It's a nickname.'

I sit up. 'A nickname? Meaning what?'

'Not necessarily meaning anything.'

'I don't understand.'

Janie sighs, but I can tell she's enjoying herself. She isn't an expert on much, Janie, but get her going on Japan, crystals, Indian medicine or cats, and she's away. 'How can I explain this? Look, you know that Japanese actor, Kimura Takuya?'

'Like a brother.'

'Shut up. You must. He's one of their most famous TV stars.'

'Janie, I have a basic Sky package. Japanese TV is a mystery to me. What about him?'

'Well,' she says, leaning against the door. 'He's known as Kimutaku. It's a nickname. Combining his two names, see?'

'So you reckon "Itotaki" is something similar?'

'Sounds it. A combination of two names.'

'Great. Which names?'

'Mac, I have no idea. "Ito" is a name in itself, but the "taki" part could come from almost anything.'

'Like what?'

She shakes her head. She's bored now. 'Like anything at all. Who knows? Why do you need to know?'

'Work,' I tell her, and turn to face the wall. 'Thanks anyway.'

She hesitates for a moment in the doorway. 'I'll call you, okay? About Mum's day?'

'Yeah,' I say. 'Right.'

'Your thoroughly superfluous arse . . .'

How would you go about identifying a random Japanese businessman armed only with his nickname? Well, yeah. Exactly. Back at work on Monday morning, I google him. Not helpful. Google knows of a mere seven Itotakis. Of these, three are in Japanese, one is a character in a student play, and the other three appear to be photographs of rivers. Or rocks in rivers. Or people on rocks in rivers; I'm not too sure – the captions are all in Japanese. Either way, it's hard to see how any of them could have any connection whatsoever with a celebrity trinket collector, or the jeweller Jackson Pirelli, or the mysterious figure in London that Greebo told me about.

Pirelli himself, by contrast, merits literally thousands of pages. It seems he is related to the tyre-making Pirellis, but only very distantly. He's more famous for getting a certain type of rich-but-brash celebrity (Jennifer Lopez. Catherine Zeta Jones. Ivana Trump. You know the sort. Anybody whose name ends 'of

Monaco' or, at a push, 'of Kent') to wear a certain type of jewellery. He doesn't actually *make* this jewellery, of course. He just *brokes* it.

Most pages concern him being instrumental in getting Celine Dion to wear that vast Chanel rock around her neck when she sang the *Titanic* song at the Oscars. He's been 'at home' twice for *¡Hola!* and three times for *Ciao!* According to various society blogs (ugh), he seems to pop up now and again in the diary pages of *Tatler* and *Harper's*, so I email the library downstairs and ask them to send up any cuts they might have kicking about. He dated the Duchess of York for a couple of months in the late nineties (just before she sucked that foot) and is currently married to one of those insanely leggy Russians that suddenly seem to be popping up everywhere. He does indeed, it seems, own one of Elvis's toes, and also the Mini that Marc Bolan died in. He doesn't, as far as I can tell, have anything to do with Japan. At all.

'Whatcha doing?' says Rebecca, appearing by my shoulder.

I click off the monitor and whirl around. 'Nothing. Research. Nothing.' Philip is just behind her, awkwardly grinding the toes of his right foot in a circle on the floor. I frown. 'Where have you two been?'

Rebecca rolls her eyes. Philip looks embarrassed. 'Um . . . conference,' he says.

'*Um . . . conference*,' I snap back, in a whiny, sneery voice. Philip goes pink. I stare at him. 'What, really? You were in conference? Why?'

'They, um, wanted somebody else. Other than Becks, I mean. They thought that she . . .'

I am enraged. 'Somebody else? I'm somebody else! Why didn't you take me? *Becks?*'

Rebecca crosses her arms, her body language, somehow, oozing scorn. Plainly she has a far better recollection of Friday night than

I do. 'Don't be so pathetic. I just thought Philip ought to be a bit more involved in things. He's not your assistant, you know.'

I stare at her. 'Yes he is.'

'No he isn't. He's my assistant. As are you.'

'I am not your assistant.'

'Oh Mac.'

'Don't bloody "oh Mac" me. I'm not. I am your equal. In fact, no. I am your superior. You're Willie's deputy, and I'm in charge of . . . this.'

'This'. What is 'this'? Once upon a time, back when I was first employed, 'this' was very much a diary column, and Daniel was very much the boss of it. Then the column went, and our stories began to masquerade as news, and then Daniel went and I began to masquerade as him, but without the job description. I became an appendix. And one that could be removed without any complex surgery at all. Half the stories I file vanish into a black hole. Were it not for Fingers, I might as well not exist.

'There is no "this",' snaps Rebecca. 'It's about time you realised that. There is this one story, just this, and you are researching it abominably. This is massive, Mac. Everybody is running it, everybody is talking about it. And we're having to run your snide, speculative *crap* on the front page, because you haven't managed to find anything else. Do you know how bad that looks?'

I turn my back on her. I'm not having this.

Nor is she. She grabs the back of my chair, and spins me around.

'I am better than you,' she hisses, and her dreadlocks flail, like the snakes on a gorgon. 'I work harder than you. I'm helping you on this ridiculous story, against my better judgement, mainly in a doomed attempt to save your thoroughly superfluous arse. Think about that. And don't ever let me catch you browsing for porn again.'

———

Rebecca disappears and doesn't return until lunch time. Philip is keeping his head behind his monitor and, unless I'm imagining it, even making an effort to breathe quietly. I'm not bothered. I log on to the paper's online newspaper archive, and trawl my way through every English-language article mentioning Jackson Pirelli I can find.

It passes the time, but it's all ultimately useless. He was born in Florence just after the war, but spent much of his childhood in Singapore. He used to have a big house in Mustique (at the Mick Jagger end, as opposed to the Princess Margaret) and, for a while in the 1980s, played host to people like Duran Duran, Queen and Spandau Ballet when they fancied taking coke in the sun. He sold it in 1995, perhaps because of tax. Reading between the lines, it sounds a little like he's bisexual. Or perhaps that's just me leaping to conclusions. Either way, he spent a lot of time with Freddie Mercury, and there's a rather arch line from *Londoner's Diary* about him being spotted playing Frisbee 'till dusk in the long grass of Hampstead Heath' with a hugely famous actor, of sexuality both uncertain and widely debated. He's also mentioned in the credits of several movies which, in this context, it might be legalistically unwise to name.

One particular anecdote stands out, but only because it sounds like the kind of thing that could have happened to me. In an interview with *Bild* (which I've translated using AltaVista's online Babel Fish thingy, and thus could be misunderstanding entirely) he described one party he threw on a yacht. I don't think it was the same yacht that Greebo's boyfriend stayed on, though, as he mentions that it was a sailboat, and that one was too big for anything other than an engine. Maybe he's had several yachts.

Anyway, this yacht was 'parked' (berthed? Docked? The German word is very long) just outside St Tropez harbour one summer night in the mid 1990s. As I understand it, it had been right by the 'High Street' (Surely it has a more poetic name than that? 'Boulevard', perhaps?) earlier that evening, but had moved away, because of noise restrictions (*sic:* 'volumnising'). Pirelli claims to have met a huge bunch of people in one of the town's 'discotheques', and invited them back to have a party. One, an Englishman, was 'as drinked as a camel of thirst', which, I don't think I'm unreasonable in assuming, is pretty damn 'drinked' indeed.

This Englishman had arrived at the party with a well-known semi-aristocratic English model. *Bild* doesn't name her, but there's enough information for somebody like me to guess. Suffice to say, you'll have heard of her. I see her at parties about twice a month, although I've yet to pluck up the courage to speak to her. She's a few years older than me, but I don't think it matters. I have it on good authority from Neil (who has it on good authority from somebody else) that, come the end of the night, she'll go home with *anybody*.

Anyway, the model seems to have been as 'drinked' as the Englishman. Night had just fallen, and the yacht was 'yolked' (anchored, I assume) to a very small rocky outcrop. This inebriated couple appear to have slipped onto this outcrop and . . . well, embarked upon the only respectable course of action to be embarked upon when an inebriated Englishman and a semi-aristocratic model find themselves alone on a rocky outcrop, somewhere off the coast of St Tropez. Trouble was, they weren't alone. They were accompanied by a small automatic lighthouse. Even if they noticed this (which, however wasted, they *must* have done), they apparently failed to notice their silhouettes – a pornographic shadowplay plastered, periodically, not only over the loose-flapping mainsails of the yacht they had just left, but also right across the frontal façade of the Hotel Byblos. Fantastic.

———

It's while I'm reading this that I get an email from Elspeth, the first I've had in ages. I feel a wild, almost childish excitement in opening it, but this quickly fades. She obviously meant to send it to somebody else. '*Fine,*' it just says. '*See you there.*' Part of me resents this mystery person she's about to spend her evening with, before savagely rejoicing that, as he hasn't got this email, he'll probably stand her up. But the rest of me, most of me, just gives an affectionate smile and thinks '*Duh!*'

Rebecca returns from lunch at around three and from then on, at periodic intervals, keeps taking Philip outside for secret little chats. My assumption is that they are just fascinated by what I'm doing. It does look pretty good. About an hour ago the kid from the library brought up the last ten years' worth of glossy magazine cuts which have any link to Jackson Pirelli. They're mainly party or diary stories, and they're mainly in Foreign, but it's still fascinating to see this guy I've spent the day reading about in context.

I'm scanning through a US *Vogue* spread about a Tall Ships piss-up in Hong Kong when my mobile rings. For some reason, I'm convinced it's going to be Elspeth.

'Yo,' I say, imagining myself as Gordon Gekko in *Wall Street.* 'Talk to me.'

'Colombo?' says somebody, who very much is not my ex-girl-friend.

'Greebo, baby,' I croon, and Philip and Rebecca both look up from their screens, like a pair of peckish ostriches. I ignore them. 'Just thinking about you.'

I shouldn't do this kind of thing to Greebo. 'Why?' he snaps, immediately panicked. 'Why me? Who've you been talking to?'

'Nobody, nobody. It's just I'm browsing through some old pictures of our friend with the yacht.'

'Oh yes?'

'Yeah,' I say, stopping at a shot of Kim Basinger in a very plunging dress. 'And there was one particular picture. I was wondering . . .'

'What?' screeches Greebo.

'Well,' I say, twisting the page for a better angle on the breasts, 'whether it couldn't be your boyfriend, Gustav. It's certainly how I imagine him.'

'It wouldn't be wouldn't be wouldn't be G . . . him,' says Greebo, with characteristic suaveness. 'What does he look like?'

'Oh no.' I muse, tracing Kim's hips with a forefinger. 'It's somebody else entirely. Silly me. What can I do for you, Greebo?'

'I spoke to him.'

'Who?'

'Gustav. My boyfriend. I asked him if he knew any more about the thing we were talking about. Itotaki. The contact in London. Jackson Pirelli.'

To hear what Greebo has to say, I am itching. To hear what Greebo has to say, I would walk across hot coals, or chew gravel, or listen to an entire album by Victoria Beckham. But if Greebo knew this, he'd be on the phone for an hour.

'Oh,' I say, airily, forcing myself to continue scanning photos to give an impression of disregard. Jackson Pirelli is air-kissing Grace Jones. Jackson Pirelli is posing beside an ice sculpture of a swan. 'That. I'd almost forgotten about it. What did he say?'

'He remembered something else about the contact.'

'Mmm.' Jackson Pirelli is drinking Budweiser with Mickey Rourke. Jackson Pirelli has an arm around Michael Flatley. 'Really?'

'Yeah,' says Greebo. 'He remembered that Pirelli said it was a journalist.'

'Jesus fucking Christ!'

'I thought that would get your attention.'

But it hasn't. Jackson Pirelli is drinking cocktails with a man who looks like an Asian Bond villain.

'Shut up for a second.' A caption: *'Jackson Pirelli with Ventrama President Ito Takamura'*.

Itotaki. An abbreviated nickname. Itotaki. Ito Takamura.

'Greebo, what's Ventrama?'

'What? I've no idea. A journalist, I said . . .'

'A journalist. Yeah. Great. What time is it in Japan?'

Greebo is positively stuttering with outrage. 'Colombo, I've no . . .'

'You don't know? Aren't you meant to be a banker? What about the yen, damn you?'

'I think it's nine hours ahead. But . . .'

'So, what? It's 1 a.m. there? Bugger.'

'Are you going to tell me . . .'

'No. But a journalist. Great. Thanks Greebo. I'll call you.'

I slip the phone into my pocket, and see Rebecca and Philip staring at me in consternation.

'Are you going to tell us what that was all about?' asks Rebecca.

I blink at her for a moment. 'On balance,' I say, 'no. Sorry about that.'

'Who the hell is Mark?'

I sneak out at about half four, when Rebecca's alternate cajoling and threats, and Philip's betrayed, bulging cow eyes are beginning to get on my nerves. I'm not budging on this one. Like I tell her, the investigation is at a critical stage, and I don't trust the pair of them not to jeopardise it. Plus, I'm intrinsically smug, resentful, and unhelpful.

At any rate, they grow preoccupied. As of this afternoon, the froth surrounding Fingers has taken a new, and rather silly turn. Joe Bastin, flamboyant veteran of all things pop, has just issued a shameless press release to announce that, at his Greatest Hits bash this coming Thursday, he will be riding the Silver Grub. The Grub, a silver-plated Vespa once owned by James Dean, normally lives in a vault at Coutts. Bastin bought it at auction, and at vast expense, last February. According to a spokesman from the Metropolitan Police, removing it from its vault is 'unwise in the current climate'. Bastin's PR people obviously disagree. Fingers has become a marketing tool.

Like half the press in the land, Rebecca is now going spare, trying to get hold of an invitation. I already have one, but I'm damned if I'm letting on.

I'm meant to be going to some party in Clapham with Lucy tonight, so I call her from downstairs to see if she fancies bunking off a bit early. Initially, she doesn't. In fact, she's shocked at the thought. It's one of my favourite things about her, this wide-eyed marriage of a chirpy tart who's up for anything and a prim little girl who does everything by the book. I tell her this, and it pleases her so much that she agrees to pretend to feel ill, and meet me in the Whittington in five minutes.

The barman looks like Tosh from *The Bill*, that podgy moustachioed bloke who died, or got written out, or got stuck behind a Sun Hill desk a few years ago.

'Whisky, mate,' I say to him as soon as I arrive, and then knock it back fast and order a pint.

I buy some fags and wander over to a corner booth, snatching Tosh's copy of the *Evening Standard* off the bar. It's a mistake. Honestly, you'd think there was nothing else happening in the world. You'd think that there weren't bombs pitting the Middle East, and diseases prickling out of Africa. You'd think that Fingers was the only movie in town.

The latest thing is for politicians to chip in, either slyly professing admiration for the thief, or criticising each other for failing to condemn him. Take Ken Livingstone. Late last week, he did an interview in *JockySlut* or *Dazed* or *Sleazenation* or some other such worthy theatre of debate in which he said that the robberies had been great for London's profile in the world, were thus great for tourism and were thus great for London. Or take Boris Johnson who wrote, quite unequivocally, in the *Sunday Telegraph*, that Fingers was a true *Boy's*

Own hero and that he (Boris) was quite insanely jealous of him.

Today, such is the way these things work, is the turn of the worthies. This is why Alan Milburn was on BBC *Breakfast* this morning, doing such a good impression of outrage. This is why Norman Tebbit (whose mortal slumber, if the picture by-line is anything to go by, has been deliberately interrupted) popped up in *The Times* to have a crack at the 'immoralities' of New Labour. This is why the main front-page headline of the *Standard* – a real, reputable newspaper – is 'WIDDERS WADES IN'.

I'll tell you what's odd, though. The papers are full of this stuff, but none of it is actually about Fingers. It's all about the hubbub *surrounding* Fingers. In documenting the hubbub, all this is (as the *Guardian*'s Marina Hyde rather wittily pointed out about herself this morning) in itself contributing to it, so the spiral goes on and on. Nobody is writing about the actual story. Nobody appears to be even trying to track down *who this guy is* any more. Or if they are they're rubbish at it. They haven't even done as well as me. There's no mention of collectors, no mention of Japan, nothing. Just a bloke stealing stuff and what we all think about it. That makes me feel . . . I don't know. At once somehow lost and alive.

Suddenly my pint is snatched from my hand, and Lucy is sliding into the booth hard against me, her legs knocking my knees together with an audible clack. She kisses me, slides a hand up my thigh, and asks me why I don't finish my drink and take her home.

The thing is, and I'm not being funny here, but I'm already regretting having called her. I'd rather spend the afternoon by myself. With a book.

We make small talk in the taxi, but we're both squirming a little. In the flat, in my tiny ridiculous flat, she pushes me against the wall (I only have one wall. The others are taken up by a kitchen, a window and a bed). She bites me on the ear, takes a step back, and undoes the top button on her white blouse.

'Where are we having supper?' she asks. 'Mirabelle?'

I blink at her. 'Uh, I hadn't actually . . .'

She undoes another. 'The Ivy?'

'Well, it's very hard to . . .'

She sighs and takes my right hand, pulling it into the top of her shirt and scooping it under one side of her smooth cream bra. 'Or Hakkasan?'

'Oh. Maybe.'

My shirt goes up and my belt is loosed. 'Momo?' she ponders. My flies are opened. 'Petrus?'

'Both. Very possibly both . . .'

'Sketch?'

'Mmm.'

Now she's on her knees, kissing my belly. My fingers grip the back of her hair. 'Aubergine,' she murmurs. 'Assaggi.'

'The Cinnamon Club?' I suggest. 'Gordon . . . Ramsay's at . . . ah . . . Claridge's?'

The last thing I hear is an indistinct 'Nobu?' and then she doesn't say anything for quite a while.

As it turns out, we go to Luigi's, a rather shitty caff just around the corner. Lucy doesn't seem best pleased by this.

I tell her that Madonna and Guy Ritchie have been known to snack here after shopping at Harrods, but I don't think she believes me. We eat pasta and drink a bottle of wine, but something somehow feels wrong. I realise that this is the first time we've spent any amount of time together after sex. We're not flirting, and we're not feeling each other up. Thinking of the small talk in the taxi this afternoon, I realise that this is all we've ever done.

It is as though we've got nothing real to say to each other at all. God, imagine the old days. How often this must have happened to people just after they got married.

Things don't improve in the tube on the way to the party. I do get the feeling that Lucy is a bit annoyed that we aren't in a taxi, but Christ, it's a long way to Clapham.

I don't own any shirts from Burton's, and I don't own any patent-leather slip-on deck-shoes with little silver bits just below the tongue. This means that, once we get to the party, I feel a little out of place.

Lucy's friend answers the door herself. 'You must be Mark,' she says to me, after squealing and giving Lucy a little hug.

'Mac,' I correct her.

'Mark,' she agrees. 'I'm Mary.'

I tell her that my sister is called Mary, which isn't, I suppose, actually even true anymore, and then she turns away.

'Bring Mark through and introduce him to people,' she tells Lucy. 'I'll be in the kitchen.'

Lucy steps away, but I catch her wrist.

'Who the hell is Mark?'

She snatches her arm away. 'What do you mean?'

'What do you think I mean? Who's Mark?'

Lucy stares at me. 'You're Mark.'

'Mark? Christ, Lucy. I'm called Mac!'

'Mark.'

'Mac!'

'Maaark. Like they say in Liverpool? Are your parents from there?'

I stare at her. 'It's short for Macaulay. How can you not know that? We've known each other for weeks. Haven't you ever seen my by-line?'

'Your what?'

'My by-line. My name, in the paper, next to things I've written.'

Lucy giggles, not even very apologetically. 'I don't read the paper,' she says.

This conversation, brief and infuriating as it might be, is probably the highlight of my evening. Lucy takes me through into the living room, where a variety of largish men observe me with barely disguised suspicion. This is not, I begin to realise, a venue at ease with cutting-edge male fashion. My big hair, vintage Levis and chocolate Ugg boots do not mark me out as a wise and interesting free-thinker. They mark me out as being marooned in that unhappy no-man's land between 'ponce' and 'poof'.

I remember people like this. I grew up with them. The girls mislead you, with their fluffy coats and their trainers, and their piercings in belly-button and nose. It's only when you meet the male of the species that you realise what is going on. Here's me imagining that Lucy is my bit of rough, and it turns out that, actually, I'm hers. These people. They're like racists who listen to reggae. I'm alone and adrift.

I'm taken over to an IKEA sofa by a fireplace with a lava lamp in it, where I meet Colin, Martin, Sanj, Debbie and Isla. Debbie and Isla are both quite sexy, in a Girls Aloud sort of way. The boys frighten me.

'And this,' says Lucy, very carefully, 'is Maahk.'

'Malc?' says Colin.

'Mike?' asks Sanj.

'Merc?' suggests Debbie.

Lucy scowls at them. 'No,' she says. 'Maahk. It's short for Maakhally. Don't you know anything? He's from Liverpool.'

———

Lucy leaves me with these people and follows her friend Mary to the kitchen. I'm having a horrible time. Sanj, as it turns out, actually is from Liverpool. Unhappily, he decides that I must be taking the piss when it emerges that I, plainly, am not.

'Why d'you pretend you are, then?'

'I didn't. I don't. It's a misunderstanding.'

'I thought she was your girlfriend.'

'I think she is.'

'You'd think she'd know where you were from, then.'

'Mmm. You would, wouldn't you?'

'Markly isn't even a Liverpudlian name. Did she mean Barclay?'

'No. No. It's Mac. Macaulay. It's Scottish.'

'You don't sound Scottish.'

'Don't I? Well, more than I do Liverpudlian, eh?'

'You don't sound Liverpudlian at all.'

'Yes. Yes I know. I'm not.'

This is an abbreviated version, by the way. The actual conversation goes on for far longer than you could possibly imagine.

Lucy is nowhere to be seen.

Eventually, the conversation turns to jobs. Well, I say turns. Actually, I steer it there. We've covered transport, and house prices, and the fact that, in Colin's experience, all fat girls like anal (not nearly as interesting as it might sound), and I honestly can't think of another thing to say to anybody. It turns out that Debbie and Sanj work in something called 'sales', Isla is a trainee solicitor, Martin – her boyfriend – works in a Pitcher and Piano, and Colin (who appears to be considered something of a Renaissance Man among the group) is a photographer specialising in weddings.

'I'm a journalist,' I tell them.

'Uh oh!' guffaws Colin. 'Tabloids is it? *Sun* and all that?

Investigative? Better watch what we say, eh guys? Find it all in the paper tomorrow, eh?'

I smile, thinly. 'Not exactly. Although our readers, I'm sure, would be . . . fascinated by every aspect of your lives. No. I do more showbiz stuff. I'm writing about Fingers at the moment.'

'Fingers?' says Martin. 'What's wrong with thumbs, mate?'

'Ahaha. No. The thief. The one stealing from all these celebrities. You must know. Everybody is talking about it.'

Colin snorts. 'Everybody without their own life, maybe. Eh Sanj?'

Sanj isn't saying anything.

'Wait,' says Isla. 'I know what you're talking about. He nicked a wedding ring off that slapper, didn't he? The one who had all those boob jobs. Turino.'

'Phwoarr,' says Colin, unsurprisingly. 'Do her. Do her right up the . . .'

'Kind of,' I interrupt. 'Although it turned out that he hadn't. She was making it up. For the story.'

'Ooh!' says Isla, and nudges Debbie. 'Insider knowledge! Isn't that interesting?'

I start to tell her that, actually, it was on the front page of the *Evening Standard*, but Debbie interrupts.

'I know who you are,' she says. 'You're the painter.'

I stare at her.

'Yeah,' she continues. 'You're the one who's doing that picture of Lucy, innit?'

Oh my God. 'You guys . . . ah . . . know about that?'

'Course we do,' says Debbie, looking thrilled.

'Yeah,' says Isla, and giggles. 'I remember. She told us the next day. We all reckoned you were just making it up to get her into bed.'

'Well that's what I do,' says photographer Colin, immediately, giving me a matey we're-all-men-of-the-world wink. 'Just tell 'em I'll make 'em famous. Don't I, Sanj?'

Sanj looks puzzled.

I'm blushing. 'Of course not. Make it up . . . hahaha. Not at all. Lucy is an . . . excellent model.'

'Has she seen it yet?' asks Debbie, who seems rather smitten with the idea.

'Not . . . not yet,' I stammer. 'I . . . uh . . . rarely show my work.'

'Fuck this,' says Sanj, suddenly. 'Painter?'

'Um, yeah.'

'You're full of fucking shit. You were a journalist a minute ago.'

That pretty much wraps things up for me. I spend a good twenty minutes trying to find Lucy, but she's vanished. It's not a big enough house for her to still be here; she's left me. Why? Who with? I get out, tipsy and annoyed.

I've missed the tube, so I catch a stinking nightbus from the stand on the Pavement. I've had enough of this. It was meant to be a drunken shag at the Diamond Ball. It wasn't meant to turn into me, weeks later, catching a nightbus somewhere in South London, alone and wondering who she's with. That's not Lucy's role in all this. That's not what she's *for*.

Up on the top deck, I give in to a whim and dial Elspeth's flat. She's out. No doubt she has just gone out, only seconds before. No doubt the door is barely closing as her telephone starts to trill. This is how it has become with me and Elspeth. We are like those apocryphal ships in the night. Were things different, by only a metre or two each way, we'd collide or collude, and exist in tandem. But they aren't, and we don't.

Perhaps this never actually happens with ships, I muse, as the streetlights outside fade into streaks of neon. Perhaps one ship always sees the other, but cuts its lights and pretends it doesn't, and lets the potential liaison drift by, quite deliberately unfulfilled.

'That would be much better, dramatically.'

n the film they are to make of my life, it turns out that I am
not to be played by Jude Law at all.

I am to be played by Dean Gaffney.

Dean fucking Gaffney, can you believe it? Once Robbie Jackson
from *EastEnders*. Brother of snotbag Sonia, and owner of the gender-
indeterminate Wellard, Britain's answer to *Neighbours'* Bouncer. In
person, he's probably lovely. In character, he had hair like a footballer and skin like a leper in an oil-slick. In the film they are making
of my life, it seems that I'm not all that important.

I learn this just before lunch, when Trevor Brainchild summons
me to his office. I don't like being summoned to Brainchild's office.
It smells of Brainchild; by which I mean of raisins, and of dandruff,
and of acrid vinegary sweat. But this morning, it smells of something else. Nivea moisturiser.

'Ah!' booms the smell's source. 'Hello! Felicity Straps! Channel
4! Delighted!'

'Hi,' I say.

'Mr Lewis,' says Brainchild. He touches his fingertips together and suddenly, in the real film of my life, I see how he should be cast. Not John Prescott at all. That bloke from *The Matrix*, the agent, the one who was the elf in *Lord of the Rings*. He'd have to fatten up and go greyer, but it's perfect. *Missss-ter Lewissss. Missster Anderssssson.*

'Misssss Strapssss,' continues Brainchild, 'is here from Channel 4. Stardom beckons, Mr Lewis.'

Felicity Straps does a daunting laugh, like a foghorn. You know her sort. Early thirties, blonde and head girl-ish. Built like a swimmer; think Sophie Raworth on steroids. Thoroughly sexual, but in the kind of way I normally avoid. Basically, she brings out the simpering girlie in me. Brimming with testosterone. Terrifying.

'Stardom? Stardom how?'

'We're thinking of making a drama,' says Straps, growling the last word like a talking lion. 'Based on . . . all this. Of course, it's all extremely preliminary at this stage, but we'll probably need a journalist character, and it seemed sensible to model it on you.'

'A drama? Based on what? The *Gazette*?'

'No, no,' she booms. 'Based on the robberies. Fingers. The thief.'

I'm thrown, albeit delightedly. 'You're making a drama about him?'

'Yes. Possibly.'

'But you don't know who he is?'

'No.'

'So how will it end?'

Straps shrugs, her shoulders moving like geography. 'That's not so important at this stage, I'm sure we'll come up with something if it goes into production. For now, we're just looking into it. That's how we do these things. It's important for us to be right on the *zeitgeist*.'

I think about this, brain awhirl. 'I see. But what if I never find him? What if somebody else does? Would that mean it would never get made?'

The TV lady frowns. 'I don't follow.'

'Well. How can you begin dramatising me on the trail of Fingers, if it might turn out that somebody else gets to him first?' I regret saying this almost instantly. 'Not that I think that's likely, of course.'

Straps stares at me for a moment, and then starts to laugh. 'Oh dear me. It wouldn't be about *you*!'

Brainchild sighs, theatrically.

'What? What? Who would it be about?'

'Well, the police, of course. Young chap by the name of Tom St Eccles. He's on the case. Very dashing.'

'Eccles,' I hiss.

'Oh, you know him?' Straps seems delighted. 'Splendid!'

I feel as though somebody has just promised me a Ferrari for Christmas, and then handed me a Matchbox toy. 'He calls me sometimes,' I mutter. 'We talk on the phone.'

'Is that all?' muses Felicty Straps. 'That's a shame. I had this darling notion of the pair of you meeting in shadowy pubs, covertly swapping tips and secrets. That would be much better, dramatically.'

I freeze. 'It would?'

'Oh yes. It's a relationship with so much potential. It would be a shame to allow it to trickle by, almost unnoticed, as mere telephone conversations. But don't look so upset, Mr Lewis! It's my job to think of these things. Real life rarely has much obvious dramatic potential.'

'Mine does!' I blurt. 'I have a colourful ethnic background and my grandfather once had a fight with a sword! I gatecrash parties and I live in Knightsbridge and I wear cool clothes and I take drugs and I'm haunted by a former girlfriend and I have loads of sex and my mother . . .'

I close my mouth with a snap. Brainchild is staring at me with frank disbelief. Felicity Straps looks embarrassed.

'I think that's rather more information than we need, dear,' she says, kindly. 'It's only a bit-part.'

'*Bit-part?*' I whisper.

'Yes. Well. A little better than that. More of a cameo, really. We were thinking of somebody relatively high-profile for the role.'

I perk up slightly 'Who?'

She answers. I perk down again.

Back at my desk, I find a note from Philip which says that he and Rebecca have gone out for lunch, but pointedly doesn't say where, or that I should join them. That's it. It's officially a shit day now. I think about popping down to see Lucy, but then remember that we haven't spoken since she abandoned me at the party. My life is awful. Everything is awful.

How can they make Eccles the star? Why am I not the bloody star? How Channel 4 is Tom St Eccles? He's positively Granada. A photogenic good-egg policeman. What is this? 1955? Even his name is like something out of Enid Blyton. Has he ever been anywhere *like* Paxy's? Did he have a grandfather who went after racists with a sword? I bloody doubt it.

Perhaps this is my fault. I can see that now. Straps was right. It would have been much better, dramatically, if we had met in pubs, to swap tips. Brown envelopes. Intellectual jousting. I've wasted him, keeping him at bay. How much more interesting my story would be if I had invited him in! I should have cultivated him as a sidekick. The comical plod, feasting on whatever scraps of information I can dangle before him. I'd have told him about Itotaki, he'd have told me about . . . well. Whatever he knows about. And who cares if he doesn't know anything? It's a classic device, and I'm a damn damn fool.

The modesty of my father, as I may have said before, astounds me. It bothers me sometimes that we men don't fight anymore – at least, not nice middle-class men like me. There was the Jensen thing, sure, and once, in Paxy's kitchen, I pulled a sleazy banker off a frightened schoolgirl and hit him in the crotch with a sandwich toaster (oh! The crumbs!) but I've never done anything like that. To fight, with blades, alongside your *dad*. I'm in awe, really. Absolute awe.

I'd never even heard about it until that night, at Jakey McLean's wedding. Jakey is Elspeth's oldest brother; he got married about eight years ago to this stunning girl from Sri Lanka. The wedding, in the old Caledonian, was this truly odd mix of Church of Scotland Christianity and Tamil Hinduism – quite bizarre. Think vegetarian haggis and reels in saris. Elspeth and I weren't really speaking for the first part of the night. She'd slept with somebody else instead of me at a party the night before, and I'd admitted that I minded, which really goes to show just how long ago it was. Now she wanted to get high, and break into a suite upstairs. I was sulking, so made a big show of preferring to get drunk with her grandfather.

We'd made up by the time the band started (translation: I'd backed down), but I kept going back to Mad Old Graham. Fascinating old pervert, that man. He came up to me at the bar and started telling me that he'd been in the subcontinent himself, back in the war. He was in some kind of Japanese POW camp on the Indian side of Burma, but managed to avoid the railways. His lasting regret, he claimed, apropos of nothing, was that he'd never quite managed to have sex with the camp commandant's teenage daughter.

'Tasty wee houri,' he mused. 'Always giein' us the eye. Some o' the lads reckoned she'd've had one o' they sideways fannies. Don't suppose there's ony truth in that, though?'

'Not to the, uh, best of my knowledge,' I told him.

He revelled in my discomfort. 'Tell me. You Hebrews. Issat true about the hole in the sheet?'

This actually made me choke on my Glenfiddich. 'Um, not to the best of my knowledge,' I repeated, as pink as Philip.

'Ladies' man, though, aye?'

'Er . . . well, you know.'

His rheumy eyes twinkled. 'Thought so. Runs in the blood. Ah remember yer Grandaddy. Auld sod'd shag a keyhole if the door spoke nicely enough to him.'

This was not quite the image I'd previously had of my comical, kilted Grandpa Johnjohn. But it seemed that, at one point, Old Graham had known him quite well. Ginger or not, it seemed Johnjohn had been quite a hit with the ladies. From the stories Graham told, I began to see not only my grandfather, but also my sombre, silent, black-clad grandmother in a whole new light.

'Seems to have missed my dad's generation, though,' I'd ventured, after a time.

Elspeth's grandfather winked at me. 'Dinnae ye believe it. Ah remember the time he brought yer ma home. Johnjohn wis proud as punch. Fine wee minx, yer mum. Always had the pick o' them though, wee Petey. Local hardman, him, afore the uni softened him up.'

That was how we got onto the Battle of Lewis Tartans. I couldn't believe it. I'd never previously considered myself to have any kind of colourful family background at all. I was thrilled. Can Tom St Eccles beat that? Bastard.

———

I've only asked my dad about the battle once, a few weeks after that. It didn't go well. I knew he wouldn't want to talk about it, so I waited until I'd have him captive. I waited until we were having supper.

There was me, my dad, and the Princess, Janie having decamped Newcastle-wards for Psychoanalysis and Massage some months previously. The Princess was scraping some kind of omelettey muck out of a pan (the 'Jewish Wife' transformation hadn't quite started yet) and my dad was judiciously sharing out two cans of Diet Coke. I waited until my sister had sat down, and then I hit him with it.

'Graham McLean was telling me a story about you at the wedding, Dad.'

'Oh yes?'

'Aye. Something about a fight outside the shop. You and Grandpa Johnjohn, and a bunch of vandals. Years ago.'

My dad put his fork down. Then he picked it up again, and stood up. 'That old fool tells too many stories,' he said, and swiped his plate off the table and went to eat in the sitting room.

The Princess stared at me. 'What was that about?'

I was a little shocked. 'I don't know. Just a story Mad Graham was telling me.'

'I guess he doesn't want to talk about it.'

'Guess not. Shame. Sounded really cool.'

'Perhaps you could ask mum,' said the Princess, although we both knew I couldn't.

Google only knows about one Ventrama, and he's some kind of Hindu deity. Probably not who I'm after, then. There are no entries at all for Ito Takamura. After a few moments twiddling my thumbs, I call International Directory Enquiries, and ask for any companies by that name in Tokyo. Nothing. After another few moments and a quick look at the office atlas, I do the same for Osaka. Nowt or, as the Japanese would apparently say, *mu*. A while later, I try Kobe, then Hiroshima, then Yokohama. And then Kyoto. When the operator says that they have an entry, I almost drop the phone.

Ventrama Import Exports. Kyoto, Japan. The phone number has more digits than a barcode. And they're out.

'And I didn't send one to you . . .'

Here's a thing. When you watch a red-carpet event on TV, and you see the air flicker with the glares of a thousand flashbulbs, did you know that most of what you are seeing isn't actually flashbulbs at all? No? Well it isn't. It's a strobe light.

That's right. A strobe light, like the ones they overuse in night-clubs to goad you into throwing a spasm. Sickening, isn't it? You see those celebs on the news, wandering up that scarlet aisle, pouting and turning, pouting and turning. You see them stopping every few steps, putting on their toothy, glazed expressions and sticking one foot out pointyways in order to make their arses look smaller. What you don't see is that, usually, they are doing this for the benefit of a mere eight or so actual photographers. The TV cameras are far more important these days, and they don't flash at all.

I'll never forget the way I laughed when I first discovered this. It was the premiere of *Eyes Wide Shut*, back in 1996 or so. Neil,

Ray and I had come down to Leicester Square for one of our first proper grommets. I miss grommeting sometimes. When the strobe started up, Tom 'n' Nicole started flipping around in it as though there were a hundred cameras, rather than under a dozen. I was confused for a moment, and then I started laughing so hard I could barely breathe. Ray had some toothpaste in his bag, and tried to use it to make his mouth foam. It didn't work – just made his spit all lumpy and blue. Although we never quite got round to doing it, we promised ourselves that next time we'd bring along a nice thick piece of ham, so he could cough it up and pretend it was his tongue.

Tonight, at Joe Bastin's Platinum Hits party at the Gretchner Hotel in Mayfair, the carpet is pink instead of red, and at times there are two strobe lights. Wonderfully, invitations appear to have been staggered. The less impressive guests – think Blue, Gary Lucy, Jo Brand, Gillian Taylforth, Susie Amy, Natalie Cassidy, June Sarpong – well, they just get the single strobe. When the bigger names start arriving – Neil Tennant, Richard Curtis, George Michael, Helena Bonham Carter, Paul Daniels and Debbie McGee (I know. No idea how they slipped through the net) – they switch on the second. It works rather well, actually, giving the impression of excitement building to a fever pitch. Excessive, perhaps, but nothing less that one would expect from the man who once described himself as 'the rich man's Elton John'.

This is not an awards ceremony. Nothing like that. This is not even the event at which Bastin will be presented with the platinum disc of his *Greatest Hits* – he's had it for over a month. This is Bastin's own bash, simply celebrating the fact that he's sold as many records as he thought he would. As something like the fifth most successful British solo artist of all time, he can throw a party pretty much whenever he pleases, and he pleases pretty regularly. Tonight's theme is the fifties, because this is the decade in which Bastin was born. The place is seething with Teddy Boys and girls in twinsets dressed up as Marilyn Monroe. My invitation was addressed to Daniel, but I noticed the return address on the back of the envelope, and swiped it from his redirection pile. It was made of cheap card, said 'PRESS' along the top, and informed me, in a coolly no-nonsense copperplate, that I was expected not to turn up in costume.

This is a shame. I quite fancied battering the 'fro into a duck's arse, and getting hold of a Marc Almond-style biker jacket, but I'm not sure they'd have let me in. Instead I'm still in Daniel's foul old suit that I haven't got around to giving back yet. In this context, my look screams 'PRESS'. It couldn't scream it more if I wore a trilby and stuck the invite in the hatband.

As it turns out, I'm rather relieved. Bastin himself isn't here yet, so the lights are still up full, bathing everybody present in a rather pissy yellow glow. You can get away with that if you're a twentysomething hack in his work clothes. For a thirtysomething cheerleader with a beehive, it's distinctly unflattering. I grin my way to the bar, and order a Grouse.

'Drunk already?' says a laconic female voice.

I turn. It's Whatshername. That friend of Jessica's who used to live with Elspeth. The one who hates me – Carolyn Somethingorother. She's wearing a floral dress that's slightly too small, grey tights, and pearls. She looks like a sluttish GI's wife from a wartime porn film. In the movie of my life, she'll be played by Keira Knightley, provided that Keira can lose about a stone.

'Getting there,' I tell her, noting the way her collar bone pokes from the front of her dress. Very heroin chic. I raise my glass. 'Nice to see you. Going to join me?'

'No,' she says, crossing her arms. 'I'm working.'

I stare at her. She cocks her head to one side and stares back. She smiles, but only with her mouth.

'Working? Working how?'

'Working here.'

I look around, seeing only waiting staff and uptight celebrities in silly clothes.

'Oh,' I say. 'What is it you actually do, again?'

She rolls her eyes. 'You're impossible. You honestly don't remember what I do?'

'You're a journalist,' I tell her. 'No. A PR. You're a photographer. You make things. Shoes. No. Wait. You're not a milliner, are you?'

'You're shameless,' she remarks, and yawns. 'I bet you don't even remember my name.'

'Of course I do. It's Carolyn. Is Elspeth here?'

'Probably. Carolyn what?'

'Carolyn . . . Somethingorother. I don't think I ever knew your surname.'

'You don't think you ever knew my surname,' repeats Carolyn. She repeats it very, very slowly.

'No. Or your job, actually.'

Carolyn's fingers rap on a bicep. 'Unbelievable. We had a very long conversation.'

'We did?'

I see her knuckles whiten. She wants to hit me, and I don't know why. 'At the house? Brian's house? Last summer?'

'Brian. Brian. Brian?'

'Oh, Jesus Christ. At Paxy's house, Mac.'

Ah. Things click. I slept with Carolyn at Paxy's house. Or at least, I think I did. Something like that. It was a Friday, one of the nights I usually avoid. I'd kind of met Carolyn a couple of times before, once when she was living with Elspeth, and once at Paxy's, but we'd barely spoken. That evening was different. I arrived very late, and very drunk, and somehow ended up cornering her on the stairs. I remember very little of anything. The next morning, I woke up in one of the upstairs rooms. Quite a nice one, actually. I hadn't been in it before. I must seek it out again some day.

'Oh!' I laugh, uneasily. 'Then! Right. Yeah. Bit wasted that night, actually. As you probably spotted. Remind me. You work . . . ?'

Carolyn bares her teeth. 'I work for Joe Bastin, you stupid little turd,' she says. 'I'm his PA. I sent out the invitations. And I didn't send one to you.'

Awkward. I think I talk her round, though. At least, she doesn't throw me out. I explain about Daniel, and the fact that he's not my boss anymore, and the fact that I'm too much of a slacker to let any of the PR companies know about it.

'It's a front, isn't it?' she says, and looks around. 'I'd better go sort out these bloody lights.'

I'm staring at her chest again. 'Hmm? What's a front?'

'You. This slacker business. You do it on purpose.'

'I wish.'

Carolyn shrugs. 'That's what Brian says, anyway. He says you're actually very diligent. Geekish, he says. Focused. You just pretend otherwise. Mind you, he also reckons that he doesn't have a drinking problem, so what would he know?'

This Brian chap again. Brian Paxton. I can't think of Paxy as a Brian. I shrug. 'Whatever. Listen. You getting burgled tonight?'

'I beg your pardon?'

'The thief. Fingers. That press release was shameless. Is he coming?'

Carolyn's eyes do something rather wicked. 'You tell me,' she says.

I put down my glass. 'What's that supposed to mean?'

'I knew you'd be here tonight. I just didn't expect you to be quite so . . . brazen about it.'

'Oh Jesus.' I take a deep breath. 'You too? You think I know something about all this? You think it's *me*?'

'Listen.' Carolyn leans over and whispers close into my ear. 'Joe will be arriving on the scooter in about ten minutes. He'll do a circuit of down here, and then it will be taken up in the lift and left in room 302. That's the internal corner suite on the third floor. There're guards in the corridor, but I doubt that they'll be a problem. And I should imagine that *somebody* will forget to lock the door. Got that? And look, if you can't actually get away with it, at least make it look as though you've tried, okay?'

I stare at her, speechless. She pecks me on the cheek, and then she's gone.

Two whiskies later, and I'm still fuming. What is wrong with everybody? I'm not bloody Fingers. I hate Fingers. He's ruining my life and my career. If I was wandering around with thousands in hot diamonds, I wouldn't be on the verge of being sacked from a pointless job on a dying newspaper, would I? I'd be . . . I'd be . . . Where would I be? I've no idea. Somewhere better.

I'm going to nail this bastard. He's mine. I've had too much whisky, too quickly, so I stagger away from the bar, and make my way into the Oriental-themed courtyard behind the dining area. Security in the corridor, eh? Well sod the corridor. She said it was an internal corner suite. From this quadrangle, outside, I should be able to see up into the room itself.

Looking up to the corner, on the third floor, it's obvious which one is 302. The windows are wide open, and stick-thin people mill inside, wielding things that look like make-up pens and glasses of champagne. There is a bench behind me and I back towards it, staring up.

'Yeeaaaaah!'

I leap into the air like an altar boy who has just mistaken his priest for an armchair. There's somebody already sitting there. Detective Inspector Tom St Eccles.

'Evening, Mr Lewis. Taking in the night air, are we?'

I'm shaking. 'Holy buggering fuck, Plod! What are you doing here?'

He moves along to share the bench. 'Don't call me Plod, Hack.' I think he's grinning. His chin, square and powerful, gleams leading-mannishly in the orange lights. He's wearing exactly the same Greaser outfit that I would have donned, had I been allowed. I hate him.

'Surveillance,' he says.

I nod up at window and sit down. 'Wouldn't you be better up there in the corridor? What can you survey from out here?'

Eccles gives me a meaningful look. 'You can survey,' he says, 'who else is out here surveying things. Didn't see your name on the invite list. Care to explain that?'

'I shinned up a drainpipe,' I tell him, 'before skulking across the rooftops, climbing into an air vent and taking out a waiter with a Vulcan death grip.'

He just stares at me.

I deflate. 'Work invite. Had my boss's name on it. Daniel Kemp. He'll be on the list. Any chance I could see it? I'm sure we could both benefit from sharing information.'

The light in 302 goes out. Eccles doesn't take his eyes from the window. 'I seem to recall saying just that to you, not so long ago. You didn't seem so keen on the idea. And it happens to be considered rather rude not to return phonecalls, you know, in my profession.'

I shrug. 'Really? It's pretty much *de rigueur* in mine. Anyway, I've changed my mind.'

'Have you indeed?' Eccles looks unimpressed. 'I never had this sort of runaround from the lovely Miss Leighton. How is she, by the way?'

'Rebecca? Hellish. Seriously, Eccles. I may have some information for you.'

'You may?'

I think of Itotaki. 'There may be a foreign connection.'

The sound of an engine drifts through the open doors to the dining area, to be quickly drowned out by throbbing music and cheering.

Eccles sighs and stands up. 'May, may. Names and places, Lewis. That's what I need. You show me yours, I'll show you mine.'

'Hey!' I shout, as he walks away, following the sounds of party. 'It's been great. Let's chat again soon, yeah?'

Maybe he smiles. The light is too weird to see. I settle back on the bench and stare up at that darkened window. I am alert and determined. I am the sleuth to end all sleuths. Screw Eccles. Poised like an eagle, I am pure leading man.

'Just describe the feet . . .'

wake suddenly and abruptly, much as Rip Van Winkle might have done, had his half-century of innocent slumber been brought to a savage and abrupt close by a discotheque-full of coked-up soap stars. I'm wet and I'm drunk. I've been asleep on a bench in the Gretchner courtyard, in the rain, for God only knows how long. People have come and gone; there are fresh wine glasses by my feet. The meal has passed, and the music has begun in earnest. The dining area has been cleared and transformed into a disco, sound and steam throbbing out from the open garden doors. It was a strobe light (yes, another one) that woke me up, I realise. It makes the whole inner wall of this court-yard glow white, and shoots through the rainy air like lightning. Droplets are transfixed, freeze-framed. The moon and stars cannot compete. I feel like I'm on a sinking ship and, also, dreadful.

My cigarettes are soggy, but I light one anyway. I need to wake up. The windows of 302 are lit and populated.

'Oi! Mate!' says a passing somebody. He has elaborate and

rat-like facial hair, and I think he was once in East 17. 'Gorrafag?'

'No,' I mutter. 'Go away.'

'Gorrenycokethen?'

'No. Listen. What's the time?'

'Party time!' he cackles. It's like he thinks we've practised this.

I call him a cunt, which offends him so much that he wanders away. Then I pull out my mobile. 9.35. I've been asleep for about an hour and a half. The people in 302, I decide, don't look like you'd expect people to look just after a silver Vespa worth a couple of mill. had been stolen. Even if they had wanted it to be. They're mainly young women, with a couple of guys. They're laughing. They're smoking and drinking champagne. Oh. Hold up. They're leaving. The main light goes out and another triangle of light across the ceiling shrinks to nothing as they shut the door.

Now what? Do I go up to the corridor and keep watch? Do I break in? Or do I stay down here and hope that if Fingers comes along he has the decency to turn the lights on? I stand up, and my feet sink into a waterlogged flowerbed. Pain. Cold. Wet. Drunk. Pain.

'Oi!'

It's the boybander with the ziggyzag beard, over by the garden doors. He drops his trousers and slaps his bare white arse in my direction.

'Is that what you make your living with these days?' I shout, but it's a bit too convoluted an insult to be audible through the rain and bass. He sneers, tugs his keks back up, and steps inside, whipping the shimmering curtain aside. I turn away, yelping, as the incomplete circle of the strobe light's bulb burns itself on the back of my eyes. Almost in tandem, my cigarette singes the insides of my fingers. I'm completely fucking sick of this.

Everywhere I look, red horseshoes dance. I turn away, rubbing my eyes and staring into shadows. And I freeze. Up on the fourth floor, at a darkened window where one would never think to look if one hadn't just been blinded by a curtain-twitching Walthamstow has-been, a figure is standing in a window. With what looks like binoculars. Trained on room 302.

For a moment I'm transfixed. Then, with a squelch and a stumble and, to be honest, a bit of a cough, I'm running.

Have you ever tried to sprint through a room full of gyrating celebrities? I shouldn't imagine you have. It makes you realise that these people are shit at real dancing. Put them on a podium, and they might look fantastic. Stick them on a dancefloor, and it's a nightmare. Everybody dances as though they expect their peers to form a circle around them and start clapping.

I shoulder-barge past more soap stars than I could possibly list, and then I'm out into the lobby, tripping drunkenly across the shag-pile carpet. I fall across a golden suitcase-carrying trolley thing, and send it crashing against a wall. I hear somebody shout something from behind a desk and, in turning to see what, or why, I career straight into one of those ancient, walnut-faced blonde women who lurk in the lobbies of posh hotels like cockroaches do in third-world toilets. She shrieks, stumbles, slashes at me with taloned claws. Then I'm past her and I'm leaping up the stairs. Pulling myself along by the banister, I can make out faces down in the stairwell below. Eyes are wide. Mouths are 'O's. I'm making a scene.

On the first-floor landing I come face to face with a porter carrying a suitcase. He goes to his left, I go to my right. He goes to his right, I go to my left. We prance like excited dogs.

'Get out of the way!'

'You shouldn't be up here!'

'Piss off!'

And there, the matter rests.

The second flight passes without incident. When I round the

corner of the third, I see a gang of four roadies coming the other way, carrying a drumkit. This is absurd. What next? I have visions of a pair of Brooklyn workmen carrying a sheet of glass across the corridor, or a Welsh shepherd struggling to control a flock of sheep. I leap the snare, duck a high-hat and use the cymbal stand to pole-vault over the bass.

Well, no. I about-turn, stab at the lift button and hurl myself inside.

'Christ!'

I trip over some fishnetted ankles, and lurch into that moody bloke from *The Bill*. He shoves me away, and starts scrabbling at his flies. I think that might actually be one of those girls from Pop Idol on the floor, wiping at her mouth.

'Sorry,' I mutter, and press the button for the fourth floor.

'It's Mac, isn't it?' says the actor, who, now I remember it, is married to a semi-famous popstar, who isn't the semi-famous popstar on her knees . 'You wouldn't . . . you aren't going to . . .'

The doors ping open. 'You must be mistaking me for somebody else,' I tell him, and leap out. I run five paces to the left, stop, shake my head, and run back to the right. This hotel is a basic square around the courtyard below, but I'm suddenly totally disorientated. As the doors close I catch sight of the actor, with a pragmatic look on his face, nodding at the girl and meaningfully eyeing his crotch.

The carpet is lurid and the walls are cream. I have no idea what room I am supposed to be running towards. A corner room, diagonally opposite 302, but a floor up. The last room before the corridor bends is 412. I hurl myself at the door.

It's dark in here, and it takes a moment for my eyes to start working. The windows, hung with cheapish net curtains, flash from the strobes downstairs. I can here music, muffled but drifting up. There is, evidently, nobody here. I move over to the window, hoist it up, and lean out.

There's a fine view of 302 from over here, but something feels slightly wrong, slightly different. I look down. There is a row of windows below me, but there is another row to my right, before the corner. It's the corner room I'm after, so I'm in the wrong room. I glance sideways, and gasp. In the corner room, in the *right* room, somebody is leaning out of the window. And although the light is bad, although I can only see a silhouette, I'm pretty sure they're looking at me.

I duck back inside, whirl around, trip over the bed, scramble over the counterpane and roll onto the floor at the other side. Then I'm on my feet, out the door, and running. The first room around the corner of the corridor is 414. If it looks out onto the same side of the courtyard, it must be L-shaped. I'm at the door in ten seconds, and through it.

It's a big room. A suite. Right in front of me the window is curtained and closed. The room is L-shaped and, around the corner, the window is open. The net curtains billow. A cigarette – which for some mad, disjointed reason makes me wince and think 'fire risk' – is still smoking in a soap dish on the carpet. There's nobody here, but a door to the left is open, and moving. I leap through it and find myself back in 412. It's where I've just come from. Interjoining rooms. Bugger it, bugger it, bugger it. The door, which I had left open, is slowly swinging closed. Leaping the bed this time, I'm through it and back, again, in the corridor. Around the corner to my left, where I've just come from, I hear the sound of running feet.

By the time I get around that corner, a shadow is disappearing around the one at the far end. I speed up. My lungs are burning. One more corridor before the staircase. He'll be in full view then. Provided I get there in time.

I'm way too drunk for this, but I'm gaining on him. As I round the penultimate corner, hitting the wall with a bang, I get a flash of a grey leg slipping around the bend onto the landing. I'm sprinting now. I'm utterly out of control. Just an instant too late, I spot a supper tray, on the floor, just by the door of room 446.

They don't half polish their supper trays in the Gretchner Hotel. The thing is silver, or maybe pewter, and when I step on it it sets off like a bobsleigh. For a moment I'm still upright, travelling even faster. Actually, it's something of a relief not to be running anymore. It's almost serene. Then I'm spinning through the air, in all manner of surprising directions, before landing on my ribs in a Hiroshima of cheesecake.

I scramble up, half crawling, and then I'm at the top of the stairwell. I'm too late. I howl like a wolf, and stumble down the stairs. From the bottom, I can see the door of room 302.

And that grey leg is snaking inside.

I take the rest of the stairs on my heels, juddering forward like a Geisha in tiny boots. Then I'm in the corridor and I know I've got him.

302 is a senior corner suite, which means it has an entry hall, a bathroom, a dressing room and a bedroom. The entry hall is empty, except for a spindly, jagged dining chair, which I manage to fall over, rather spectacularly. It cracks, like gunshots, and I'm suddenly sprawling amongst twigs. I roll on my back, towards the bedroom and those damn, damn grey legs are right there. Then the bedroom door slams in my face. Literally, in my face. It strikes me across my left cheek, and I howl again.

Seconds later, face numb, I'm on my feet and in the bedroom. It's empty. Two other doors lead out – one presumably to the bathroom, and the other to some kind of dressing room. I stare at them for a while, looking from one to the other. Then I pick up a leg from the broken chair, and push open the door to the right.

A bathroom. Empty. I see myself in the mirror, brandishing my chair leg. I look less like Luke Skywalker with light sabre than I would have hoped, more like a tramp with a passing interest in carpentry. I'm flushed and beetroot red. I turn around and, hefting my stick in front of me, approach the other door.

It resists my push. It's locked, from the inside. I kick it once, twice, three times, and it swings open.

It is a dressing room. The dressing room contains a window, with curtains drawn. It contains a wardrobe and a sink. It contains Joe Bastin's actual platinum disc, which is leaning against a thatched white stool. The dressing room also contains a silver-plated Vespa, which is taking up most of it.

The dressing room does not, quite obviously, contain any kind of thief, gentleman or otherwise.

I drop my stick, and lean against the door frame. I blink.

'Eh?' I say, out loud.

Behind me, somebody clears their throat. I spin around.

'I believe the phrase is "'allo, 'allo, 'allo",' says Tom St Eccles. 'What have we here, then?'

For a few moments I just gape at him. Eccles, the great, chis-elled, Indiana Jones slab of beef that he is, just sticks his hands on his blue-jeaned hips and raises his eyebrows.

'Listen,' I say, desperately. 'I was chasing somebody. They were watching me, from upstairs. I chased them all the way down here! I did! You can check! I . . . I . . . knocked over a trolley and I fell down stairs and . . . well. They came in here.'

Eccles steps past me and yanks at one of the curtains. The lights from the party downstairs dance on the roof. 'You were following somebody?' he says, quietly.

'Yes,' I nod. 'I saw him. He came in here. Look at my face, Eccles! He slammed the door in it!'

He peers at me. 'Looks like you fell over, to me.'

'No! Well yes. I did. But afterwards. And also before. But . . .'

'Lewis,' says the policeman, quietly. 'Shut up. Listen to me. I'm downstairs, right? I'm mingling. I'm *working*. Then the hotel manager comes to tell me that there's some drunken . . . prick running around upstairs, breaking things and throwing food around. So up I come. And what do I find? You. Here. Why?'

'I told you. I was chasing somebody. I followed him from the fourth floor. I chased him through the corridors, and down the stairs, and we ended up in here.'

'But there's nobody in here, Lewis.'

I look around, rather desperately. 'Well, no. But there was. The door was locked.'

Eccles examines the door. 'This door?'

'Yeah, Plod. That door.'

'This door doesn't lock.'

I look at it. He's right. Why did I start kicking at the door? Did it really never occur to me to turn the damn handle?

'Oh,' I say, weakly. 'Then he must have gone the other way, while I was in the bathroom. Didn't he come past you?'

'Nobody came past me, Lewis. There wasn't anybody to come.'

'There was! And don't look at me like that, you flat-footed arsehead. I chased him! I saw the man, okay?'

He looks interested at last. 'You did? Describe him.'

I deflate. 'Well. I only saw his feet.'

'Describe them.'

'Describe the feet?'

'Yes, describe the feet.'

'Is that what they teach you at police school? To get people to describe feet?'

'Just describe the feet, Lewis.'

'Fine, Sherlock. Black shoes, slightly muddy. Lace-up. Grey trousers with a turn up. Oh, for God's sake, don't look at me like that. Do you want me to describe the mud as well? Elementary,

205

my dear Eccles. Dirt or clay? Plainly a gardener or potter, what? After all, when one has discounted the impossible . . .'

Eccles interrupts. 'I'll tell you what they teach us at police school. They teach us that, at times of high excitement, the brain is as unreliable as a story in your newspaper. Grey trousers? Muddy shoes?'

'Yeah, Quincey. That's what I said. Grey trousers and muddy shoes.'

'Quincey was a doctor. You're thinking of Colombo.'

Now I'm thinking of Greebo. Why do I feel guilty that I haven't told the Plod about Greebo?

'Don't patronise me.'

Eccles yawns. 'You just described your own feet, Lewis. Look at them.'

I stare at my reflection in the silver Vespa. He's right. Those feet, in their muddy black shoes and slate grey trousers, with turnups, stare back. One of them taps, as though embarrassed. Those feet, Fingers' feet, are my own.

'I'm cracking up,' I mumble.

'Possibly,' says the policeman. 'Or you're drunk, or you're taking the piss. I don't much care which. You want some friendly advice? Piss off home. I see you here in ten minutes, and you're spending the night in the cells.'

'Grease is the word,' I mutter, but I also leg it, while I can.

But here's something funny. Obviously, the silver Vespa doesn't go anywhere that night. Who's going to steal a moped from the third floor of a hotel? It's still there when Eccles and I leave the room, it's still there when the party ends, and it's even still there very early the following morning when the men from Coutts come back to pick it up. Joe Bastin's platinum disc of his *Greatest Hits*, on the other hand, isn't. Exactly when it goes, nobody knows for sure. But it's gone.

'I'm not talking about the thief.'

Six forty-five a.m. I've just heard the news, and Lauren Laverne is playing Carter USM's 'Only Living Boy in New Cross' on XFM. In my tiny shower cubicle (which doubles, rather inelegantly, as my flat's toilet), I wonder why I am awake so early. It must be enthusiasm. A lust for life, and a love of the job. I don't feel mad anymore. Fingers was definitely there, and so was I. And I nearly caught him. Front page, here I come.

I step out, towel off, and kick Daniel's horrible, pudding-smeared suit from the wear-again-if-necessary pile (most of the floor) to the wash-damn-you-wash pile (under the bed). With a yawn and a stretch, I travel the two steps into my kitchen and open the curtains. The tatty white buildings nearby all look a kind of watery yellow, and shadows of swaying trees fringe their lower floors. The streets are quiet enough to hear the sounds of individual cars. The odd bird, even. Is it always like this at this time in the morning? I had no idea.

As I dress and catch the lift downstairs, I'm actually humming.

I'm hungover, but in a rather wild, excited way. It's going to be a good day. I'm feeling quite so chipper, I even risk conversation with Lenny, the porter.

'Morning Lenny.'

Lenny looks up from behind his desk. His eyes are marble yellow affairs, lurking behind puffy eyelids that could be bloody scallops. 'Morning Mr . . . Sir,' he says.

This is deliberately rude. I've been living here a year. Lenny sees both me pass, and the name on my post, every day. He knows exactly what I'm called. He just wants to make sure that I realise he doesn't think I'm important enough for him to bother with. Wait until he sees tomorrow's newspaper. Arsehole.

Outside, though, my mood is Lenny-proof. Big green delivery vans are reversing past Harrods. An unmarked minibus is unloading traffic wardens on the corner of Sloane Street. This is London, preparing for the day, with a smell of damp bananas and newsprint. There's something rather inclusive about it all. I'm smiling. I think I'll walk to work. It's mornings like this that make me wish I knew how to jog.

By the tube, I run an eye over the headlines in the news stand. Nobody has anything about the theft of Bastin's platinum disc. It must have only happened a couple of hours ago. The *Gazette*, I notice, has a very small box on the front page, written by Rebecca and explaining that the heavy police presence at the party meant that the event passed without incident. I wonder where she got that from. I also wonder how I'm going to be able to get through the day without laughing outright in her smug, ill-informed face.

I head down Sloane Street, and cut in towards Belgravia. The streets are still surprisingly quiet, at least around here. I suppose that's because it's a residential area, but a residential area that's quite so posh that most people either don't have to go to work, or went to work hours ago.

Assuming that I one day make friends with somebody who lives within a mile of my flat (Daniel is my closest friend, distance-wise, and he lives near Victoria), I could really get used to living around here. I could really feel I belonged. Perhaps that's just the romantic in me. I used to get the same sensation in Brixton, with its burnt-out cars and yellow signs boasting homicides. Not so much in Hampstead, though. Perhaps it would have felt different had I not been living in a commune of swingers. Who can say?

A chill wind hits me as I enter Belgrave Square, but it's the kind of chill wind that lifts your spirits. It's fresh and new. Life is good. I find myself lighting a cigarette, which is kinda sick at this time in the morning, but just feels right. For a couple of months, during my Brixton days, I was seeing a girl who lived around here. Tamzin. Dumped me eventually for a guy she had known since she was three. Posh as a corgi in a tiara. She wanted to be a writer, and I could never escape the sensation that I was just some kind of character study. I'd just got my first job stuffing envelopes for *Poshbird Monthly* at the time, which was something that she and her slightly hellish friends found hysterical. 'You of all people!' they used to bray, as though I was a direct descendant of an actual pit pony. I think I was the most working-class person they had ever met, save for people like gardeners and driving instructors. They had no concept of middle class. Quite seriously. I remember there was one of her friends who had the wrong sort of posh genes – big arse sort. Emily or Emilia, I forget which. Anyway, she once asked me if I ever carried a knife. True story.

It's good to walk. I should do it more often. It gives you a chance to think. I feel refreshed and quick-witted, and as I turn down the street towards the *Gazette*'s office, it's still only 8.10. Even Rebecca probably won't be in yet.

———

But she is. She's lurking at her desk, half-concealed behind a monitor in a manner which suggests, somehow, that she's been there quite a while. I feel a flash of annoyance as I sling my jacket over the back of my chair, but suppress it.

'Morning,' I say.

'Hi,' she says, looking towards me and then doing a double-take. 'Sorry. Thought you were Philip. What the hell are you doing here?'

I play dumb. 'What? Have I been sacked?'

Rebecca nods towards the clock above Brainchild's door. 'Not yet. But the little hand and the big hand are still obtuse. I don't usually expect you until they get distinctly acute.'

'What?'

'The time, Mac. It's early. Have you heard?'

I should imagine I stick out my chest. I tend to, at such times. 'I have done more than merely *heard*, my dear. I was *there*.'

Rebecca stands up. 'You were what?'

'I was there,' I tell her. 'I had a ticket all along. I was magnif-icent. I staked out the room. I saw somebody acting suspiciously, and I gave chase. I damn nearly caught him as well. It'll make a great piece. There was this moment when I tripped . . .'

'You prick,' says Rebecca, and she's almost smiling. Not a nice smile, though. 'I'm not talking about Fingers.'

I am derailed. 'What are you talking about?'

'I'm talking about my rapist,' she says, and my day begins to collapse.

Void is a new bar in the deepest, darkest depths of Chelsea. In fact, Void *is* the deepest, darkest depths of Chelsea. That's the gimmick. It's a labyrinthine and cavernous place, and almost entirely devoid of light. There are three small strips of LEDs running along the floor – a dark red strip in the middle to stop you from walking into walls, a line of pink arrows on one side leading to the ladies, and a line of blue ones on the other leading to the gents. Aside from an occasional bit of subtle back-lighting, the hazy cherries of cigarettes, and the jagged sparks of Fulhamite Zippos, that's pretty much it. Punters are expected to bump, grind, snog and lick, or at the very least talk loudly about the, like, existentialness of it all. Dreadful. I went there a couple of weeks ago, just after it opened. That's 'opened', by the way, with a small 'o'. It hadn't yet 'Opened'. It 'Opened' yesterday.

It was a very middle-ranking affair, this Opening. No celebrities of note, but then it's not meant to be that kind of bar. It's for young professionals, workies like me, with the odd smattering of West London trustafarians thrown in. It's owned by a guy called Mick Home, who I've run into at Paxy's a couple of time. Essex lad on the make. He knows his market, does Mick. Accountants, lawyers, bankers, architects, medics and advertising types, all trying to pretend they are still at university. You know the kind of night? Pretty much our entire junior staff was invited, but I don't think many bothered to go. I'd have gone, had I not been at the Bastin bash.

At the back-lit glowing violet bar of Void, at around 9.30 last night, something happened to the vodka-based cocktail of a girl whose name we all now know, but are not allowed to use. Somebody put a pill in it.

What followed couldn't have happened if it hadn't been so dark. There was a girl, who we shall be calling 'Miss X'. Miss X is twenty-seven, works as a lawyer, and lives at the more fashionable end of Shepherd's Bush. She's the sort of person who, while you probably won't have heard of her, you might have heard of her parents if you read the right society columns in the right Sunday newspapers. She's an Almost – she could have been a lowly 'it girl' if she hadn't inherited not only a trust fund but also a brain, and thus decided to have a crack at real life instead.

Miss X was out with friends – some of whom you might very well have heard of. They'd been to a bar in town before, and were planning to end up at Bijous afterwards. They started on vodka Red Bulls, and from then on began to experiment. Vodka and orange juice. Vodka and cranberry. Vodka and Baileys, vodka and white wine, and, ultimately, vodka and something quite different. Miss X's friends say they last saw her chatting to a guy by the bar. I can't tell you his name either, but that's because I don't know it. He was tall, he was wearing jeans, a blazer and a stripy shirt. They couldn't say any more. They didn't see any more.

Miss X's friends only noticed she was missing when they all piled out to a taxi, en route to their next port of call. It's not easy to find a missing friend in a nightclub without any lights. They searched the bar, they searched the dancefloor, they searched the booths. They even searched the toilets, male and female alike. Nothing. They assumed she had left, and marched on to Bijous regardless. Later, one of them was snapped by a guy from the *Mail* with a telephone camera, sitting on the knee of Prince Harry.

Void may have opened, but it wasn't entirely finished. There was a small area, tucked behind the cigarette machine, that was going to be turned into a cloakroom, or into more booths. Mick hadn't decided yet. Either way, it was as dark as the rest of the place – darker even, as it didn't even have the LEDs. To get there, you had to climb over a chair. In the subterranean gloom, nobody was even aware of it.

That's where the cleaners found Miss X. Drunk, drugged and asleep, with her Miss Sixty fishnets around her ankles.

Quite knocked my thief off the front pages, let me tell you.

'Take me somewhere sensational.'

'Rebecca!'

I glower into my monitor. I need a quote, any quote. I am battling, deep in a world of Ventrama Import Exports, Kyoto, Ito Takamura, and Japanese directory enquiries. After calling the buggers something like forty times, I am beginning to suspect that the number international directory enquiries gave me was old, incorrect, or maliciously false. I may have found his home number, but I may not. It's hard to be sure. Japanese directory enquiries are not, I am discovering, the easiest people for a non-Japanese-speaking UK journalist to deal with. Either way, there is no answer. So, along with knocking out the odd paragraph about footballers' wives and politicians' dogs, I am spending my day as I spend so many of my days – trawling through web pages I do not understand, hoping that one of them will have a keyword and a phone number. I am beyond caring what is happening to Rebecca. I am beyond even looking up. I do not mind that she is the centre of attention. I have no interest in the endless lines of colleagues who are sidling up to her, for her attention, or approval, or to share a theory or a contact. I don't care. I feel nothing. I am beyond it.

'Rebecca! Just heard from a chap at the Yard. Definitely Mr Spike. They say they've got a DNA match!'

'Rebecca! Terribly *pleased* with how *diligently* you're *approaching* this. I must say it makes a lovely *change* to see this kind of *professionalism*.'

'Rebecca! Just in on *BBC News 24!* They're questioning Mick Home!'

'Rebecca! *Reme tene; verba sequenter!*'

'Rebecca! Darling! Nice to see we'll have a sensible front page for once.'

'Rebecca! How can I help?'

'Rebecca! Any ideas for illustrations?'

'Rebecca! Have you spoken to that policeman Eccles yet? He's been calling for you all day.'

'Rebecca! Woman on the phone says she's been date-raped fourteen times. Wrote a book about it, and did a play. Wants to know if we want a side-bar. Any views?'

'Rebecca! We've had a chap outside Miss X's house all day. We've got a snap of her in a tracksuit, taking out a binbag. We'd have to black out the eyes, and we'll get complaints, but nobody else is going to run it. What do you reckon?'

'Rebecca! Mick Home has been released without charge!'

'Rebecca! Channel 4 on the *phone*. Lady called Felicity *Straps*. *Head* of *Drama*. Wants to have a *chat* about your search for Mr Spike. Can you see her *tomorrow?*'

That's it. That's fucking it. I slap the off switch of my monitor, shove my notebook into my pocket, and storm off to the lift.

———

Where I meet Lucy. She looks startled to see me.

'You didn't call,' she says.

'Neither did you,' I say.

'How are you?' she says.

'Shitty,' I say.

'Are you going home?' she says.

'Yes,' I say.

'Can I come?' she says.

'If you want.'

Afterwards, we sleep, wake, and get stoned on the remnants of Ross's pot. Idlewild are on my stereo and my lights are dimmed. Lucy sits at one end of the bed in my holey green Cure T-shirt, rolling, licking and twisting. I'm at the other, hands behind my head. It's a heady, greying night – think London, think summer, think of the way that warm dust drifts across the mosaic entrance halls of those faded whitewashed stucco townhouses. Now and again an edgy breeze will invade through the open window, making me shiver, although pleasantly. There's a sense of resigned contentment in the air. Or maybe just in my mind. Things are fragile, but okay.

'Listen,' says Lucy, and as my fingers close around the joint, she grabs them with her other hand. 'I want to see my painting.'

I stare.

'My painting,' she repeats. 'I want to see it.'

'Oh.'

'But it doesn't seem to be here.'

'Ah.'

'And last time I stayed here you told me it was getting framed.'

I take a drag, and nod. 'Yeah. Yeah, right . . .'

Lucy looks out the window, to Harrods and Hyde Park and

215

heaven. 'But I can't think why that would take two weeks. Or, really, why you'd bother.'

'Babe, I swear . . .' I have no idea what I swear.

'And also, I was speaking to Julie.'

'Julie . . .'

'Julie from two desks down.'

'Julie from two desks down . . .'

She sighs. 'Julie who you fucked the night they sacked Daniel Kemp.'

'Oh right. Julie.'

'Yeah.' Barely looking at me, Lucy retrieves her joint. 'Julie. Julie says you painted her, too. And Julie says she never saw the painting. And Carole Pickles, that sub, and you must remember *her*, because you sat next to her for a year, and fucked her too, the night *she* got sacked, well, Julie said you painted her as well. So I phoned her and guess what? She never saw her painting either.'

I close my eyes, and watch the crazy stoned swirl on the inside of my eyelids. But this isn't going away. 'Look,' I say. 'Julie . . .'

'Lucy.'

Jesus. 'Lucy, right. I just . . . I just don't like to . . .'

'So either – and I've thought about this – you've got this vast, secret horde of paintings of various people you've fucked, hidden away somewhere in this tiny flat, or you've never really painted anybody at all. Because some people, who you haven't fucked, like Margaret who does the front desk, and Jenny, the editor's PA, they say you've offered to paint them, too. So either way, I feel a bit of an idiot, you know?'

'Oh Christ. Look, Lucy. I'm just . . . I'm not a very . . .'

She hands me the joint. 'Answer me just one thing. Is it here?'

I inhale, staring fixedly at a point high above her nose.

She says it again. 'Is the picture here?'

'No,' I say.

Lucy flops back on the bed. I put a hand on her ankle, and she doesn't shake it away.

'Take me somewhere sensational,' she says, suddenly, distantly, and I'm afraid she means Mauritius or the Seychelles. But then she adds, 'not the Met or Rex or anywhere like that. Somewhere different. Somewhere sensational. I want to have the wildest night of my life.'

I let go of her ankle and blow a smoke ring at the ceiling. 'What day is it?'

'It's Friday,' says Lucy. I still can't see her face. 'It's the weekend. I want to go somewhere sensational.'

'Get dressed,' I tell her, and because I can't think of anywhere better, because I fancy going there myself and, frankly, because I'm a bit of a bastard, I take her to Paxy's.

'Mr Mac! Thank heavens you've come. Do you know, there's simply not a person here worth speaking to?'

Friday night at Paxy's. The host himself answers the door, squatting in his hallway, swaying between the walls. He's wearing velvet slippers, underpants and a tie. His right hand sticks out, formally, to shake my own. His left is fumbling to contain a bottle of Grouse, one of those skinny cigars with the white plastic mouthpieces, and the left heel of the utterly naked redhead he is balancing on his back. Friday night at Paxy's. I really haven't done this for a while.

'Paxy,' I say loudly, to be heard over the shrieks, crashes and, oddly, Def Leppard blasting out from inside. 'Thought I'd drop by. This is Lucy, by the way.'

'Enchanted,' growls Paxy, giving a curt nod.

'Oh my God,' says Lucy, faintly.

'What's with the music?' I enquire.

Paxy shrugs, cumbersomely. 'Isn't the strangest thing? Blame Mr Bolton, if you can find him. He's just got back from a sojourn with the *norte americanos*. Brought some guests with him. They do move well, I have to say. Squadron of table dancers from some place like San Diego.'

'Santa Cruz,' squeals the redhead.

Paxy tilts his head. 'I don't believe we've met,' he remarks.

'Candi,' his passenger coos, 'from Santa Cruz.'

'Hmmm,' muses Paxy, and moves away, past fluttering candles in slicks of wax and fallen bottles of Oddbins wine glugging their contents onto the floor. A male couple in suits are huddled on the floor by the coat-stand, kissing violently. Three girls in halternecks share a joint by the bottom of the stairs; one licks Candi's leg as she is borne past. On the mezzanine landing, two naked men fence with walking-sticks; all around people dance, kiss, cartwheel, disrobe.

Lucy clutches my arm. 'What *is* this place?'

'Friend's house,' I tell her, leading her inside. 'I use to live here. Like it?'

She pushes past, stepping ahead so that she's leading me. 'It's amazing,' she says, and for some nameless reason, I suddenly feel slightly sad.

We end up in the drawing room, whereupon I briefly abandon Lucy in order to commandeer a bottle of Finlandia vodka from the secret drinks cupboard by the bookcase. By the time I glance back across the room, she's ensconced on a sofa, deep in conversation with somebody I can't quite see, who is either a girl or dressed as one. Not fussed, frankly.

Bony fingers grip my elbow, and I spin around. It's Carolyn Somethingorother, in a clingy silver shift dress that makes her look like a supermodel. She says something indistinct, and then slaps me in the face so hard that my head whips to the side.

Anywhere else, this would attract attention.

I grab her wrist in case she does it again. 'Hell was that for?'

Carolyn is giggling, plainly wasted. She leans in towards me, close. 'I've got a bone to pick with you,' she says.

'How so?' I ask. She shouldn't talk about bones, this girl. She's too bony to talk about bones.

'Even after,' she begins, effortfully enunciating each individual word, 'our little chat, the scooter didn't go. Did you notice that? Big silver scooter, just waiting to be stolen. Insured and everything. Perfect. But no. No. You had to steal a bloody disc. Rude, Mac, rude.'

'Not me,' I tell her.

Her head lolls. 'Whatever. Your friend, then.'

'Nothing to do with me whatsoever. Barely even made the paper, though. You notice that?'

Carolyn nods, or sways. 'Oh yes. Joe was furious. You here alone?'

I point a thumb over my shoulder. 'With Lucy.'

'Ah yes.' She sniggers. 'Lucy *Denton*. Your *girlfriend*.'

'Yes. No. Just a date. You?'

'My date is currently trying to get into the pants of your date.'

I turn, curious. Oh. The girl on the sofa is Melissa, the boyish blonde whose tights I so unsatisfyingly mauled on my last visit here. 'I see. I had no idea you were . . . so inclined.'

'Melissa inclined? But aren't we all?'

I close my eyes, feeling seedy. 'Same sex inclined, I meant.'

'So did I,' says Carolyn, and suddenly she doesn't seem that drunk at all.

I'm beginning to remember why I don't much like Carolyn. She pushes past me, towards the sofa. I turn my back on her, and decide to explore.

'Overexposure.'

n the kitchen, I find Neil. He's standing on a chair with his camera, taking photographs of a group of girls posing by the microwave. 'Mac,' he says, and nods towards the table. 'With you in a moment. Have some absinthe.'

I abandon my vodka, and sit down among a group of American men, all with leather trousers and noses like Ronnie Wood. They're silent, but not unfriendly. One passes me a bottle of murky green stuff, apparently mixed with twigs, and I grab a shot glass and a sugar bowl with a teaspoon in it from the centre of the table.

Ray, Neil and I developed quite a thing for absinthe when we were living in Brixton. I think it's the paraphernalia aspect that appeals – it's such a complex process to consume, that you get an extra glow of self-satisfaction, alongside the alcohol, simply by knowing what to do. It works thus: you pour a shot into a glass, and balance a sugar cube on your teaspoon, before lowering the spoon into the liquid, and holding it there until the sugar cube is soaked and translucent. Then you set fire to the sodden sugar cube, until it melts into a gloopy syrup that looks like Fairy Liquid. This you mix into the glass, and knock the whole thing back before it cools. Once, in Brixton, our sweet old lady neighbour saw us out the window, mixing some up in the garden. She was never quite so friendly again. I think she thought we'd gone a bit *Trainspotting*.

The Worzelish Americans seem to approve of my competence, and one offers me a Lucky Strike. I accept it, wordlessly. Men. We are Men. We drink, we smoke, and we do so silently. Neil finishes taking his photographs, whispers something to one of the girls and joins us. He drinks. I drink. We all drink.

Oscar Wilde was a fan of absinthe. What was it he said? 'After the first glass you see things as you wish they were. After the second you see things as they are not. Finally you see things as they really are, and that is the most horrible thing in the world.' I'm not sure that's true. I've had five now, and things are all still looking pretty rosy.

'Come upstairs,' says Neil, suddenly. It must be the first thing anybody has said to me for almost an hour.

'Why?'

'My bag is up there. I've got some pictures to show you.'

I nod and follow him from the table, pinching another Lucky as I go.

Lucy, Melissa and Carolyn have all vanished from the sofa, but Paxy's is still in full swing. We pass it all, and make our way up the stairs. I have to tug myself up by the chipped wooden banister, which has given me terrible splinters in the past. Maybe it is doing so now.

Neil says he left his bag in a second-floor bedroom, but we find it on the landing outside. The bedroom itself is locked and, doubtless, occupied. I'm thinking of that living-room sofa, on which Lucy, Melissa and Carolyn were no longer sitting. Are those giggles? Or am I imagining them?

'How thoughtful to leave it outside,' murmurs Neil.

I'm breathing shallowly. It must have been the climb. 'What are these pictures?' I manage.

'They're from that MOFO thing,' he says. 'When Sophie Gerad had that choker nicked. There's some of you, some of me, and some of . . . well, all kinds of people. I wanted to see if you recognise anybody I don't. He must have been there, right?'

This smacks of co-operation, and I am instinctively wary of it. Nonetheless, I nod. He must have been there. The photographs are large and black and white. Neil shakes them out of an envelope. There's me, there's him. There's Carolyn, there's Jessica. There's Freddie Windsor, Clarissa Mountejoy, Iain Bovery, Petrina Khashoggi. I recognise almost everybody. And if I do, and Neil doesn't, then whatever he says, he's going to be furious.

'I recognise almost everybody.'

'So do I,' says Neil, rather too quickly. 'But look. What about him?'

I peer. 'That's a guy called Douglas.'

There is an intake of breath. 'Is he famous?'

'Not at all. He's a friend of Paxy's. I wonder what he was doing there.'

'Paxy was there, too,' says Neil.

'Was he? Really? I had no idea.'

'Well,' says Neil. 'You were wasted. You didn't have a clue. There was one guy you were insisting was Jean Paul Gaultier's boyfriend, and it plainly wasn't. What about this guy?'

'That's Will Ramsey. He's a journalist. I was at school with him. Paxy knows him as well. He's sometimes here.'

Neil makes a note of this. 'Any chance he's our man?'

'Will?' I laugh, which turns into a hiccough, which turns into a wheezing cough. 'I doubt it. He's an indie kid. Not into the glitz.'

'And him?'

I frown. It's a slightly weird side profile. 'That's just Jensen, isn't it?'

'Who?'

'That arsehole Jensen. Jensen Randall.'

'It could be, I suppose,' says Neil, turning the picture on its side. 'But isn't it pronounced Yansen?'

I feel sick. 'Whatever.'

Neil scribbles. 'Oh,' he says finally. 'And there's this one. This is my favourite.'

The photograph looks like it was taken in a snowstorm. There is an explosion of brightness from behind, and a pair of indistinct silhouettes in the foreground.

'Wow,' I manage.

'It's a mess, isn't it?' muses Neil, as if in agreement. 'I hope they weren't anybody important.'

Whoever they are, one is plainly a woman, and the other is a man. The man is in a suit. The woman is wearing something high-necked and Oriental-ish, and there is something about the provocative set of her shoulders that I half-recognise.

'I think that could be my friend Elspeth,' I say, pointing, 'from Edinburgh. But I couldn't be sure. The other person could be anyone.'

Neil chuckles. 'It could be, couldn't it? I could have a photograph of Fingers here, couldn't I? He could be wearing a bloody mask and carrying a swag bag, and I'd never know.'

This is true. I study the picture from a variety of angles. It almost hurts to stare at it. 'What went wrong?' I ask.

'Overexposure,' says Neil. 'Too much light.'

Two people, posing at a glitzy party, and behind them the bomb finally drops. Is this how the world will end?

'I thought light was meant to be a good thing,' I mumble.

Neil shrugs. 'You can have too much of a good thing,' he says, and takes the photographs back. 'Well, that's the lot. Let's go get fucked, heh?'

I don't follow him. Instead I stand still, swaying, watching him go. Is that a giggle? I'm sure it is. I clench my fist, ready to know, and then think better of it.

This old house is a creaky old house and up here, strangely, it's quiet enough to hear the walls move. Perhaps it's because it's falling apart, with floorboards either bare or covered with scraps of rugs, and plasterboard walls with cracks in them so big that you can see the thin strips of wood that the Victorians used as insulation. We had wireless internet here, I remember, and a hacked NTL box and a Playstation. We had a table tennis table in one of the spare bedrooms and we spent hours, Paxy, me, and an Australian girl called Jane, piling magazines under the legs in order to make it perfectly flat. We did all these things, had all these things, thought to do all these things, and yet we never thought to plaster the walls, or even wallpaper them. There's something truly horrible about that, don't you think?

Things were never this bad, though, when I lived here. Even the rugs are threadbare now and, through the wooden plank floor, I can see the occasional glimmer of light from the festivities downstairs. I am walking, I realise, away from the stairs, along the second floor corridor that leads towards the narrow step-ladder up to what used to be my room, in the attic. I wrap my arms around myself – I'm only wearing a thin T-shirt and I'm suddenly freezing. At the end of the corridor, I see, a window is missing a pane of glass. There's a pile of leaves and moonlight in the corner, and a smell like dead birds.

The stepladder to the attic is fractured and precarious. I used to have the walls up here lined with sarongs and posters, with rugs on the floor, low tables and a futon. I had a disco ball, and a switch that made it dance. I used to feel like Mick Jagger in this room, Puckish and Moroccan, impossibly sexy. I had my laptop on a table by the window, and a coat stand by the door.

Only the futon remains, coffee-stained and seedy in the corner. The light switch does nothing but emit a faint spark of blue. The window here, also, is cracked, and the walls are as bare and brittle as the floorboards. All I can hear now is the wind. I step across through the gloom, towards the futon, and sit down, curl into a ball. I'm shivering. Is there even a party downstairs? Is there? Really? Or am I a madman, perhaps, turned suddenly sane, alone and freezing in a derelict house?

Perhaps, I muse, this is what happens when one enters these rooms alone. I could come up here with Lucy, or Melissa, or even Carolyn, and this place would seem flushed with warmth. Patterns would billow once more from the walls, soft carpet would caress the underside of my padding feet. My mother read me one of those kids' horror stories once, about vampires living in a paradise of lush palaces, where they drank wondrous wines and wore the finest robes. Only when they stopped drinking their daily blood, these vampires, would they realise that the palaces were stinking shells, the wines were ditchwater, and their clothes were rags.

I'm startled to realise that I'm crying. This is downright embarrassing. I'm drunk, and I'm being absurd. I topple to one side, and I sleep.

The next thing I know, I'm in the bathroom downstairs, it's a while later, and I'm being violently sick. I'm short of breath, and my legs feel springy – perhaps I have been running. Perhaps I awoke upstairs, felt sick, and ran down here to the nearest bathroom. That seems perfectly possible. I just can't remember it happening.

Out in the corridor, I gouge at my eyes. I am a crocodile, with a second set of translucent eyelids for swimming underwater. I'd make a lousy crocodile. Mine are misty and blurred.

Somebody pushes past me, and I feel an elbow in my chest. There's an apology, and a rush of air. I am no crocodile. I am an old man, fucked in a war.

I must have been asleep for a while. The house is quieter now, the music has stopped. There are plenty of people around, huddled chatting in corners, dozing against walls, but there is an atmosphere of afterparty, rather than of party itself. I don't know what time it is. My mobile is in my pocket, but I can't be bothered to look. I should go home. Or I should go into the living room and sleep on a sofa.

Lucy. I came here with Lucy. What happened to her?

There is already somebody curled up on the big sofa in the living room.

'Sorry,' I mumble, and slump into a chair.

'Mac?'

'Lucy?' No. Not Lucy.

The somebody is leaning forward, looking concerned. 'Are you okay?'

'Tippity top,' I answer, brightly. 'And you're . . . Rebecca?'

'Of course I'm Rebecca,' says Rebecca. 'You don't look tippity top. Are you sure you're okay?'

I feel cunning. Heavy-lidded, admittedly, but cunning. 'Are you sure you're Rebecca?'

'Are you on drugs?'

'You're a dream. How do I know this isn't a dream? Maybe I'm still upstairs, in the bathroom.'

Rebecca curses, and I feel a stinging sensation in my cheek.

'Did you just slap me? Why did you slap me?'

'I'll fucking punch you in a minute,' snaps Rebecca, and I open my eyes, properly, and become properly awake.

'Oh,' I say, and because I can't think of anything else to say, I say it again. 'Oh.'

Rebecca is still in her work clothes, and holding a huge glass of red wine, which is the same dark oxblood as her shirt. She looks tired, but fresh, which makes me suspect she hasn't drunk very much of it. Suspicious behaviour, at this time on a Friday.

'What are you *doing* here?' she asks. 'I always knew you were a slag but . . . Jesus Christ, Mac.'

'What are *you* doing here?' I bitch back, defensively.

'I'm working,' says Rebecca.

I sit bolt upright. A challenge. 'No,' I say. 'Listen. No. That's not allowed. This place . . . this place . . . no . . .'

Rebecca tells me to relax. She's not working that much, she says. She's not going to write anything. She just thought she should check the place out. She came with friends. As it happens, she's been having quite a good night.

'Oh,' I say, and I suppose I leer. 'So have you been . . .'

'I have *not*,' she snaps, rather savagely, and then her tone softens. 'Have you?'

'No,' I tell her. 'I don't do that. I used to, but I don't anymore.' This is true, and I only realise as I say it. Or maybe it only becomes true as I say it. Either way, it's true.

'Of course.' Rebecca curls her legs up underneath her on the sofa. 'Lucy. The girlfriend. Quite enough to tempt any man to chastity, I should expect.'

I grimace. 'Don't. She's here somewhere. I think. She wandered off with . . . with a couple of people.' I hesitate for a moment. 'I think we may have a problem, she and I.'

'It does sound that way,' agrees Rebecca.

'No.' I shake my head. 'Not just that. Her friends are awful. Really awful. Scary awful. And she seems to show no interest in mine at all. Except for this evening, obviously. And that's the wrong kind of interest altogether. I suppose she might just think my friends are awful. But we aren't *awful.* Are we?'

Rebecca looks amused. She sips her wine. 'Are you suggesting that we're friends?'

'Oh leave it, Rebecca. You know what I mean. Anyway, it's not just that. The girl knows nothing about me. She doesn't even know my name. She calls me "Maahk".'

'Maybe she thinks you're somebody else.'

'Maybe. God knows.' I yawn and stretch and spot a half-smoked Benson in an ashtray by my feet. Rebecca makes a disgusted choking sound, but still tosses me a book of matches. 'Thanks,' I say, catching them. 'So who are you dating these days? A Formula One driver? Robbie Williams? Jensen Randall?'

She snorts. 'Nobody. All single men are drunks or idiots.'

I nod, sadly. 'I suppose we are. Ah well. You're not my type, anyway.'

'Yeah, I can tell. You like them dimmer and blonder, don't you?'

I frown. 'Elspeth is a brunette. And she's cleverer than me.'

'I thought she was called Lucy.'

'Someone else. Anyway, Eccles fancies you. I'm sure of it.'

'Tom St Eccles?' says Rebecca. 'The policeman?'

'Yeah. Very dashing. That chin.'

Rebecca shakes her head. 'Isn't he married? He must be. He's so calm and responsible.'

'I'll find out. Listen, why *are* you here? You don't think this place could have something to do with your Mr Spike?'

Rebecca blinks, and puts her eyes on mine. 'Well don't you?'

'Not at all.'

'Really? Bunch of promiscuous posh kids in a wanky media hellhole like this? You don't think it's worth a look?'

I take a drag, which tastes of charcoal, and I cough. 'No. Although I can see why you think that. But no. It's not *cool* here, Rebecca. It's not even properly depraved. It used to be. But now it's not. It's just kinda silly.'

'What changed?'

I shrug, and then start to laugh. 'Overexposure,' I tell her. 'Too much light.'

Rebecca frowns. 'I should be very surprised,' she says, 'if our nice friendly rapist had never sat in this very room.'

'Oh really?' I'm laughing at her solemnity. 'Got a lead, have we?'

'You honestly think I'd share it with you if I did?'

'Go on. You tell me yours, I'll tell you mine.'

There's a gleam in her eye. It might even be humour. 'I don't want to know yours. Why would I want to know yours?'

I'm still laughing. 'Oh, I see. I'm stuck on yesterday's story, with all its attendant glitz, fluff and nonsense, and you're dealing with the real, hard-hitting future. Am I right?'

'Damn right.'

'Bitch,' I say, and she actually laughs. The last year feels like a waste, suddenly.

'I don't get you, Mac,' she says.

'Yeah you do. That's the problem.'

'No.' She shakes her head. 'I don't. You know what's going on. You know everything that is wrong with your life, but you make no effort to change it. You revel in it. All these girls. What are you doing chasing some bauble-stealing nobody? You know stuff. You're educated. You should be doing my job. You'd be great at it, if you wanted to be. You might even be better than me.'

I'm shocked. 'You're being very . . . nice.'

'No I'm not. I don't do nice. I'm just baffled. I know you think I've got a . . . a stick up my arse, or something. I care about stuff, Mac. I was brought up to. This rapist guy, he's not just a diversion, you know. He's not just some rival story. He's a guy, going round London, drugging women and having sex with them. Why doesn't that matter to you, Mac? It's *bad* that he gets knocked off the front page. It's *wrong*. You're just so *flippant*.'

I honestly cannot think of a non-flippant way to reply.

'I don't think you've got much longer, Mac. You know that, don't you?'

I close my eyes. 'Kind of,' I say.

'You just piss off too many people. And you haven't got any allies. The only one you ever had was Daniel. There's Hargreaves, maybe, but he won't be around for ever. But they don't want to sack you. It's expensive. They're hoping you'll leave.'

I open my eyes. 'Why would I leave?'

'Developments,' she says, portentously.

'What developments? And why did you say that portentously?'

'*The Talk of the Town*,' she says, but she says it in a funny accent, like the voiceover at the beginning of an action film.

'What is that supposed to mean? Are we talking about Jensen?'

'I can't tell you. Or rather, I could, but then you'd leave now, and they'd know that it must have come from me. I don't want that.'

I gaze at her, balefully. 'So what do you think I should do? What would you do if you were me?'

Rebecca smiles at me, in a way that seems entirely genuine. It probably is. I suppose that's how she can be nasty so often, because that's genuine, too. 'Well, starting on Monday, I'd make sure I caught that pointless bloody thief. Although I might start clearing out my desk and backing up my email, as well.'

'And starting tonight?'

'I'd go home. And sleep. I'm in Vauxhall. Shall we share a taxi?'

I yawn, loud and long. I do, really, want to get to bed.

'I should find Lucy,' I say, half-heartedly.

Rebecca stands up. 'Will she really want to be found?'

'I'm not sure. Maybe. She is meant to be my girlfriend. It is *kind* of serious.'

Rebecca arches an eyebrow. 'It can't be that serious if she calls you Mark.'

I shake my head. 'I never said she called me Mark.'

'Yes you did.'

'No.' I shake my head. 'You misheard. I said she calls me Maaahk.'

Rebecca stares at me for a moment. 'Yes,' she says, finally. 'That's a lot better, isn't it?'

'See what you mean. Let's go.'

'Let's.'

And we do. And the whole way back, I don't even flirt. I certainly don't lunge. And we talk, about nothing much, like friends do. And when the taxi pulls up outside my ridiculous flat, I give her twenty quid and tell her I'll see her on Monday. And she smiles, and I smile back. And that's that.

'I need buttons.'

Because the Jew Ball will be chock full of Jews, they had to have it on a Saturday night, rather than a Friday. And because they're having it on a Saturday night, in the summer, they have to wait until 10 p.m. before it can start, so that the Sabbath can end first.

The Princess, however, has been cunning. The ball is being held in the Samfried Hotel, near Heathrow, and the smart wee minx has arranged for a trainee rabbi to hold an evening service in one of the function suites upstairs. This means that guests who are unconcerned about such things can start drinking at nine, those who are a bit concerned can turn up, have a drink, go pray and then start drinking again, and those who disapprove of such convenient frivolities altogether can make their devotions else-where, and still not miss too much of this whole Semitic shindig.

Janie, whose core lunacy seems to have solidified into a brittle serenity in recent weeks, calls me at about 9.30 a.m.

'Wstfgrap,' I answer, chipper as ever.

'Rise and shine!' sings Janie, and I can just picture her, standing in her hideous kitchen after going for a jog, perhaps hopping from foot to foot in a headband and a pair of cheesecloth hotpants.

'Go away, Janie,' I tell her, head thudding like a length of wobbling cardboard. 'Can I call you back in like, six hours?'

'Oh Mackie!' she keens. 'It's a beautiful morning! The sun is shining! You can smell the blossom! Even the grass looks happy!'

'Sounds hideous.'

'Listen to the grumpy man! Is it a hangover? Were you and Elspeth out on the tiles again?'

'Janie, I barely know Elspeth anymore. What do you want?'

'I wanted to check about tonight.'

I let out a deep, shuddering sigh. 'Janie, I'll be there, okay?'

'You have sorted out your dinner jacket, haven't you? You aren't going to come in that horrible kilt?'

'No, Janie. I'm not going to wear my kilt. It's all ready. It's all clean. I just need to buy a bow tie. I was thinking of a flashing red one, that revolves . . .'

Janie is as shrill as a plummeting aeroplane. 'Mackie!'

'Kidding. Kidding. I'll be smart as you like, and I'll be there by ten.'

'Eight thirty,' corrects Janie. 'I want to show support. It's a big day for Miriam.'

'Who? Who? She's called fucking *Mary*, Janie!'

'Eight thirty,' says my sister, firmly.

'No! No! It doesn't even *start* until nine! We'll just have to stand around, doing nothing, with all *Mary*'s new friends, having to be nice about Israel and discussing . . . bagels. I just won't.'

'Perhaps the time has come,' says Janie, grandly, 'for us to embrace our culture.'

233

'Christ above.'

'And less of that. You'll offend people.'

'Who? Why?'

'Eight thirty,' says Janie, again, and eventually, as usual, I give in.

There's not much hope of me getting back to sleep after that, but I roll fitfully around in my bed for a while, just in case. Half an hour later I am wide awake, and exhausted. I'm also feeling strangely detached. Because it's early, I decide to put into a call to the number that might be Ito Takamura's home. I do it on my mobile. I can claim it. A woman answers, and then hands the telephone to a man. I don't understand a word either of them says. When I introduce myself, the man screams something that might be 'Never again!' and then hangs up. I am confused. Probably a wrong number. Probably got the time zones wrong. Probably the middle of the night.

I loll back in the bed for a while, and try to read the *Economist*. It is beyond me. Eventually I rise, and wash, and dress, and decide I might as well go out.

Thanks to the voice of our generation (see earlier chapters) my dinner jacket is in a dry cleaners by Victoria Station. I'm not really feeling up to the jostle and sway of public transport, so I decide to walk. I'm in my leather jacket with the high collar, and, because it's bright, I have a huge pair of sunglasses on, over my normal glasses. I'm aware that this probably looks odd, but I don't consider that to be my problem.

Absinthe leaves a legacy, I'm remembering. It gives you dreams of razor-blades, sugar-coated in an emerald fairground gloop. And it detaches the brain, sometimes for days. I'm finding strange things amusing – bicycles, pigeons, manholes, the rich. By the time I get to Victoria, I have stopped still and laughed out loud on four separate occasions at nothing at all.

At Victoria, the young Nigerian girl in the drycleaners eyes me with unabashed distaste, and asks for photographic ID before she'll give me my suit. I show her my press card. Every one of my actions seems monumentally significant in some way. At the back of my mind, I'm trying to piece it all together. I'm trying to figure out what it all means.

I'm feeling more confident by now, so I decide to risk the tube. Across the forecourt, past the beggars who sleep outside *Starlight Express*, down the steps still slick with the footsteps of the night before. In the brash interior of the tube station, I buy a travel card, rather than a single. This feels like a little victory.

The escalators are out, so I find myself trudging into twilight down the frozen steps, which are so ingrained with dirt and grime and London that I wonder how they ever moved. Then I'm on the platform, smiling at a tiny black mouse, and then I'm on the train, feeling the encrusted tufts of the velveteen seats itch against the small of my back, where my jacket has ridden up to my hips. Then I'm squinting across the aisle at the guy opposite me, with the beard and the stripy jumper, who is smiling.

'Ray,' I say. 'Hello. This is the Victoria Line, isn't it? You've just come up from Brixton.'

'Indeed I have,' says Ray, and sticks out his hand. 'You're looking a lot better than you were last time I saw you.'

I brighten up and grab it. 'You've no idea how much that means to me. Am I really?'

'No. Not really. But less drunk. You know you're wearing two pairs of glasses? How are you, Mac?'

I snatch one away, and the twilight dissipates. 'I'm . . . complicated. I never called, did I? I was going to.'

'No probs,' says Ray, and by his smile I can see he means it.

'You're doing well, aren't you? Been reading you in the paper. Regular Sherlock Holmes. Who is it, then, this thief? The boys in the house reckon it's one of those footballers. You reckon it's a footballer?'

I wince. 'Don't really want to talk about that, Ray. What about you? Last I heard, you were in Nepal. What are you up to now?'

Ray makes a face. 'Just drama school,' he says, easily.

I stare at him. Ray spent years trying to get into drama school. Ray spent more time trying to get into drama school than I've spent trying to get into Rebecca Leighton. It's not the kind of thing I'd expect him to drop into the conversation, easily. 'You're kidding? Whereabouts?'

'Round Covent Garden way. It's okay, actually.'

'RADA? You're at *RADA*?'

'Mmmm. Where you heading now?'

'Blimey. Uh, town. I need a bow tie. Not sure.'

'I need buttons,' says Ray. 'Let's go to John Lewis and pretend to be a couple.'

So we do.

Afterwards, we find ourselves in the Cock on Great Portland Street, and I tentatively order half an Ayingerbrau. I find it hard. I'm still laughing. I'm not sure what should be so funny about pretending to be gay in John Lewis, especially considering that back in my university days it genuinely was touch and go for a while, but it never fails to crack me up. I think it's just the pretending. Ray and I used to do it all the time – pretending to be Russian, pretending to be ornithologists, pretending to be posh, pretending not to be. And God, he's a good actor. I think I can only see it now because I don't know him so well. He has this gift for making people feel uncomfortable. He exudes unsuitability. When he knelt in front of my chair outside the changing rooms and fumbled, outrageously, with a succession of bow ties around my neck, even I felt that it was something we ought to be doing in private.

One half is followed by another, and I notice that my conversation with Ray is turning into something remarkable. We're talking shit. Not newspaper politics, or even real politics, or who is making what album or who will be at which party with whom. We certainly don't talk about Fingers the Thief. We do talk about his work for the briefest of moments (I ask why he needs buttons, he tells me) but mainly we just talk stuff. About people we used to know, about people passing in the street. About froth and nonsense.

'Are you in a hurry?' he asks, eventually.

I gesture at my suit and the bag containing my bow tie. 'Not at all. I've got six hours and all I need to do is get dressed. Why?'

'I'm meant to be going to Streatham, to meet some mates in the pub. Want to come?'

Streatham. Has there really been a Streatham all these years? Just up the hill from Brixton. We used to go bowling there. A place of prams, taxi drivers and old people. It's been so long since I had anything to do with it, I'd almost forgotten it existed. There's a Streatham *and* a Knightsbridge? How can that be? We take the tube back down to Brixton, stand around with the nutters for a while, and then get bussed up through Brixton Hill to old Saint Wreatham himself. Ray's friends, none of whom I have met before, are in a grimy yet welcoming pub just past the station. David, Alex and Phil. Nice guys. I don't ask what they do, and they don't ask me.

We drink Coke, and talk about women. Then we move on to Carling, and talk about Freemasons. We go around the corner to Phil's house, where there is a Playstation 2 and two sofas, and a large coffee table with a bong in the middle of it. This is thrilling.

What have I been doing with my life? Why spend my evenings in horrible clubs, drinking warm champagne, with people I either don't know or despise, when I could be spending my life doing this? I'd forgotten life could be this way. We used to nod in this direction at Paxy's, now and again, but there were always hundreds of people everywhere, and some kind of predatory agenda to be stuck to. But this? This is idyllic. We spend an hour or two on a four-player shoot-em-up called TimeSplitters, then we watch this weird French kung-fu movie set in the Middle Ages. We talk right through it, but it's still great. I feel like a student.

'Dude,' yawns Ray eventually, when the conversation turns to supper and sending out for a pizza. 'Aren't you supposed to be somewhere? Like, with the suit and the bow tie?'

He's right. I turned my phone off during the movie, but when I turn it on again it tells me that it is quarter to nine. I'm already fifteen minutes late for Janie, not dressed, and in Streatham. As I gape, my phone goes all *Reach for the Stars*. Janie's not *angry*. She's just *disappointed*. I borrow a white shirt from Ray (it's a polo shirt, and short-sleeved, but I think I'll get away with it), dress and leave the house at a dinner-jacketed run. Not the way you want to travel through Streatham, believe me.

'A tough match for an eleven-year-old.'

t's just after ten when I get out to Heathrow. In the Samfriend, the Jew Ball is loud and alive. There's a smell of champagne and perfume in the air, and I spot Janie almost immediately. She's sitting at an otherwise deserted, round, white-draped table and wearing, I note with a slight jolt, a sari. She's gazing around the room with a blissful smile that is almost proprietary, and when she notices me, her face crinkles. I swipe a couple of glasses of something from a passing somebody, dodge through the throng, and wink at her.

'You're impossible,' she tells me, over the music from, I think, the wedding in *The Godfather*.

'You're wearing a sari,' I tell her.

'It's from India. The south. Kerala. There's a strong Jewish presence there. Margaret told me.'

'Who's Margaret?'

'Never mind Margaret. Mackie, you're late. You're impossible.

You're really, really late. I wanted us all to be together, you know? It's Mum's birthday.'

I wince, and sit down next to her. 'I doubt Mum would be too bothered,' I say, and filch a cigarette from an open packet of Silk Cut somebody has left on the table. 'I'm sorry, okay? I'll hang around late at the end. We can all be together then. I promise.'

Janie just rolls her eyes at me.

'This is really impressive, actually,' I say, looking around. 'It's huge.'

'I saw Dani Behr,' says Janie.

'Super.'

'And that girl from S Club 7. And the woman from *The Mummy*.'

'And have you seen the Princess?'

Janie looks at me for a moment, and her nose twitches in the beginnings of a snigger. 'Which one?'

It is insecurity, I know, that makes us mock this way. There is much beauty on display here tonight. The Hampstead girls, with their diamonds and fingernails, are about as bling as a Missy Elliott video, all cleavage, legs, highlights and hip-swaying walks. It is a look they work extremely well. I'm thinking of Mary's friends who I met for breakfast in that deli a few weeks ago. If that's the effort they put into a Sunday breakfast, then they've little excuse for looking anything other than mind-blowing tonight. That said, most of this lot have about as much to do with rabbis as Christina Aguilera does with the Pope. Mary's crowd are altogether more demure, with high necks and long sleeves. Hendon's answers to Audrey Hepburn.

Mary herself is looking stunning. Janie points her out to me, drinking champagne beside a grand piano. She's in a very Zeta-ish sleeveless dress of fierce, scarlet red, with her suspiciously straight black hair piled up on top. She looks scarier than I have ever seen her. Nancy Dell'Olio scary. She's surrounded by a gaggle of similarly chic models of perfection, all of whom I shoulder-barge through from behind, in order to pick her up by the waist and spin her around like a puppy.

'Mackie!' she screeches before she's even seen me, arms flailing and pointy stiletto heels hammering into my thighs. I set her down and she turns, snarling.

'Hey baby,' I say.

Out of the corner of my eye, I can see people staring, putting hands to their mouths. The Princess smoothes her dress. 'Don't *do* that!' she hisses. 'You're impossible! I'm meant to be in *charge* here! You do know that?'

'Obviously. Who else could organise a bash like this?'

She softens, although not as much as I would have hoped. 'You like it?'

'Of course. I'm in absolute awe. It's like Madame Tussauds in here. Is that really Vanessa Feltz over there?'

'Don't be snide.'

'Sorry.'

Mary is looking around, filled with a kind of nervous glee. 'Tony is really impressed,' she says. 'I think I'm going to get to run the Wrexham House awards thing.'

I stare at her. 'You what? Wrexham House? *The* Wrexham House?'

'Sure. Tony has been putting it together for years.'

'Christ. Sorry. *Gosh*. My own sister. Running the Wrexham House party. Who is it this year, anyway?'

'A documentary-maker. Somebody Cuppitt. He made that documentary about that orphanage. Place with a funny name.'

241

'Sounds thrilling.' A thought strikes me. 'Hey. Does that mean you can get me a ticket for my girlfriend?'

The Princess rolls her eyes. 'Speak nicely to Tony.'

'Tony, Tony, Tony. Who the hell is Tony?'

'My boss. Haven't you met him? Tony Manstell. The guy over there.'

'Him? He looks like the Hideous Penguin Man.'

'He is considered quite a catch, Mackie.'

'By zoos?'

'Am I going to have to ask you to leave?'

I laugh, and I can see she's struggling not to. 'I'm sorry. This is all great. You've done good. How did you get all these people?'

'Your friend did it,' says my sister, nodding to her right. At first I think she's gesturing towards that blonde, Sarah, who, it must be said, is diverting an embarrassing proportion of my attention in a black choker, black gloves, and something floor-length and cream. Then I realise who she is talking about.

'Oh right,' I say. 'Daniel.'

'He's been great,' says the Princess, and calls him over. 'Danny! I was just telling Mackie how brilliant you've been at sorting this all out. Knowing who to invite, how to get hold of them, everything. I can't thank you enough.'

'Well done you,' I tell her, brightly, 'for thinking of him. It's not like you know anybody else with contacts, is it? Oh wait . . .'

Daniel winks at me. The sod.

'I was even going to ask him how I could get hold of this Thief guy,' continues Mary, 'but I didn't want him to rob somebody he wasn't meant to.'

'Well now,' says Daniel, and winks at me again. 'I suspect you would have been better off consulting young Macaulay about that.'

242

'Yes you would,' I retort, angrily, and then think about what I've just said, which isn't the best way round of doing things. 'But not because I know anything about him that anybody else doesn't know. And you can stop fucking winking at me, Daniel, because it's true, okay?'

Mary wrinkles her nose, an expression which seems to convey, with fluent despair, that boys are just silly. Then she kisses me on the cheek, and wonders off to argue with the band about an Abba quota.

Daniel and I stare at each other for a few moments, and there's an aura between us, like we are competitors. I guess we are, in a way. 'Forgot you were doing this,' I say, eventually.

Daniel shrugs. 'Have to do something.'

This makes me feel guilty, and it shouldn't. It's not my fault I've got his job. It's his, for being crap at it. 'I thought you were, uh, dealing,' I say.

'Uh, dealing? Uh, dealing what?'

'Dealing. Drugs dealing.'

He laughs. 'Heavens no. I am but a poor out-of-work hack, waiting for somebody to give me a big break.'

'Daniel. I don't know what you think I know.'

'No?'

'No. And if I did, I'm frankly at a loss as to why I should share it with you.'

'Ouch!' Daniel rolls his eyes. 'How quickly they grow! How quickly they turn!'

'Oh, leave it. Can we talk about something else? I'm frankly sick of him, okay? I really, really don't want to talk about it. How have you been? You back in touch with Michelle yet?'

He isn't. We sink a few cocktails by the high, white trestle table that is functioning as a bar tonight, but I can tell that he's keen to go on the prowl. Despite the advantages I have over him, ethnicity-wise, I'm not really in the mood for prowling myself. I stay put, and hit the whisky.

A couple of times, I try and fail to get the Princess dancing, and a couple more times, Janie tries and fails with me. I'm not sure I have ever seen the Princess dance. Janie, despite her slender frame, dances like a fat comedy Arab in an Indiana Jones movie.

She's done herself proud, has the Princess. Every North London chiropodist with a dinner jacket must be here. There's a strange buzz of flirtation in the air, of a whole different sort to the parties I usually go to, or the cat-eyed lasciviousness of Paxy's. This lot, I suppose, aren't looking for a casual one-nighter. They're looking to breed. I spot the blonde, Sarah, drifting around, leaning in close to various expensive-looking men. She ends up on the dancefloor in a clinch with Tony, the Princess's boss. Even Leoni, my sister's friend with the face like a pug, seems to be having a much better night than me. I am, I realise as the night wears on, both too scruffy and too young to deserve any serious interest from anyone.

Here and now, and probably solely because of the whisky, it makes me terribly sad that I don't feel a part of this, at all. I'm not after kids, personally, but still. These are my people. I ought to feel some kind of affinity to them. Mary clearly does, although I suppose she's been working at that all her life. But from her nodding enthusiasm, Janie seems to as well. Why should that be? Oughtn't she to be even more divorced from these aspects of our background than I am? She's made a conscious decision to abandon it, after all. I've just drifted away. Mind you, stick her among a group of Mormons or Moonies and she'd probably be equally enthusiastic. She's just the cultish type. It's a wonder that she's never properly joined one.

It is when people are beginning to leave, at about 1 a.m., that Janie waves me over on the way back from the toilet. She's sitting at a table, with the Princess. Both are curiously upright and drawn.

'Listen,' Janie says as I sit down, and through my drunken haze I spot that the Princess has a few sheets of airmail in front of her, and is frowning. 'Listen. I've got something that you ought to read.'

'Let me guess,' I tell her, carelessly. 'It's a book about how I'm from Mars, right? And you're from Venus. And Mary . . . sorry, Miriam, is from, like . . . Pluto, and we can never properly understand each other unless we confine ourselves to a diet of biscuits made from crushed weevils. By monks. From Bali. Am I right?'

'No,' says Janie. 'It's a letter from Mum.'

I start to stand up, only to be caught around the wrist by Mary, in a grip like a coat-hanger snare.

'Sit down,' she says quietly.

I can feel myself going red, swelling, squeezed from the neck like a crimson balloon in a fist. 'Bollocks,' I say, meaninglessly, and then I shout it. 'Bollocks, bollocks, bollocks . . .'

The Princess yanks my wrist, and I crash down into my chair. 'Bollocks,' I say, weakly.

'Read it,' says Janie.

'No,' I say.

'I'll read it,' says the Princess. 'She says she's well. She says thanks for your letter. She says . . .'

'Your letter?' I interrupt. 'Your fucking *letter*, Janie?'

'Oh, grow up,' says Janie. 'I've been writing to her for almost a year.'

'How lovely!' I trill. 'Is she well? Happy? New chap still treating her well? Any pets or anything? Any *kids*?'

'Don't be stupid,' says Janie, calmly. 'We're her kids. That's why

245

she wants to know us. Never mind, Mary. I'll tell him. She and Ben have moved to a new kibbutz. It's closer to . . . Well. It's more convenient. And bigger. More room for visitors. She was wondering if we wanted to . . .'

Now I'm on my feet. Mary goes for my wrist again, but I snatch it away. 'You're an idiot,' I tell Janie. 'You're an idiot, and Mum's an idiot as well. Princess, why are you listening to this?'

My little sister is quiet for a moment. 'I'm going to give her a call,' she says.

'Oh fuck off, the pair of you,' I say, and I leave.

I'm still drunk when my taxi gets me home, drunk enough to pick up the telephone and dial.

'It's me,' I say.

'Macaulay?' My father sounds alarmed. 'What's happened?'

My lights are off, and I'm sitting, fully clothed, on my bed. I draw my legs up to my chest, and start fumbling for my cigarettes. 'Nothing has happened. Why does anything have to have happened? I just fancied a chat.'

'It's past two, Macaulay! Are you drunk?'

'Aye, a little. Were you asleep?'

My dad sighs. 'Well no, actually. I wasn't. I was reading. I tried to call you last week, you know. I left a message. Are you okay?'

'I'm fine. I didn't get it. Listen. I wanted to ask you about Mum. About when she left.'

'Jesus, Macaulay! You can't just . . .'

I light one. The flare hurts my eyes. 'What?'

'You don't just . . . you can't . . .'

'What? Ask you about this? Why not? Because I'm drunk? Seems the perfect time to me.'

My father is silent for a moment. 'Can't this wait until morning?'

I shake my head for a few moments, until I remember how telephones work. 'No. I'll be sober in the morning.'

'Christ,' says my dad, and then he's silent for a moment. 'Well, you were there. What do you remember?'

What do I remember? I remember the gash in the woodchip of our yellow-flecked hall. I remember the shards of broken pottery in the carpet, and the way one of them, only as thick as a wire but an inch long, leaped, as if from nowhere, out of the carpet and into the sole of my left foot almost a fortnight later. I remember the cold air from the open front door, and the smell of twigs, and rain and bonfires. I'm sure I remember the squoosh of wet tyres sluicing past on the road outside, and, if I really try, I can remember hearing somebody, possibly Mary, sobbing her tiny, childish tears down at the other end of the corridor.

'Is that all?' asks my father.

Not quite. I can remember my father, bellowing, fighting to escape the bear hug that Dougie McLean had him in against the living-room door. I can remember the kick I gave Dougie, hard as I could, just below the knee, and the way he swore at me, but held fast. I remember trying to do the same to the short, swarthy, black-haired man who was leading my mother towards the front door. And I can remember the slap she gave me, backhanded across the face, to keep me away.

'Dougie was limping for three days,' says my father. 'He reckoned you'd have killed him if you could. And Ben, too. Although you might have had your work cut out. Israeli army, and all that. Bit of a tough match for an eleven-year-old.'

I'm thinking about swords and skean-dhus, and a battle outside a shop.

'None of it was Ben's fault,' says my dad. 'I liked Ben. He was just what she wanted. I wasn't. Some people just don't match, Macaulay. God knows why your mother and I thought we did.

She looked like Mary, but she was like Janie inside. Can you imagine being married to somebody like Janie? Christ, lad, don't you remember her *clothes*? It wasn't working.'

So why did he fight? Why did he try to keep her?

'God knows,' says my father. 'Men do. I don't actually remember a second of it. Your story is a lot like Dougie's, so I guess it must be pretty right. I was pissed. Complete blackout. Knew something had happened. Didn't know what. Woke up and she was gone.'

I blow a smoke ring towards the window, and then another, smaller one that dances through the middle. I get that, I tell him.

'It's why I stopped drinking,' says my father. 'It comes from your grandfather. He could spend days in that bloody shop, tanked up to his eyebrows. He never had a clue what was going on. That's why he fell off the ladder. I remember once, he hit some lad with one of those ornamental swords. Damn near took his arm off. Flatly denied it when the police came around, and didn't even know he was lying. Kept denying it until they found the blade and showed him the blood.'

I tell him that I know about that fight. I heard he stabbed somebody.

There's a long silence. 'Not tonight,' sighs my dad. 'You want to know that one, you'll have to get pissed again and call me tomorrow.'

I might well, I tell him, and say goodnight.

'An inquisition . . .'

'We're back,' says Philip, when I arrive at the office on Monday

'How do you mean?'

'You haven't heard? They've found the Thimbles. And they've arrested somebody. In Japan.' His eyes are shining. 'We're back,' he repeats and, at that point, so far, there's no indication that he's utterly, utterly wrong.

Itotaki. I guess he must have been getting desperate. The police in Kyoto raided his penthouse. A huge place, apparently, overlooking the Nintendo building. It makes for an odd feeling, reading about it. All this info, right here, and it's taken me a fortnight to get his phone number. Apparently Ventrama was once a very rich company. Not any more. The current Itotaki is the heir of its founder, and, according to this report, he has spent much of his life pissing his late father's fortunes away on ludicrous schemes. There was a robot dog thing, and an electric bicycle thing. There was a print-your-face-on-a-CD thing. There were a few straight-to-laser-disc porn things, including one – *Tunic Teens Lick for Grades* – that I think I remember seeing a poster of, that one time I was in Jensen's horrible home. Then there was a cocaine thing, although as that just involved Itotaki sticking as much of it up his nose as possible, as quickly as possible, I doubt even he really considered it a business plan.

In recent weeks, though, the Japanese police seem to have been thinking otherwise. Their narcotics squad has been tailing him across the country, between meetings with various Yakuza-types. Reading between the lines, when they raided him last night, they must have expected a major haul. Fortunately for Itotaki, they only found around ten grams. Less fortunately for him, they also found the Bushman's Thimbles, a 'selection of jewellery', and a collection of indecent photographs that appear to have made the stars of *Tunic Teens Lick for Grades* seem positively wizened. It's the latter that looks likely to send him away for the longest, but it's the Thimbles, obviously, that are the story over here. 'There is no suggestion,' the story concludes, 'that Takamura has visited Europe at any point in the past year.'

I'm just reading this last line, on a printout from the BBC website, when Trevor Brainchild and Jensen Randall come stalking up.

'Have you seen it?' Jensen is shrieking. 'Some bloody Jap's got the baubles!'

I nod. 'We've seen it.'

'What's his name? Tukymora! We need to get hold of his people, right now!'

'Ventrama Import Exports, Kyoto, Japan,' I tell him, idly. 'I think I've got his home number. And you're pronouncing his name wrong, Jensen, old lad. Can annoy people, that sort of thing.'

'*Yan* . . . ,' he begins to retort, and then stops. 'How do you know that?'

'Happens to me all the time,' I say, airily. 'You're lucky, with that bog-standard, unpretentious moniker of yours.'

'How do you know,' breathes Jensen, 'his home number?'

I'm feeling wild. 'It's called journalism. I've been onto him for weeks. He put the phone down on me . . . oh, three days ago, maybe. His friends call him Itotaki, and he runs an import/export business called Ventrama. He's certainly not the thief, but it does sound like he might be the fence. He's been pestering his contacts in Europe, trying to shift some stolen jewellery from London.'

Jensen stares at me. Brainchild, who has been reading a printout of his own, slowly straightens. Philip has his head in his hands, and Rebecca is looking at me strangely.

'Oh Mac,' she says. 'What have you done?'

'Don't feel bad,' I tell her, with a grin. 'I'm sure you'd have got there eventually.'

Brainchild turns his back on us. 'My office,' he says. 'All *three* of you. Now.'

'You *knew* about this,' he begins, once Philip, Rebecca and I are lined up in front of his desk. I feel smug as a medallist. The other two are fuming. Jensen is sitting at a smaller desk in the corner, fiddling with a computer.

'Oh yes,' I tell Brainchild. 'For a couple of weeks now. I even spoke to him. I think. He wasn't very helpful.'

'How did you get his name?'

I grin. 'Tip-off from a contact.'

'Which contact?'

'I'm afraid I can't tell you that, Trevor.'

Brainchild looks at Rebecca. 'Can you tell me about this contact?'

'I,' says Rebecca, 'know nothing about any of this.'

'Philip?'

'I . . . er . . . I . . . er,' contributes Philip.

Brainchild rubs his gawping Mekon eyes. 'I'm disappointed with both of you. You're meant to be a *stabilising* influence. But *you* . . . what is *wrong* with you, Lewis?'

My grin slowly fades. 'What?'

'You say you've known about this for a *fortnight*. Yet our *readers* have not. Why?'

I feel a cold bolt shoot down my spine. 'I . . . I wasn't there yet. I didn't expect him to get busted, did I? I thought it would hold. It was just a tip-off. I hadn't, like, confirmed it or anything. I was researching. I didn't have anything concrete.'

'You have a duty to tell us these things,' says Jensen, loftily, from the corner.

I open and close my mouth a few times. 'Why are you even here?' I manage, eventually. 'What have you got to do with anything?'

One of Brainchild's eyes gets even wider. This is not human. He gestures at Philip and Rebecca. 'You have colleagues, Lewis. Many hands make light work. You didn't think to *share*?'

'Well . . . no. They wouldn't have shared it with me. It was my story.'

'It was *our* story,' says Brainchild.

'Excuse me,' says Rebecca, wearily. 'You realise he's probably making this up? He'll never have heard of this guy until ten minutes ago. He's just after the attention.'

I whirl. 'I am not making it up!'

Philip's elbow hits my upper arm. 'Might be better if you were making it up,' he mutters.

'Oh right. Good point. Yeah. I'm just doing it for attention. I'm totally making it up.'

'Are you?' demands Brainchild.

Jensen stands up. 'He isn't. Half his internet history over the last fortnight has been about this Takamura guy, and Ventrama. And somebody called Jackson Pirelli. Who is Jackson Pirelli?'

I am outraged. 'You've been checking my web history? You can't do that!'

'It's not hard. Who's Pirelli?'

Before I'm even aware of moving, I'm right in front of Jensen, my face inches from his. 'Shall we do this now? Shall we do this right fucking now? Because you're really starting to . . .'

'Lewis!' barks Brainchild, and I can feel Philip's hand, unexpected and restraining, on my arm. '*Control* yourself. You are behaving like a *child*, and you are a *whisker* away from walking out of this office and not coming back. Do you *understand* me?'

I step away from Jensen. He's grinning. Somewhere, in the wobbly mania of my mind, I'm remembering what Rebecca said, that evening at Paxy's. They don't want to sack me. It's expensive. They're hoping I'll leave. Would they sack me if I snatched out Jensen's voicebox, like a poacher grabbing a wobbly fish? Do I want to find out?

'Jackson Pirelli,' continues Brainchild, 'is a *jewellery* agent, is he not? An *Italian*.'

I nod, just as Robin Hargreaves bursts into the room. 'What's going on?' he says.

'An inquisition,' mutters Rebecca.

Brainchild rubs his eyes. 'Lewis. You will *tell* me, right now, how Pirelli fits into this. You will tell me *everything* you know about this Takamura. You will tell me how *long* you have known these things, and *how* you found them out. Do I make myself clear?'

I nod again. 'I'm not sure Pirelli does fit into it,' I tell him sullenly. 'My contact didn't seem to think he was really connected. Takamura has been trying to shift some hot trinkets from London. That's all I know.'

'Takamura,' mutters Jensen. 'That name sounds familiar.'

I think of the poster in his flat. 'The porn angle?' I suggest. 'Perhaps he's employed your mother.'

Jensen curls his lip. Brainchild's eyeballs throb for quiet. 'Who is your contact?' he asks.

'I can't tell you that,' I reply.

There is a pause. 'You will *tell* me your contact,' says Brainchild, 'or you will *get* out.'

'And go back to my desk?' I suggest, hopefully.

'No,' says Brainchild. '*Not* go back to your desk. Tell me your contact, or you will *never* go back to your desk.'

Hargreaves makes a worried, chirruping sound. 'Ah, Trevor? I'm not altogether happy with the way you are . . .'

'Objection noted,' says Brainchild, and if he had a hammer, he'd bang it down, the fat prick. 'Lewis?'

I'm breathing a little heavily. 'No,' I say. 'And I should warn you, I'm a member of the union.' This is a lie. I stopped paying my NUJ subs when I got satellite TV. It was one or the other. Damn.

There is a long pause, at the end of which Brainchild actually claps his hands. 'Okay! Enough! From *all* of you. Out. I'll be *speaking* to you all individually later, but for now, get *out*.'

'Back to my desk?' I ask.

'Just *go*,' says Brainchild.

On the way out, I nudge Philip. 'Hey tiger. You were pretty nifty back there.'

'Fuck you,' says Philip, and turns his back on me.

Hmmm.

———

So as it turns out, we aren't back at all. I try to laugh it off. I tell Philip and Rebecca that we're like Gibson, Glover and Russo in *Lethal Weapon III*, and the DA has finally managed to take our badges. It doesn't help.

Every television in the office is blasting out facts that, only twenty-four hours ago, I was desperate for. On Sky they have a graphic of the Mandarin Hotel, like a level from a 1980s computer game. On the tail end of BBC *Breakfast*, Natasha Kaplinsky and Dermot Murnaghan are sombre, like they are discussing the death of a royal. According to Moira Stewart, unconfirmed reports on Japanese television indicate that Ito Takamura has already given his own police a full statement. Apparently, he considers himself to have been an unwitting stooge in the whole business, manipulated from the start by a shadowy London media figure, possibly a journalist. Kaplinsky seems stricken by this, and personally apologetic. This cheers me up immensely. Maybe it's her.

Greebo calls at about eleven. I don't answer and he doesn't leave a message. He'll have heard. Poor sod's probably frantic.

Already, even before lunch, there is a printout of tomorrow's front page sitting in the recycling bin. I have had nothing to do with it, not even so much as a consultation. It's not by-lined, which makes me think that somebody senior and managementy must have written it. 'NAIL THIS SICK BEAST!' blurts the headline, and I find myself feeling a sudden burst of forlorn empathy with this faceless, fallen folk hero. There is a box at the bottom of the page, which gives an 0898 phone number. 'CAN YOU HELP US BUST THE THIEF?' it fairly screams, 'HUGE REWARD! SEE INSIDE!!'

I toss it across onto Rebecca's desk.

'What?' she says.

'Have you seen this dross? Hardly a vote of confidence, is it?'

'Mac, I'm busy, okay?'

'But look at it! It's like a *tabloid!* It's pathetic. Since when did the *Gazette* do this kind of thing?'

Rebecca raps a pen against her teeth a couple of times.

'Since now,' she says. 'I happen to think it's a rather good idea, actually. I was in favour of doing it a fortnight ago.'

I pull a face. 'It's a bit Channel 5, isn't it? How much is this reward going to be?'

'Lots. But it doesn't mean anything. Somebody would actually have to virtually stick the guy in a box and lead us to him for us to have to pay out. And even if they did that, it's probably cheaper than keeping on some pointless idiot to write about trinkets and parties, isn't it?'

I stare at her. 'Are you aware of what you just said to me?'

She won't even look at me. 'You've made your own bed, Mac.'

I glance at the empty desk next to her. 'It's also Philip's bed. Figuratively speaking, that is. And yours.'

'It's not my bed.' She flicks a bottle of pills with her fingernail. 'This is my bed. My old bed. A bigger, better, more worthwhile bed.'

'What's that?'

'Rohypnol, the date-rape drug.'

'I see. Doesn't that make this whole bed analogy a little inappropriate?'

'Oh, piss off, Mac.'

I start to walk away, but think better of it. 'I thought we were friends. I'm fucking dying here. Why are you being like this?'

Finally, she looks up. 'You should have told me. About this Japanese guy.'

'You'd have taken it away from me.'

'At least it would have been me,' says Rebecca.

'Full medical back-up.'

People come and go. Daniel calls twice, but I don't answer. Greebo calls so many times in a five-minute period (seven) that I turn my ringer off, and don't turn it on again. I get a terse text from the Princess instructing me to meet her for dinner in Chinatown tomorrow, which I have the nerve to ignore for almost *three minutes* before acquiescing, meekly. Rebecca goes, comes back and then goes again, this last time with Philip, who appears to be joining her for lunch. Nobody speaks to me, not even him. From their conversation and his phone calls, I gather he is helping Rebecca set up a laboratory-conditions experiment. This is how far downmarket we have sunk. She's planning to take her Rohypnol, in a safe environment, and then write about how it makes her feel. 'Full medical back-up!' is the phrase Philip keeps squeaking down the telephone. I can tell what he's up to. He'll wait until she is at her most pliable, and then hit her with the suggestion that he should be given my job. Treacherous little sod. I can see the little vial of pills is right there, sitting next to the pen pot on her desk. Perhaps I could switch it for arsenic.

If need be, I can hang on here for weeks. Willie Fowler did, simply taking refuge in ever expanding lunch breaks. And I'm no Willie Fowler. I'm good at my job. If they aren't going to let me do it, that's their loss, not mine.

And yet, there is something in me that yearns to be proactive. I have the entire facilities of a medium-sized newspaper at my disposal. Surely there is some way in which I can make my mark? It's only when I'm standing over Rebecca's monitor, flicking the cap off her pill box with my thumb, and wondering resentfully what male hormone pills look like and whether I can get some by the time she's due to start popping these, that an idea strikes. I'm going to steal her feature. I'm going to take some of these demonic little blue tablets myself, live the experience, and then write the arse off it. I can do it better than her, and they'll have no excuse not to run it.

I stick a couple on my tongue, and scurry over to the water cooler.

There can't be a man alive, I have often thought, who doesn't find himself feeling a tiny bit guilty about the whole date-rape drugs phenomenon. Of course, the vast majority of us would never consider it, but that doesn't mean we haven't . . . that doesn't mean we wouldn't . . . well. It's a rare man who has never encouraged anybody to drink more than they were intending to, or smoke more than they had been planning, or whatever, in order to help their inhibitions . . . slip a little, isn't it? Is that such a shocking confession to make? I don't think so. I'm not talking rendering people incapable of making a judgement, after all. I'm just talking about helping them make the right one. Or the wrong one. Whatever. Women do it, too. They've certainly done it to me.

An hour later, I have no idea how I feel. Perhaps a little spacey, but with nobody else here, staring alone at an empty screen, it's impossible to tell. I have nothing to do, nothing to write, nothing to say. At first I lurk online, chatting on the *NME* message board and Googling myself, but then I remember that people like Jensen have full access over my web history, and I stop that kind of thing, pretty smartish. Is it the pills that made this take so long to click? Or is it extreme boredom? Hardly killer copy either way.

For a while, I entertain myself by preening away at my email. Rebecca was right on that front – such things are important if I'm soon to be sacked. I forward selected bits of my inbox and sentmail folders to my Hotmail account and set about deleting everything else. As an afterthought, I log into the goss@gazette.co.uk mailbox, to see if any of the nutters or wags have sent anything even mildly entertaining our way.

Four messages. Pretty poor, considering it must have been two months since I last checked. Oddly, they are all very recent, within the last two days. And they are all from an address called it@ventrama.jp. Har-de-fucking-har. Popbitch again. Confessions, no doubt. Declarations of complicity with Shergar, Elvis or Lord Lucan. My aching sides.

But no. They are all very short. Single sentences. '*Call me,*' says the first. '*Please call me,*' says the second. The third deviates in theme slightly with '*Return my call immediately!!!!!*' and the last is an altogether more ominous '*Do not turn your back or you will regret it.*'

Weird stuff, even for a nutter. Could they be genuine? Perhaps they are. Perhaps Takamura relented, after screaming at me down the telephone, and was on the verge of confessing all before he was busted. But how would he have got this email? And what's all this 'return my call' business? I have had no calls. And I didn't even give him my number. Is my mobile broken? Or does he mean my work phone? But I never use my work phone for anything. I hardly ever even give out the number.

Something is growing within me, a black tide rising like a panic. Have I missed the scoop of a lifetime? There have been so many calls I haven't got recently. There was Neil, trying to get my help for his magazine spread. There was Lucy, apparently, that afternoon last month. There was my dad. Is my telephone broken? Is the little flashing red message light simply not flashing anymore? Can something as mundane as that have dealt the death blow to my ailing career? This is awful. I'm freaking out. I'm panicking. Is this the drugs? But I don't feel suggestive at all.

With a trembling hand, I lift the receiver. It's been so long since I last used the thing that it sticks slightly to the base. I press the *retrieve* button.

'*You have no new messages,*' elucidates the android voice. She sounds rather like Elspeth's friend Carolyn. Well, of course I don't. How could I? It's plainly just . . .

'. . . *and twelve saved messages. To hear the first saved message, press or say "one".*'

I'm so shocked that I don't press or say 'one' for ages. Then I do both. Who has been saving my messages? I haven't been saving any messages. What's going on?

The first message is months old. It's from Neil. The second and third are also from Neil. They sound more annoyed. There are a couple from Brainchild, wondering where I am, there's one from Mary, agreeing to meet me in the pub (what?), and one from that American girl in the blue vest I met at The Zekes' gig, who says she thought I was nice, and wondered if I wanted to give her a call later that week. And there's one from Philip, telling me he's going to be late. Six weeks ago. The rest are all from PR people, except for the last. I know who that is from straight away.

'You call me!' a Japanese man is shouting and he sounds drunk, or enraged, or quite possibly both. 'You promise not to call me and you call me! The lady she is not my wife she know I take call from London journalist shit! Now I go to fucking jail!'

It goes on. I don't quite catch some of the words, and I don't quite understand others. Basically, this man isn't happy. He isn't happy because he had been promised that certain goods were untraceable, and this appears not to be true. He isn't happy because his more serious problems are being splashed across the papers, and this is why. He wants the stories stopped. He wants advice. Mainly, I think, he just wants to shout. He wants to shout at me, and I don't know why.

The telephone beeps and the android voice starts telling me to please replace the handset. I can't. I am physically unable. Over and over she says it, and I cannot move. I don't know what this message means. I do know what this message means. I just don't know how it can possibly mean it.

This message is for me. It must be for me. Because I did call him, and there was a lady. It can't be for Philip, or for Rebecca, or for anybody else. It must be for me. But how can it be?

Everybody has always thought that I knew who Fingers was. Even the guy who Fingers has been selling his stuff to thinks I know who Fingers is. Are they *right?* Am I cracking up?

What was it Eccles told me? He said I described myself. I thought I was chasing the thief, but I described myself. It was my leg. I'm thinking of my blackouts. I'm thinking of my father's blackouts, and Grandpa JohnJohn's blackouts. But those are *blackouts*. Those are momentary. This is . . . episodic. This is insane.

And, God, that's not the worst thing. It's such a *cliché*. That's the worst thing. I'm a cliché. The film they make of my life will be a hackneyed film, a remake of a thousand others. This is awful. I'm insane. This is awful. I'm a cliché.

I have to calm down. I'm panicking. This is absurd. It's those drugs. I'm not thinking clearly. I would never be thinking this way if I was thinking clearly.

I drop the phone and stand up, trembling. Then I pick it up again. Systematically, I go back through every one of those twelve messages, and delete them. 'You have no more messages,' says the android, Carolyn, and I could kiss her bony forehead. Then, still standing hunched over my desk, I go through the goss@gazette.co.uk mailbox and I delete every message. Then I empty the trash. Should I format the hard drive? No. Pointless. It's stored remotely. If they wanted to, they could still find these. But dear God, why would they want to? Nobody has ever used this address. Nobody. Except for me.

A hand clasps me on the shoulder, and I very nearly scream. Philip. It's Philip. He's staring at me. 'You've heard,' he says softly.

I spin away. People are rushing past me, lurching diagonally, like a cheap horror film. Rebecca is there too, moving ominously towards her desk. 'I've heard nothing,' I tell him. 'Nothing.'

Philip frowns. 'I thought . . . you looked . . . never mind. The column? You haven't seen it?'

'I know nothing,' I say. I think I say it staunchly. I certainly intend to.

Rebecca's head snaps up. She's holding her pill pot. 'Some of these are gone,' she says slowly. 'Somebody has . . . oh Mac. You didn't? How many?'

'Oh my God.' Philip is pale. 'He wouldn't have . . . You should have told him. You should have told him about the column. Mac? Tell me you didn't . . .'

'I didn't do *anything*!' I scream, and notice that Philip is backing away. 'What? Wait! What column?' He's holding a paper, and I snatch it from him. It's open at a column about Fingers. I'm scanning the words. 'Noooo,' I'm muttering, 'Nooooooo.'

Journalist suspect, it says. Insider London knowledge. Takamura's English accomplice. Well-known media figure. This is awful. And it gets worse. Police closing in. Strong lead. DNA evidence likely. Reward offered from *Gazette*. Half a million pounds. Contact Jensen Randall. New column begins today. Thread sample from the Gretchner Hotel. Grey suit. Forensic tests. Cannot escape. Nationwide neighbourhood watch . . .

Hold on.

I wheel on Philip. 'What the hell is this?'

He glances at Rebecca. 'You didn't know? He didn't know? Then why . . . ?'

'*The Talk of the Town*,' I read. '*The new daily showbiz column from Jensen Randall.* Jensen Randall? Showbiz column? That fucker is meant to work in marketing!'

'Mac,' says Philip, urgently. 'You need to calm down. You're making a scene, and we need to get you to a doctor. How many did you take? What did you . . . oh no.'

I follow his glance. Jensen Randall is coming towards us. Before I'm even properly aware of it, I'm striding towards him.

'Oi!' I shout. 'Jensen! You stole my job! You stole my job!'

'Yansen,' he says, looking right at me. 'It's pronounced Yansen.'

'I don't care! I don't care how your stupid fucking name is pronounced! Do you understand me? We went to the pub! I pulled you off that fat bloke! And you repay me by stealing my job? You do know you'll be shite at it? You witless prick.'

Jensen goes a little red. 'You ought to listen to your boyfriend,' he says. 'Calm down. And watch what you say.'

'And you ought to have your face smashed in! This is well

overdue. I'm going to take your nose, and twist it, and ram it right up your . . .'

I'm raving. Philip steps between us. 'Jensen,' he says. 'Wait. Don't hit him.'

'How many did you take?' says Rebecca, and turns to Philip. 'He's not lucid. Where does he think he's going to put his nose?'

'Up its own arse!' I shriek, and shove Jensen in the chest.

He has that fixed-smile, bobbing-voicebox thing going on. His arm swings back, but Philip grabs it. 'Stop this!'

There are people everywhere. Brainchild has appeared, as if from nowhere. '*Lewis!*' he barks. 'Are you *incapable* of spending as much as a *morning* in my office without creating a *riot*? What is going *on* here?'

Jensen is trying to shake Philip off, almost methodically. His eyes are oddly shiny. On balance, I decide, there doesn't seem very much chance of him not hitting me. Perhaps I should hit him first.

'Please!' implores Philip, clinging onto his arm. 'He doesn't mean it! He's been taking pills! We need to get him to a doctor!'

I freeze. 'What?'

'It's okay,' says Philip, very quickly. 'He's not going to hit you. Nobody is going to hit you. We know why you took those pills. We understand that this is a cry for help.'

I stare at him, and I can feel my fist unclenching. 'You tit,' I say. 'This isn't a cry for help. This is a feature.'

'What?' says Philip.

'I only took two. I wanted to test them. For a feature. To describe the experience.'

'Ooooh!' squeals Rebecca. 'That's my bloody feature! Do hit him! Hit him now!'

And Jensen tries to, but Philip gets in the way. And then I hit Jensen, and Philip doesn't. And then I'm not sure what happens, but I'm pretty sure I hit a couple of other people, Brainchild among them. Rebecca is holding one arm, and Philip is holding the other, and I'm screaming and I want to kill. I couldn't tell you what actually happened, to be honest. I'm my dad, in our hallway. I'm my granddad, and I'm defending my shop. And I know that's a little tacky, and I know that, to shoot it with any sort of cross-referencing flashbacks in a film would be frankly unforgivable, but that's just the way it is. It's just the same as either. Although without the swords, obviously.

Then I'm in a police car. And that appears to be that.

'Foul, but free.'

wake to the sound of a bolt being drawn back, and the sight, a few seconds later, of Detective Inspector Tom St Eccles. I'm fully clothed, lying on top of a rough green blanket that smells of compost.

'Oh Christ,' I manage, rising up on my elbows. 'Not you.'

Eccles sound cheerful. 'Only the guilty sleep,' he begins, 'Did you know that, Lewis? That's one of the first things I learned on this job. Let's say you arrest three guys for the same crime. Stick them in a cell overnight. Next morning, whoever is sleeping is your man. If you're guilty and you know you're caught, you let your guard down. You follow?'

I rub my eyes and shift uncomfortably on the flimsy yoga mat thing that the police stick in these places and call a mattress. Not nice. This is not my first night in a police cell, but it's the first time I've ever been actually aware of one. Last time I was locked up was in Cambridge, after an Elspeth-related episode in which they found me shouting drunkenly, by myself, in a mid afternoon city park. The first thing I remember is being upright and bleary in the reception area, while a man who called himself a Warrant Officer gave me back my shoelaces. I didn't feel as dreadful then as I do now. This is like a hangover, but worse. In fact, now I concentrate, it is like a particular hangover. It's like the hangover I had the morning after the Piss Streak Planes party at Thrust. The same burning in the ears, the same crazy heartbeat. I blacked out, that night, didn't I? Was I drugged then as well? But why?

'That's from a film,' I tell him. 'I do know that's from a film, Eccles.'

'*Usual Suspects*,' says Eccles, and I notice he's carrying two mugs. He proffers one in my direction. 'You were sleeping like a baby. That's coffee, by the way. Milk, no sugar. It's foul, but free.'

I accept. 'Thanks. But that doesn't mean I'm guilty. It must have been the drugs.'

'Not the best of excuses to offer to a policeman, Lewis.'

I shake my head. 'Not real drugs. Date-rape drugs.'

'Better and better.'

'Oh fuck off. It was research. We had a licence for them.' I think about this. 'Probably.'

Eccles laughs, pulls a plastic chair from next to the wall, and sits in it. The right way round, I am slightly disappointed to see. 'Sure you did. Anyway, I shouldn't worry. You're free to go. You're not being charged.'

I blink at him for a few moments. 'What, exactly,' I say, carefully, 'am I not being charged with?'

'What, exactly,' retorts Eccles, 'haven't you done?'

I open my mouth, and then close it again. For some reason I think of Orca, Janie's foul cat, and the time I saw him padding anxiously across a fresh snowfall in her back garden. He was prodding at every patch of snowy ground with a hesitant foot, as though worried about tumbling into something very, very deep.

'All sorts of things. Almost everything.'

Eccles smiles. 'How is your coffee?'

I sip. 'Awful,' I say, shocked. 'Wow. Really, really bad.'

'Told you so. If you must know, you are not being charged with assault, grievous bodily harm, being drunk and incapable, or resisting arrest.'

I touch the snow lightly. 'That's all?'

'That's all. What else have you done?'

'Nothing whatsoever. I didn't even do any of them. Did I hear a GBH in there?'

'You did.'

'That's pretty cool. Was it on Jensen?'

'It wasn't on anyone, Lewis. That's why you're not being charged with it.'

'Makes sense. I suppose I should be off. They didn't happen to mention whether I still had a job, did they?'

'They did.' Eccles drinks his coffee, and bares his teeth. 'And you don't.'

I nod. This also makes sense. 'Are you going to show me out, then?'

'Sure,' says the policeman, but he doesn't move a muscle. We look at each other for a few moments. I crack first.

'Okay,' I say. 'What's going on here? Why you? There are lots of policemen in London. There's simply no reason why you should be involved if I get picked up for being drunk and disorderly.'

'Drunk and incapable.'

'Whatever. I know what kind of thing you work on. Why are you here?'

Eccles smiles. 'I decided to drop by. I thought it might be

useful for us to have this chat. Because I know the kind of thing *you* work on. And I think it's pretty similar.'

'Well,' I say. 'I don't work on anything any more.'

'I wouldn't actually say that,' says Eccles.

Here we go, I think.

Except we don't and I leave, twenty minutes later, baffled. I don't even get around to asking him if he's married or not. This is all too bizarre. I couldn't even quite say what Eccles thinks I know. I don't think he thinks I'm the thief, but I do think he knows who the thief is. It's impossible to say. He reminds me that I mentioned Japan to him, at Joe Bastin's party, and wonders where I can possibly have got the information that led me to do that. Then he reminds me that Itotaki is claiming that he had a journalist as an accomplice. He reminds me that the Joe Bastin theft turned up a thread sample from a grey suit and, while he doesn't specifically mention that I was wearing such a suit that night and we even had a conversation about it, it's very much a given. All this must, I'd have to concede, point the finger at me pretty strongly, but Eccles doesn't quite seem to be directly suggesting this. It's more like he thinks I know something I'd quite like to tell him, and he's trying to make it easy for me. And, God knows, maybe he's right. Maybe I do.

It's only once I'm out, and gone, that I can start to think properly about the past twenty-four hours. Out here, Fingers is everywhere. And there's none of the jovial, congratulatory affection of the past few weeks. Headlines on every news-stand are barbed, and affronted. 'JAIL HIM' says the *Sun*, bleakly, while in the upmarket press a sense of betrayal is masked with dry legalese.

'EXTRADITION OF ACCOMPLICE UNLIKELY,' seethes the *Telegraph*, before striding off, briskly, to talk about gypsies, death and the cost of a decent au pair.

I don't want to go home, but I've got nowhere else in particular to go. I'm not meeting the Princess for dinner for another eleven hours. Perhaps I'll cancel. Or just not turn up. I cut across St James's Park and go down Whitehall towards Trafalgar Square. Do policemen never sleep? It's drizzly and cold, and offensively early, so the only people around are binmen, workmen, and the more militant sort of tourist. The Horse Guards' Parade smells of dung and sawdust, and at times, if you squint properly towards the shiny heads and backs of the Life Guards in the Arch, it could be a century ago. I could be the original Raffles, striding home after a night on the steal. As opposed to the new one, after a night in the cells.

But this is absurd. In fact, in the cold light of day, it is more than absurd. It is tacky, clichéd, and downright implausible. In my blearier moments, I can theoretically accept that there can be things that I do which I can fail to remember. Events even. Punches. But a parallel life? A whole separate existence? Christ, what would I do with all the *stuff*?

In Trafalgar Square the Japanese are already posing for photographs. A couple wear plastic policeman hats, folding their arms and grimacing, inexplicably, beside the lions of Nelson's Column. Mornings like this let you see the tourists' London. It's a London of buildings and palaces, of soldiers in red, Rolls Royces and bridges. For them, the Thames isn't an irrelevance. It's all black taxis, double-decker buses and Big Ben. That's Fingers' London. Much as I sometimes like to pretend, it's not mine. He can't be me.

From the Europa by the corner of Whitehall, I buy a pack of twenty Bensons and a box of matches. I climb up over the base, past the lions and the Japanese and, sitting with my back against the square trunk of the beginning of the column itself, stare down towards Parliament Square and smoke one. I have no idea what to do, what to think, how to fill my day. So I do what I always do when I feel like this. I go to Paxy's.

The tube is empty in my direction and packed in the other. Similarly, when I get to Hampstead, I am the only person in a suit who is walking up the hill. I'm like a salmon, going the wrong way on a river. The funny thing is, I've not done this walk in daylight in years. It makes me feel like I've been away.

Something has happened at Paxy's. It's not such a surprise to see that the front garden is a mess of bogweed and undergrowth, but I don't expect the gate to be cracked and hanging from its hinges. And I certainly don't expect the front door to be missing, or that length of police tape to be stretched across the doorway. There's a crumpled scrap of plastic-coated paper on the step. I peer down. It's from Camden Council. Paxy's is scheduled for demolition. I was here only a week ago. How can this have happened?

I duck under the tape and wander inside. This place is a ruin. Broken bottles and glasses line the skirting boards and empty light sockets hang from the ceilings. The walls are stained, rumpled and bare.

'Hello?' I call, but there's nothing.

It's not just dirty here, but dusty, too. I know nobody ever cleans, but this is a bit much. Well, isn't it? Scraps of paper and worn rugs litter the floorboards. The banisters are chipped and broken. The door to the dining room has a splintered hole in it, and inside there's a broken window and the remnants of what I'm pretty sure was once a pigeon.

'Hello!' I shout again.

I back out into the hallway, and bluster into the downstairs bathroom. Black water in the bowl. White flecks on the mirror. Is it always like this? It could be. It's usually night-time and packed with life. It's usually too dark to see into the damp corners of the rooms, where the carpet turns up, and the walls swell and touch.

But the broken gate. The demolition order. The lack of door, and police tape by the doorway. It's not always like that. Or is it? I think of that dark, awful moment upstairs, when I came here with Lucy and lost her. Was that clarity? Do I come, alone, to an empty house, and party, alone, like a madman? Is there no Lucy? But Rebecca was here, too. There's surely a Rebecca. Isn't there?

I'm running now, down the hallway and towards the living room. There's a door here, and I hit it with my shoulder.

'Mac?' says somebody. 'Is that you?'

It's Carolyn. Carolyn Somethingorother. She's jutting out of a small yellow dressing gown and she comes flying at me from the corner of the room like a bony, sobbing comet.

'I thought nobody would come,' she's saying. 'I thought nobody would ever come again.'

'Hey!' I say, and as I hold her, I notice that this room, at least, looks moderately familiar. There are sofas, and there is the drinks cabinet. It's shabby, but comfortable. Just like it always was. 'What's going on? What's happened?'

'We got raided,' whispers Carolyn. 'Somebody died, and we got raided.'

I push her away, and hold her by the shoulders. 'Somebody *died*? Who?'

'I don't know. Some girl. She'd taken something. It was upstairs, two nights ago. Brian found her. He freaked out. He dragged her outside, and tried to put her in a taxi. The taxi driver called the police. They arrested him, and stormed in here. Hundreds of them. Loads of people got arrested. Faisal had just scored a lot of coke. He was selling it on. Everybody had some. But most of it was in Brian's room. He hasn't even got *bail*, Mac. I need to call my dad in South Africa and I *can't*. I just *can't*.'

'Jesus,' I say. 'But why do you need to call your dad? What's it got to do with him?'

She collapses back into me. 'It's his house. But he hasn't been here for years. He doesn't even know we've been living here. It's meant to be empty. He's no idea that his kids have been having a party in it . . .' she starts laughing, but raggedly, '. . . for the past five years.'

Carolyn Somethingorother. Carolyn Paxton. She's Paxy's sister. Of course she is. I knew that once, and I forgot it. This is like one of those dreams, where strange things start to mesh together towards the end. She's still crying, sobbing so much that she's shaking like a washing machine. I stroke her hair, and without warning she lurches sideways, tumbling us both onto the sofa.

'You're going to stay, aren't you?' she whispers, and kisses me, hard and suddenly on the mouth. She's straddling me. I'm utterly taken aback. 'Tell me you're going to stay. Everybody else has gone. I've been here by myself, and everybody has gone. Please, Mac. Stay.'

'Listen,' I say, and raise a hand. She catches it, and pulls it inside her dressing gown. I feel cold ribs, a tiny breast and a hard, almost scratchy nipple. 'Oh God. Look. Carolyn . . .'

'Please stay,' she says, and her face is right in mine. She's squirming on me slightly. 'They've gone. Don't go.'

Carolyn has a coldsore, I notice. Her dressing gown is filthy, smeared with patches of brown. There are bags under her eyes, her hair is wild, and her lips are bitten. Her teeth are stained bloodish with red wine. She's rocking now, grinding her bony hips into my own. I suddenly feel like I am about to vomit. I snatch away my hand, and knock her sideways into the sofa. Then I spring to my feet.

'I've got to go,' I say.

She's on her hands and knees now, dressing gown hanging open. Even her breasts look sick, like triangular pouches of skin. I turn and I run and she starts shouting for me to come back. As if. I'm down the corridor, under the tape, and into the street within seconds. This is . . . what? Utterly fucking mental, that's what.

Or maybe I am. Because as my pace slows and my breath returns, only a few minutes later, I'm already wondering whether I imagined the whole thing. When my phone rings, I answer, even though I can see that the caller is Daniel. He says he wants to see me. I don't have the strength for this anymore. Everybody thinks it is me. Maybe it is me. Maybe it really was an empty house. Maybe there is no Carolyn. You can't judge these things. When you start questioning things like this, you can't judge anything at all. Because it's the bit of you that makes the judgement that needs judging itself.

Back on the tube, and I'm bewildered enough to be crying. I don't understand anything anymore. It could be me. I'm really mad enough that it could be me. I don't care if it's a cliché. I am. I truly am.

I stumble out into the light at Victoria, and very nearly find myself heading for work instead of for Daniel's flat. Righting myself, I duck through street and alley, smoking constantly, until I come to his door. I'm shaking. I don't feel well.

He doesn't answer his buzzer at first. I'm furious. I find an empty Tango can in the gutter, and hurl it up onto his balcony.

'Let me in!' I shout. 'Let me in! I'm here. I've come! Let me bloody in!'

The door finally opens. I run up the stairs and burst into his flat. Daniel is also in a dressing gown, and also looks terrible.

'I was on my way,' he says, in a flat, tired voice.

'Daniel, it's me,' I tell him, before I have a chance to stop myself. 'Fingers. It's me. You were right. Everybody was right. It's me. It's been me all along.'

Daniel stares at me, and then peers wildly out into the stairwell. 'Are you on drugs?' he says. 'It's not bloody you.'

'But you can't be sure!' I wail. 'How can you be? You can't be sure of anything!'

'You bloody fool,' he says. 'I can be perfectly sure. It's me.'

'I just got sick of it.'

'I just got sick of it,' says Daniel. He's sitting hunched on his balcony in his dressing gown and a pair of over-sized, Jackie O sunglasses, that I can only assume were left here, weeks ago, by Michelle. He didn't want to come out here, but I made him. I live a life of pizza boxes and fag packets, but the interior of Daniel's flat is an environment which even I find distasteful. It's odd that he can be outwardly so dapper, and inwardly such an outright slob. But I digress. 'I just got sick of it,' he is saying. 'Bloody sick of it. Sick of it all.'

'I don't follow,' I tell him, and I really don't. I can barely even hear.

'Oh, you should,' says Daniel. 'You of all people. We spend our lives chronicling the fads and foibles of people who are stupider than us, less interesting than us and, most of all, lazier than us. Just because society has dictated, for whatever thoroughly banal reason, that such people are newsworthy. How can it not drive you insane?'

I fish out the last cigarette from the packet in my pocket. 'Something seems to have,' I tell him. 'Didn't realise it was that.' I start to light the wrong end. I drop it. I pick it up.

'Of course it's that. What else could it be? But you're still relatively fresh, aren't you? You probably think you're above all that, that you love the glitz and froth and stupidity, don't you? You love it. Only, pretty soon, you'll start to realise that you only love it because you think you ought to love it. Then you'll realise that it's not love. It's obsession. You need to know this stuff. You go mad if you don't. And you kid yourself that you're at least better than the people who don't even get paid for obsessing about it. And you're not. You're far worse. You are devoting your life to something worthless. And it doesn't even begin to love you back. Do you understand me?'

'Have you been drinking, Daniel?'

'Of course I've been bloody drinking, you cretin. I've been doing nothing else for two days. I'm a damn fool. I wanted to beat them at their own game. All I really wanted to steal was their column inches. For something more worthwhile.'

'But you did,' I say. 'Fingers did. You shook things up. You really did something different.'

'I did not!' shouts Daniel. I wonder if I've heard him shout before. I can see that he has, indeed, been drinking for two days. 'I did something exactly the same! People were shocked for about *half a week*! Then they started *patronising* me! They turned me into one of them! I was like a new bloody pop band, or a trendy watch! A *fashion statement*.'

I draw hard on my cigarette. 'I . . . uh . . . may have had something to do with that.'

'You amaze me, Macaulay. But why wouldn't you? It's what you are. It's what I made you. It's what I am.'

We stare at each other for a few moments. 'I hated you,' I

begin. 'Not you. Fingers. Whatever. You consumed everything. You stole my life. Yeah, I liked the idea at first, but I didn't end up *patronising* you. I wanted to destroy you. I hated you. I did.'

'We champion, then we destroy,' sighs Daniel. 'We build up and we pull down. It was ever thus.'

I'm on my feet now. I march over to the edge of the balcony, I march back. I'm furious. 'You know what? I still hate you. You. You've ruined the whole story, Daniel, you know that? This is my story, not yours. Nobody is going to empathise with you. You're too old. You're too posh. You've got this *totally* cunty Noel Coward thing going on, and you're about as sexual as a . . . as a pissed camel. Who wants to shag a spindly fucking mess like you? This isn't the 1970s, you know. You can't *make* films like this anymore! You're not like me. You're a useless old, washed-up arsehole.'

Daniel laughs, like a chimp in a tea advert. 'Oh, don't hold back, young Macaulay. You let it all out.'

'Fuck you. This is my movie. You've fucked my movie. We don't all get the chance to live one. I did, and you've fucked it. It wasn't meant to end like this. Two jobless idiots bickering. Can you understand me? There was meant to be a chase. Me and Fingers. A rooftop showdown. Lightning and stuff. I'm meant to be about to expose you, and you're meant to want me dead. You explain all, and then we fight. Don't you *know* that? That's how it is meant to be!'

Daniel leans forward. With his cigarette, he gestures at me, the London skyline, and himself. 'Oh Macaulay,' he says. 'Look around yourself. A rooftop showdown? Where do you think you are?'

Look. I do know how dramatic tensions are meant to work, but I'm going to be honest here. I'm not entirely convinced by this.

Still, I resolve to sit tight, at least until he's done the 'explain all' bit. Should I be worried? Should I be consoling myself that the Princess will miss me if I don't turn up for dinner, and raise the alarm? I don't think so. He's in a dressing gown and women's sunglasses. His balcony is only three storeys high. I reckon I can handle myself.

Daniel knows about Itotaki, but Itotaki doesn't know about Daniel. Daniel has been very careful about this. He first contacted him the week after stealing the Bushman's Thimbles. Since then, he has communicated with him only through the goss@gazette.co.uk email address (logging in remotely in that way that I knew was possible, but have never bothered to learn) and by, when absolutely necessary, dialling in and receiving messages left on my answerphone.

'I spent a lot of time in internet cafés,' says Daniel. 'Ghastly places. Particularly that big orange one by Victoria. I've been careful. Even your telephone was a safe bet. I know how late you get in. I dialled into it every morning, and deleted any messages that I didn't want you to hear.'

'You missed the last few,' I says.

Daniel shudders. 'He didn't call? Couldn't pluck up the courage to check. Worried somebody might answer.'

'I deleted them. I thought they were for me.'

'Thanks,' says Daniel, and then peers at me, sidelong. 'You have a strange self-obsession thing going on. You know that?'

'I know that.'

Daniel did actually meet Itotaki once, years ago, on a yacht. That was how he knew about him. It was a rather dodgy yacht, he tells me. A couple of Russians, an American who had something to do with oil, a pair of suspiciously dapper Colombians, an Arab or two, and an old Etonian with arms connections, who later ended up in jail in one of the Congos. It sounds terrifying. Daniel says he was only there because of a very short-lived fling with his then girlfriend, a certain semi-aristocratic model who was a friend of the yacht's owner, one Jackson Pirelli.

'Hang on,' I interrupt. 'You went out with *her*? And she took you to Jackson Pirelli's yacht?'

'Yes. Well. One of his yachts.'

'In St Tropez harbour, wasn't it? Moored just by a little light-house?'

Daniel sweeps his hair out of his eyes. 'And just how on earth would you know about that?'

'I read about it,' I tell him. 'In *Bild*. Jesus. It *was* you. Silhouetting your cock across the Hotel Byblos.'

Daniel chuckles and I join in, and for a few seconds we both forget that we are meant to be maintaining an air of suspicion. We both catch ourselves at exactly the same time. It's a little embarrassing.

Itotaki loved the idea of being a fence, he tells me. He didn't seem to care that he didn't know who Daniel was, that appeared to just add to the excitement. Once the Thimbles arrived for him by courier ('They'll never trace it,' says Daniel. 'Gave my name as Randall'), and a week later Sophie Gerad's choker did the same, he was utterly sold. Between them, they agreed that Daniel would do the stealing, and Itotaki would do the selling. The businessman paid him twenty per cent of whatever the trinket in question was worth, mailed in dollar bills to a PO box outside a newsagent on Warwick Way.

'That's some discount,' I say.

'Buyers' market,' says Daniel.

Daniel doesn't know if Itotaki ever actually managed to sell anything. All he knows is that he received, and paid for, the Bushman's Thimbles, Sophie Gerad's choker, the artist's ruby pendant, the Froth.com pearl, and Willy Zilder's cane before calling a rather panicked end to their arrangement.

'What about the rest?' I ask him.

'There wasn't much more,' says Daniel. 'Topaz Wilton's safe had a little bit of cash in it, which I spent on drugs, booze and far too many flowers for Michelle.'

'Oh yeah. Michelle. What happened there?'

'She left. She thought I was dealing.'

'I thought you were dealing.'

'Wish I bloody had been dealing. Wilson had some jewels as well, but they turned out to be fake. Can you believe that?'

'These people,' I sympathise.

'I know. Aside from that, there was just Joe Bastin's disc.'

'And where's that?'

He laughs, mirthlessly. 'Under the bed, Macaulay. Next to the hoover.'

Daniel redirected his post from the office, and kept getting invites to all these parties because I hadn't gotten around to telling all the relevant PRs that he shouldn't be. When I stole his invite to Joe Bastin's party, he simply phoned them up and got another one. He already knew where all these celebrities lived through work, and most weeks, figuring out what to steal was a simple matter of reading the papers.

'But how did you *do* it?' I ask him. 'It's all . . . there was just so much . . . you were like a *magician*, Daniel. Can you really climb up the outside of a building without being seen? Have you really been abseiling into airvents? You just don't seem the type.'

'I'm not. All I have ever done is walk into places and take things. Newspapers exaggerate these things.'

'Bollocks,' I say. 'Bollocks. I chased you at that Bastin thing. You were inhuman. You ended up in that dressing room, but when I got there, you'd gone. How?'

281

'I hadn't gone,' says Daniel.

'You bloody had! I had that policeman coming after me. I told him I'd been chasing somebody, but there was nobody there. I looked a right tit.'

'I was hiding,' says Daniel, 'behind the curtain.'

'What?'

'That's it. Just behind the curtain. But you wanted to believe that something unfathomable had happened, didn't you? Something newsworthy.'

'But they had a thread sample! From a suit like mine! From a room I wasn't even in!'

'Your suit was my suit, remember? Jermyn Street. Bit expensive for the likes of you. I have several.'

I feel like my head is shrinking, like I am falling backwards through my own eyes. 'Okay then. What about the Thimbles? How did you do that? You just strolled up and grabbed them off the front of Gemma Conrad, did you?'

'Natrel Plus,' says Daniel.

'Excuse me?'

'Natrel Plus. Of all High Street deodorants, it is the coldest. That's because it has the highest percentage of solvents. Did you know that?'

'Did I . . . no. Well yes, actually. Elspeth and I used to snort it, through a towel. Daniel, why are you telling me this?'

He grins. 'I found out beforehand that the gems were stuck on with this waxy gum stuff. A bit like Blu-Tack. They used glue on everything else, but you can't use glue on a diamond. And backstage, it was pretty dark. Just before she went on, I gave her a blast of the stuff across the tits. The nipples hardened, the gum shrank, and the things just toppled off. I knew it would work. I'd performed tests, at home.'

'On yourself?'

'No Macaulay, not on my . . .' Daniel stops for a moment, and looks at me. 'Yes. On myself.'

'Am I stupid? Do I look stupid?'

'Oh shush. Yes, I had an accomplice. A lady. Satisfied?'

'Of course I'm not satisfied. Who was it? Michelle?'

Daniel laughs. 'Are you joking? That woman has a loose . . . if skilled, tongue.'

'Then who? Somebody I know?'

'It's not important. Our connection has been severed. She'll know that by now. We were meant to be doing a final hit last night, at the Dana Marion launch.'

'The what?'

'You really have let things slide, haven't you? Quite the hottest place to be on a Tuesday night. At the Rex in Soho. It was to publicise the new range by Dana Marion, the milliner.'

I feel simple despair. 'Not another milliner. Why are we even interested in *milliners*?'

'Who can say? The status of hatmakers is something that I have never been able to understand.' Daniel looks thoughtful for a moment. 'You know, it may well have been milliners who pushed me over the edge.'

'Which one is she again? The one who denied sleeping with the Gallaghers? Or the one who posed for Lucien Freud?'

'Neither. She's the South African. Diamond links. The centre-piece of the show was a turban with a gemstone fringe. Very twenties.'

'Sounds ghastly. I can't imagine why you'd want the thing.'

Daniel yawns. 'Well I don't anymore, do I? That's why I stayed in. My friend will have got the hint. I'm out. Finished. Done.'

'Who is she, Daniel?'

Reaching behind his sunglasses, he rubs his eyes. 'Forget about it, Mac. This game is played. I am spent. It is over. '

I extract one of Daniel's Dunhills from a packet on the arm of his chair. He'll be too drunk to notice. He's talking in threes, after all. 'Not necessarily. Not if they track you down.'

Daniel looks away. 'Rather hoping they'll forget about it. Or, failing that, pin it on somebody else,' he says airily.

'Who?'

'You.'

I'm on my feet in an instant, but Daniel's hand is round my wrist like a claw. Pretty fast for a drunk.

'I could make half a million quid,' I hiss, 'by telling the *Gazette* it was you.'

'And I could,' says Daniel urgently, 'by telling them it was you. Listen! Everything I did, it all traces back to you more than it does me. It wasn't intentional, but it's just the way it happened. The telephone. The email. The parties I went to, and the things I stole. We're in this together.'

I recoil, but he's not letting go. 'The fuck we are.'

'We are. You know we are. Nobody would believe either one of us. It's all about who squeals first. And it will be me, unless you help me. I don't know what I'm going to do, but I do know I need your help. There's nobody else. And you haven't really got a choice.'

I sit down, abruptly. He's right. Is he right? I'm suddenly unfathomably tired. I don't know what to think anymore. 'What about your accomplice?' I say, heavily. 'I could find her.'

'You think she'd corroborate your story? She couldn't, Mac. She doesn't know enough. She's a party girl. She's just in this for the kicks.

'You really need to tell me who she is,' I say.

'I'm really not going to,' says Daniel.

'There was a card, just like before . . .'

What is it with orthodox Jews and Chinese restaurants? It's like there has been a collective community decision, throughout the ages, to utterly overlook them when it comes to dietary law. Obviously I'm no expert on the Torah, but I'm fairly confident that it doesn't say THOU SHALL SHUN THE PIG AND THE SHELLFISH AND EAT OTHER MAMMALS CULLED ONLY IN A SUITABLE MANNER – UNLESS THOU ART IN A PARTICULAR SMALL CORNER OF SOHO, IN WHICH CASE ALL BETS ARE OFF. Not that I've checked, mind you. Perhaps Moses was a prawn cracker fiend.

Half of Soho smells of piss, and the other half smells of monosodium glutamate. There's that line that you cross, if you come from Oxford Street, just a few blocks down. Nothing looks any different – the same skimpily over-dressed girls leer in doorways, the same ragged hobos huddle in the streets – but you can't miss it. It crinkles the nostril hairs, coats the eyes in an oily sheen, and makes the belly rumble. When I left Daniel's, I had no appetite at all. Hurrying, now, to meet the Princess in a restaurant, I could eat a horse. And by the look of some of these places, possibly soon may.

Back when I used to work at *Poshbird Monthly*, I felt a part of Soho. Admittedly, I had to take an *A–Z* to work for the first fortnight. Our offices were in the middle of it, in one of those surprisingly lush green squares that you only ever stumble across when you are hopelessly drunk, and can then never, ever find again. Pretty soon, though, I felt a Soho stalwart. It's an area that thrives on bright-eyed youngsters in utterly menial, slightly overpaid media jobs. We thronged the pubs, we crowded the bars, we spilled into the restaurants just before closing time, and we ordered all the cheap stuff.

Crossing Shaftesbury Avenue now though, I see that I was wrong. Soho isn't about young media sluts at all. And it's not about the Chinese, with their insulated, inexplicable lives. It's about weird, ageless men who look like they've spent the afternoon sleeping in their shapeless suits, on their foppish former boss's sofa. Nobody makes movies about these men; the best they can hope to be is a villain's sidekick. And their stories aren't clear, but tangled and amoral, the stories of men who twitch in the sunlight, who hurry, and frown, who wear sunglasses over their glasses and are obviously and inevitably and unavoidably, going down.

'Mackie! You look deathly! Where were you last night? In a park?'

The Princess is immaculate, black power-suit that makes me think Chanel at a pristine white table cloth. Her hair is ramrod-straight but rigid; it doesn't hang, it pokes.

'In a cell,' I tell her.

'You *are* joking?'

'Do you want me to have been joking?'

My sister sighs. 'You're impossible. You aren't drunk, are you? The whole point of this was that you wouldn't be drunk, and wouldn't have an excuse to get drunk. Tell me you aren't drunk.'

'I'm not drunk,' I tell her, and glance around the room. 'Although I wouldn't mind a beer.'

'I've ordered you a Diet Coke. We have chicken and sweet-corn soup, followed by sweet and sour chicken and crispy beef with plain rice. Is that acceptable?'

'Ja, Kommandant.'

She scowls, prettily. 'You're being very strange. I spoke to Dad. He said that . . .'

I interrupt her. 'What about Mum? Have you spoken to her? How's good old Mum?'

'Mum's fine . . .'

'And *Ben*? How's good old *Ben*?'

'Ben is dying, Mackie. Ben has cancer. Happy?'

Ben is a human wall. In my mind, Ben is five and a half foot, both tall and wide. Dark brown skin with thick black hair all over it. In the film that they make of my life, Ben would be played by Pete Sampras, but stretched sideways and shrunk down. When Ben first came to Edinburgh, first started coming round to our house, he could hold me by one ankle and swing me around the garden like a lasso. How can something like that be dying?

'I'm not bothered,' I tell Mary, stonily, 'either way.'

'I don't believe you. He's having chemo. That's why they moved to another kibbutz. They're nearer the hospital now. But he's going to die. Whatever happens, he's going to die. That's why Mum got in touch with Janie, and that's why we've been in touch with her. But that's not what I want to talk about. Like I said, I spoke to Dad.'

'I spoke to him as well. Just the other night.'

'I thought you must have done. Did you have an argument?'

287

I shake my head. 'Not at all. Quite the opposite.'

Our food arrives. We tip, spoon, combine. I am lousy with chopsticks. The Princess is flawless.

'What's the opposite of an argument, Mackie?'

The beef is very good. And the chicken is also very good. This is all very strange. Airless. A conversation happening at no specific time. I feel as though I have stepped out of my life, momentarily, to meet my sister for lunch. 'Just a chat,' I say. 'What did he tell you?'

'He didn't tell me anything. He was being subtle. You know what he's like when he's being subtle.'

I nod. 'Excruciating.'

'Exactly. He kept trying to drop you into the conversation, innocuously. How your job was, whether you were still seeing Elspeth, whether you were happy. That kind of thing. I think he thinks you are cracking up.'

My sticks collapse, like a foal's legs. This is messy. 'Does he know about Mum?' I ask. 'That you've been in touch, I mean. And about Ben.'

'Yes. Janie told him, ages ago. Before we told you. He didn't want to talk about it.'

'And?'

'And we didn't talk about it. That's his prerogative.'

'But not mine?'

'No.' Mary is annoyed now. 'But that's not what we're talking about. Dad's worried about you, Mackie. And so am I.'

I feel hot, suddenly. 'Because you think I'm cracking up?'

She rolls her eyes. 'Of course not. You're like me. We don't crack up. People like Mum and Janie crack up. You're not mad. Just unhappy, perhaps. I know our lives are different, but that shouldn't matter. I want us all to talk to each other a little more. Regularly. Like a family.'

I laugh. 'Listen to yourself. You sound like Janie.'

'Fuck you,' snaps my sister, the prim, proper little Jewish princess, and I actually guffaw. After a few seconds, she titters. This is a victory.

'Okay,' I say, and I wipe my eyes. 'Let's talk. Honestly. Right now. Pour out our hearts. We're going to be rubbish at it, I warn you. What do you want to know?'

The Princess scowls. 'You're mocking me. I can tell. I meant in general, Mackie. Not necessarily now.'

'Why not now? Ask me something.'

'Like what? I can't think of anything!' Just for a moment, her composure is ruffled. This is the panic of a job interview, or an exam in music theory.

'Ask me about my girlfriend.'

'Okay. Fine. Macaulay? How is your girlfriend?'

I grin. 'You need a slightly more crazed smile. Show me infinite patience and love, but make sure you still somehow leave me nursing the suspicion that you're not really listening. Still, not bad at all.'

'Answer the damn question.'

'Haven't got a girlfriend. We split up.'

'Mackie! Why? Not Elspeth again?'

'Of course not. Lucy was just a dick. Next question?'

Mary flaps her eyelashes at me. 'You can't just leave it like . . .

'Next!'

'Job. How's your job?'

'Haven't got a job. Was sacked.'

'*Sacked?* Why?'

'I was a dick. Next question.'

'No,' says Mary, and puts down her chopsticks. 'Stop this. This game is stupid. Tell me everything.'

It takes a while. I have to run out and buy cigarettes and I have to whine at her until she does let me buy a beer. And I don't tell her everything, obviously. I leave out the last part, about Daniel. But I tell her almost everything else. I haven't really spoken like this with anyone since the Diamond Ball, since Act 1, when the film began. It feels good.

'You know who it is,' she says to me, once I have finished.

I blink at her. 'No I don't.'

'Yes you do. It's obvious. The way you tell the story. Is it someone I know? One of your horrible friends from that horrible house?'

'No! Mary, I don't . . .'

The Princess drips with disdain. 'Yes you do. Are you going to turn them in, and get the cash?'

I collapse. 'Maybe. It's not that simple.'

'No,' agrees my sister, thoughtfully, and waves at a waiter for the bill. 'I assumed it might not be, or else you'd have done it by now. So what are you going to do? How are you going to live?'

I shrug. 'I'm not sure, yet. Perhaps I'll move home. I guess you're going to have to be the successful one for a while.'

Mary snorts. 'Me? I gave my notice two days ago. In a month, I'll be in the same boat as you.'

'How? Why?'

My sister gives a wry smile. 'Next question.'

'What's happening? I thought you were doing really well. The Jew Ball was a triumph, wasn't it? And what about Wrexham House?'

'That,' says Mary, heavily, 'is the problem. It was meant to be mine. I've done all the work. I've booked the caterers, I've sent out the invites. I've had Nigel bloody Cuppitt's name engraved on the cup.'

'Who?'

'The winner. That documentary maker. He made that thing about the orphanage in . . . where was it? Turbolikstan? Something like that.'

'Oh, he's that one. Sure. Saw it on BBC4. It's not actually called Turbolikstan, surely?'

'Whatever. It's near Turkey, I think. Mackie, listen to me. You did ask. I've hired the security guards and I've even learned how the bloody burglar alarm works. But Wrexham House has been stolen from me. By that strutting little bitch Sarah.'

'Who?'

'The blonde? The one you always drool at? She pulled the boss.'

'The Hideous Penguin Man?' I am appalled. 'I saw them dancing but . . . eeeuuw. That's repulsive.'

'You should have thrown a bucket of water over them. Then she wouldn't suddenly be number-one girl, and I wouldn't be looking for a new job.'

A thought strikes me. 'But you used to be number-one girl. Does that mean you and Tony . . . ?'

Mary raises an eyebrow. 'If I wasn't your sister, I'd slap you for that. But no. I think it is safe to say that Reuben would have minded.'

'Ah yes. Reuben. I never ask about Reuben, do I?'

'No,' says Mary.

I'm stepping off the tube at Green Park when my mobile rings. I see the name flash up on the display and very, very nearly decide not to answer. But I do.

'Evening, Tiger,' I say, airily. 'Let me guess. Rebecca has you working late, and couldn't remember where they keep the paper clips. Bottom left, old bean. Behind the staples.'

'Mac,' says Philip, and there is something wrong with his voice.

'Listen. I wanted to tell you before . . . before somebody else told you. There's been a . . . development. He's struck again.'

I stop walking so suddenly that one of those scary old Knightsbridge ladies clatters into my back, dropping her yappy little dog. At another time, I might have had the presence of mind to stamp on it. I think of Daniel when I left, drunk on his balcony, head lolled forward onto his chest.

'He can't have done.'

'He has,' says Philip. 'Mac, he has. It was at Dana Marion's launch, last night.'

'*Last* night? But . . . are you sure?'

'They've only just let us know. There was a card, just like before. The thing is, it's pretty nasty. The girl. She's . . . well. She's somebody you know.'

'A girl? Why is there a girl?'

'She was attacked,' says Philip. 'She was drugged and attacked. Not raped, we don't think, but beaten up, certainly. It's not quite clear. But she . . .'

'No. Shut up.' I feel upside down. I feel like Ben has swung me by my ankle, and let me go. 'A girl? A card? Who are you talking about, Philip? Fingers? Or Mr Spike?'

'Both,' says Philip. 'It seems pretty obvious that they're the same person. We should have thought of it. It's the same world, isn't it? The same sort of targets.'

'No way,' I say.

'Yes,' insists Philip. 'He left a card. He virtually confessed.'

'This can't be true.'

'It is true. But Mac, the girl . . .'

'What fucking girl?'

Philip sounds like he's about to cry. 'The girl who was drugged. Mac. It's your friend from Scotland. It's Elspeth.'

'Everything?'

It takes me under fifteen minutes to get back to Daniel's flat, which, considering I'm on foot and a physical ruin, is pretty impressive. I'm about to stab the buzzer with a finger, as a warrior monk might, for example, stab the voicebox of a mortal enemy, but at the last second I think better of it.

I don't want Daniel to realise I am here.

Or rather, I do want Daniel to realise I am here, but I want him to realise it at the precise moment I descend from behind him like a wraith and split his skull open onto his plasterwork. I'm thinking of the eye-gouging slaughter at the end of *28 Days Later*. I'm thinking of the way that brain comes apart in *Platoon*. I'm thinking of a bar-room beating from *Once Were Warriors*, or of what the talented Mr Ripley does to Dickie Greenleaf with an oar. I step to the side of the door, and set about climbing the drainpipe.

I'm actually rather good at drainpipes. I used to have to climb them fairly frequently, back when I lived at Paxy's. It was so rare that the place would be empty, that the front door would even be locked, that nobody ever bothered with a key. Presumably Paxy had one, but I never saw him use it. Periodically, we'd return home, as a mob, from some other party, or nightclub, or one of our outreach woodland jaunts (have I mentioned the outreach woodland jaunts? Not nice) and the place would be dark and shuttered, locked down like a missile silo. My skylight didn't lock, so the duty invariably fell to me. An ancient iron pipe by the corner of the house, a scramble up a slate-tiled roof, another pipe, and then a victorious descent through a deserted, conquered house.

The trick is to lean back, to make the gravity outward, rather than downward. Then you put your feet flat against the wall and simply walk up, feeding the pipe hand over hand as you climb. I developed quite a knack for it.

Daniel's drainpipe is made of thin grey plastic. Six feet up, the thing sheers off from the gutter and dumps me on my back in the street, like a stranded woodlouse. Now I'm really pissed off. I roll to my feet, and lean the broken section against the wall diagonally. I run up it, ignoring the creaks and cracks, and leap for the railings of the first-floor balcony. I pull myself up, stand on top of the railings, and leap for the one above. I do this three more times, and at no point do I fall off and die. Then I'm on Daniel's balcony, and I'm stepping through the open door to his flat.

He's not in the living room, and he's not in the bedroom. I kick open the bathroom door and he's there right in front of me, dressing gown open, sitting on the toilet. He starts to rise but I kick out, catching him on the collar bone. He crashes back into the cistern, one elbow triggering the flush. I step forward, with the sound of water suddenly roaring through the tiny, white-tiled room. I'm planning to hit him, punch him, send his head crunching back against the porcelain, but one of his flailing arms turns out to be flailing by design, rather than accident, and scoops up an open bottle of Old Spice. It catches me on the forehead and splashes everywhere. I step back. My eyes are streaming, I'm spluttering, I can barely see. Through a blurry haze, I see him reach for a shaker pot of Johnson & Johnson's talcum powder, and squeeze it, hard. A white cloud suddenly envelops my head. The stuff is clinging, like a paste, to my face, my eyes, my tongue. I gasp and step back again, only for my legs to collide with the side of the bath. Then I'm on my backside in the tub, and I'm sneezing.

'Nice move,' I croak.

'Thanks,' says Daniel, and turns on the shower.

'It wasn't me,' he tells me, a few moments later. He is sitting on the toilet again, and smoking. I, for want of anything better to do, am settling back into my moist and foamy nest.

'I knew you'd say that,' I tell him.

'But I do know who it was,' he adds.

'Who?'

'Jensen Randall.'

'You're sure?'

'I'm sure.'

'Tell me everything.'

'Everything?'

'Tell me everything.'

———

295

Elspeth is Daniel's accomplice. Well, of course she is. They've been working on this, together, from the start. Elspeth needed the money, and so did Daniel. Daniel had the contacts, and so did Elspeth. But mainly, as with anything, Elspeth was in it for the kicks.

Elspeth is an actress, but she doesn't really act very much. She spent a couple of years at drama school, nowhere special, and since then she's been in a few adverts, and a couple of pop videos. She was even in a play once, at that arts theatre in Elephant. It wasn't very good. I don't think she really cared. Elspeth is only an actress because she has to be something. Really, she lives off men.

Her flat in Marble Arch belongs to a Russian, who visits her once a month. Her car, still a convertible, but now a BMW, belongs to an Italian. I've no idea if he knows about the Russian, or the Russian about him. There are other men, too. Perhaps they all know about each other. Elspeth always has money, and she always has new clothes. She once told me that her grandmother would have regarded her as a prostitute. Although this didn't bother her, she preferred to think of herself as a muse. I wasn't happy with 'muse'. I suggested she use the term 'geisha'. She suggested that I was a pretentious idiot.

'Muse' fits, though. Originally she was a groupie, although 'groupie' really doesn't do her justice. Elspeth was the kind of groupie that explains why pop stars become pop stars. She moved, seemingly effortlessly, through New Wave, Britpop, and that whole arthouse scene, and every band she was with did their best work while she was bedhopping between them. I really don't think you could say she was exploited. Imagine a handsome man, prowling London Fashion Week and picking up models. Is he being exploited?

I don't know when she made the move from music to money. I do know that she didn't find it so rewarding, car, flat and allowances aside. Although Daniel doesn't say as much, I'd guess her partnership with him was her attempt to do something for herself, to stop her dependency on Russians and Italians and God knows who else. Maybe not, though. Elspeth wouldn't have seen it as dependency. That's the whole point, really, isn't it?

She and Daniel originally met, through me, at a party after a charity auction. I forget what it was for, exactly. Limbless orphans, out-of-work theatre directors, dogs with cancer, something like that. Hugh Grant was the auctioneer, I do remember that. I think he was promoting a film at the time. Whatever, it was over canapés and warm white wine. I'd just started at the *Gazette* and I thought Daniel was a genius, and I hadn't seen Elspeth in months, and I was thrilled with the whole situation. I'd imagine I was using each of them to show off to the other. There is something so blithely asexual about Daniel that beautiful women can't help responding to, and they clicked, obviously. I suppose I was dimly aware that they kept in touch, but I never really thought about it. Elspeth knows everybody I know. Elspeth knows everybody I will ever know. It didn't really register.

Daniel tells me he took her out for dinner, a week after he was sacked, and laid his cards, literally, on the table. He needed an accomplice. The rewards were high, and the risks were limited. He would do the thefts, the selling, the planning, everything. All she had to do was plant the cards. Write them, and plant them

So she did. At the Diamond Awards at the Mandarin, she slipped backstage, switched the nominations envelopes, and then dragged me into the toilets as an alibi. Elspeth walked past the shoebox on Sophie Gerad's doorway thirty seconds after Daniel had taken the *Collier d'Or* out of it, and put a Fingers card in its place. The courier who delivered the card to the *Evening Standard* after the Turino hoax was a real courier, whom Elspeth had found at Piccadilly Circus twenty minutes earlier. Wearing sunglasses, she paid a Japanese tourist ten pounds to give him fifty pounds, an envelope and an address.

One committed the crime, the other provided the evidence. The thinking was, if Daniel was never caught with a card, then, at least until he'd lifted whatever he was lifting that night, he could never be fingered as Fingers. And even if Elspeth was caught with a card, she could pretend she'd found it, or been given it, and while there might be suspicion, there would be no evidence to prove her wrong. The one time they deviated from this plan was when they burgled Topaz Wilton's safe. There were two cards in that robbery, one in the handbag from which her house keys, car keys and safe keys were filched, and one in the safe itself. Elspeth went to the party, and dealt with the bag. She slipped the keys to Daniel, who drove to the house in Wilton's own car, left a card in the safe, and drove back again. It all sounds highly fun and *Mission: Impossible* and my main emotion on being told about it, frankly, is to feel utterly left out.

That was why Elspeth had cards on her at the Dana Marion party last night. Daniel, in his sodden paralysis, had never called to tell her that the job was off. She must have guessed soon enough, when he didn't turn up to the party, but she still had the cards. She took them out of her bag, just in case, and put them in her bra. Then she had a couple of drinks.

Jensen Randall must have been chasing her for weeks. I saw him bending her ear at the MOFO party weeks ago, and he must have cornered her elsewhere, plenty of times. She wouldn't have slept with him voluntarily, I'm pretty sure of that. He might be rich, but he's too young and too . . . vile. The skin. The eagerness. The creepy, bright-eyed blankness. She just wouldn't.

As Daniel talks, I keep picturing that time in the pub around the corner from work, when Jensen tried to bottle that accountant. We were drunk, but not drunk enough, and the guy had come in with some friends, and was staggering towards the bar, drunker. We were either talking about women or office politics, and I was gradually learning that everything he said about either, however outrageous it might sound, was entirely genuine. And then they came in, and they were making a din, and they knocked over a small table and had ties wrapped around their heads, and I said, probably by way of simply changing the subject, that guys like that, occasionally, stirred within me the desire to kill. And Jensen nodded, amiably, jumped up, walked over to them, and smacked the fat guy in the face with his bottle of Grolsch. And when the guy went down, but the bottle didn't break, he leant over him, as though he was about to do it again.

And I pulled him off and bundled him out of the door, and I was shocked with him, and he didn't understand why. He really didn't. He just laughed, a little awkwardly. He didn't get it at all.

Could Jensen Randall be Mr Spike? I suppose he could. He goes to all the right clubs. He was surely invited to the opening of Void. He was at Thrust that night, when I faded out while speaking to Rebecca. He pulled me off her when I lunged, didn't he? Was he after Rebecca? And Rebecca and I were doing rounds that night. Did he try to spike her, and end up spiking me?

Dana Marion's party was at a function room in the Metropolitan, and attracted an eclectic crowd. In the midst of hat-lovers such as Sadie Frost, Jacquetta Wheeler, Laura Bailey, Rufus Sewell, Tracey Emin, Freddie Windsor and David Mellor, Jensen Randall slipped a pill into Elspeth's margarita and, eventually, followed her upstairs to the toilet. Then he bundled her, semi-conscious, into an empty boardroom.

According to Daniel, she was drugged, but not drugged enough. She woke up semi-naked, with Randall on top of her. She slapped and screamed. He punched her in the face, and kept punching. And, God, I can just imagine it. I bet he was wearing that fixed plastic grin while he hit.

It takes more than a few punches to subdue Elspeth. I've seen. Once, when we were children, and cycling to get ice cream, we got jumped by a gang of feral Craigmillar kids who wanted our bikes. But Jensen kept punching, and Elspeth kept slapping and screaming, and eventually he punched her so hard that she felt something red hot go click between her right check and her temple, and she blacked out. She woke up ten minutes later, choking on blood and teeth and wearing only her pants. Jensen was sitting in a swivel chair, watching her shiver and retch. He had five Fingers cards in his hand, spread out like a fan. They had been folded up inside her bra.

Elspeth didn't scream anymore. Jensen mentioned me and my articles, cocaine and paedophilia, Itotaki and Japan. He mentioned Elspeth's line of work, inasmuch as he understood it, and remarked upon how much all sorts of newspapers were going to enjoy writing about it, once she was linked to everything else. Elspeth was scared, drugged and probably concussed. She was done with screaming. She didn't have a hope.

Daniel doesn't tell me what Randall did to her, but he does say that it wasn't as bad as it could have been. When he was done, he made her swallow another pill, and then another, and then he gave her one of the cards, and made her sign it, as Fingers would. Then he sat on her until she passed out, with the note still clutched in her hand. Then, as her eyes began to puff and close, and the blood caked around her nose, he left her for the cleaners.

———

I'm out of the bath now. I'm standing in Daniel's stinking living room, and he's run out of Dunhill.

'Is she okay? She's okay, isn't she? How do you even know all of this?'

Daniel is grave. I think he might even be sober. 'She came out of hospital, just after you left, and called me. She's bruised, and she's lost a few teeth. They think she might have cracked an eye socket. It's not disfiguring, Mac. A few tiny scars, maybe.'

'I'm going to kill him. I'm actually going to kill him. I could get a gun. Or a knife. Or just a shovel, or something . . .'

'Mac. You have to listen to me. She told the police she didn't remember a thing. That's how she wants this. It's her call.'

Daniel sounds different, shaken. I can hear an accent on the edge of his voice, like South African, but softer. I've never noticed it before.

'Fuck her call. I'm going to kill him. Then I'm going to the police.'

He leans forward, and catches me by the shoulder. 'She's given them a statement. She told them she was attacked. She hasn't told them by who, and she doesn't want to. She wouldn't even let them take DNA samples. Listen. If she tells them the truth, Randall might go to jail. But she had the card, Mac. So there would be trouble. Publicity, at least. And Elspeth lives a private life. Jensen was right. Newspapers would love her. All those Russians and pop stars. She doesn't want that.'

I knock the arm away, grab Daniel by the lapels and slam him against the wall. Stacked empty wine bottles spin away like skittles. 'This is your fault!'

He doesn't fight me off. 'I know it is. It all is. I don't know what to do. I'm worried he might do it again. Worse. To somebody else. I want to go to the police, too. But it's her call. It has to be.'

I slam him again. I can feel myself starting to cry. I'm thinking of Elspeth's face, the way her cheeks are always slightly flushed. 'Jesus, Daniel. Her eye socket?'

Daniel closes his eyes. 'She'll be fine. I know it sounds bad, but she'll be fine. Mac, I'm sorry. It was never meant to turn out like this.'

Something catches me in the way he says this. 'The Jimmy Choo,' I say slowly. 'That was hers, wasn't it?'

He looks stricken. 'Yes. I almost told you. It was a one-off. Well, a two-off. But it's over.'

I'm expecting rage, or jealousy, or all the other familiar boiling furies that bubble over when I hear about Elspeth and other men. But I just feel sad. Empty, and very sad. I let go of his dressing gown and push the heels of my hands into my eyes.

'This is too mad. Where is she now? At home?'

'She didn't want to go home. She didn't want to come here, and she didn't want to go to a hotel. She said she had to go somewhere safe.'

'So where is she?'

'Where do you think she is?'

Elspeth is in my flat. It's taken two years, but she's finally used her key. She's left a note with the night porter, who is every bit as friendly as that human gargoyle Lenny, and she's deadlocked the door. Just before I bang on it with my fist, I check my watch. It's 1.45 a.m. I hesitate, and then I go back outside.

Knightsbridge is deserted. There's a yellow moon, bloated and smeary, hanging up over Hyde Park Corner. Over there is the West End, with its clubs and bars and hotels. A little bit further is Paxy's house, now cold and empty, perhaps with Carolyn floating around in it like a crazy wraith. It's all wrong. It doesn't fit. This isn't how my movie is meant to be at all.

A death, a sacking, and a sexual assault. It's not me. It's not my story. Not even nearly. It's the wrong genre altogether. My movie is meant to be cheerier than this, lighter. It's meant to be all about mindgames between equals, about scaling walls and fleeing down corridors. It's meant to be an adventure, and it is meant to be without consequence.

I sit down on my building's front steps and I breathe, very carefully. Then I dry my eyes, stand up, and call Daniel.

'It's me again,' I say. 'Listen. He's not going to do this to anybody else. We're going to put that fucker in jail. But she'll be fine, and we'll be fine. We're going to get your job back, and we're going to make a lot of money. I don't know exactly how we're going to do it, but I'm going to work it out. Everything is going to be all right.'

Daniel's answerphone, clearly unconvinced, does not reply. I go back upstairs, bundle up my jacket to make a pillow, and lie down in the corridor outside my front door. My eyes are closed, but I don't sleep for a very long time.

'What do you want?'

've always expected to end up with Elspeth. Not quite consciously, just as a sort of lingering assumption at the back of my mind. Elspeth was my first. Elspeth is the reason I have done almost everything. I can't imagine life any other way.

We were seventeen, and I wasn't Elspeth's first, not nearly. She had a succession of boyfriends who were slightly, but not sickly, older, and she used to run rings around them all. I used to tease her about it, rather longingly. She, in turn, used to tease me about the longevity of my virginity. I quite liked this. It was intimacy, of a sort.

Weird as it might sound, I never wanted to sleep with her. She wanted it to happen; I didn't. Well, I did, but I also didn't. It was only the fact that we'd never had sex, I felt, that kept our friendship on an equal footing. Otherwise, I'd have been competing with all those bass players and DJs. This way, I was unique.

In a loaded, teenage, understated way, it was laughingly understood that, should things get ridiculous, should I be about to head off to university, say, without having BECOME A MAN, she'd assume the responsibility. This made the prospect of sex with Elspeth carry with it a whiff of failure, even though it was often the thing I wanted most in the world. We're barking mad as teenagers, aren't we?

I'm older now. I understand that Elspeth was terribly mixed up, and that this was her way of letting me know that she did, actually, like me. At the time, I just didn't have the nerve to believe it. We'd sit up together, late at night, on the brown corduroy sofa in what had once been Nina's attic room, watching godawful films on Betamax and smoking, squeezing ever closer together. Frequently, my cock was a swollen titanium rod, hidden under a coat, tucked under my belt, or even pressed against her side, through the clothes between us. She knew about it. Finally, after she'd split up with a boyfriend, and we'd spent the evening watching *Planes, Trains and Automobiles*, she cried and pulled my trembling hand into her yellow elastic knickers. Later, she unbuttoned my black, baggy jeans, and wanked me off into a cushion.

Around a week after that, on a balmy, summer, Sunday evening, we went round to the back of Duddingston Loch. We had a secret place there, where we used to get stoned and drink cider, a place where you had to scramble down a steep bank, and you found yourself in a tiny secluded grove, with thick willow branches overhanging the channels they'd cut into the reeds to encourage the ducks to breed. She'd brought a bottle of vodka. Her hair was in two tiny buns, and she had a Courtney Love babydoll dress on over her jeans. We sat on neighbouring boughs, laughed at the ducklings, smoked her Craven A, and got drunk. She made sure I was drinking a lot more than she was. I didn't mind.

At one point, she dropped my Zippo into the water. She rolled up her jeans before jumping down to fetch it, but the water was deeper than she expected. She climbed back up, pulled them off, and stood on my branch, draping them over her own to dry. Then she straddled me and pushed down my trousers. It was as matter of fact as that. I can still hear the ducks, the wind in the reeds, and the tinny zoom of the distant cars. The feel of her legs, slightly wet, against my own. She took my thumb and rubbed it across her flushed cheeks and swollen lips. We didn't kiss, but we did hug a lot.

That was the summer we spent fantasising about moving to London. I miss Elspeth. I should remember that summer more often. It's not true that she only ever made me feel bad about myself. Whatever I might sometimes seem to suggest.

Even in the morning, I don't wake her. I'm up with the lark, or at least I would be if Brompton Road had larks. Up with the maids, perhaps. Up with the au pairs. Either way, I'm up early and I head around to Monkle Street. Here, under the Greek Cypriot drinking den where I met Daniel that time, a Turkish Cypriot runs a greasy spoon. I have the full English – bacon, eggs, tomato, toast, and a deceptively spicy sausage. While digesting, I make some notes on the back of a napkin.

I have three missions today. One will take me to the British Library, one to Liverpool Street, and one to Hendon. Two of them require me to make phone calls in advance. I make them, then I pay up, step outside, and jump on the bus up to King's Cross.

'Somebody would have to stick him in a box and lead us to him.'

Rebecca said that. I've got my thief. Now I just need to find my box.

Have you ever been to the British Library? Wonderful place. They let me join just after I quit at *Poshbird Monthly*, when I had a brief and unsuccessful stab at freelance journalism. I had to show them a few articles I'd had published in the last year, and they gave me a card that would allow me to get past the reading-room guards for the next five. I couldn't believe it. Only three articles, and for the next half-decade I would always have a warm, well-lit, middle-class place to spend my days. For a few months I used to go there quite a lot. I never actually needed the books, but like all libraries the place positively seethes with flirtation and sexual tension. I used to sit at my desk, fantasising about noisy sex with one of those kinky PhD students in leather boots, or a dressed-down young novelist in a half-unbuttoned shirt. It's all bollocks, of course. People stare, people blush, people look away, but nobody ever actually says a single word to another human being. Only once did I ever even attempt to pick anybody up there – this trendy travel writer, cute as buttons, with long brown hair shot with gold. We got talking in the café, but her boyfriend turned up after twenty minutes or so. He was a scruffy little writer, like a shorter, uglier version of me. God knows how he managed to end up with somebody like her. There's no justice.

At the computer terminal in the vast Humanities One room, I discover there are only two books on Wrexham House. The first is a glossy guide brochure, from 1979. The other, from 1952, is a history of the Wrexham Prize. I order both, return to my desk, and wait.

Midday, the Golden Heart, Spittalfield's Market.

'You married, Eccles?'

Detective Inspector Tom St Eccles holds his chin in both hands, like Desperate Dan. 'Now why could you possibly want to know that?'

'Humour me. Wife? Kids? Pint?'

'Not while I'm on duty, thanks. And no. I was engaged, but I'm not any more. Why?'

I give him a coy schoolgirl look. 'My friend fancies you.'

'I think I'd rather give your friends a miss, Lewis. No offence meant.'

'I bleed.'

'I'm sure you do. What do you want? I'm sure you didn't drag me all the way out to this greasy hellhole just to set me up with your friend.'

'You don't like it?' I gesture around, vaguely. 'It just felt right. Smoky air. Old men drinking. Beer. Isn't it exactly where the likes of us ought to meet to swap tips?'

'Thank God,' says Eccles, and rolls his eyes skywards. 'We're swapping tips. I was afraid you'd come over all Cilla Black. We do have grubby pubs nearer the Yard, you know. Ever been to the Elusive Camel? Positively filthy.'

I grimace. 'Damn. That would have done, yeah. You know, I very nearly set this up for a park bench instead. St James's Park? By the ducks? But it might have rained.'

'We could have used umbrellas.'

'I don't have an umbrella.'

'I could have brought two.'

'It doesn't matter. This is perfect. The two of us, meeting out in the world, sharing our leads. Off the record. Incognito. We could be anybody, just having a drink.'

'You'll have noticed I'm in uniform today, Lewis.'

'Mmm. Disappointing.'

'Sorry.'

'I'll get over it. I have information for you, Eccles. We can help each other. You get the arrest, we get the story.'

'We? I thought you were out of a job.'

'I didn't say we.'

'You most certainly did.'

'Royal we. It's not important. Go on, Eccles. Get us a Staropramen. On the taxpayer.'

Eccles buys me a half. Twenty minutes later, he leaves smiling. And not just because he has Rebecca's mobile number.

Four p.m., Starbucks, Hendon High Street. I almost don't recognise the Princess at first. Her hair is back in a pony-tail, and she's wearing a black polo-neck and a knee-length tweed skirt.

'You look different from yesterday,' I tell her. I'm sipping a mocha latte. I arrived early. Almost a first.

'How so?'

'Dressed down. Casual. The jumper. Are those *trainers?*'

The Princess scowls and sits down. 'They're Dolce & Gabbana. And this is cashmere.'

'I'm not knocking it,' I tell her, quickly. 'I think you look lovely.'

'I'm off duty,' she says, and softens. 'But thank you. That was a very sweet thing to say. Even if I do think you are quite mad. Listen, I haven't got long. I have some applications to get through. I'm not used to seeing you this often. What do you want, Mackie?'

I tell her.

'That's easy,' she says.

'Just for me,' I say. 'Daniel already has one.'

'Daniel?' she frowns. 'What does this have to do with Daniel?'

I curse, inwardly. 'Can we pretend I never mentioned Daniel?'

Mary looks at me, levelly, for just a moment. 'Fine. Is that all?'

I swallow. 'No. I also need a few details. How many security guards will there be? In what sort of case is the Wrexham Cup being held? Does anybody take it out? Oh, and what areas do the burglar alarms cover?'

309

My sister blinks. 'Oh Mackie.'

'Please, Mary. You planned all this. I wouldn't ask if it wasn't important.'

'I could lose my job.'

'You've already *lost* your job. I wouldn't ask if you hadn't. I'd be trying to get Sarah into bed or something.'

'You already tried that.'

'Well, yeah. Penguin Tony, then.'

Mary smiles, but unhappily. 'Mackie, be honest with me. Is it going to be obvious that somebody told you all that?'

'All that? No.'

'But?'

I swallow. This is the tricky bit. 'But. I also need something else. I need the alarm code. Not for everywhere. Just for the room with the Wrexham Cup in it.' I think back to the books I found this morning. 'The East Gallery, rebuilt in 1887, after a fire.'

My sister just stares at me. A couple with a pram move behind her, towards the counter. Through my soles, I can feel the wheels judder over the floor tiles.

I speak hurriedly. 'Please Mary. You told me you knew how they worked. Nobody will ever know.'

'Nobody will ever know?' the Princess is almost squeaking. I have never heard this noise before. 'Somebody deactivates the alarm and steals the cup, and I'm one of . . . of, like *ten* people who knows the code, and you are telling me that *nobody will ever know?*'

'Nobody is going to steal anything,' I say, quietly.

'Oh Mackie. I'm not stupid.'

'I swear it. If anything quite the opposite.'

'The opposite? Oh, right enough. You're going to break in and *give* them things?' Mary isn't happy. Mary is unhappy enough to be sounding Scottish.

'Trust me,' I say. I'm her big brother. She should trust me. 'Nobody will ever even know the alarm was switched off.'

'You promise?'

'I promise.'

'There will be no stealing going on?'

'No,' I say, and then think about this. 'Not as such.'

'Really? Nothing illegal at all?'

I hesitate. 'I didn't say that.'

'But there's no danger of anybody being caught?'

'I didn't say that either.'

'Oh Mackie,' says Mary again, but she also, eventually, says yes.

And finally, Philip. This one is a phone call. I make it at home.

Home smells of Elspeth. She's left me a note with the porter apologising (why?) for last night, and saying that she'll be out most of the day, collecting belongings from her flat. Ships in the night, even now.

My bed is made, and my holey green Cure T-shirt is folded on the pillow. I pick it up, hold it to my face and inhale. I can tell she wore it last night. Thinking about what she has been through, the action makes me feel guilty. On the pillow, also, I notice a tiny fleck of blood. I fold the T-shirt and replace it where it was.

My kitchen space is clean and she has dragged my easel out from behind the curtain. The nonsensical daubs I made while pretending to paint Lucy have been turned face down. She's painted a smiling stick man with glasses and dandelion hair, holding hands with a frowning stick woman with a mouth like an upturned U. Elspeth is either utterly bonkers, or very, very bored. But then, I've known that for years.

I leave a note for her, to say that I'll be up late with Daniel, and will spend the night there. I tell her to call if she needs anything. I start to say that I have a plan, and that I'm looking forward to seeing her, but it sounds inane. I score it out and just write, rather lamely, that everything is going to be okay.

And then, Philip.

'Hey, Tiger,' I say.

'What do you want, Mac?'

'Just wanted to check. You guys are going to Wrexham House tomorrow, aren't you?'

'Of course we are,' says Philip.

'Splendid,' I say.

'It was all bullshit. Media hype.'

'The trick,' I say to Daniel, 'is to lean back, to make the gravity outward, rather than downward. Then you can put your feet flat against the wall and simply walk up, feeding the pipe hand over hand as you climb.'

Daniel just stares at me. We're in the flickering central courtyard at Wrexham House, and we're in black tie. Our hands . . . well, never mind our hands. It's raining, slightly, and we're sharing an edge of hysteria. It's a quarter to ten.

Around a hundred metres away, through the windows on the other side of the courtyard, is the West Gallery. In there, the annual Wrexham House bash is in full swing. We're too far away to make out faces, but we can hear music and the buzzing hubbub of voices. There's no way that anybody inside can see us. It's too bright in there, and dark out here.

We're outside the parallel East Gallery, home of the Wrexham Cup. It's deserted, but the windows on the ground floor are locked.

313

There is a balcony above us, however, with a pair of huge French windows. I'm pretty sure that they won't be.

'Simply walk up?' whispers Daniel. He sounds horrified. 'You say that like you read it in a book.'

'I am an old hand,' I tell him. 'Trust me.'

Daniel tugs at the drainpipe uncertainly. 'Then what?'

'Then we go through the French doors on the balcony, and we're inside. The East Gallery is a mirror image of the West. There's a walkway around the top, and a staircase by the door. It'll be easy.'

'What if the windows are locked?'

'They won't be. At least, there's no reason why they should be. There's no way into this courtyard if you haven't come through the building. At any rate, this building is listed to high heaven. I was reading about it, yesterday, in the British Library. They'd never have got permission for anything too modern or effective.'

'Alarmed, then.'

Obviously, there is an alarm. As I have learned, the East Gallery is not just home to the Wrexham Cup. It is also home to two Constables, a Picasso sculpture, a medieval tapestry, and a display case of bronze-age pottery. According to the Princess, there's a state-of-the-art motion-sensor alarm down on the ground floor. This is where the cup is now sitting – in a case, on a trolley, ready to be wheeled next door. But she seemed pretty confident that the upstairs walkway wouldn't be alarmed. There's ordinarily no way to get to it. There's no point.

I explain this to Daniel. 'The alarm won't be triggered until I get down the stairs,' I say. 'And I have the code. I just need to get to the box by the door.'

'In thirty seconds?'

'Yes, in thirty seconds. I told you that already. I used to be able to do four floors in thirty seconds. This is, like, four metres. Easy.'

'Listen to yourself, boy. I'm meant to be the cat burglar here.'

I giggle. 'So act like one. Pull yourself together. Why are you being so jittery?'

Daniel flaps his arms around his ridiculous frame. 'I'm just cold,' he mutters. 'Pay me no heed.'

I'm on the balcony in under a minute. Good solid cast iron. If time wasn't quite so pressing, I might nip down and do it again, just for fun. 'Your turn,' I murmur.

Daniel reaches then stops, reaches then stops. Grumbling, he shrugs off a layer of clothing. His shirt flares off-white in the muted moonlight and I can clearly make out the thin, yellow climbing rope, wound around his waist like a cummerbund.

'. . . fuck are you *doing*?' I whisper.

'This damn jacket,' he hisses. 'Too bloody small.'

Let's step back a bit.

Daniel and I arrived separately. From the moment I stepped out of the cab (*seventeen quid* from Farnham, the bastards) the annual Wrexham House party was everything I had ever dreamed it would be. Dancers with psychedelic bikinis, ironed hair, and not a flicker of self-consciousness were writhing in oversized marble vases all down the white chalkstone driveway. Waiters, all looking like butlers, greeted every guest with foot-high flutes of champagne. I came down the driveway in front of Kevin Spacey, Peter Mandelson and Trudie Styler, and up ahead I could see Erin O'Connor, Natalie Imbruglia, Debbie Harry and Sir Ranulph Fiennes. None of them had come in a taxi. Forget sloanes and fuckheads in nightclubs. This was the real thing.

Inside, there was the obligatory English-country-house curving double staircase, with a flunkey at the bottom trying to persuade people to walk up on the left, and descend on the right. There was a set of double doors on each side of the ground floor, and on each side of the landing. The ones that led to the left, the west, were open. The ones to the right were not. There was a security guard in a grey shirt and cap in front of each. I stood between the staircases, as though between the horns of a bull, and sipped at my vase of fizzy pink. I felt immortal, computer-gameish, a man on a mission. The Wrexham Cup was in there, to the right, behind security guards and closed doors. It was at the far end of an alarmed hall, in a glass case like an upright sarcophagus. And soon, I would be there, too.

I climbed up the staircase alongside Claudia Schiffer and Matthew Vaughan, and ambled onto the walkway around the West Gallery. It was a blur down there. Naomi Campbell, Rosie Byrne, Jonny Wilkinson, somebody Freud, Anita Pallenberg, Bay Garnett, Terrence Dibbley, Gary Barlow. Cat Deeley, Sienna Miller. Ricky Gervais, Tara Palmer-Tomkinson, Sting, Melanie Parker. Richard Branson. Esther Rantzen, Minnie Driver, Kate Driver, Jodie Kidd, Joanna Lumley, Annie Lennox and David Gilmour. And, at the side of a canapé table, talking loudly to a girl whose face I was sure I recognised from the back pages of *Harper's Bazaar*, was Jensen Randall. I descended, steeled myself, and approached.

'You've got some nerve being here,' I said, amiably.

He turned to me, nose poised like he was going to peck me with it. 'Lewis,' he said, with affected distaste. Joy of joys there was a bruise, cooling to purple under his right eye.

'Jensen,' I replied. 'Hullo.'

His eyes flickered. 'That's *Yansen*.'

'Isn't that what I said?'

'No,' barked Jensen. 'It's not what you said. It's not what you ever say. Yansen. Yansen, Yansen, Yansen. What are you even doing here?'

'Actually Jensen,' I said, and the girl giggled. 'Thanks. Actually

Jensen, I have an invitation. And not through your poxy news-paper either. Ironic, that. You're the hack. I am merely a well-to-do lad about town, popping by to socialise. Isn't it a scream? Perhaps I could grant you an interview.'

Jensen glowed red. We looked at each other, he and I, and something passed between us. I knew what he had done, and he knew I knew. Philip was right. I had always been a little bit afraid of Jensen. But, with Elspeth hanging between us, like a spectre, he was afraid of me.

'Get out of my face before you annoy me,' he said, quietly, and turned away.

'Sure,' I said, and slapped him on the back, so hard that his drink sloshed forward out of his glass. 'Wouldn't want you to make a scene. Not here.'

I was talking loudly now, like a drunk. Heads were turning. Jensen tried to shrug me off, but I slapped him again, even harder, and gripped the back of his dinner jacket.

'Like I said,' I continued, in my mad, amiable shout, 'surprised you had the guts to show up. At the Wrexham House! Because you're never comfortable in the club, are you? And just think, that cup, just a couple of rooms away. You can't get near it, can you? It's on the top of your godawful paper, and you think you ought to own it, but you don't. You'd have to win it. Bet that hurts. You creepy bastard, you.'

Jensen was trembling. He's no good at confrontation. 'Leave it . . .' he began.

'Why?' I yelled, actually hollering now. I nodded at the girl. 'Got plans? With her? Going to get a pill and . . .'

Jensen fairly wrenched my arm away, and I pulled back, hand balled into a fist. Just before I unleashed (and I would have done, I swear it, even though it wasn't the plan) somebody stepped between us. Daniel.

'Calm down,' my former boss hissed, and gave me a flat-palmed shove to the chest, so that I staggered and tripped and slumped against the canapé table. He turned to Jensen. 'I'm terribly sorry. He's upset. Drunk, I think. He's . . .'

'Jensen!' I shouted. 'Did I ever show you what Liam Gallagher did to me at the Brit Awards?'

Daniel leapt at me, but the guacamole was already flying.

Jensen had one of those horrible shirts on. The ones that look like a standard wing collar when you've got a jacket on, but reveal all kinds of colours and swirls on the back and sleeves once you take it off. It was yellow and green, designed to look like overlapping pages of a newspaper. Bad enough on a dance floor. In the bright brittle light of a champagne reception, it was unforgivable.

While Daniel took both jackets to the kitchen, I sat by the canapé table, cackling at him and winking at strangers. People kept sneaking secretive glances towards us, over each other's shoulders or through the glasses in their hands. Faces peered over the balcony of the walkway above. The *Harper's Bazaar* girl was mortified, but Jensen had her trapped against a pillar. He had become a party Jonah, with guacamole in his hair and a killer's eyes.

Over to my left, I spotted a few familiar faces, and started slightly. Rebecca and Philip were there, with Neil, who was clinging to a camera, and Jessica, who was clinging to Neil. They kept looking in my direction. I never knew they all knew each other. Eventually, I waved. Everybody looked away. Only Philip looked back.

'On your feet,' barked Daniel, hurrying past me with Jensen's jacket. 'I'm terribly sorry,' he told him, as the girl dodged politely between them, and set off at a run, 'I think I got most of it out. Mine was far worse. I'm sure he didn't mean to get carried away like that. I'll keep him away from you.'

Jensen slipped gratefully into the jacket, covering up his foul shirt. 'I throw a good punch,' he said. 'He should know that.'

I lunged forward, but Daniel caught me again. 'Fresh air!' he roared, and I allowed myself to be frogmarched away like a child.

After ten paces, I ducked my head and switched to a murmur. 'How did it go?'

'Perfectly,' said Daniel, and I could tell he was fighting not to laugh.

We were heading for the carpark, outside. Once we were out of sight of the bouncers, Daniel stopped and let go of my arm. I bent double, and rubbed my eyes with the heels of my hands. There was a light rain falling, but I was highly strung enough to find it soothing. The worst thing was, I knew I was going to have to speak to Jensen again tonight, and I wasn't going to be allowed to hit him even then. Daniel was going to do the hitting. That was the plan. Not fair.

I felt wired, like a murderous racehorse. I wondered how Elspeth would want me to behave, were she to see Jensen and me face to face. Would she want me to attack him, like I had wanted to, or would she want me to fuck up his life, like the plan said? I grinned. She wouldn't want me to do either. She wouldn't think it had anything to do with me at all. Despite my best efforts, for almost as long as I've known her, she never thought that anything about her life did.

'All right there?' said Daniel, eventually.

'Mmm. Yes. What have we got?'

Daniel stuck his hand into his jacket pocket. Although it wasn't his jacket, of course. Daniel was in Jensen's jacket and Jensen was in Daniel's. Hence that little stunt with the guacamole.

'Car keys,' he said. 'And a wallet.'

It took me a while but eventually, inside the wallet, in the back section of the coin compartment, I found what I was looking for. Three little blue pills, just like the ones in the pot from Rebecca's desk.

'Thank God,' I said, pocketing one, and handing the wallet back to Daniel. 'Now. Where's his car?'

'Right next to mine,' said Daniel.

I didn't even know Daniel had a car. It was a Mini, an old one. He told me he'd had it since 1987, when it was new. It was a grotty burgundy thing, dating from the days before old Minis had that retro chic vibe they have today, and back to when they were simply cheap motors for grandmothers. How he fitted into the thing, I couldn't imagine. He probably didn't drive it very often. He'd have to be sober for that.

The Ferrari was, indeed, right next to it, twenty times the price and nearly twice the length.

'Gloves?' I said, as we drew near.

Daniel pulled a packet from his trouser pocket, and tossed it over.

I looked up at him. 'Are you taking the piss?'

'What?' he said.

'Daniel, I'm not going to have sex with the thing. Give me some fucking gloves.'

The master thief shrugged. 'I haven't got any,' he said. 'I normally do, but I used them to paint a window frame the other week. The fingertips withered. Don't look at me like that, Macaulay. I had to stop at a pharmacy on the way here. I consider these a stroke of genius.'

'I consider them Femidoms,' I told him, and snatched the car key out of his hand. I clicked the burglar alarm tab, and nudged open the Ferrari's boot with my toe. Daniel advanced on the back of his own car, and then stopped, looking stricken.

'What now?' I snapped. 'Get it out.'

'It's locked,' said Daniel, slowly.

'So bloody unlock it.'

'They keys are in my pocket.'

'Then get them out and . . . oh. Oh Daniel.'

Daniel's keys were in Daniel's pocket. And Daniel's pocket was part of Daniel's jacket. And Daniel's jacket was on Jensen Randall.

Surprisingly sturdy, the backside of a Mini. I'd kicked a hell of a dent into the thing before long, but the boot still resolutely failed to spring open. Daniel had to stop me from breaking a window. Apparently you can't open a Mini's boot from the inside, anyway.

'What are we going to do?' he wailed.

I lowered my foot and glowered at him. I had a battered shoe, mud-spattered trousers and clammy prophylactics on my hands. 'You're fucking useless at this,' I said. I was amazed.

'I know,' said Daniel, and glanced around nervously. 'Are you surprised?'

'No. Well yes, actually. You're Fingers. You're the Gentleman Thief. You've led half of London on a merry dance for months. You're supposed to be a cross between Raffles and the guy out of the Pink Bloody Panther. I was expecting you to have at least a modicum of talent at this kind of thing, Daniel.'

'I told you,' he said, miserably. 'It was all bullshit. Media hype. I never had to do anything like this. I've no idea how to even get into a locked car. I got this thing for my eighteenth, you know. Aren't there any tools in Jensen's boot?'

I found a screwdriver. I kicked in Daniel's Mini a little more, and then worried at the catch until it popped. Then I took Joe Bastin's platinum disc out of the Mini and put it into the Ferrari. I was a better Thief than the Thief. I was rather pleased.

I took the brand-new thin yellow climbing rope out of Daniel's boot, ripped it out of the packet, dropped the packet into Jensen's boot, and handed the rope to Daniel. He wound it several times about his waist, and closed his – Jensen's – dinner jacket around it. Then we went back into the party, each knocked back a drink, and sneaked out into the inner court-yard.

So, that was before. That was how we got to be out here, in the rain, climbing up the side of a building and onto a balcony with a pair of ornate French doors. Which I cannot open.

'I thought you said they didn't lock,' growls Daniel.

'They shouldn't do. This is appalling.'

'Of course it is,' agrees Daniel.

'How dare they? This is a listed building.'

Daniel looks like he's going to hit me. 'What are we going to do?'

I think for a while. Then I take his jacket from him, wrap it around my hand, and punch it through one of the paperback-sized glass rectangles. Then I reach around to unlock the door.

'Well that seems to work.'

It's a little too dark to see exactly what happens next. As I open the door, there is the sound of it striking something, and that something striking something else. Then there is the sound, the remarkably discernible sound, of something rolling across the wooden floor of the East Gallery walkway and then falling, with a strange rattle, onto the downstairs floor below.

The alarmed, state-of-the-art, motion-sensor-heavy floor below.

'This is really, really bad,' I say, and duck inside.

Inside, it is dark. I run two metres, and then trip over a stool. Then I run another two, and almost put my foot through a painting. In theory, this was all so simple. In practice, it's awful. As I bounce down the stairs on my heels, I have about twenty-four seconds left.

Down on the flat I'm floundering, because it's darker than I expected it to be. There's a beeping sound, but a faint one, coming from somewhere near the door. It is the sound of my time running out. I'm sprinting, waving my hands like a cockroach's antennae, a desperate yet lazy strategy which somehow fails utterly to detect one of the nine-foot-tall, six-inch-wide pillars that anchor the balcony to the floor. It smacks me about the head for a while, and then deposits me on the floor. From here, I can see the blue LCD of the burglar-alarm control panel. I scramble to my feet, flip it open and, although it isn't easy in my sticky mittens, punch in Mary's code. Then I press enter, and the beeping noise stops.

For a few moments I just stand and shake. Then I make my ponderous way back across the floor, up the stairs and along the balcony to tell Daniel it is safe to come inside.

He looks harassed. 'Did you manage it?' he whispers.

I stare at him for a moment, trying to summon up an expression that conveys, with a single look, the marked absence of wailing sirens, flashing lights, pounding feet, shouting security guards, popping flashbulbs and the rubbernecking of everybody next door.

'Yes.'

———

We have an argument about it, and eventually we half open a curtain. The party across the courtyard gives us some light to work by, but not nearly enough. For a few moments we guide ourselves with Daniel's Zippo, but then a thought strikes me and I smack it shut.

'Smoke alarm?' says Daniel.

'Possibly. And I think I was melting my *glove*. We should have brought a torch.'

'I brought a little Magilite,' says Daniel, miserably. 'But it's in my jacket.'

'Of course it is. Hold on. Give me Jensen's keys.'

There's a tiny bulb on the door key, triggered by squeezing the fob. It's not much, but it's enough to prevent us from falling over anything. I hold it like a firearm, and wave it across the floor until I spot what it was that fell and triggered the alarm. It looks like a snooker cue. I pick it up, and lean it against a pillar.

The cup's case stands bold in the middle of the room. It's like that bit in *2001: A Space Odyssey* when you see the monolith. We should be dancing around like monkeys, praying.

'This is it,' I tell Daniel. 'They'll be coming to get it in an hour or two. We don't want to waste any time.'

'Is it that Inuit jockey guy this year?'

'That was last year. This time it's a filmmaker. The BBC4 thing about the orphanage. What's it called? Turbolikstan?'

'It can't be,' he says. 'Where is it? Near China?'

I shrug. The case is on wheels. It's wooden on three sides, like an oversized coffin, and glass on the front. Some kind of black felt paper has been taped over the glass.

'That's an unexpected bonus,' I say.

'How so?'

'Well. It means they might . . . never mind. They probably won't.'

'They probably won't what?'

'Doesn't matter. Leave it. Let's get a move on.'

With our sheathed fingertips, we worry the heavy wooden lid off the Wrexham Cup's case.

'Where's this going?' he grunts.

I shine the torch towards the far wall, and grin. There is a dumb waiter there. The book from the library had promised, but I hadn't quite dared to believe it. 'Over there.'

Daniel leans the plank against the wall and slides open the dumb waiter's door. 'Seems functional,' he says, and gives the operating rope an experimental tug. 'Why couldn't we come up in this?'

'The basement is alarmed,' I tell him. 'The Princess told me. It's on the same circuit as up here. And you'd never have hoisted me up in time.'

Daniel snorts. 'Me? Why couldn't I have been hoisted by you?'

'I doubt you'd have fitted in,' I say, peering inside. 'You're too tall.'

'Only just, I hope,' says Daniel, fingering the sleeves of Jensen's jacket.

'Only just,' I agree.

We put the plank in the dumb waiter and lower it down. Then we close the half-opened curtain and leave, the same way we came in.

'What about that?' says Daniel, pointing at the broken window.

I hesitate for a moment. 'Not a problem,' I say, finally. 'He has to get in somehow, doesn't he? Let's get out of here.'

'What happens now?'

'You go down to the basement. I'm going bury a hatchet. Shallowly.'

I pull the Femidoms from my hands, with a snap.

'You haven't got a story. You can't prove anything.'

Rebecca watches me approach, much like a medieval princess might have an oncoming leper with whom she once shared a drink, in his pre-leper days. She turns to go, but Philip catches her by the arm. Good old Philip, always catching people by the arm. He looks less shifty than before, more solid. Less Gunther, more Vladimir Putin. Perhaps my absence has done him good.

'I told you Eccles wasn't married,' I say, and Rebecca, perhaps despite herself, smiles slightly. Before I can follow this up, I suddenly find myself launched suddenly sideways. My tumbler of Grouse sloshes over my fingers.

It's Jessica. Pretty and petite as ever, and in a purple dress that looks like nightwear. Is there anything more terrifying than an angry Newcastle woman in stilettos? She comes forward, to shove me again, but Neil catches her, also by the arm. I don't have anybody to catch by the arm, or anybody around to catch mine. It makes me feel rather sad.

'Thought you'd be in a cell by now,' snarls Jessica.

I'm a little startled. *But we haven't done anything yet*, I almost say. 'Why?' I manage.

'Elspeth could have been killed,' snaps Jessica, and Neil pulls her close.

If you're so concerned, I want to say, *why isn't she staying with you?* My eyes meet Philip's, but Philip isn't saying anything.

'How's Carolyn?' I ask.

Jessica sneers. 'Who's Carolyn?'

'Carolyn. The blonde. The one I always see you with. She wasn't well when I saw her last. Not well at all.'

'I've no idea. I barely know her. I thought she was a friend of yours.' Jessica puts on her thinking face for a moment. 'Maybe I met her at Paxy's.'

'She's Paxy's sister,' I say. 'Didn't you know that?'

She didn't. Nobody did. There's a lesson in that. It's so easy to go through life thinking that you are the only one who isn't paying attention, that the world is a system that somebody else is holding together. But nobody ever is. Everybody is peripheral. There's nothing holding anything together, and nobody gives a shit.

It shouldn't make me happier to realise that. But it does.

Jensen, perhaps because he's not been having the best of nights, is drunk. This is a blessing. I spot him over by an ice sculpture, laughing with two cheaply expensive-looking blondes. Even from here, I can see the light sparkling from the glitter on their cleavages. As a waiter passes with a tray, one of them reaches for a mini Yorkshire pudding canapé. Her two-inch nails clatter uselessly on the tray for a few seconds, and then she picks it up between her palms. Like a squirrel.

The taller of the blondes says something in Jensen's ear and leads the other away by the hand, looking back over her shoulder and giggling. Momentarily, he's alone. I grab two bottles of Budweiser from a free-standing bar, thumb the blue pill from Jensen's wallet out of my pocket, and slip it into the top of one of them. I give it a slight swish, and set off across the room.

He looks up when he sees me coming and, almost defensively, raises his glass. Daniel's jacket is slightly too big on him, hanging in that teddy bear/George Bush sort of way. I can't imagine he's noticed.

'I come in peace,' I say, and gesture in an expansive I'm-such-an-idiot-let's-have-a-hug kind of way. Then I hold out a beer. 'Here. Have one of these.'

'Go away,' he says edgily, but he takes the bottle. 'We have nothing to say to each other.'

I laugh. 'Going to have to work on those clichés, Jensen.'

'Yansen,' he says but he looks puzzled. 'What do you mean?'

'Clichés,' I say, and I realise this is going to be even easier than I expected. 'You need to start thinking about things like that. Now you're a *columnist*.'

Jensen glares at me, darkly and drunkly. 'I can see what you're trying to do,' he says. 'It won't work. I'm not going to do that bit.'

'What am I trying to do? What bit?'

He knocks back the rest of his first drink and hands the empty glass to somebody passing by. Not a waiter, just somebody passing by. He's an arsehole.

'You're trying to convince me that I can't do your job,' he says. 'Like you always used to in the pub. All that rubbish about commas and paragraphs. Can't be bothered with it.'

'You can't be bothered with commas and paragraphs? Isn't that going to be a problem?'

'Patronising fuck,' says Jensen, and I'm momentarily grateful that he gave away his empty glass. 'It won't be a problem, because I'm not doing that bit. So there.'

'Which bit, Jensen?'

'Yansen. The writing bit.' He sneers and takes a swig. 'I'll get the poof or the jungle queen to do that.'

I have to play this carefully. I'm treating him with kid gloves, but I cannot let this pass. 'You're going to be a columnist and not do the writing bit?'

'No,' says Jensen and grabs me, suddenly, by the shoulder. 'I'm going to do the parties bit. The girls bit. The *getting Macaulay Lewis sent to jail* bit.'

'Not a chance,' I say.

Jensen does his gleaming vicar smile. 'I saw the cards. I have the emails. You're Fingers. You're the Thief.'

'You're Mr Spike,' I say, but I say it softly. His beer is half empty now. 'You're the rapist.'

He doesn't stop smiling. 'You can't prove it,' he says. 'I can get your fag friend to write what I know about the Thief, and get you sent to jail. That's going to be my big story. You haven't got a story. You can't prove anything.'

'Elspeth can.'

'Who?'

'I think you met the other night. At the Metropolitan.'

'The whore?' says Jensen. 'She can't. There's no evidence that points to me. There's just the cards, and they point to you instead. So, who's going to believe her? You can do what you like with *whores*, Lewis. Didn't you know that?'

If it wasn't for tonight, for the plan, for Daniel down there, still waiting in the basement, I do believe I'd ram my bottle into his mouth, and punch it, again and again, until it dropped in shards down his throat. Instead, I grin. It's a struggle, but I do. 'They don't point to me,' I say. 'You're wrong. I'm not Fingers.'

'Oh yes you are,' says Jensen, and, as our eyes lock, I get a vision of this, of now, from the perspective of whatever warped little mental engine lurks behind his. I see what is going on here. This is an intellectual joust, a hero and a villain, meeting like Bond and Blofeld at a drinks party. This is the moment I've been waiting for all along.

But this is the problem with real life. This is why it is different from fiction, from the film. In the real world, the bad guys don't know they are bad guys. Jensen thinks he's the hero and I'm the villain. He's a psychotic rapist with no friends and terrible hair, but he genuinely considers himself to be in the right. Real life is complicated.

I lean forward, close. 'I'm not,' I whisper. 'But I know who is. He's here, tonight.'

'Piss off, Lewis.'

'It's true. Listen. That Elspeth girl. The *whore*. I don't give a shit about her. I don't like what you do, but that's my problem. I'm offering you a deal. I just want my job back. You can do that, can't you?'

'No,' he says, but he says it in a way that obviously means *maybe*. His beer is very nearly finished. 'Why should I believe you?'

'Because it's true. Because there's no reason you shouldn't. Because, if you'll help me, we can nail him, tonight, together. I told you, he's here. That's why I'm here. He's here, and he's going to steal the Wrexham Cup. Come on, man. Let's do it. Let's get him. All I want is my job back.' I stick out my hand.

Jensen looks at it like I've offered him a fish. 'If it's not you,' he says, 'who is it? Who is it, and how do you know?'

'Daniel Kemp,' I say. 'It's been Daniel Kemp all along. And I know because he thinks I'm helping him. He's in the basement right now, waiting for me. Are you in?'

Jensen looks at me, and his bright evangelistic face is as transparent as Cellophane.

'I'm meant to be meeting those girls,' he says, equivocally.

I tell him that Daniel is going to text me. I tell him that he is going to come down in the dumb waiter, with the cup, and text me to collect it. I tell him to keep an eye on me, but subtly, and to follow my lead. I tell him that we have to be subtle, because this is our story, and we didn't want to lose it to anybody else.

'Listen, Jensen,' I say. 'Daniel is a big guy. There's a lot of strength in those spindly limbs. I couldn't take him by myself, and nobody would believe my word over his. I need you on this. So, look. Are you in?'

'Yansen,' says Jensen, but he shakes my hand. He's in.

He does as he's told. When I turn away, nonchalantly through the crowd, Jensen watches me. While I stand at the bar, sipping at whisky, he watches me. When I whip out my phone and study the screen, cupping it surreptitiously between my hands, he watches that, as well. I start moving towards the door, and by the reflection of the mirrored ball beneath the central chandelier, I can see Jensen Randall doing the same. There he is, behind David Furnish and Bobby Gillespie, pushing between Bob Geldof and Liam Fox, slipping past Pete Waterman and Vic Reeves. He's following me.

As soon as I'm on the stairs, I start running. I need him to be following me, but I need to get there first. I catch the banister at the bottom in the entrance hall, and see him picking his way across the landing above. I give him a meaningful nod, then I leap through the service door towards the cellar stairs.

There's a corridor at the bottom of the stairs, before the basement door. I wait at the end of it until I see Jensen's foot, just like I saw Daniel's foot, that time in the Gretchner Hotel. Then, knowing that he has seen me, I dive into the basement itself.

It's dark in here, as dark as a childhood fear. A cone of light spreads across the floor as I step inside, and then dwindles to a line as the door swings shut.

'Hi,' I say, and I hope that, somewhere in the darkness, Daniel is there to hear me.

The line swells again, as Jensen bursts through behind me.

'Now!' I hiss.

There is a thump, and the door swings shut.

'Aaaah!' shouts Jensen.

'Oh my God,' mutters Daniel.

Jensen curses. 'Lewis? Did you just hit me with a . . . with a *plank?*'

'Hit him again!' I shriek.

There is another thump.

'Why do you keep *doing* that?' roars Jensen.

I move through the darkness, doing my cockroach thing again with my arms. I feel the lid from the Wrexham Cup's case, held by Daniel's trembling hands. I wrench it away and swing with all my might, edge first, towards Jensen's roar. There is another thump, and then a smaller one, and then silence.

Absolutely nothing happens for almost thirty seconds. Then I hear somebody breathe.

'Hands up,' I say, hefting my plank, 'who is still alive.'

Daniel's face appears, pale as a Halloween mask, lit up from below by the bulb on Jensen's keys. 'Me,' he says.

———

Jensen isn't dead either, of course. At least, I don't think he is. He's just out cold. By the light of the Ferrari key fob, I can see that my roundhouse blow caught him on the side of the head. There's a cut, and a little blood, just above his right eye. There's no evidence that either of Daniel's blows did anything to him at all.

'Bastard,' I breathe, and kick him in the belly. He doesn't even twitch. If Daniel wasn't here, I'm not sure I wouldn't kick him a little bit more.

'Sorry about that,' mumbles my former boss. 'Took me by surprise. Dozed off a little. You were ages. Is he okay?'

'Who cares?' I grab the splayed ankles. 'Can we get him upstairs now, please?'

We bundle Jensen into the dumb waiter, and while I hoist him to the top, Daniel goes the long way, through the party, up the drainpipe and back to the room with the cup in it. It's a lot of responsibility for him. I have a nasty five minutes, straining at the dumb-waiter rope, convinced that he must have been arrested, or got lost, or got stuck talking to one of those semi-famous harridans who back you into a corner and won't let you go for hours. Maybe he got nabbed by those blondes. Will Jensen's little blue pill have kicked in yet? I'm terrified that he is going to wake up inside the dumb waiter. What happens then?

Eventually the pulley goes slack, and the dumb waiter comes whirring down, empty. I climb inside, and it's Daniel's turn to hoist me into the East Gallery.

We don our Femidoms, lug Jensen up to the walkway, and wheel the Wrexham Cup's display case until it is just underneath. Looking down from above, from the walkway, I can actually see the cup itself, a flash of silver in the darkness. I lean the case's lid against the wall and stamp on it, until it is broken into two. Then I drop both halves into the display case, down alongside the cup.

Jensen is the tricky bit. He's going in there, too. We heave him over the railing and, holding an ankle each, lower him down head-first. The arms give us some trouble, but after a while we manage to scrape them against the sides of the case in such a fashion that they fold up neatly, by his sides. He's still wearing Daniel's jacket.

We'll be resetting the alarm in a moment, and we have to make it look as though Jensen managed to get in here, into the case, without knowing the code. We wheel the case back to its position in the centre of the room. Things are a little easier now. Daniel has his torch now, the one he accidentally gave to Jensen along with his jacket. It's no flare, but it's enough.

Daniel unwinds the rope from around his waist and we tie it to the banisters on the walkways, on both sides of the room. It should look as though Jensen tried to use it to monkey-crawl across from walkway to walkway, to reach down for the Wrexham Cup from above. And it should look as though he fell, bursting through the lid. Had he landed on the floor, the alarm would have gone off. But he didn't. He landed, square on, snug as a bug, in that coffin-sized glass case. In a box, just like Rebecca said.

Daniel surveys our handiwork. 'It wouldn't have been easy to crawl along that rope,' he says.

'Have some faith, Daniel. This is Fingers. He's the Gentleman Thief, the devilish cat-burglar who has terrorised London society these past three months. People will want to believe this. Newspapers, especially. Now, let's get out of here. Have you got the Fingers cards?'

'The Fingers cards . . .' says Daniel, faintly.

'Are they in the car? You didn't forget the cards? Daniel, this whole thing hinges on the cards! Without the cards . . .'

'I didn't forget the cards,' says Daniel, in a hollow voice. 'They're in my pocket.'

'Great,' I say, and pull him towards the door. 'Just where they need to be.'

'No,' he says, and points towards the prone Jensen. 'That pocket.'

'That pocket?'

'That pocket.'

'The pocket in the jacket that Jensen has been wearing all night? The pocket into which he could have put his hand *at any point*?'

'Yes,' says Daniel, and laughs, sheepishly.

I don't laugh. I'm feeling cold, suddenly. Frightened. Almost everything about this has gone wrong at least once. We shouldn't be here. We don't deserve for it to work.

'Why weren't you in jail months ago?' I ask him.

'I quite honestly have no idea,' says Daniel, and we do it all again.

'You might as well get them out.'

It ends that Saturday, at the annual ball at the Wrexham House. Everybody sees it. The Duchess of Cornwall, Duncan Starr, Mohammed Al-Fayed, everybody. There will be epilogues, of course, and repercussions and reinterpretations, but nobody could argue that this is, fundamentally, the final act. Tomorrow, the *Sunday Times* will describe this evening as 'formerly prestigious'. The *News of the World* will opt for 'posh disaster'. The *Gazette*, of course, doesn't publish until Monday. A blessing. For them.

Look around. You ought to know how this works by now. Look one way and you'll see Kevin Spacey and Peter Mandelson, holding a hushed conversation that must be a gossip journalist's wet dream. Look the other, and there's Keira Knightley and her mum, taking it in turns to smoke the same cigarette through the same perfect pout. There will be a photo of that, somewhere, tomorrow. Although, these days, even the *Telegraph* is starting to prefer Natalie Portman.

Look. There's Richard Madeley, half hidden behind an ice sculpture, bending the ear of Sir Trevor Macdonald. There's Christian Slater, in his hat, joining Keira and her mum. There's Charlotte Church, watching all three of them with slitted eyes. There's Sienna Miller, Rupert Everett, Parker Tracey, Ian Hislop, Sir Roger Moore and Michael Parkinson. There's Geri, still with her damn little shit of a dog. And there, cutting through the cocktail tables, heads down, clutching microphones and purposefully heading towards a pair of lecterns by the staircase double doors, are this evening's hosts. Our old friends. Graham Norton and Gemma Conrad.

She's moved on, has Gemma Conrad. Once the world had seen her nipples, after the Diamond Ball, it could have gone either way. The trajectory, for once, went right. There were chatshow appearances, the obligatory glammed-up, smokey-eyed spread in *Sunday Times Style* (essential weekend reading for your middle-class masturbateur) and a slot as a slightly rubbish contestant in a follow-up to *Strictly Come Dancing*. That was the clincher. Gemma Conrad spun and flailed her way into the nation's affections, and next week (and really, this is meteoric) she's due to be on *Desert Island Discs*. Tonight she's wearing purple satin. Lots of gold, lots of hair. The Princess would approve. Less Jordan, more Kaplinsky. A metamorphosis.

If you know what he looks like, you might spot Nigel Cuppitt, the man who made the documentary about those orphanages in somewhere that was called something like Turbolikstan. He's a sort of dishevelled, pre-diet Peter Jackson type, and he, too, is being led towards the doors. If you've been paying attention, you might recognise the girl leading him. She's slim and blonde, and could pass for that girl from All Saints. It's Sarah, that other princess who took the Princess's job. You might also notice her passing a short, grotesque guy (who genuinely does look a bit like a penguin) and flashing him a saucy smile. Then looking away, and letting it fall from her face, like an avalanche.

There is a screech of feedback as Norton and Conrad reach their podiums on either side of the doors, and the plummy hubbub begins to subside.

'My Lords, Ladies and Gentlemen . . .' begins Conrad, and at that exact moment the doors open. Two uniformed security guards are wheeling the display case out from the hall. That dark, felt paper is still over the glass.

'Ooh,' says Norton. 'We have been premature.'

Everybody laughs. You have to, when Graham Norton says a sentence with the word 'premature' in it. It's almost primal.

The display case comes to a stop. Conrad starts talking about the Wrexham Prize, and the glorious history that lies behind it. It's fairly dry stuff. Norton is largely silent, evidently aware that there's a limit to the number of knob gags you can get out of a orphanage from a country with an unpronounceable name. He must loathe Gemma Conrad, with all her sudden and affected worthiness. He's probably wondering why he took the gig.

At this exact moment – and I'm not even slightly ashamed to admit this – I'm miles away. Literally. I slipped out to the gents half an hour ago, where I washed my hands and flushed four Femidoms down the toilet. Pausing only to decline the offer of a pure skunk spliff from a diminutive former youth-TV presenter – who, for legal reasons, I should point out was absolutely not Dermot O'Leary – I set off for Farnham Station in Daniel's clunky battered car. Tightrope walking on the alcohol limit, I'm sure. By now I am on a train, halfway to Waterloo.

'That's right, Gemma,' Norton is saying. 'And this year, following on that fine lineage, we have Nigel Cuppitt, director of this fantastic documentary about Turk–*bolik*–stan!'

There is an embarrassed hush.

'I'm sorry,' says Norton, quietly. 'I think I am genuinely incapable of saying that word without making a pun out of it. Clearly I must never go to Former Yugoslavia.'

Conrad frowns. 'North Africa,' she corrects.

'Actually,' ventures Cuppitt, in a shaky voice, 'Central Asia. And it's pronounced . . .'

Conrad hands him her microphone, and he speaks. About his documentary, about the orphanage, about some kind of disappointing conversation he has had with the Foreign Office. And out there, out in the bear pit – where the women wear expressions of scheming flirtation by default, and the men keep their money in clips, where a woman leers at wealth and a man leers at youth, where nobody, ever, is content to be stuck speaking to the person they are speaking to – out there in the swamp, the muck, the inferno, people are growing bored. Look at them. Pop stars and soap stars, book stars and film stars. Political stars and theatrical stars and stars who are just stars who are just stars who are just stars. Glassy-eyed. Waiting, tortured, for something to tell each other about.

The only exceptions are the staff of the *Gazette*. Not Rebecca and Philip. Brainchild, and his lot. They look triumphant. This is a vindication for them. No breasts and flashbulbs. It's not quite their gig, but they benefit by association. You can, actually, buy class.

And then Cuppitt stops speaking, and everybody applauds. And Conrad steps forward and rips the black felt paper away from the case. And there is Jensen Randall, like a kitten squashed into a pint glass, upended and bloodied. And then there is silence.

Then a glass hits the floor, like a gunshot. A group of people are moving across the room. It's a travelling commotion, made up of Daniel Kemp, Detective Inspector Tom St Eccles and three or four uniformed policemen. Daniel holds a bundle of Fingers cards out in front of him, like a pass. He's shouting. Something about a jacket, a switch, a revelation. There is a hubbub, suddenly, as everybody, simultaneously, understands, and the cameras start flashing.

And still, poor, sweet Gemma Conrad is standing there, still with the same fixed smile on her face, hand pressed to her demure silky bosom, not quite able to comprehend.

Graham Norton sighs into his microphone, almost kindly. 'Oh, go on, love,' he says. 'You might as well get them out.'

'Hello.'

In the film they are now making about my life, it seems pretty likely that I am to be played by Jude Law.

Rebecca is to be played by Naomie Harris, Philip is to be one of the geeks from *American Pie*, and Trevor Brainchild is to be played by the guy who used to be Mr Bronson in *Grange Hill*. As casting goes, this last is truly inspired. I can't imagine why I never thought of it before. Jensen Randall is to be played by Martin Kemp. He isn't nearly as fitting a choice as Joaquin Phoenix would have been, but he's both older and less famous, so I'm kind of okay with that.

I heard all this from Daniel this morning. He got it from Felicity Straps. They had a meeting at Horseferry Road last Wednesday, and they seem to have hit it off pretty well. She's terribly excited about the whole thing. Jensen's arrest, Daniel's discovery, the fact that it was all televised – it's all turned Fingers into a much, much bigger story than he was before. The rape

341

accusations are the big criminal matter, obviously, but it's Fingers that makes it showbiz. They're pressing ahead with the film, as quickly as they can, and they are now thinking cinema release, right after the trial. Nothing so big has happened in this city for years, and everybody wants a bit of it. The thinking is that it will be a very London affair, cameos all over the place. Hence Jude Law being so keen, I suppose. He'd only be on screen for five minutes, tops. Because it's not the story of my life at all. It's the story of Daniel's. He's going to be played by Ewan McGregor.

I know, I know. Ludicrous. 'We have the same colouring,' Daniel said to me, rather pompously, when we spoke this morning. He is having a fine time. The *Gazette* haven't paid him the reward for his scoop but he's taking them to court and they may have to. In the meantime, he's got a column in the *Sun* lined up, and a regular slot on the BBC3 news. He's a happy man. And soon he'll be a famous one. *Fingers : The Movie* (or whatever), the story of dashing Detective Inspector Tom St Eccles and his love interest, up-and-coming hackette Rebecca Leighton, in a battle of wills against fallen hack Daniel Kemp, as they race to unmask the villainous Jensen Randall as the evil thief and rapist he is. Me, I don't even really come into it. Nor should I. Like I said, it's not my story. It never was.

It all turned out so much better than we had even planned. Daniel was supposed to wait for the delay, and then lead the police through the party to the East Gallery. That would have been good enough. I still can't believe that nobody looked in the case before they wheeled it out.

Jensen is denying all knowledge of the thefts, obviously. He's also denying all knowledge of the rapes, though, and there's plenty of forensic evidence to link him to them. All the evidence that marks him out as Fingers is circumstantial, but it's pretty strong. He was upside down in a display cabinet, after all. The cards were found in his pockets, Joe Bastin's disc was found in his boot, and Jensen had access to Itotaki's lines of communication at the *Gazette*. He also did, indeed, have a poster of *Tunic Teens Lick for Grades* on the wall in his horrible Vauxhall apartment, but I can't claim any credit for that.

As far as I can figure, the only people who know what really happened are me, Daniel and Elspeth. And maybe, although I couldn't be sure, DI Tom St Eccles. The thefts are a minor affair, as far as the courts are concerned. At most, they'll add six months onto Jensen's sentence. Has Eccles figured it out? Maybe. I'm not sure he's bothered. He's doing almost as much telly as Daniel these days. And he has that stunning new girlfriend of his: the beautiful journalist whose mum is a top human-rights lawyer. Yes, her. He's pretty content. Anyway, I bet the police fix stuff up like this all the time. Criminal cases have to work, like gossip journalism. True stories often don't. They meander. They go where you don't want them to, and have split ends, flapping loose like pages slipped from a spine. They leave weeping girls, in stricken, broken houses, and never, ever go back.

I haven't actually seen Daniel since the Wrexham House bash. I slept on his sofa that night, but he never made it home. I saw him on *GMTV* the following morning, still in black tie. I watched it, and I laughed, and I sent Elspeth a text to make sure that she was watching, too. Then I tubed it up to King's Cross and got a train back to Edinburgh, to see my dad.

That was ten days ago, and I only left there this morning. We talked a lot, but mainly we walked. Up over Arthur's Seat, all around the Pentlands. It seems my dad has a dog these days. And also, although it took until day nine for him to admit it, a girlfriend. Janie and the Princess have known about this for ages, and are going up there this weekend to check her out. I've promised that I won't be gone too long.

There have been calls, of course, and offers of work. Two broadsheets and three tabloids have asked me to write about my experiences following the story, and I was even invited onto *This Morning* for a brief slot. I turned them all down. For one thing, I'm not entirely certain that my official version of events would tally with Daniel's. And for another, I'm just not that interested. I'm just not.

The only person I've spoken to from the *Gazette* is Philip. He called a couple of days ago, to let me know what was going on. The editor has gone, of course, as has Trevor Brainchild. This will have been a blow for old Trev. He's been angling so diligently for the succession for the last couple of months. He can't have imagined that a broadside like this would knock him off the rails. One could almost feel sorry for the man. Almost.

The board haven't picked out a new editor yet, but it's looking pretty likely to be the ever-dapper Hargreaves. Rebecca's profile has rocketed, so it's very possible that she'll be his deputy. Old man Randall won't make a fuss about either. He's suddenly got problems of his own. Something about one of his interests in North America. Misuse of a pension fund, perhaps, or unauthorised payments from somewhere or other; I haven't really been following it. Either way, the Big Boss is stuck over there and, if things are as bad as the whispers make out, he isn't necessarily coming back. All in, I think it's fair to assume that the *Gazette* will have a pretty hands-off proprietor for quite a while yet.

Not hands-off enough to let them give me my job back, of course, but I'm not so bothered about that. I don't really want my job back. I'm not quite sure what I'm going to do. I've been thinking about the world, outside of London, and the bits of it I'm interested in. And I've been thinking about somebody else. Between texts and emails, I've been thinking about her an awful lot.

Here's another reason why it wasn't really my story: it has ended, and I'm not . . . sorted. I'm on the Heathrow Express, cutting through West London from Paddington, and I'm nervous. I'm still far too eager to please. I'm still smoking. I still have terrible hair.

I also have one of those unshakeable colds, the ones that make your nose squeak like a bird and creak like a door whenever you breathe through it. I keep reminding myself not to blow. When I do, my ears hurt and my nose gets ever redder. I'm wondering if I ought to get some foundation to dab on the tip. I really am.

I have money. Daniel gave me some, by way of an advance. I also have my redundancy, and the rent I would have to pay on my flat next month if I was ever planning on going back to it. I won't need much money where I'm going, though. And when I get back, I can't imagine I'll find myself living in Knightsbridge. I'm thinking Brixton, perhaps, or, if I can afford it, Hampstead. I'm hoping it won't be up to just me.

It wasn't meant to be like this. It was meant to end on more of an up. I still have issues unresolved. When I think of the things that matter to me, I find it very hard to stay focused. When I think of the people who matter to me, I find it very hard to hear them speak. But I'm trying.

According to the flickering yellow screen by the entrance to Terminal 4, flight BA163 to Tel Aviv leaves in just over an hour. I have the tickets in my bag, tucked into my *Lonely Planet* as a bookmark. I have the name of a taxi service, and directions to the kibbutz. Perhaps this time we'll make it work. We never have before. But maybe this time, I'll manage not to keep acting as if I don't expect it to. I've never done that before, either.

She comes through the sliding doors looking uncertain: a tiny figure, swamped in my army coat, with a yellow T-shirt and her hair in a bun. She has a bag over her shoulder, heavy enough to be bending her sideways, like an over-strung bow. I was expecting her to be later than this. She's always been late, before.

She doesn't see me at first. She's pushing some loose curls out of her eyes and scanning the check-in hall. The bruises are almost gone; she actually looks pretty good. I should step forward, or wave, or call, but I don't. I wait for her to spot me. She does, and she comes my way, beginning to smile.

'Hello,' I say.

'Hello,' says Elspeth.